Crown Of Spears

ANTHONY GARCIA

DEDICATION

For Elaine, my love, my partner in crime, who has never once flinched at the absurd, the impossible, or the wildly impractical—who has nodded solemnly at each mad idea and said, *Yes, of course you must do that.*

For Charlie Harris, the keeper of stories, the conjurer of books, the friend who makes sure my insatiable hunger for words and worlds is fed—and the one whose approval, if I'm honest, matters most.

And for the doggles, who have never read a single word I've written but nap beside me as if they have, which is more than enough. Yes, yes, you're in here too. Happy now?

CONTENTS

There was supposed to be a list of chapters here. Neat, orderly, numbered. A sensible way to navigate what lies ahead. But where's the fun in that?

Instead, let's do this properly. Turn the page. Wander into the dark corners. Chase the words as they skitter away. Some chapters will find you before you're ready. Others will wait patiently, hidden just out of sight, until you stumble upon them like a forgotten door in an unfamiliar house.
This is your journey now. Follow where the story leads.

Go on. The adventure is waiting.

ACKNOWLEDGMENTS

No book is written in solitude. Oh, the writer may sit alone—staring at the blinking cursor, muttering to themselves, arguing with characters who refuse to behave—but stories are built from the voices of others, the echoes of history, the wisdom of those who walked the path before us.

To Kris Lane, whose book *Quito 1599* opened a window into the world of Spain's South American colonies, allowing me to glimpse the past with a clarity I would not have found on my own. And to Philippe Descola, whose *The Spears of Twilight: Life and Death in the Amazon Jungle* guided me deep into the lives of the indigenous peoples of the region, making their world feel all the more vivid and alive in my mind. These books were not just references—they were compasses, pointing me toward truth in the tangled wilderness of history.

To Reno Maniquis, who once brought *Crown of Spears* to life as a graphic novel that never quite was—but in my head, still is. His art shaped the way I saw this world, the way I breathed life into it through words. Every time I pictured a battle, a face, a shadow moving in the firelight, it was his hand that had drawn it first.

And to everyone else—those whose names should be here, but whom my treacherous memory has misplaced for the moment—you are not forgotten, not really. If I have neglected to name you, know that you are written into the foundation of this book, as surely as ink is pressed into paper. You are here, in the bones of the story, in the whispered echoes between the lines.

For all of you: thank you. This book is, in some way, yours too.

Crown Of Spears

ANTHONY GARCIA

©2025

Chapter One

Dearest Esperanza. I have at last arrived at Perico, the gateway to the Pacific. The journey across the Isthmus of Panama was neither arduous nor long, a welcome relief after the crossing from Cadiz. You would love Perico, my sister, the warm ocean breeze, the gaily-decorated shops that line the marina, and the birds! Esperanza, there are parakeets here in great number and in every hue. They are in such abundance here that the island itself was named for them. I wish you could see this. My first glimpse of the Pacific was such that I shall never forget the stirring of my heart at the sight. I felt, I'm sure, much the same as Balboa felt when he first made the journey that I have so recently retraced some eighty-five years later. Great are the wonders of the new world.
December 19, 1598.
Ignacio de Montemayor. Last known correspondence.

Ignacio left the rectory at Iglesia de San Miguel. That was a laughable term. The rectory consisted of a small stone structure in which he had to share a bed with Father Antonio Ramirez, an affable and hospitable older man swept up in the fervor of Spanish and therefore Catholic conquest. The church itself was not much larger and after evening services Ignacio and Ramirez had retired to the rectory for a meager meal and brandy by the small fireplace. In spite of the circumstances, Ignacio was not judgmental after having spent months in the cramped confines of the ship that had brought him to the New World, and Ramirez had proved to be an amiable host.

The morning was bright and warm as he made his way down to the harbor, and although he didn't have far to go in the sprawling port city, he took his time savoring the fresh air and exploring the few shops that lined the waterfront. There was much to see, and there was a large number of people in the marketplace, a river of running children jostled him from all sides. Before he had realized it, he arrived at the wharf where the *San Felipe y Santiago* lay at anchor. Here the atmosphere was one of controlled chaos as crews loaded slaves, spices, silk and porcelain amidst a group of men, women and children waiting to board. Sighing at the prospect of another sea voyage, he made his way to the gangplank and joined the line of passengers.

Gaining the foot of the gangplank, he took another look at the coastal seaport. It was beautiful, he thought albeit rustic. A crescent of civilization bordered by the dense jungle that darkly surrounded it, looming and mysterious. Perico was a bustling coastal seaport serving as a vital hub for maritime trade and exploration in this Age of Discovery. While not as prominent as its Atlantic counterparts, it still played a large role in connecting the Empire with the wealth of the Far East. Perico's strategic location made it a key waypoint for galleons navigating the treacherous waters surrounding the Central American isthmus. The port itself was a harmonious blend of colonial and Old World architecture nestled in this newfound territory.

Situated in a region of lush tropical landscapes and pristine beaches along the coastline, and surrounded by dense rain forests, the settlement benefited from the abundant natural resources found in the isthmus. Towering palm trees and exotic flora provided a picturesque backdrop for the coastal town. Perico facilitated trade between the Americas and the lucrative markets of Asia. Galleons, laden with silver, gold, and other precious goods from the mines of Peru and Mexico, docked at Perico before embarking on the perilous journey across the Pacific. It was a hive of activity, with merchants, sailors, and indigenous traders engaging in a vibrant exchange of goods and cultures.

Yet it was not without challenges. The tropical climate brought diseases that occasionally ravaged the population, and the dense rainforests harbored unseen dangers. Navigating the intricate channels and tides along the Pacific coast demanded skilled seamanship, and the unpredictable forces of nature posed constant threats to maritime activities.

As he made his way up the ramp, he took his travel documents out of his pouch, wondering at the workings of fate (or God) that had brought him to this place.

Born to a noble and influential family in Seville that held a strong tradition of service to the church, Ignacio enjoyed the privileges that came with aristocratic lineage, and from a young age he had exhibited a deep piety and sense of duty. A thorough education allowed him to display exceptional intellectual abilities and a keen interest in the teachings of the Church. The priesthood was an inevitability. He had quickly gained a reputation for his compassion, wisdom and dedication. In spite of his noble upbringing, Ignacio's humility and genuine concern for others earned him the respect of both the clergy and the local community. And then everything changed.

His family became entangled in a political scandal and accusations of treason were leveled against them. Ignacio did not escape scrutiny and found himself implicated by association. In a desperate attempt to protect his family and honor, he found himself volunteering for a perilous mission to the New World, a distant and unexplored land. Ultimately, it was banishment in exchange for a chance at redemption for his family. He despaired at the thought of leaving his dear sister Esperanza, who had been his confidant and anchor through his formative years. Esperanza, the elder of the two, was the guiding presence in his life. Despite the constraints of traditional gender roles, she demonstrated an intellectual prowess and curiosity that defied the limited opportunities available to women. Ignacio, on the other hand, exhibited an early inclination toward spirituality and contemplation, drawing the attention of the Church. Yet, despite the societal norms which would have set them each on divergent paths, Ignacio and Esperanza shared a profound bond that transcended societal expectations. In the secluded halls of their family estate, they found solace in each other's company, engaging in conversations that spanned the realms of philosophy, theology, and the uncharted territories of their own dreams. Esperanza offered him unwavering support as he grappled with the weight of his spiritual calling. Ignacio, in turn, served as a pillar of strength for Esperanza, providing her with a sense of purpose and intellectual stimulation beyond the confinements of her prescribed role in respectable society.

Their parents, staunch adherents to societal conventions, groomed Esperanza for an advantageous marriage to a nobleman, securing alliances and enhancing the family's standing. Esperanza's marriage, while advantageous in securing the family's standing, marked a significant turning point in their relationship. The physical distance between them strained the bonds that had been woven through years of shared experiences. Ignacio, now fully immersed in his duties within the Church, found solace in his faith, while Esperanza grappled with the complexities of her new role as a noblewoman.

Their correspondence became a lifeline, bridging the gap created by miles and societal obligations. Through letters filled with warmth and sincerity, Ignacio and Esperanza maintained a deep emotional connection that transcended the physical separation. Ignacio, in his spiritual pursuits, often sought guidance from Esperanza's worldly insights, while she, in turn, found solace in his unwavering support.

He feared he would never see her again, begging God's wisdom to persevere. His faith and resilience would be tested in a turbulent and unknown world. It would be a very long time before he would learn if his efforts had indeed helped his family. If ever. He prayed mostly for his sister's well-being.

Coming out of his musings, Ignacio found himself at the top of the gangplank. As he stepped onto the deck, he handed his documents to the man waiting there. The man scanned Ignacio's papers broke into a wide smile.

"Welcome, Father Ignacio! I am Mariano, the Stevedore. We are so honored to have you on board. Master De Cuellar said you were to have preferential treatment." Mariano was a small wiry man with graying hair surrounding a bald pate. Ignacio suddenly felt somewhat humbled and bowed slightly with his hand on his heart.

"My regards to your master, but please, I need nothing save a place to sleep."

"Nonsense! Tonight you dine at the captain's board. Now, let me show you to your cabin."

"As you please."

Ignacio made to follow Mariano but the man was apparently in no hurry to get Ignacio below decks. Instead, he showed his obvious pride by pointing out several of the ship's features.

"She's an old ship, Father, but she'll get us to Callao safely enough. We take very good care of her and she takes care of us, eh? Hopefully, the weather will be kind to us and we'll only spend a few weeks at sea instead months. But you'll not see a finer vessel of this size and armament in the New World. Despite her size, she's fast and maneuverable. There is nothing the sea can throw at us that the San Felipe y Santiago cannot handle. And no need to fear marauders, the rumor of the firepower we carry is enough to ward off any attackers."

"I was not aware that there were pirates in these waters."

"True, it is not like the Atlantic," Mariano conceded, "but they will come and we will be ready." Recover quickly he added, "Come, take a look at these riggings, only the finest sailors in the empire serve the finest vessel in the fleet."

"I was subjected to this type of tour on the ship that brought me from Cadiz," Ignacio said as diplomatically as he could. "I would not keep you from your work any longer, Mariano. I would just like to get settled."

"Of course, of course Father, how impertinent of me to commandeer you this way. I will take you to your cabin without haste." He took a few steps with Ignacio in tow, but stopped behind a large burly man who was shouting order at various sailors. "Ho, there, Rodrigo. Meet our esteemed passenger..."

Without turning, the big man made it clear he was very busy.

"I have no time for passengers, Mariano. Leave me."

"Heh, perhaps we should move on, Father, and let the heathens work."

Suddenly the big man turned and stood facing them, his face starting to show some discomfort. Quickly adjusting to the situation Rodrigo bowed deeply to Ignacio and removing his hat.

"Forgive me, Padre. I meant no offense. At times, our Mariano is such a prankster that one tends to dismiss him if there are more important matters at hand." Rodrigo shot Mariano a look with narrowed eyes that left no doubt of his current feelings.

Ignacio raised his hand to the man and said, "I can see that you are working hard, my son. Go back to your tasks with my blessing."

Much relieved, Rodrigo stepped back to make room for them to walk by, his hat still clenched in both hands. "Thank you, Father," he said somewhat contritely. Ignacio stopped again before the big man at scrutinized his face more closely.

"The name, Rodrigo, is Portuguese, is it not?"

"An accident of birth and no more. I've lived my entire life in Murcia, Spaniard through and through."

"That is quite alright. It was a passing curiosity, nothing more. Do go on" Mariano walked away, finally enroute to the promised cabin, but keeping in character, did not do so quietly.

"Rodrigo is a good man, and a good pilot, although he's only shipped twice with us." It was evident to Ignacio that these two men were probably the best of friends. Ignacio smiled to himself at the way people reveal more of themselves to the world at large than they realize. Very quickly they were before a door and Mariano sprang forward to open it.

"Your cabin is right here, Father."

The cabin was small, perhaps even cramped although the wasn't much inside other than a cot, and small desk ant a small collection of crates in one corner. Evidently the ship's crew found storage wherever they could, even in passenger quarters. It was also very dark, the one one window covered almost completely by those same crates. This did not seem to bother Ignacio very much.

"Austere, but it will suffice. Thank you Mariano."

"A pleasure, Father. There is a lantern in the corner. We will see you at dinner tonight, Eh?"

On board and alone at last, Ignacio sat heavily on the cot and breathed a sigh. *Another voyage,* he thought and with that thought came the memory of his previous voyage across the Atlantic. That passage had been fraught with frequent storms and a surly crew. He was certainly *not* a 'distinguished guest' on that trip. That crew was well aware of the scandal that swirled around him and viewed him more a fugitive from justice than an honored passenger. His accommodations there were worse, having to share a small cabin with an obnoxious drunkard who would retch anytime the ship swayed, and he certainly was not invited to share a meal with the captain. This crew's apparent ignorance of his stature was a small blessing. Still, his mission was not to make friends with the crew. His mission lay ahead down the coast at Callao. Exiled perhaps, but exiled in civilization.

Ignacio was eager to fulfill his spiritual duties and he saw Callao as an opportunity for spreading the Christian faith in the New World. And yet, he had a very long voyage ahead of him. The voyage from Cadiz was arduous, to say the least. By the end of it, the mere thought of yet another voyage weighed heavily on his mind.

He opened his pouch and brought forth his journal but the lighting the room was not suitable for writing. Standing, he reached for the lantern and struck a flint to light it. The room's shadows jumped back and as they did so, Ignacio caught a small movement in the corner and let out an involuntary yelp. A face seemed to appear amongst the crates, a dark face in a scowl topped with a mop of hair cut into a bowl shape, adorned with feathers and what appear to be a stick piercing the apparition's nose.

"Madre de Dios!"

He swung the lantern around but the shadows refused to be dispelled.

"Who is there? Who are you?"

He thrust the lantern into the corner but there is nothing there, only the crates, a stack of bedding and a pitcher of water with a bowl.

"Nothing! What madness is this?"

Ignacio, already shaken, nearly jumped out of skin when there came a sudden knock at the door. Mariano had apparently still been nearby and he now cautiously opened the door and peered inside.

"Father Ignacio? Are you alright? I heard you cry out."

Ignacio peered at the man as if not recognizing him at first, his hand still holding the lantern at the corner of the cabin. Mariano looked at him questioningly.

"Is there something amiss?"

Ignacio regained his composure, somewhat. Obviously the apparition was a trick of light and shadow. An illusion and nothing more. Still he turned his face back to where he had seen it. Slowly he turned back to Mariano and placed the lantern on the desk.

"No, no. I am quite alright. I'm sorry to alarm you. I was merely...that is to say, I merely struck my leg on the desk and cried out in pain." Lying was not one of his many talents but there was no point in relaying any of this to Mariano. Especially not to Mariano. Sailors were already a superstitious lot to begin with. No sense in divulging his encounter when he wasn't sure himself if he had actually seen what he thought he saw.

"Then I am sorry to intrude. Forgive me," he said as he backed out the door, still eyeing Ignacio with no small level of suspicion.

Ignacio closed the door on the retreating man and leaned with his back against it. His eyes searched corner again warily but there was nothing there. The illusion had been broken. Still...what if Mariano had not come in when he had? Ignacio shuddered to think. *Bless you, Mariano.*

Chapter Two

Almighty Father, whose divine providence guides our paths and whose boundless mercy sustains us in our endeavors, we stand before You on this eve of our departure. As we embark on this perilous journey across the vast expanse of the ocean, we humbly seek Your divine protection and guidance.

Bless, O Lord, this vessel that shall carry us through the rolling waves and tumultuous seas. Grant strength to the hands that navigate her course, and wisdom to those who command her. May Your celestial light pierce through the darkest of nights, illuminating our way and ensuring safe passage through unknown waters.

Look favorably upon this crew, a fellowship of brave souls bound by a common purpose. Grant them courage in the face of adversity, unity in times of discord, and fortitude against the challenges that may assail us. Bless each member with a steadfast spirit and resilience to endure the trials that lie ahead.

We beseech You, O God, to extend Your merciful hand over the passengers who have entrusted their fates to this vessel. Comfort their hearts, allay their fears, and grant solace to those who leave behind familiar shores in pursuit of distant horizons.

As we set forth on this expedition, let Your divine providence be our guiding star. May it steer us away from treacherous rocks, shield us from raging tempests, and lead us to the haven of our destination. In times of uncertainty,

may Your unwavering love be our anchor, grounding us in hope and faith.
Finally, O Lord, grant us a spirit of gratitude for the wonders of Your creation
that surround us—the vastness of the sea, the brilliance of the stars, and the
majesty of the heavens. May we, in our journey, witness the marvels of Your
handiwork and be reminded of Your omnipotence.
In Your holy name, we offer this vessel, its crew, and all who sail upon her. May
our voyage be a testament to Your glory and an exploration of the boundless
mysteries of Your creation. Amen.
Ignacio's Invocation and blessing, December 19, 1598

* * *

At last the journey has begun. The tide is in and the second, most important
part of my adventure lays before me. As for my experience in the cabin, I
consider it less an omen than perhaps my own anxiety at work. The ship rides
heavy in the water. We have a fair complement of passengers, some 80 soldiers
bound for the barracks at Callao, as well as contraband silks, textiles and
porcelain from the Far East. One hundred and twenty slaves in the hold on
their way to permanent drudgery in the expansive cane fields, vineyards and
mines of Peru. The ship's master, Alonso Sanchez de Cuellar, appears a
formidable man. He does not bark orders. His crew knows what is expected of
them. For my own part, I relish the sea breeze in my hair. Perhaps I should have
been a sailor, but, alas, God has willed otherwise. That is of course a bad
attempt at humor. I already long for solid ground under my feet. I miss you
desperately, my dear Esperanza, but I fear my life may be here in this new
world.

-Letter to Esperanza, never posted

At last the ship was ready, the anchor hoisted and the myriad flags on
the masts unfurled. The San Felipe y Santiago was towed from its slip on the
tide and its sail immediately bellied with the wind coming off the mainland. It
was all done without fanfare, no crowds of well wishers on the shore to see
her off. It was, after all, business as usual. Very soon, if anyone were watching,
it became a hazy smudge on the horizon.

In the dark hold, African slaves stared blankly at each other, rattling
their myriad chains quietly. Men, women and children without hope,

numbly accepting whatever fate awaited them.

On the bridge Captain De Cuellar stood with Rodrigo who was manning the wheel. De Cuellar is a portrait of the ship's master...a proud man with proud bearing.

Ignacio was at the rail, his eyes already at the horizon as the sun sets, while Perico fades behind him. The days slipped by swiftly as the ship and its crew fell into routine. The seas were calm, the winds favorable and they made considerable progress. It seemed to Ignacio that his prayers had indeed been answered and that his arrival at Callao was imminent. He knew better of course, the journey was barely a week underway, but as the breeze ruffled his hair, his apprehension of the voyage began to lift. He glanced at the horizon where a line of angry clouds had assembled, but Mariano assured him that nothing would come of them.

"They are angry we are here," Mariano had told him, "but they will do no more than watch." He appeared to be right as the clouds had maintained their distance on the horizon for several days.

On Christmas Day Rodrigo met with Captain De Cuellar in the captain's quarters. They stood at a long table strewn with navigational tools; charts, writing instruments, compasses and rulers. They were busy discussing their course when they were interrupted by a knock at the door. Rodrigo had just managed to say, "--and this portion is unknown to me. There are no proper soundings--." De Cuellar cut him off with a slash of his hand.

"Enough! You will chart them as you go, Pilot.." Turning to the door he said, "Enter."

Rodrigo made to leave the room as Mariano entered. With him was Don Francisco de Arobe.

"Don Francisco is here, my Captain."

"Ah yes, Señor Arobe. Come in, come in!

De Arobe was a short man of dark complexion. A man who obviously had a larger opinion of himself and his opulence than was warranted. He was, as always, dressed in the fashions of the Royal Court, ruffled collar and fine silks. De Cuellar maintained a cordial but stern demeanor as he motioned de Arobe to a chair. He eyed the foppish man with mild disdain.

"Please, make yourself comfortable, Don Francisco. I will only take a moment of your time," he said as he sat across him, clearing some of the navigational items out of the way. "I am sorry, Señor, to bother you on this Holy day."

"If I can be of service to you, Captain, I will. We missed you at Mass this morning."

"Mass, yes. I'm afraid the *San Felipe y Santiago* is a selfish mistress, Señor. Some things must come before even God. However, I was not the only one missed this morning..."

"Domingo is a young man, still exploring avenues of excess. Where is he now?"

"He is in the hold with the Harquebusiers. It appears he was found with the Africans...one in particular. Exploring his avenues of excess, as you put it. You must agree, we've been at sea only a week. Surely, discipline can be maintained for a journey of less than a month?"

"I beg your indulgence, Captain. I will watch over him like a mother hen. Release him to me and I promise you, he will cause no more trouble."

The captain sat back and gave the little man a stifling glare. To himself, he was enjoying himself immensely. He disliked the pretentious nobility affected by the current crop rich merchants who felt they had ascended to some perceived seat on the Royal Court. And now he had caught this one in an embarrassing situation.

And yet, it was not only the claim to nobility that rankled de Cuellar. It was that de Arobe and others like him in the region were not true Spaniards. He was of mingled blood from the early settlers that had spawned people like de Arobe. De Arobe had not been born in Spain, had never traveled there or even been educated in the Empire's institutions. How could he ever be considered a true member of the Empire when half his family traced their roots to the indigenous natives of this savage land?

To add to the insult, there was the matter of de Arobe's other son, Pedro, also part of the ship's passenger manifest. Pedro, who was in appearance even more native than his father, was an unapologetic drunkard. That he had maintained his composure on the journey so far was only a small blessing in de Cuellar's eyes. He had no doubt that before the voyage was over he would have another discussion with de Arobe about Pedro. Bad blood, bad people.

"It is customary that some form of punishment be meted out, to serve as reminder as it were. The crew and soldiers may find their own castigations undeserved if I were to let young Arobe loose from his crime. Do you agree?"

De Cuellar did not wait for an answer. He stood and made a dismissive gesture towards the door. De Arobe sat there with his mouth gaping like a fish.

"I..I..I..," he stammered but nothing more came out.

"Come, come, Señor. I see you are quite embarrassed by the whole affair. I will be lenient this time and spare you the humiliation. After all, boys will be boys, eh?" He ushered de Arobe out the door where there was a soldier waiting. "Thank you for your cooperation in this matter, don Francisco. I trust the rest of the voyage will be somewhat less eventful, yes?"

"Yes, of course, Captain." De Cuellar nodded and smiled a little smile. He had had his small victory.

Once outside cabin door, de Arobe looked back as if he had something more to to say, and indeed he does. But all he can manage is one word.

"Bastard."

Suddenly seething, he brusquely motioned to the soldier to lead him. They quickly came to a hatchway that led a passage to the hold. Here it was dark and low ceilinged with few lanterns to light the way. Ahead, in a lighted alcove was his son Domingo, looking a little haggard but none the worse for spending the night sleeping on a rough bench. His face brightened as he saw is father when the soldier guarding him had moved out of the way.

"Father!"

"You dare be familiar with me, insolent whelp!" With that, de Arobe backhanded his son, knocking the boy's he against the wall. The soldiers moved in quickly preventing him fro further violence.

"Do you know the embarrassment your tawdry antics have created? Have you any idea?" he screamed at his son. He wrestled out of the hold the soldiers had on his arms, brushing his sleeves as if contaminated with filth. He stormed away, back the way he had come, rubbing his hand all the way. Calling back to the soldiers he said, "Clean him up and bring him to my cabin. I will not be seen with him."

Coming back onto the deck, he blinked back the tears from the sudden bright sunlight. Sunlight or something more? He stood there for a moment swaying involuntarily while he tried to get his emotions under control. Domingo had been a source of irritation to him for some time now. Ever since his coming of age he seemed hell-bent on embarrassing his father in every way possible. Drinking and debauchery seemed to be the signposts in Domingo's life these days. *Perhaps I indulged him too much. Perhaps I encouraged him to embrace his status as a noble. Perhaps I made him this way.* Taking a couple deep breaths, he managed to calm himself a bit. He wiped away the sunlight induced tears and smoothed his robes. Truly, he did love his son but he loved his position in life more.

He made to return to his quarters and await Domingo's arrival but noticed Ignacio standing at the railing. The priest was apparently writing in his journal. Loathe to disturb the man but longing for a sympathetic ear, de Arobe walked up to him. He coughed softly to gain the man's attention. Ignacio turned and smiled.

"Ah, don Francisco. A thousand pardons. I was engrossed in my own musings. Have you been here long?"

"No, not long, Father Ignacio. I do not mean to interrupt your... musings. I just happened to see you here."

"The ship is not that big. You are bound to 'just see me' anywhere. Can I help you in some way?" Ignacio noticed the man was a bit fidgety. He seemed to be about to ask a favor but would obviously rather be anywhere else. Ignacio decided to spare him the trouble by asking first. "This has, in some way, to do with your son Domingo?"

"So you've heard. Yes. It does indeed. It is not easily that I burden you with my familial miseries, but if you would be willing to help..."

"Of course! I serve not only God but also my fellow man."

"...if you could just speak to him, show him that his father is only interested in his proper upbringing." De Arobe paused and ran his hand through his hair. "I cannot make him understand what it means for our family to have been given lordship over our lands. Our mixed heritage puts in a tenuous position with the Crown and our subjects. We are just returning from our audience at Veragua. We need to carry ourselves as lords, not as besotted rutting beasts!"

"I see."

"I am sorry. I should not have used such language, Father, but the boy arouses such a passion that I sometimes forget my manners."

"It's quite alright, don Francisco. I hear much more terrible things at confession."

"Then...will you talk to him?"

"I most assuredly will, however, it must wait until morning. I must attend to my ablutions before dinner and I fear young Domingo will require more time than I have available at the moment."

"I thank you, Father. I too must make ready for tonight's banquet."

"God's peace be with you, don Francisco. I am looking forward to seeing you and your son tonight. Perhaps I can establish a rapport with Domingo ahead of our appointment."

De Arobe walked away and Ignacio turned back to the railing. Those same dark clouds still haunted the horizon. A few feet away, Rodrigo and another sailor, whose name Ignacio had come to know was Pico, were doing soundings, playing out a long rope with a weighted end. Ignacio chuckled to himself as he overheard them.

"Pico! How are we doing?"

"Holding steady at thirty braza. How long must we stay at this, Rodrigo?"

"For as long as I say. Our charts show no soundings for this course and the Captain has us following the shore. Would you like me to tell him how tired you are?"

"No, I would like to tell him how tired I am of *you*."

Chapter Three

In the hallowed glow of this sacred evening, as the stars above shimmer with celestial delight, let us gather around this table, bound by the ties of camaraderie forged amidst the vast expanse of the sea.

O Almighty Father, whose divine light guides us through the turbulent waves and tempests, we humbly bow our heads in gratitude for the bounty before us. Bless this feast, a communion of souls adrift on the vast canvas of your creation. As we partake in the sustenance graciously provided, may our hearts be filled with warmth and compassion. Let the bonds of fellowship forged in the crucible of the voyage strengthen, transcending the confines of this humble vessel.

On this blessed day, we offer thanks for the journey undertaken, for the safety bestowed upon us, and for the camaraderie that blossoms within these wooden walls. May the spirit of Christmas infuse our hearts with goodwill, and may the love shared here echo in the corridors of eternity.
In your divine grace, O Lord, we find solace and courage. Bless the hands that prepared this feast, the hearts that share it, and the journey that binds us as one. Amen.

-Ignacio's Christmas Day blessing, December 25, 1598

Rodrigo was a simple man. Not in terms of intelligence, as he was a first rate helmsman and navigator, but in the sense that he did not ask too much of life. A life at sea, regular meals and ample wine satisfied most of his immediate needs. He was happy with his station in life and he was not plagued with overly ambitious thoughts. He did not view serving Captain de Cuellar a burden, in fact, he regarded the man highly.

Having served with many captains previously, most of them driven by their egos to be near maniacal, he considered de Cuellar a just and stable man. A leader he respected and admired. However, he could not get past the nagging feeling that the Captain's latest course seemed somewhat foolhardy. Rather than plot the course traveled routinely, which would have put them farther out to sea, the Captain had him hugging the coast through waters that could present any number of dangers.

One of them, of course was depth. Further out, this would not be a problem but for some unknown reason de Cuellar had him sailing through uncharted waters with the jungle encrusted land just in view. This required constant soundings and constant corrections that pushed Rodrigo's talents to the edge.

He could faintly hear the merriment coming from the Captain's quarters below him as the Captain and the important personages celebrated their Christmas dinner. *Oh, to be there with a big glass of wine rather here, worrying with every turn of the wheel.* He looked toward the darkened shore, shuddering at the thought of what could be lurking under that impenetrable wall of jungle unmarked by any light or settlement.

There was a sudden shout from Pico at the sounding post at the rail.

"Rodrigo! We're losing depth! The bottom's coming up quickly!"

"Give me a number, you fool! How quickly?"

"Wait...wait...It's leveled off now. Less than fifteen braza and holding."

Rodrigo wiped the sudden sweat on his brow, "I will nudge her seaward a point. Give me constant readings," he called back to Pico. To himself he thought, *Damn de Cuellar...making me sweat.* Rodrigo made the necessary corrections and after several minutes made another. He checked his compass bearing and managed a small smile. *We are exactly on course, in sight of the shore and in deep water.* Now he just had to confirm that his course change had the expected result.

"Pico! What news?"

"Back to thirty! God has smiled on us, my friend. He knows good sailors when he sees them."

"I'm afraid that doesn't include you, Pico. You are an endless pain to my backside."

"Hah! Perhaps if it were not so broad..."

Below Rodrigo, the Christmas dinner had gotten underway. The long table was strewn with a variety of foods, perhaps not as varied as one would find if one were not at sea, but welcome indeed and plenty of it. There were dried meats, beef, pork and fish, hard tack and biscuits with gravy, dried fruits and nuts as well as a selection of hard cheeses. Most importantly, there was wine. Ignacio found himself seated next to de Cuellar, while opposite him was the elder de Arobe and his two sons. Further down the table were several other prominent passengers whose acquaintance Ignacio had not yet made; Doña Isabella de Montoya, a wealthy Spanish noblewoman, Don Diego de la Vega, a military officer freshly assigned to a posting in Callao, and Señora Rosa Alvarez, a young widow seeking a fresh start in the New World after the death of her husband.

Introductions were made and group settled into innocuous small talk. Presently, the stewards began filling wine glasses and Captain de Cuellar took the opportunity to address the table.

"It is, without question, an honor to play host to such a fine group of fellow travelers. As we navigate the vast expanse of the sea and chart our course through the unknown, let this Christmas be a symbol of unity and resilience. Thank you, Father Ignacio for a most wonderful blessing. May the bonds forged here withstand the challenges that lie ahead. To new friendships, shared adventures, and the promise of a prosperous future in the New World!" Raising a goblet he added, "Now, we must try this wine, from don Francisco's own vineyard!"

"A humble gift for our table. I hope it pleases you."

The captain took in a mouthful and made a supreme effort not to spit it out or make face. It certainly was not what he had expected, and his reaction to it was not borne of dislike for de Arobe. It was...different. *Good God, does he used beets in his distillery instead of grapes?* Ever the gentleman he merely said, "Delightfully rugged, don Francisco." Feeling he should give praise where none was due, he added, "I must have some for my personal stores.

"You are too kind, Captain, but I'll make sure a case of it finds its way to your quarters."

"Thank you, and make sure that dog Rodrigo doesn't see it! He would drink it out from under me," thinking, *Not even Rodrigo could stomach this swill.* On reflection, *He probably could at that.*

Keeping his promise to de Arobe, Ignacio began to engage Domingo in conversation, saying to the young man, "How fare you, don Domingo If not for daily Mass one would not see you for days."

"Well enough, Father. My father strives to make a gentleman of me. He watches over me like a mother hen."

Ignacio gave a short laugh at this. He saw Domingo cast his eyes downward somewhat shamefully but still managed to smile. Putting him at ease, Ignacio said, "My own mother did much the same. Look at me now. I've gone somewhat beyond gentleman."

"I know what you mean. That is what happened to my brother, Pedro." Pedro, overhearing this decided to interject. In a very short amount of time, he has become a bit tipsy and he poked Domingo in the side with his elbow.

"Tell him, Father. Tell him that once he is a gentleman he can buy his own slave girls. Or is it slave boys you are after?

"Be still. Pedro," said Domingo, chiding his brother. "Ignacio is a man of God. There is no place for your drunken talk at the dinner table."

"Nonsense! Issa party! I will..."   "You will be quiet," Don Francisco said sternly. "This is not the place for one of your incoherent outbursts."

"Humph. It was not I who was found in the slave pit."

"Enough!" said de Arobe, raising his voice. "My apologies, Father, Captain. If you would like, I will send Pedro back to our cabin."

"No need, no need, Señor," said de Cuellar diplomatically. "Young Pedro is correct. This is a party, but perhaps we should slow down the consumption of this fine wine and give the food a chance to compete." He passed a plate of cheese to Pedro who looked at it dourly. "Try the Manchago, it is a wonderful companion to the wine."

A hush fell upon the table momentarily as everyone paused to see what would happen, but Pedro dutifully cut himself a piece of cheese and piece of bread and soon the level of discussion rose up to its previous level. Ignacio took this as an opportunity to resume his conversation with Domingo.

"I know it must be somewhat difficult for you not having peers your age onboard other than..." At this he gestured with his eyebrows to Pedro, who to his credit was digging in to the plate before him and did not notice. "If you would like, I would be happy to be a confidant of sorts to you while we are trapped together on this vessel."

"I would like that Father. I suppose it has been established that I have a bit too much free time here with few diversions." He added sheepishly, "Although your efforts may be wasted. I already know what is expected of me and I will work to better myself."

"That is good to hear, Domingo," said Ignacio without prejudice, "We need not talk of matters of that ilk. Perhaps we can have topics that are of interest to both of us. Perhaps we share some things in common yet undiscovered."

"That would be most agreeable, Father. I will be sure to seek you out on the morrow and learn what we can from each other." Next to him, his father, overhearing the exchange, smiled. *Perhaps there is hope for this one after all.*

The small social crisis had been averted, it seemed, and everyone resumed the festivities. De Arobe did his best to monitor Pedro's wine consumption discreetly and for once it seemed to be working. Presently, the meal was over and the stewards began clearing the table, but refilled the wine goblets. De Cuellar signaled a steward to bring him a small cask from his desk. Opening it, he offered his guests a variety of tobacco, a relatively new commodity and immensely enjoyed by sailors. There were cigars, loose tobacco and an assortment of pipes in cask which made its way down the table. While not all the guests partook of the offer, notably Ignacio and the women, there was soon a haze hugging the rafters.

"A most wondrous discovery this was," said de Cuellar as he leaned back in his chair with a large cigar. "I find nothing more relaxing after a meal than a good smoke, and I am sure it is just the beginning of what we have yet to discover here in this new wilderness," There were nods and sounds of approval around the table as the group settled into postprandial comfort. Eventually, the festivities appeared to be nearing its end and Ignacio prepared to make his exit when he felt a tug on his sleeve. Turning he saw Señora Rosa Alvarez smiling at him.

"Pardon me, Father," she said sheepishly. "If I could ask you something of a personal nature."

"Of course Señora," he said hesitantly. "What would you like to know?"

"Well," she began sheepishly, "I was wondering if you remember me."

"I don't quite understand, Señora. I have seen you here every day since our departure."

"What I mean is, you are Ignacio de Montemayor of Seville, are you not?"

"I am indeed. I have made no secret of it." Ignacio suddenly had an inkling of where this was going. Rumors of the scandal that surrounds my family have followed me here to the edge of the world. He was soon to be put as ease as Rosa continued.

"Of course not. I just wanted to assure myself that you are indeed the same man I met some years ago."

Ignacio looked at her closely. "You *do* look somewhat familiar, now that I look at you, but truly I cannot place you."

"It *has* been some time, I admit. I was close friends with your sister, Esperanza, after her marriage to Miguel. We used to call you Nacho, and you knew me as..."

"Rosalilly! Yes, my goodness! I'm ashamed I did not recognize you straight away. In my mind you were still on the other side of the world." He clasped her hands in his own and added, "It is so good to see you again. We must make time for a prolonged conversation. There must be many stories about Esperanza that I have not heard heard." After a pause, he reflected. "I am now doubly sorry for your loss, Rosalilly. To lose a husband at such an early age..."

"Don't be. My husband was a good man, but foolish and headstrong. He lost his life defending some imagined slight and that duel ended him for no good reason. Still, I have survived. I was left with enough money and opportunity to strike out on my own and here I am!" She looked at him with a twinkle in her eye. "And yes, I do have stories of Espy, some of them quite salacious."

"I have no doubt that you," He said laughing, "but you can keep those..." He was not to finish his words. A sudden boom reverberated through the ship, with a long violent shudder that threw the table and all the furnishings at the wall and everyone along with them. Ignacio instinctively threw his arms around Rosalilly as they quite literally flew through the air.

Chapter Four

This blessed Christmas Day finds our vessel, the San Felipe y Santiago, sailing steadfastly along the uncharted coastal waters of the New World. Our course, a deviation from the routine, has been met with mild objection from Rodrigo, who is a slave to routine and procedure but has complied with orders. Despite the challenges posed by these perilous waters, the crew remains steadfast and in good spirits. The evening sky is clear, and the winds favor our sails, a sign that Providence smiles upon our journey. Our esteemed passengers, including the noble Don Francisco de Arobe and the pious Father Ignacio, grace the Captain's table tonight for a celebratory Christmas feast. All goes well and charts indicate we are indeed ahead of schedule. If all holds, we should arrive in Callao in four weeks.

Captain Alvaro de Cuellar
Onboard the San Felipe y Santiago
December 25, 1598

Once, it had been an island. Not a very big island, never more than a few yards across and perhaps a half mile long. For millions of years, it had stood a little ways above the waterline, playing host to lichens and various marine mollusks, but the erosion had already begun. It stood amidst a strong coastal current that cut its sides narrower and narrower. It had enjoyed the peak of its island status during the ice age, when ocean levels had dropped significantly. Then, it had become a sanctuary for a variety of sea birds that used the island as a breeding ground, but it never had plant life of any import except for the lichens that had called it home for a millennia of millennium.

Then the glaciers of the world began to melt and the waters got deeper. The tiny island was then submerged, perhaps never to rise above the waves again. Yet life had not given up on it. The parts that had been underwater had always been a haven for corals and shelled invertebrates, and now that the summit had been engulfed, these creatures laid claim to new territory and soon surrounded the erstwhile island in a coat of calcium rich armor. Protected then from further erosion, it lurked under the waves, its razor-sharp edges waiting. A sanctuary for some, a bane to others.

The *San Felipe y Santiago* did not strike the outcropping straight on. Instead, it scraped its hull against its sharp edge tearing out a seam of lumber and iron fittings almost twenty feet long. No amount of soundings could have given the crew any warning. The death of the ship had come quietly and decisively. The ship still had forward motion which only added to the destruction below the water line, bringing the moment of its eventual sinking that much closer.

The guests began to get back on their feet, on a floor that now had a considerable angle to it. Ignacio helped Rosa gain her footing, still holding her in his arms.

"Are you alright, Rosa?"

"I...I think so. What happened?"

At the far end of the room, de Cuellar stood somewhat dazed. His forehead sported a significant gash from which blood flowed into his face. A second later his face showed a mixture of shock and outrage. He knew immediately what must have happened.

"We've been hit!" he cried. "Everyone out on deck!"

The cabin door burst open as the guests made their way out onto the deck, where it seemed everyone else on the ship was now assembled in a loud chaotic frenzy. De Cuellar immediately went in search of Rodrigo.

"Rodrigo! Where are you, fool? What have you done to my ship? I'll have your hide if I find you've been sleeping!"

Ignacio grabbed the first soldier he encountered, yelling, "The slaves! They must be unshackled before we sink!" The soldier gave him a look that quite clearly said the slaves were not on his immediate list of priorities. Ignacio was astonished by the bland look he received. "Damn you, soldier! I will do it myself!" Turning, he saw Domingo. "Domingo! Quickly! Follow me!"

They made their way to the slave hold, descending by ladder that was no longer vertical, and instantly encountered bedlam. There was a monstrous rent in the side of the hold where sea water was pouring through unabated. The slaves themselves were panicked, trying to free themselves from their bonds. Many of the unfortunate, who had been shackled by the fractured wall, now lay dead or maimed on the water that was almost chest high. Ignacio looked about frantically as Domingo pulled uselessly on the slave's bonds. The imprisoned throng was shouting and screaming for help. Ignacio had to scream himself to get his voice up above the fray.

"Domingo! There must be keys! Help me find them!"

Domingo came to him, swimming more than walking and together they entered the adjacent guard cabin. Everything that was not bolted down was strewn everywhere, but behind a fallen cabinet, Ignacio found what he was looking for. They made their way back to the prisoners, whose situation was now much more dire. They had unlocked perhaps half of the shackles they could get to when they ran out of time. The bulkhead gave way and the hold was now completely inundated. Ignacio ond Domingo had no choice but to make for the ladder hoping that at least some of the freed slaves would make it out. Making their way out of the hatchway, they helped pull out a little more than a dozen people, but there were many more below.

"Give me the keys, Father! I can do it!" but Ignacio held him back.

"No, Domingo, it is too dangerous. You will be lost as well," Ignacio said, wiping the wet hair hair from his face. "It is too late for them. We must help wherever else we can." He looked up at the bridge where de Cuellar was ineffectually pummeling Rodrigo with closed fists as Rodrigo cowered. Ignacio quickly got up and ran toward them.

"You fool! You imbecile! You were to sound the depths! Now you've killed my ship!"

"We're in deep water, my Captain. A..a rock! It was a large rock hiding under the waves!" As Ignacio pulled de Cuellar away, Rodrigo added, "I followed your orders exactly even though I warned you against this course you set us on."

This enraged de Cuellar further as he struggled against Ignacio's arms.

"I will have you flogged, you dog! I will..." Ignacio spun him around and shouted in his face.

"We don't have time for this! We must get everyone off this ship!"

The ship gave a sudden lurch. It had lost most of its forward momentum and the current was now pushing them up against the rocks again. The deck was tilted even more now and the end was imminent. Mariano slid his way toward them.

"Captain! There is only one boat! We must have lost the other in the crash."

The madness left de Cuellar's eyes. He looked about, perhaps seeing the true situation for the first time. He was again, in command. "Get the women on the boat!" he barked. "Everyone else must swim to shore!" Ignacio stiffened at the word 'women'. *Rosalilly! Where is she?* He cast his eye about but did not see her. He jumped from the bridge, ignoring the now useless stairs, scrambling to gain his feet on the sloping deck. Calling her name frantically, he finally spotted her coming out of the captain's cabin.

"Rosa! What are you doing here? We have to go *now*!" She seemed somewhat confused but she held on to Ignacio fiercely.

"Oh, Miguel, I knew you would not leave me."

"Miguel? No, it is I, Ignacio. It is not safe here we must get off the ship!"

She clearly was not seeing him and continued to ramble. "Do you remember when we took that trip to Galicia, that little town Ferrol? You made fun of me then because I was afraid of the water...because I could not swim. Instead I left you there and went shopping in the town. I found such pretty things."

Cannot swim? Ignacio took her by the shoulders and shook her but her eyes refused to focus. Against his own volition, and instantly regretting it, he slapped her hard across the face. The force of it drove her to the floor. With dismay, Ignacio helped her up. When she was again upright, looking at Ignacio with a puzzled look but her eyes were clear.

"Nacho...what...what..."

"Never mind that! Come with me." He looked at her then and notice she was holding on to something. "What do have there?" he asked sternly. She held out the thing to him and he beheld the pouch which contained his journal and a few other items. His only true possessions in the world. At the moment it was the furthest thing on his mind and he certainly not gone back for it himself. Still he took it from her and slung it over his shoulder.

"I am sorry for striking you, and I thank you for my pouch, but there is no time for gathering treasures. We have only moments to get off this ship."

He fairly dragged her to the railing, where the sea was now ominously close. Straddling the rail, he grabbed her by the waist and said, "Take a deep breath." With that he let gravity take them down and into the water. He knew they had to get away from the wreck quickly lest the suction of the drowning vessel pull them under.

"Kick, Rosalilly! Kick!" And his thoughts reminded him, *Cannot swim?*"

On the bridge, de Cuellar hung on to the wheel in a vain attempt to right the foundering ship. He was largely alone now, a few stragglers taking their own plunge into the water, which was now strewn with planks, barrels, crates and more than a few bodies. *Where are my men? Where is Rodrigo, Mariano? They abandon me when I need their help most! Cowards! Disloyal dogs!* The ship began to break apart. The uneven weight of the water that flooded the holds stressed the structure of the *San Felipe y Santiago* to the breaking point. The mast before cracked with a sound like an explosion and fell toward him with inexorable speed. He only narrowly managed to side-step it and avoid being crushed. The sails, that had been fully unfurled before the crash fell on him covering him in their canvas embrace.

Mariano and Rodrigo were manning the one lifeboat afforded them after the crash. It was filled with more than just the women from the ship. In their madness, everyone who could had piled onto the little vessel which was now riding dangerously low in the water. Further, there were many others clinging to the gunwales making rowing decidedly difficult. In spite of this, they managed to clear the wreck and make noticeable headway toward the shore.

"Pull, Mariano! Pull!" yelled Rodrigo between his labored breaths. Before the little man could reply, they heard a sound like thunder that filled the air. They looked back then and saw it. The ship folded over on itself like a tent without its support poles. Soon there was nothing above the surface to indicate that a once proud galleon had been there. They stopped rowing and gaped in amazement.

"Holy Mother," Mariano managed to murmur. Turning to Rodrigo he said, "Do you think the captain managed to get off?"

"We cannot worry about that. We have our own troubles to attend to. Whatever happened, the captain's fate is beyond us. He is in God's hands now."

Ignacio struggled with what now seemed to be dead weight. Rosa had become unresponsive since entering the water. Whether it was stress induced or fear of the water, Ignacio did not know. He paddled as well as he could with the one arm he had free but it did not seem to him that he was getting anywhere. Doing the best he could, his main concern was keeping Rosa's head above water, which was becoming increasingly difficult as the water had become quite choppy from all the falling debris.   The moment he had been dreading came; the final death throes of the galleon. The hull slipped noisily beneath the waves and immediately Ignacio felt the pull of the current against his legs. Shifting tactics, he pushed Rosa ahead of him making use of both his arms. Gradually, he managed to gain distance and the suction he felt lessened. Still there was still the problem of dodging the debris that drifted into his path. He hoped for something large enough that he could use it to keep Rosa afloat but so far, nothing useful had presented itself. He was tiring and the shore seemed no closer. At this rate they were more likely to drown and become just more flotsam. He was on the verge of giving up.

Oh Lord, in this hour of trial and tribulation, I humbly beseech thee for thy divine mercy. If it be thy will, grant me the strength to persevere through this tempest and reach the safety of solid ground. The waves buffet me, the darkness of the abyss looms before me, I place my trust in thee, O Lord, and surrender my fate unto thy hands. Have mercy on me.

Then he saw it. Just ahead was barrel, half submerged. Whatever it contained, it contained a fair amount of air as well, allowing it to bob on the water. With a final burst of energy, he made his way toward it, pushing Rosa ahead of him as he went. It was another ordeal getting Rosa's limp form onto it but he persevered and it was accomplished. Hanging on to one end, he allowed himself to finally rest. His face was wet, whether from tears or salt water, he did not know. *Thank you, Lord,* he thought to himself over and over.

He must have fallen asleep for a while as he suddenly found himself submerged and came up sputtering for air. How long he had slept he did not know and looking at the shore he saw that it was much closer than he remembered. He pushed off again, this time pushing the barrel instead of Rosa. The sudden movement caused Rosa to moan softly and Ignacio was heartened to know that his efforts had not been in vain. Dawn was now fast approaching and he redoubled his resolution to get to shore. His joints and back ached but now the end was in sight. *I do not know what I will find when we get there but it will be better than this, I hope.* He realized this might just be the beginning of an adventure he might not survive. Waiting at the shore was an unexplored country with unknowable perils. *So many people have already died, Lord. Please do not let it all be for naught.* Already the water was shallower and he knew they would make. Whether Rosa would recover from her swoon was another matter to be considered later and Ignacio pushed it out of his mind.

Chapter Five

Field Entry:
Date: May 15, 1973
Location: Ruins of Santa María del Oro, Spanish town near Shuar territory
Description of Discovery:
Today, while excavating the ruins of the old Spanish town near the border of the Shuar lands, our team made a remarkable discovery. Among the debris and rubble, we uncovered what appeared to be the remnants of a journal. The manuscript was badly damaged, with pages torn, mildewed, and even partially burned. Despite its poor condition, it was evident that this was a significant find.

Upon closer examination, we determined that the journal belonged to a Spanish priest who likely lived during the late 16th century. The entries within the journal provide valuable insights into the experiences of a ragtag group of survivors of a shipwreck off the coast, and their interactions with the indigenous peoples of the area. Further analysis and preservation efforts will be necessary to extract as much information as possible from this invaluable historical artifact. It is my hope that through the careful study of this journal, we can gain a deeper understanding of this pivotal period in the history of the Spanish colonization of the Americas.
-Dr. Elena Ramirez

The boat with Rodrigo and Mariano was the first to reach the beach. They jumped out and pulled the boat onto the sand as people jumped out of it. Those that had been holding on to the sides began wading in as soon as their feet touched bottom. The oarsmen flopped onto the sand, exhausted from their efforts. De Arobe had been one of the people on the boat while his sons had drifted alongside. He waited on shore as his sons waded in and embraced them both.

"Thanks be to Heaven that we have all made it," he exclaimed as the ocean released the rest of the passengers. Looking about he saw soaked bedraggled people, the few women with them were plainly afraid, panicked and crying. Others were helping the last few stragglers out of the water. He stepped over to where Rodrigo and Mariano were stretched out.

"We must take the boat out again and rescue as many as we can, as well as as many stores as we can salvage." Rodrigo rolled over and looked at de Arobe, shading his eyes from the brightening day.

"You are right, don Francisco, but I cannot do it. I cannot speak for my companion here," indicating Mariano, "but I do not think that he is in any shape to help either." Next to him Mariano groaned in agreement.

"Your man Pico was manning the rudder. He must be in better shape then you two." He turned to his sons and appraised them. Presently, he said, "Domingo, go with Pico in the boat and salvage what and whoever you can." Domingo nodded and trotted off to where Pico was assisting those in need at the shoreline. Pedro, meanwhile, let out a sigh, obviously thankful that his father had not picked him. However, his father saw this.

"Do not just stand there, Pedro! Help where you can." He pointed to the surf and said, "There is plenty wreckage that drifted with us. See if there is anything of use to us, even if it is only fragments of wood. We will need it later to make a fire." Pedro cast his eyes down and shuffled off to do as he was bid.

Presently, Rodrigo got himself up to a sitting position and he assessed the situation. *So few of us remain. The sea has swallowed many good men.* He looked out to sea but there was nothing much he could discern. The endless blue sky met the ocean in a great blue bowl. Well, not totally endless sky. The bank of dark clouds that had dogged their voyage were now decidedly closer, Rodrigo observed with a frown. To either side of him, the beach stretched on until it was lost in the early morning haze. Mariano managed to stand beside him, shakily holding his arms around himself as if he were chilled to the bone.

"What of the captain," he murmured. "Do you think the waves took him as well?"

"I know not, Mariano. Last I saw of him, he was still on deck as well as the priest, Ignacio. I doubt either of them would abandon ship as long as there were anyone onboard...or until they had no other recourse." He bowed his head. "Pray for them, Mariano. Pray for them."

The boat was pushed back into the water, with Domingo and a soldier manning the oars and Pico at the rudder. They soon were lost to view and the survivors were left to wait. Occasionally someone would wade into the surf to retrieve some sort of debris to add to their growing pile. It was during one of these excursions that someone noticed there where swimmers approaching and everyone went to help them. It was a large group of African slaves that had finally made it safety. The slaves were subjected to a barrage of questions to which they had no answer. *The Captain! Where is Master De Cuellar?* they asked repeatedly forgetting that the Africans had no language in common with the Spaniards. Many walked away in disgust and the slaves were left to huddle by themselves and attend to their own needs.

It was now about midday and the sun was high in the sky when the boat was spotted returning to the beach. The survivors huddled around the vessel as it made its approach and was dragged up onto the sand. In the boat were five people in addition to the three that had set out. One was another African, another was a soldier and a child. The two remaining rescues were Ignacio and Rosa who seemed to have recovered remarkably well.

"Is that all you found?" asked Rodrigo.

"No," said Pico as he jumped out of the boat. "There were many more, most were drowned, but sharks, Rodrigo! Sharks are having the feast of their lives out there. We did what we could but...but..." He fell to his knees weeping from the terror and futility he had endured. After a few moments he composed himself enough to add, "Supplies...we gathered what we could, but the current had taken most of that away. I am afraid there is no more...and no one to be had."

"That is ill tidings indeed," said Rodrigo. "Still we must keep trying. Push that thing back into the water! We'll find the Captain or die trying!" A voice suddenly boomed out, "Belay that order! We are here and safe, it seems." Unseen by anyone, distracted as they were by the arrival of the boat, they failed to see Captain de Cuellar rising out of the water like a waterlogged apparition. His men were instantly cheered and rallied around him. They carried his bedraggled form to higher ground where he fell limply onto the sand.

"Rodrigo is right," said Ignacio. "The boat should be pushed back out. We need to salvage as much as we can."

"Then make haste!." de Cuellar said. "The current, sun and the tide are against us."

The boat was emptied of the few things they had managed to recover, mostly odds and ends, boxes and bags that had been in the various holds, but none of it was food. With this realization, the boat was pushed out quickly with two soldiers at the oars and Pico once again at the rudder. Meanwhile, the dark clouds that had been on the horizon for many days were now nearly upon them.

The Africans, keeping to themselves, began digging a pit further up the beach and lining it with stones. Between the clouds and the westering sun, darkness was fast approaching. They filled the pit with such pieces of wood they could find, supplementing with twigs and foliage from the edge of the forest. As none of the other survivors offered flint, if they indeed had any, they set about rubbing sticks together in an effort to ignite the kindling they had gathered. De Cuellar suggested to his people that they should perhaps do the same and soon a separate but equal project was underway.

Hours passed and the darkness was now complete except around the two competing fires. In the distance, the sound thunder added to the sense of isolation they now all felt. The occasional flash of lightning made them all huddle a little closer together, Ignacio decided it was time to confront the obvious. The small boat had not returned.

"Pico and the others will be hard pressed to navigate in dark," he said to de Cuellar.

"Have hope, Father. They have two bright fires to guide them to shore. Surely by now they have salvaged what they could and even now are returning."

Ignacio did indeed have hope, prayers and faith in his arsenal, but doubt and fear still held their sway. He looked at de Cuellar's profile in the firelight and opted to change the subject.

"We shall hope for the best. Do you have any idea where we are?"

"If I remember my charts aright, the settlement of Portoviejo is no more than two days march from here."

"It is a miracle that we've survived the shipwreck. However, I fear that an extended march will bring naught but misery."

"Two days," countered de Cuellar. "Three at most if we are slowed by the weakness of those not used to hard labor." Ignacio chuckled at this.

"I acknowledge, good sir, that you include me in that list. I promise I will do my utmost to pull my weight and the weight of those that need it." Ignacio poked the fire with a stick. "Is it at all possible that during those three days that another ship will pass?"

"Nay, unlikely," said de Cuellar. "We are the only ship on the Callao run." De Cuellar gazed thoughtfully into the fire. Presently, he added wistfully, "Even if there was another ship nearby, it is doubtful they would follow such a course as we did. The main routes are far out to sea. They would not even see our fires." They sat in silence as the fire crackled merrily. "We will assess our situation better in the morning," said de Cuellar. "The boat will be back shortly and we will take stock then. In any event we cannot just sit here waiting for a miracle. Our only option is to make for Portoviejo."

Miracles do happen, thought Ignacio, stretching out before the fire, his pouch a rough improvised pillow. *Yet we are not in control of when or how they will be dispensed.* The events of the day caught up to him and he fell into a fitful sleep.

The morning broke grey and misty. It appeared Ignacio was one of the last to awaken and looking around he immediately felt the unease emanating from the others. He rose and made his way to Rosa who was standing nearby.

"What is the problem? Has something happened?"

"That is the problem, Nacho. Nothing has happened. The boat has not returned."

Ignacio looked toward the sun. Dawn was far behind. In his exhaustion he must have slept longer than usual as he was usually awake at the first hint of light. Around him, people were looking out to sea, and in spite of the coming storm, the ocean was flat and calm. That was soon to change.

"Perhaps they made landfall further down the beach. The current out there is strong and they could have drifted off course." De Cuellar overheard this and stepped closer to the pair.

"One can only hope that is the case. If it is, then we should encounter them as we progress south along the shoreline if they are not already making their way north to us."

"But how would they know?" asked Rosa. "This stretch of beach looks no different from what we can see on either side of us. They may assume we left without them."

"As I said, Señora, One can only hope. I for one, believe they are lost, never to return. The odds are stacked too high against them. In the meantime, we must take stock of what we we have and who is left to us." He called to the others and had them gather around him. The San Felipe y Santiago had a contingent of eighty including passengers and crew, while the slaves accounted for a further one hundred. Ignoring the Africans for the moment, de Cuellar quickly assessed that there were sixteen people missing, not yet counting Pico and his two oarsmen.

"We could have done far worse," he proclaimed. "We shall no doubt mourn those we have lost, but we now have a challenge before us. We have no food, lest we venture into the forest and I will ask for volunteers to do just that. We have no water, although judging from the sky that will not soon be a problem. We must gather whatever meager possessions we have and begin our trek south. I believe the port of Portoviejo to be some two days journey from here and the sooner we depart, they sooner we will be saved." Unfortunately, as we shall see, the captain was quite wrong about this. Portoviejo lay some five hundred kilometers to the south, and arduous undertaking even in the best of conditions and conditions were not the best. Yet, what else was there to do?

Those assembled seemed to be in agreement with the plan but for one who stood apart. It was one of the soldiers who, having discarded his armor in the swim to shore, was not immediately distinguished as such.

"It seems we mostly all made it ashore, no thanks to the noble crew that put us in this predicament in the first place," he said loudly to everyone. "Why should we put our trust in them now?" He address de Cuellar directly. "As for your own crew, I'm surprised they can swim if I were to judge them by their seamanship.

De Cuellar's crew bristled at this and quickly made to surround their captain, while the soldiers did likewise for their spokesman.

"Have a care, Sirrah!" de Cuellar shot back. "Soldiering did not help us at sea! For better or worse, we find ourselves here together and together we must work if we are to survive.

"Aye, ship-master, but it will be on the backs of soldiery that we will prevail! I stand ready to assume command."

"And who are you to make such a claim?"

"Diego Martinez. I was lieutenant to our Captain Sanchez, who your crew had a hand in killing." At this the factions seemed intent on killing the other and the ones who were of neither quickly backed away. Ignacio quickly stepped between de Cuellar and Sanchez and attempted to defuse the conflict.

"Stop this, I beg of you. We shall all do what is required of us, but enough of this petty bickering! It is not only on soldiers that we will depend. We have many strong men among us including the Africans and yet even such as these must be freed to fend for themselves and us all. Not on the backs of soldiers shall we survive but on every back here! Including my own!" As he pointed back to where the Africans had built their fire, many eyes looked, and then looked again in disbelief. The Africans were not there. They had somehow disappeared during the night. A quick search produced no indication of their whereabouts or even what direction they had taken. The sand offered no clues.

Chapter Six

Like a toucan on the highest tree
I shall leave my enemies far down below me.
My enemies...who gather together...who spread vile gossip about me...who
enrage me.
I shout "cuan", "cuan"! Far down below me...My enemies disappear.
Umáru, áya tátsumeash áya tátsumeash. Penké tiúsa jeártamsui.
High above everyone else...my hair fluttering in the wind
Like flickering flames. Bright, so bright.
No one can reach me. No words can do me any harm.
I let my enemies disappear...like an anaconda...which devours everyone.
I fly with the wind...and show them...nothing but the tips of my feet.
Beaten, they fall back.
I am Toucan.
-Shuar curse.

Someone *did* see what happened to the Africans. And they had been watching the survivor's drama unfold from the time the first of them washed ashore. Five of them there were, just beyond the tree line, their painted faces and bodies blending with the trees and foliage. They were not hiding. They did not have to. They were one with their surroundings, their kingdom, their home. Five pairs of eyes looked on the tableau with interest, not ready to interfere in the slightest, neither to help or to hinder. At the moment, they watched with interest and a measure of humor. These were not the first white people they had encountered. Nor were the blacks for that matter. But they were still alien and that sparked their suspicion.

De Cuellar was not willing to send anyone in search of the Africans, although some of the soldiers were at the ready. They wanted the blacks punished and put to work for the group. Typical narrow thinking, he thought. They think about putting others to work when in fact they have done us a mercy. There are now fewer to feed, fewer to water and fewer to discipline. Although his stomach was growling, what he missed were his cigars. At that moment, a deep smoke was more inviting than any morsel to be found nearby.

A short while was spent gathering themselves and their things and without fanfare, they began their southward trek. They were very loosely knit, this group, some quick in pace, some slower. Here and there certain people walked together, sharing some commonality, others preferred to be alone. But everyone moved in the same direction. And with them, in the forest, the eyes moved as well.

It started to rain. Not as much as the sky promised, but a fine drizzle that soaked them nonetheless. There was much grumbling and soon de Cuellar acceded to their complaints by moving the group to shelter in the treeline, but he was quick to point out that their comfort was hampering their journey unnecessarily.

"It is bound to get much worse than this," he admonished the group. "This storm is coming in, not going out. While we take refuge here, we are not advancing as we should. If we just take the rain in stride, we will hopefully be in sight of Portoviejo before the bulk of the tempest hits us." He was largely ignored, until it became noticeable that the trees did not offer much in the way of keeping dry. Rather the leaves served as funnels that would occasionally dump their contents onto their heads without warning. Moreover, rivulets of water began streaming out of the forest soaking their feet more than their heads. It soon became obvious that wet was wet, here or on the beach, they could not escape it and grudgingly they resumed their trek.

The road ahead was hazy and ill defined due to the mist caused by the rain. After several hours of trudging through the precipitation, it appeared to the eye that no progress had been made. The same wall of forest to the left, the same restless sea to the right, and an endless stretch of sand ahead. There was nothing to relieve the monotony of the terrain. The sky grew dark, but whether the sun was setting or the storm was intensifying was a mystery that had no bearing on the situation. They plodded along mindlessly until sheer exhaustion overwhelmed them. They huddled together, with no hope of starting a fire when someone with keener eyes saw something further down the beach, De Cuellar and Ignacio looked and although it was indistinct, there was definitely something there.

"Perhaps it is Pico and the boat," someone said. Another said, "It could be some of our wreckage washed ashore." In spite of their fatigue they rushed to the apparition ahead. To their dismay and consternation, they quickly found that their hopeful outlooks were shattered. What they found was a picket line of poles stuck in the sand extending across their path. Atop each pole was head, shrunken, withered and dark.

Ignacio took a closer look at one of the heads. Its eyes and mouth were sewn shut, a sharp stick had been shoved through the nostrils, yet Ignacio realized with a shudder that it resembled the apparition he had seen in his cabin when he first boarded the San Felipe y Santiago. Until this moment he had given no more thought, thinking it only a trick of light and shadows confusing his tired eyes. Now he was not so sure. Rosa walked up to him.

"Hideous things are they not? What do you think it means?" She looked and him and saw his pained expression. "Ignacio, what is wrong? You look as if you seeing the devil himself." He seemed at first not to hear her, and he was several moments composing himself.

"Yes, hideous indeed," he said finally. "The only meaning I can derive from this is ominous at best."

"Clearly a warning of some sort," said de Cuellar further down the picket. "My guess is that someone does not want us to go further."

"If not further, then where?" said de Arobe. "We certainly cannot go back, and to venture into the forest is folly. We would be immediately lost and no one will ever hear from us again." He shook his head, adding, "No, no, as much as I despise the thought of this endless march, we must continue on."

"I quite agree," said de Cuellar. "The simplest choices to make are when there are no other choices. Still it will be prudent to be careful as we go on. We will begin posting sentries at night while the rest sleep. We have been quite negligent about that even though we have landed in a strange unknown place. But no more."

"Captain! Captain!!" The cry came from a few that had ventured past the picket. Looking in that direction, they saw a man running toward them. He very nearly crashed into those at the picket, pointing back the way he came. "I saw one! I saw one!" he cried hysterically, his eyes wide with fear. De Cuellar grabbed the man by the shoulders and shook him.

"Saw what?" De Cuellar kept shaking him until the man looked at him directly. "Control yourself! What did you see?" The man began gesticulating anew, pointing toward the looming wall of foliage.

"A...a savage! There! Staring at us from the trees!" De Cuellar looked in the direction indicated but saw nothing. He motioned to a group of soldiers standing nearby.

"Go look. If there are indeed savages and they are only curious, they may help us."

The soldiers ran off and everyone looked on with apprehension. Mariano started laughing and said, "Oh yes, we've landed in an unknown land, inhabited by wild Indians who eat human flesh! They're curious, alright. Curious what we taste like!"

"Enough of that!" said de Cuellar sharply. "Everyone is frightened enough as it is."

"They'll cut off our heads while we sleep! Cut them off and adorn their little huts with them!" Mariano's words clearly had an effect on the group and many starting repeating variations of the wild thoughts he had spouted. Rodrigo wrestled the little man to the ground in an effort to quiet him, but not before Mariano finished. "Eat us...kill us an' eat us."

Chapter Seven

The seagulls cry as they circle overhead. Their cries are mixed with the songs of angels. And the screams of demons. They wheel, dive and snatch souls as they pass by. Why they do this, no one knows, for they serve no masters but themselves.

Elayna Hadley, Exercises in Faith, Bosley Press 1917

The deaths started a week later. Not from the much feared marauding savages that Mariano had insisted would kill them in their sleep, rather it was nature itself that had become their enemy, as it had had always been from the moment the San Felipe y Santiago had struck that malevolent rock.

After the encounter with the picket line of heads and the unconfirmed sighting of the savage, the troop had moved on, continuing their trek southward along the beach. They were tired, weak and starving as they trudged on unhappily with no sign or hint of a sign that they were indeed approaching civilization in the form of the settlement of Portoviejo. Had they known of the vastness that still lay before them before that goal was achieved, they would have panicked and fled into the forest heedless of what may be waiting for them there. Still, the plodded on day after day, scavenging what foods they could from the treeline, drinking from the occasional stream that ran out from the ominous canopy that never broke with so much as a clearing or glade.

At length, there were stumbles that became more frequent as people became weaker, particularly among the women and the few children that had survived thus far. A sudden cough came among many members and the pace slowed considerably. They were all suffering from exhaustion, exposure and hunger. The rain clouds had relented and the sun glared down on them unmercifully. There was again a line of dark clouds out on the horizon seaward, but that was no comfort to those that were beginning to show signs of heatstroke. Moreover, drinking from streams had caused a bit of flux among an already depleted company. Many began to say that crossing the line of heads had cursed them to a living purgatory with only the prospect of death as release. De Cuellar and Ignacio did their best to abate the fears and the increasingly occasional squabbles that broke out among those that still had the energy to do so, but it quickly became an exercise in futility.

Inevitably came the day that one stumbled and did not get up. Ignacio had been near the front of the group with his arm around Rosa, helping her as best he could as she was suffering as much as the others when a commotion arose behind him. He quickly helped down to the sand and ran back to see what the outcry was about. Arriving, he saw that it was a woman who had fallen. When he turned her over, her face was pale and mottled and a light froth came from between her lips. She was quite dead and the stoic Ignacio found himself crying at the sight of her. He knew her of course, but could not remember her name. She had been at the Captain's table not so long ago and now she was nothing more than a limp rag.

De Cuellar and de Arobe made their way back to him with the two de Arobe sons trailing behind. So consumed was Ignacio with the poor woman's fate that he did not notice the men come up behind him. De Cuellar called his name and called it again but Ignacio did not respond. It wasn't until de Cuellar put a hand on his shoulder and shook him that Ignacio came out of his reverie. De Arobe helped Ignacio shakily to his feet as he tried to focus on the men before him through watery eyes.

"Come away, Father," said de Cuellar softly, "There is nothing more that can be done here."

Ignacio wiped the tears from his eyes and glared at de Cuellar angrily.

"Nothing more?", he cried, his voice hoarse. "She should not have died! *We* should not have to die here on this endless quest for a city that may or may not be around the next bend. That is all we have been hearing from you for countless days now."

"What would you have me do? Our course is clear to us. We have ocean to one side, a dangerous forest to the other. We have no choice."

"The choice we are pursuing is clearly going to kill us," said Ignacio angrily. "In the forest there is food, shade and water. We need to get off this wretched beach for our own sakes."

"Come now, Father. You are beginning to sound like Mariano. You know there are infinitely more perils within the forest. Savages and animals that may hunt us."

"We know nothing about the savages. We have only conjectures about what dangers they pose to us."

De Cuellar stepped back and started walking away. "We don't have time for this, Ignacio. I will forgive your outburst this once. If the people are unwell, it would be best to get them where they need to be and that is yet ahead of us. In time, you will come to see that I am right."

Ignacio called to his receding back. "We must at least bury her!"

"As I said, we do not have time for this," said de Cuellar without a backward glance. "I doubt you will find anyone with strength enough to dig a hole for you."

"Then I shall dig it myself!"

"Do as you will."

Ignacio clenched his fists and stepped toward de Cuellar. He was stopped by a gentle yet firm hand on his arm. De Arobe stood by his side.

"My sons and I will help you, Ignacio." Ignacio nodded and turned back to the woman. "He is mad."

"That may well be," said de Arobe sympathetically. "We will have time to debate that further once we attend to this luckless woman."

* * *

It was a shallow grave, but a grave nonetheless. When the last stone had been gathered and placed atop the mound, Ignacio turned to de Arobe and said softly, "Thank you Señor for your help and your sons as well," nodding to each in turn. "And I must apologize for my outburst earlier. I was somewhat overcome with emotion and I am afraid I lost my temper."

"No need for contrition, Father," de Arobe replied. "You merely expressed the thoughts that have befallen all of us. I myself am not immune. There is only one among us who does not share our concerns, and misplaced as our trust must be, he is the one leading us."

"It is not my intent to suborn his authority nor do I pretend to have answers to our plight. I have prayed constantly for clarity and guidance, yet my thoughts are not clear and I fear we are misguided."

"And yet we need one more prayer to set this woman's soul on it's way."

Ignacio rose and wiped the dirt from his hands. "Indeed we do," he said with more conviction. "If it is my duty to stand over those who fall, I shall not leave them wanting." He took his place at the foot of the grave and looked around. Aside from de Arobe and his sons, who stood nearby with their heads bowed, no one else seemed to care about the proceedings. Whether it was from exhaustion, apathy or ennui, Ignacio could not tell. Perhaps they all feared their turns would come soon enough. He bowed his head, raising his hands in supplication, and began to intone his prayer for the newly deceased.

"O Lord, in Your infinite mercy, we commend to You the soul of our sister who has left this earthly life. Though her journey in this world was filled with trials and suffering, we trust that she now finds rest in Your eternal embrace. Grant her peace, O Lord, and may Your perpetual light shine upon her. Forgive her sins and welcome her into the company of Your saints, where sorrow and pain are no more. As we lay her to rest, may we be reminded of the brevity of our own lives and the hope of resurrection in Your Kingdom. In life and in death, we are Yours, O Lord. Guide us through our own trials, and keep us ever faithful to Your will. Comfort those of us who remain with the assurance that we will meet again in Your presence, where all tears will be wiped away. Through Christ our Lord, Amen."

As the Arobes echoed the final amen, Ignacio took in the sight of the beach, seeing it with renewed vision. Many of the company lay strewn on the sand, or sitting on rocks, some wandered aimlessly. They were all visibly near the end of their endurance. *I must talk to de Cuellar,* he thought. *If nothing else, these people need time to regain their strength. We must risk a foray into the forest. At the very least to get some fruit.*

It was then that his thoughts were triggered and he remembered leaving Rosa limp on the sand. He began to hurry toward her leaving the Arobes looking dismayed at his receding back. As he hastened through the sand, he passed Rodrigo who was cradling Mariano's head and weeping. Ignacio paused a moment to evaluate what was happening.

"Alas Rodrigo, has something happened to Mariano?"

"No Father, I deem he is only sleeping but he appears tired to the point of death. It's not just this forced march we are on but the madness that burns within him is draining him body and soul."

"We are at risk of that, I fear. And I do not believe that he is the only one to be afflicted with this malaise of madness."

"Yes, you speak of the Captain. I would have never said it before, but I believe he had a touch of it ere we ever left the ship."

"Perhaps that is true. I must first check on the Señora Rosa, then I shall seek out the Captain and see if we can not end this folly." With that, he continued his pace back to Rosa. As he approached her, he was immensely relieved to see her sitting upright playing idly with the sand at her feet. She looked up as he approached and gave him a smile.

"Nacho, where did you run off to? Is something amiss?" Ignacio hesitated a moment and then sat down on the sand next to her.

"There have been many things amiss since we arrived here," he said in an exasperated tone, "but yes, we have had a bit of trouble. A woman has died, apparently from sheer exhaustion."

"A woman? There are not many of us," she said with alarm in her voice. "Who was it?"

"I am ashamed to say that even as I recognized her, I could not for the life of me remember her name." Rosa began to get up.

"I must see her! I will know who she is." Ignacio gently pulled her back down.

"No Rosa, it is too late. We have already buried her as the Captain has given to us that we must move on with haste. I will go to him and try come to a reasonable comprise that may lengthen our journey but decrease the danger imposed upon us." He lay back on the sand, shielding his eyes with his arm. "But not this moment. We have just dug a grave with our hands as we have no shovels and I need but a few minutes to regain my strength."

"Yes, rest Nacho. I will alert you should the Captain come near." But Ignacio did not reply except in soft snores. Rosa looked at him and again smiled. She then looked toward the sun and wiped the sweat from her face. "How I wish I still had my parasol and fan."

When Ignacio awoke, the sun was already kissing the horizon. He saw that Rosa was still next to him fast asleep. He got to his feet with a groan and scanned the beach as he stretched the stiffness out of his limbs. Nothing much had changed. He spotted Rodrigo and made his way over to him.

"Evening, Rodrigo. How fare you?" He glanced and saw Mariano was not with him. "What of Mariano," he added, "Has his discomfort passed?"

"Hello Father," replied Rodrigo somewhat blearily. "I do not know if *his* discomfort has passed but *mine* certainly has not. He has indeed awakened but he now wanders mindlessly mumbling to himself. I spent some time following him about to keep him from harm but as he has not left the group or wandered into the forest, I chose to take respite from him." Rodrigo pointed and said, "See, there he is, just shuffling along in circles."

"Well, that seems to be an improvement at any rate. What of Captain de Cuellar? Do you know where he is?"

"I have not seen or searched for him nor do I care to. Perhaps he scouts the road before us."

"I must speak to him before ere long. For unpleasant reasons the troop has had time to rest a bit today. We should perhaps travel by night and take shelter as best we can during the day. Do you think you can gather up the company and make sure there are no strays?"

"Aye, I can do that, but what of the Captain? That has not been his way since the beginning of our trek."

"This I know, Rodrigo. I must talk to him and remind him that the greater portion of us are not soldiers and so I must appeal to his compassion. It is not just for me. We must appeal as a group"

Rodrigo snorted at this and said, "Say a quick prayer then, Father. No doubt he will regard such a suggestion as mutiny. He is steadfast in his ways, that one."

"That may be the way of it without doubt, as I have many other suggestions to present as well. Sooner is better than later, I deem, and so I shall go seek him out. Do your best then to round everyone up and meet us at the front of the line."

Ignacio made his way to the front in the direction of their path forward. He passed the group of soldiers and harqebusiers who were huddled together but did not see de Cuellar.

"Gentlemen," he said, addressing the group. "What of the Captain? What news of de Cuellar?"

"He went on ahead to reconnoiter," said one of the soldiers. "He said he would be back before night fell."

Ignacio looked down the beach. "That would be about now," he said, "yet I see no sign of him returning if that were the case. How long ago did he leave?”

"It has been hours, Father.”

"And he went alone?”

"Yes. Several of us offered to go with him but he would have none of it, and so we sit here and wait.”

"I have told the others to regroup and prepare to travel by night. Hopefully we will encounter him as he returns. Will you help?”

"Yes, of course,” replied the soldier, with his comrades nodding in assent. "It chafes us to sit here and do nothing.”

"Then let us get ready. Night is nearly upon us.” Ignacio looked again up the beach searching for a distant speck that might be their Captain, but he saw nothing. All he *did* see was a single line of footsteps leading away into the unknown.

* * *

Their pace was slow, but less fraught with despair. The air had cooled significantly and even those afflicted with the various symptoms of exposure were able to keep up. The night was inky black but a partial moon soon rose to give them glimpses of the road ahead. Ignacio marched at the forefront, keeping his eyes, as best he could, on the trail of footprints to see if they would veer into the ocean or toward the jungle and all trace of the Captain was be lost forever. For now, the footprints led straight down the middle of the strand and, try as he might, he could not discern any sign of the Captain ahead.

Rosa walked by his side, clinging to his arm as they walked. She seemed in better spirits and kept the pace easily. Ignacio had grown quite fond of her since the shipwreck. She exhibited a fortitude that many of the men in the company lacked. Rosa began humming a melody that Ignacio thought he recognized but could not place.

"What is that you sing?” he asked, glancing at her.

She looked up at him and said, "What? Oh, it is just something that came out of nowhere. Something I heard once long ago.”

"It is lovely. Do you know the words?”

"Ha! Yes, I do indeed but I am not much of a singer. I would bring shame to a beautiful song.”

Ignacio chuckled in turn. "You are performing for an audience of one, a very forgiving one I might add. Come, let me hear it.”

Rosa tightened her hold on Ignacio's arm and said laughing, "Have you not suffered enough on this journey? Very well, on your head be it. I want no complains after. It is called *El Camino Ante Mí* and I will do my best to not defile it. It goes like this:"

And she raised her voice, which to Ignacio, sounded like a voice angelically inspired.

To the road I go, not knowing the way,
The stars will guide me, I cannot stay.
With faith in my soul and the sun on the rise,
The road ahead will lead me to skies.
For every step, for every pain,
God sustains me, He is my guide.
Let the darkened path be filled with light,
And the road ahead offer its might.
Though the winds may blow and bend me low,
Though the seas may rise, I will not lose hope.
On the hardened earth my feet will tread,
The road ahead will lead me instead.
For every step, for every pain,
God sustains me, He is my guide.
Let the darkened path be filled with light,
And the road ahead offer its might.

Ignacio found himself moved to the point of tears. "That was beautiful, Rosa," he managed to utter huskily, betraying the emotion the song had laid on him. "And you indeed did it justice. More than that, it is uniquely appropriate to what we face now in our moment of uncertainty." Others had heard the song and they called out with praise and scattered clapping.

Rosa buried her head on Ignacio's arm. "Oh, I feel such a fool!"

"Nonsense. I feel it is something we all needed just now."

The stars were bright in the sky in spite of the light of the moon. El Camino de Santiago sprawled against the velvet black like a milky stain across the heavens. *If one sought evidence of God,* thought Ignacio, *there it is in all its splendor.* Ahead, the footprints went on and on, with never a break in stride or direction. *We must see some evidence of de Cuellar soon, but he seems like a man possessed. Surely, he cannot be far.* Even though they were traveling under cover of night, without the sun constantly beating on them, the pace was slowing noticeably. Rodrigo was not far off and Ignacio called to him.

"Ho, Pilot! How much longer to this night?"

"Not long now," the big man replied. "Another hour mayhap, two if I judge wrongly."

"Let us pray you are not. I feel we are flagging. Soon we must make shelter against the day." Rodrigo made no reply to this and he was once more left to his thoughts. He glanced at the line of the jungle. If it was ominous during daylight, it was doubly so now. The forest was never quiet, with bird calls and rustling, but at night there were the frequent cries of unknown beasts that shivers down the staunchest back. Ahead, the beach seemed to come to an end, but it was evident that it was merely another bend approaching. Ignacio prayed fervently that something new would be seen once they rounded it. As he thought this the sky began to lighten. Apparently Rodrigo *was* wrong but in the right direction. *We shall round the bend and then make camp.*

The bend turned out to be a little further than first thought, but it mattered little. The sun had not yet shown its face and set the sand shimmering with heat. As they rounded the bend, with Ignacio still praying for something new to see, they were greeted with the same vista they had been seeing for weeks. With one small exception. The was a man standing there a ways down the shoreline, facing away from them. Ignacio broke into a run.

In a minute, Ignacio had reached him and came to a stop in front of the Captain. "De Cuellar! Are you well? Why did you abandon us so?" De Cuellar looked at him impassively, apparently trying to focus and taking a full moment to realize who stood before him. Instead of greeting Ignacio, he merely pointed past him down the beach.

"Did I not tell you? Can you now see I was right?" Ignacio turned in the direction proffered and looked. There was nothing there but after a moment he saw it. Far away along the shoreline, a gray shadow lay across the beach.

"There," said de Cuellar unmoving, "is the city wall of Portoviejo."

Chapter Eight

The coastal ecosystems of 16th-century South America presented a rich mosaic where tropical forests blended seamlessly into mangroves and the Pacific shoreline. Here, the currents of the Humboldt and the warmth of the equatorial sun converged to create a cradle of life, from the lush vegetation of the coastal plains to the teeming marine ecosystems. The indigenous peoples, particularly the Shuar, understood the rhythms of this land, living in harmony with the tides and the forests, preserving a delicate balance that colonial expansion would soon test.

-Dr. Isabela Gómez del Valle, Ecologist and Scholar of Ecuadorian Natural History

Alvaro de Cuellar did not start life wealthy or to a noble family. He was born to a modest, yet well respected family with shipbuilding and seafaring as his heritage. His father had joined the Navy as a young man and found himself rising through the ranks through hard work and perseverance. He managed to catch the eye of various naval officials and eventually found himself groomed as officer material. Alvaro was deeply influenced by his father's career although, due to the constraints of a life at sea, he did not see much of his father through his early years. Still, as soon as he had come of age, he too joined the Navy, and due to his father's reputation and recommendation, he was immediately put into the officer program. He had inherited his father's work ethic and fortitude. The Admiralty was quite taken by young de Cuellar and favorable posts were often placed in his path.

Yet, de Cuellar's ambitions went farther. He dreamed of fame and glory, conquering new lands and new people. By his early twenties, de Cuellar had proven himself a capable leader, rose to be one of the youngest captains in the fleet. Before being assigned to the *San Felipe y Santiago* his career had already spanned two decades of service, during which he gained recognition for his sharp tactical mind and calm demeanor under pressure. He was known for his even-handed leadership and his commitment to the mission at hand. Yet, if truth be told, he was also pig-headed and stubborn. And so, he served in various capacities, from escorting treasure fleets from the Americas to defending Spanish interests in the Caribbean. By the time he was given command of the *San Felipe y Santiago*, he had earned the trust of the Spanish Crown.

The Pacific theater was new territory to him, however, and he quickly found that the distance from the Spanish Empire had somewhat diminished his prestige. True, the Pacific was indeed a coveted post offering new lands and new peoples, the very thing de Cuellar had craved, but now he was far from the spotlight and this rankled. While he was still able to to exert a fair share of autonomy, he had been relegated to ferrying soldiers, dignitaries, and precious cargo from one port to another. The New World was being conquered but de Cuellar still had not made his mark on it.

He took to creating new routes between his ports of call, in the hopes of discovering uncharted islands with innumerable treasures or enemy ships to defeat in combat. His pilots and navigators found this troubling, to say the very least. De Cuellar never disclosed his reasons for diverting from the established shipping lanes and his men were hard pressed to follow his seemingly strange and time-consuming meanderings around the Pacific. That all came to an end, of course, when the *San Felipe y Santiago* was shipwrecked. Now, instead of roaming the seas in search of glory, he found himself stranded on land in search of survival. And it rankled.

* * *

"What are you talking about?"

"You can plainly see the wall," said de Cuellar distantly. "I told you we would reach Portoviejo, and there it is."

By now the others had caught up to de Cuellar and Ignacio. Rosa and Rodrigo came up alongside them.

"You said Portoviejo was a settlement. Why in God's name would they have a fortified wall?"

"To keep out the savages, of course. It may be a settlement but it is part of the Empire, with all the resources it needs at hand."

"Wait," Rosa interjected, "of what wall do you speak?"

Ignacio pointed down the beach and Rosa and Rodrigo followed his finger. "See there," said Ignacio mockingly, "that smudge in the distance on the beach? This man says it is a vast wall surrounding a settlement. A village!"

Rodrigo shielded his eyes from the now rising sun and said, "There is something there but I cannot be sure what it is. We'll know more as we get closer. I judge it to be another day's march at best."

De Cuellar suddenly became animated. "Yes!" he cried. "Yes, we must get closer. Soon we shall be among our own again!"

"I think not, Captain," Ignacio interposed. "We have been marching all night just to get where we are now. The people need to make use of what shelter they can and wait out the day. They...*we* must have rest."

"Nay," said de Cuellar forcefully, "we are so close. Relief is at hand."

"I am afraid Father is right, my Captain," Rodrigo said. "We are exhausted, sick and hungry. If we rush this, well, several of us are nigh on to dying."

"Nonsense. Leave them here if need be. We'll have the township send rescuers for them."

"Captain," said Ignacio in a persuading tone, "You are not listening. The people are in dire needs. While I do not believe that what we see is what you say, it will go better for us to wait and go with what strength we can muster in the cooler moonlight."

De Cuellar started walking away. "Then I shall go myself," he called over his shoulder. "I will not wait for weaklings such as you!"

Ignacio and Rodrigo jumped forward and grabbed him by the shoulders. "Captain! You are in no better shape then the rest of us!" exclaimed Ignacio.

"Take your hands from me this instant, you dog!" he cried into Rodrigo's face. "This is mutiny and I will see you hang from the yardarm! I am the authority here and you shall do as I command! All of you! I will make sure you pay for this indig..."

"Forgive me, Captain," said Rodrigo as he suddenly clenched his meaty fist and plowed it into de Cuellar's chin. De Cuellar fell like limp rag doll while Rosa and Ignacio gasped audibly. "but we no longer have a yardarm." He rubbed his fist and smiled at the others. "Perhaps when his senses return, he will return to his senses."

* * *

Later in the day, while the sun was still high, Ignacio got up from his sleep pit in the sand and went to check on de Cuellar. He found Rodrigo sitting while the Captain was still stretched out senseless.

"He is still out?" asked Ignacio.

"Aye, but it is not from the blow I dealt him. He sleeps true sleep now. He was just as exhausted as the rest of us but his mania kept him going."

"Yes, his mania. Perhaps justified, perhaps not. I am concerned that the mania will spread if we are out here for much longer."

"Most of us have no energy left for mania, Father. Even Mariano has calmed down. Witless and somnambulant but calm."

Ignacio sat next to Rodrigo. "What do you make of what we saw this morning? Do you really think that a small settlement, even one that is part of the Empire, has the resources and manpower to construct such a thing?"

"I do not *what* to think," said Rodrigo slowly. "It seems unlikely, but who knows. We will be traveling in darkness so its true nature will not be apparent until daybreak."

"But would we have not seen at least some fishing boats? Especially that early in the morning?"

"Fishing boats are small. We probably would not see them at this distance." He looked at Ignacio with a bit of curiosity. "It seems to me that your mind is made about what we will find."

"I hope fervently that I am wrong, that salvation is right around the corner, yet my feeling is that if we were so near a settlement large enough to support the building of such a protective wall, we would have seen signs of it by now. Fishing boats? Sentries? Signal fires?"

"On the wall itself, you mean? You have reasonable doubts, to be sure, but if they *do* post sentries and signal fires, we are sure to see them when we begin our march in darkness."

"I pray our Lord grants me patience, Rodrigo. I want more than anyone to see this flock delivered safely." He had a sudden thought. "Is Portoviejo on the shipping routes?"

"Assuredly it is. I have never been there myself nor seen it from the sea, but I have no doubt it is serviced by ships the same as other colonies."

"But not by the *San Felipe y Santiago.*"

"No. Our route is between Perico and Callao. We occasionally make port at Veragua for refit and new orders but that is far north of here. Other ships must have Portoviejo on their route. Why do you ask?"

"Something else to look for, I suppose. If we see a ship lying at anchor..."

"It would be months between stops, Father. The chances of us arriving at the same time are not in our favor."

"I know, Rodrigo, yet at the moment, I have nothing else to muse upon. I am torn between what I hope for and what may actually be." He looked about at the others. Everyone seemed to asleep, many very near to the treeline where some measure of shade was afforded. His stomach suddenly growled, which had not been totally unusual in these last weeks, but the growl came with a wave of nausea. "Have we anything to eat?"

"The soldiers have made a short foray into the forest. They have gathered such fruits and edibles as the could. You should go to them right now before those pigs have devoured it all."

"And you?"

"For the moment, I have had my fill of fruit. I need something of more substance. Oh, that a wild boar or deer would wander onto the beach!"

Ignacio laughed as he rose. "Then bow your head in prayer, my friend. Let God hear the grumbling in your stomach for I can hear it plainly myself!"

"Aye, I will pray for wine as well. No harm in trying."

* * *

Later, the sun had finally begun to wester, but the clouds that had been hovering about the horizon began to move in, turning the sun into a pale ghost. The band began to rise as the prospect of a final march and possible salvation motivated them. Ignacio went back to Rodrigo who was still watching over de Cuellar.

"How is he, Rodrigo?"

"I was just about to wake him. I fear what he may say or do once he is roused."

"That cannot be helped. Go ahead, wake him up. We must get

moving."

Rodrigo shook the Captain and the man was easily wakened. He looked about him, clearly confused for a moment.

"Where are we?" he asked muzzily, "what has happened?"

Ignacio replied warily, "We are about to embark again. We go to see if that thing we saw is truly the wall to a city." At the mention of this, de Cuellar brightened considerably.

"Yes, the wall, by God. I remember seeing it off in the distance but I thought I was alone."

"You were, Captain," said Ignacio carefully. "We found you here and made camp. Do you not remember?" De Cuellar sat rubbing his chin where Rodrigo had struck him. There was a visible bruise.

"I do not. I suppose I must have stumbled and fallen. My chin is quite sore." Ignacio and Rodrigo glanced at each other, agreeing non verbally to not pursue this line of thought.

"Yes, that may be so," said Ignacio. "We found you that way on the sand."

De Cuellar stood and Rodrigo steadied him. "Do we yet have a full complement?" de Cuellar asked. He looked about and said, "Dark is soon approaching, we must be on our way. Perhaps we can make Portoviejo by morning." He walked off and began ordering soldiers to round the people up.

Rodrigo looked at Ignacio with trepidation in his eyes. "What do you make of that? Does he truly not remember the blow I landed on him?"

"Softly, Rodrigo. He may not recall what happened during the height of his madness. He may come to it later, but for now we will take it a divine provenance that we do not have that particular issue to deal with." Ignacio smiled and added, "But please, refrain from hitting him again."

Rodrigo did not smile back. "This I *do not* promise. I will do what needs to be done for the safety and continued survival of our group. Captain or no, I will take whatever measures are needed at any moment. His authority here is severely limited and his leadership here is more of a courtesy than anything else." He paused and mused a moment. "Leadership! Ha! He has already abandoned us once. If he goes off on his own again, I, for one, will not waste time looking for him!"

Ignacio was taken aback by Rodrigo's explosive outburst. It was not only the most he had ever heard coming from the big man's mouth, but also the most vehemently expressed. "Have a care, Rodrigo. I appreciate your feelings on the matter, but I also note that you stayed by him all the day while he slept." Rodrigo calmed and stared at his feet. "It is apparent," continued Ignacio, "that you care for him as *much* as you care for any of us. We will take it as it comes and we will treat him with compassion first." Rodrigo nodded his consent and did not comment.

Having no baggage and very little in the way of stores, the group was on the move in short order, each at their own pace. Ignacio and Rosa, being in better health, were often at front but were mindful of the others, slowing their pace to allow the others to catch up. Rodrigo was one of these, who assisted the hapless Mariano. Mariano, for his part, was doing much better. He had shed some of his catatonia and was aware of his surroundings. Rodrigo was even able to engage him in some limited conversation from time to time. At any rate, far from having overcome his hysteria was clearly regaining most of his functions of reasoning.

They were well into their first hour of marching when Ignacio had a sudden insight. De Cuellar had made no protest or comment to the revised schedule of walking after dark. He had accepted the change as if that had been how it was since the beginning, or as if he had thought of it himself. *That is more likely. Now that he has shed the mantle of mania somewhat, he probably* does *think he ordered us to walk during the night.* He crossed himself and thought, *Thank you Lord, I will take whatever scraps you throw my way.* Rosa saw him do this.

"Are you praying, Nacho?" She snickered and added, "of course you are. That was silly of me. I am sure our navigator friend over there constantly looks to the stars for guidance. You look farther."

Ignacio looked at her in feigned surprise. "Are you mocking me, Señora? I have very little in the way of tools and must use such as I have." He stopped her before she could attempt to apologize. "I jest, Rosa, much in the same spirit as you. If you must know, I was giving thanks for our continued existence in spite of the constant challenges. As for 'our navigator friend', there are far too many clouds for the stars to be of much to him."

"What if we are already in Hell, Ignacio? What if the endless walking, hunger and disease is our penance for the misdeeds of our life? What if were are damned?"

"I do not believe that, Rosa. In Hell, we would have no hope and there is yet hope for us. If we can feel it, and *I* can, then we are not yet in that place of torment."

"The only assurance I have is that you are with us. Someone such as yourself would never find himself in Hell. I cannot speak for the rest of us."

"Rosa, please clear these thoughts from your head. Doubt will only lead you astray. Have faith."

"I lose a little of it every day, Ignacio."

"Then I shall be your rock. Let us pray together."

Ignacio put his arm around Rosa's shoulder and muttering softly to each other, they walked on. Around them the clouds thickened and a light mist arose from the sea. In the distance, lightning flashed intermittently but far enough that no thunder was heard. This would not hold for long. Another storm was coming.

Not far away, a similar, yet less cogent conversation was taking place. It had been days since Rodrigo had to physically support Mariano on their seemingly endless journey, but he still accompanied him to support him in any other way he could. As they trudged along, Mariano started mumbling. To Rodrigo's ears, he seemed to be saying the same thing over and over.

"What is that you are saying, Mariano? Speak up that I may hear you."

Mariano's reply was still mumbled, but Rodrigo was able the decipher the words.

"Where are we going? We are going home, Mariano, we get closer every day."

"Home? Whose home? Mine...yours?"

"What? No, no, no. We will soon be among others, other Spaniards who will take us in, shelter us and feed us."

"Why would they do that? We are cursed, doomed, to walk this earth endlessly."

"Why would they help us? They are Spaniards, Christians. They would do unto us as we would do unto them."

"Not good. Not good."

Rodrigo tried humor to try to break through the man's fog. "No, it will be good! It will be better than good! They will ply us with roasted meats, heady wines and lusty women. You will want to stay there forever!"

"We have been here forever. I do not want to stay here. I want to go home."

"Mariano, we *are* going home. Right now. Just keep putting one foot in front of the other."

"Home? Whose home? Mine...yours?"

Rodrigo realized that the conversation would go in circles if he continued, and so he stopped responding and Mariano kept repeating his last question over and over until he simply forgot to keep asking.

* * *

The road became increasingly rocky. There were boulders strewn all over the sand, and although the walkers had encountered many stony areas on their journey down the coast, they had not yet descried such monolithic stones. And the ground had begun to rise. There was now a steep slope between them and the ocean. The clouds were unrelenting and the sounds of the storm were closing. Somewhere in front of the came the sound of crashing waves.

The group slowed to halt, all of them sensing that something was amiss. A sudden succession of lightning illuminated the scene before them and they all knew in an instant they were indeed doomed. They were dismayed to find themselves at the foot of a formidable escarpment, waves crashing endlessly at its feet. It was indeed a wall. Not a city wall, but one carved by nature long ago, and as such, impenetrable as a fortress.

As if wanting to inflict pain on top of injury, the rain chose that moment of revelation to pour down in blinding sheets of water that came down with such fury it hurt the skin. Everyone made a mad scramble to the remaining treeline to get out of the stinging deluge.

By sheer happenstance, Ignacio ended up next to de Cuellar under the trees which whipped to and fro in the sudden tempest. They were no drier or safer here than they were a moment ago. Ignacio had to shout to be heard above the tumult.

"There is no wall! No city! Where in God's name are we?"

"Ask Him yourself, priest! This is not my doing!"

"Is it not? I begged you to consider a path through the forest!"

"None would have followed you! Has God granted you vision to see what the rest of us could not? I think not! Away from me with your incessant harangue! It is I that leads this band of miscreants, it is I that shall bring them to safety! All you can promise them is milk and honey in the afterlife." Ignacio bristled at this and turned away. He nearly crashed into Rodrigo who had heard it all and had a murderous look in his eye.

"Shall I hit him again?"

They had no choice but to hunker down and wait for nature to expend its fury. Surprisingly, Ignacio was able to find sleep even as his mind roiled with the same ferocity as the storm. He dreamt uneasily that he had fallen off a cliff and was falling eternally into the blackest abyss. He jerked and quivered in his uneasy torpor as Rosa, sitting beside him, watched on anxiously. She could imagine, perhaps, what was going through the man's mind, yet she could do little more than sympathize. She wanted to wake him and comfort him, but Rodrigo had already stopped her once. He too, watched Ignacio. And Rosa and Mariano. *He is like a large guardian angel,* she thought. *I am thankful for that.* After a while, she too succumbed to slumber. And still, Rodrigo watched on.

Chapter Nine

South America's middle western coastline, spanning Ecuador and Peru, is a dynamic intersection of tectonic forces and coastal erosion. The rugged cliffs and sweeping deserts were shaped by the collision of the Nazca and South American plates, creating a landscape that is both beautiful and perilous. From the towering Andes to the arid coastal plains and verdant jungles, it is a story of relentless upheaval and adaptation and an environment where human survival depends on understanding the land's volatile rhythms.

-Dr. Emilio Vargas Montoya, Professor of Geology, University of Quito, 1967

In his nightmare, Ignacio's fall into the abyss slowly came to a halt. Surrounded by darkness he felt lost and alone. In time, a spark grew before him, expanding until he could see that it was a primitive hut, a ramshackle assembly of wooden poles and palm fronds with an eldritch light emanating from the entrance. He stepped forward and entered. There was nothing inside but a stool and on that stool a man was seated. Ignacio recoiled, instantly recognizing the apparition. Here was the same face he had seen when he had first boarded the *San Felipe y Santiago* in what seemed a lifetime ago. Frozen with sudden fear, he stood before the spirit unmoving. The man began to speak, the words rolled like thunder and shook Ignacio's resolve to the core.

"Numiátai nujús pujukaratunmi," the dream spectre intoned. *"Nunkui tatajai, uuniru wárisa. Tsérumui yajáitkau, uunt nunki natárammi. Núuka, itia wa ainta, apajú pujakatai. Itia ítaru chicharutkau, apá, yaamtai pujukaratai. Nunkui nuwai táktai. Wiaa Núka Nankái. Wiaa, yáa winiatui. Nútsa, Tsewa, ayumpi."*

Ignacio was astounded to find that, although he did not understand the language at all, the meaning to it was clear and translated roughly to his mind as: *"You walk in lands not meant for your feet. The jungle watches, and the earth remembers. Blood will stain the rivers, and the spirits are restless. The path ahead is dark, priest, and not all who walk it will see the dawn. Beware the silence that follows the wind, for it is not emptiness but a warning. Life and death dance together here, and they have chosen their partners. The earth will take what it is owed. Come to the Crown of Spears. Come and be released. I, Tsewa, have spoken"*

Ignacio awoke, sitting up with a jolt, crying out, "Tsewa!"

The outcry startled those around him, and Rosa rushed to his side.

"What is it, Ignacio? Are you alright?"

Ignacio buried his head in his hands, the terror he had felt, the paralysis in his limbs were still with him. It was a long moment before he lowered his hands and took stock of his surroundings. It was still raining heavily but clearly it was daytime. Several people were looking at him with concern.

"It was nothing," he said softly. "A dream. A nightmare, nothing more." Even as he said this, he felt the penetrating stare of the apparition boring into his soul. Rosa offered him a skein of water, which he guzzled down hungrily. Although he was, as was everyone, soaked to the bone, the water seemed to wash away some of the dread of his vision. "Thank you," he said weakly. "I am sorry to have alarmed anyone. It was, as I said, just a dream."

"You shouted something as you woke," said Rosa. "I could not make it out. What did you say?"

Ignacio knew full well what it was. The name Tsewa rolled in his head like thunder. He chose to keep that to himself as there was no way he could explain it to anyone without sounding mad. "I do not know. I cannot remember."

Rosa sat next to him and embraced him. "That may be. You were obviously dismayed by it. Now, put the comfort of faith in the forefront and calm your mind."

"That is difficult when dismay is all around us." He looked around and added, "What time is it? What else has happened?"

"I suppose it is about midday, although it is hard to be certain. De Cuellar has sent men into the forest to see if there is a way around the cliff. They have yet to return."

"Ha. So *now* he follows my advice, when there is no other course to follow." *I hope they do return*, he thought to himself, thinking of the ominous warning in his dream. *This would be a perfect place for an ambush*, thinking also how he had maintained that the comportment of the natives was an unknown and that they could be potential allies. That was before his visit to Tsewa's hut. Now he was less sure. "How long ago did they leave?"

"They left as soon as it became light enough to see. Several hours, I suppose."

"Did de Cuellar go with them?"

"You come back from your nightmare with your humor intact," she laughed. "Of course he did not go. He ordered three of the soldiers and Rodrigo to scout ahead in his stead."

"Rodrigo as well? He should be here. His best role was in helping the others in their need."

"Listen," said cupping her ear. "I am sure we can hear Rodrigo grumbling even from here."

"I just hope we do not hear him screaming from here."

Rosa looked at him quizzically, "What has gotten into you, Nacho? You are our pillar, the voice of reason that the rest of us look to for succor and assuagement."

Ignacio disentangled himself from Rosa's arms and stood. "Perhaps that time has passed. I fear there are forces working against us, and some of those forces are right here in this camp. Over-confidence of some, weakness and apathy of others. We are coming to a crossroad, I deem, and the path ahead is not as clear as it once was." He started walking away.

"Ignacio, you frighten me! Where are you going?"

"Nowhere and everywhere it seems," he said as he walked. "I will tend to the flock as best I can and see if I cannot regain a bit of my composure. Then I will confront de Cuellar once more."

Rosa was left staring at his receding back, frowning as she watched him go. *If madness claims him, then we are all surely lost*, she thought. *He has begun to break and I am left to pick up the pieces as best I can. Oh, Rodrigo, I pray you hurry back.*

It was not madness that clouded Ignacio's mind, but a sudden anger at his inability to make a change for the better. His nightly prayers were a thing of the past as exhaustion overcame him more often than not. He felt disconnected. He felt he had lost his center, and he felt that his faith might be next to go. Although the main elements of his dream had faded, the foreboding he perceived could not be shaken.

He spent the next hour going from group to group seeing their welfare. There were all cold, wet and miserable but well enough he surmised given the circumstances. As he approached, the last two, however, the now familiar feeling of dread rose in his heart. It was Mariano and the young boy. The lay side by side, unmoving and Ignacio knew straight away that they were dead. Mariano's eyes were still open, his face in a grimace. Ignacio knelt and gently closed the man's unseeing eyes. The boy looked to be at peace, almost angelic in repose, as if he had accepted his fate willingly. Ignacio did what he could for them, which in his eyes, was not much at all. He could not bury them. The now constant downpour made sure of that, nor was there anyone who could help dig a grave if he could. The fittest men in the group had been sent away, possibly on a fool's errand, to find a safe path back to beach on the other side of the cliff. Ignacio took his time, rain pouring over his grieving face, and said what prayers he could over the pair. It sounded hollow, even to him, who had recited numerous prayers in similar circumstances throughout his life.

It had been his intention to speak to de Cuellar, to come to some agreement as to what they should do going forward, but he suddenly had no heart for it. Talking to de Cuellar was like talking to the wind. The man would not be swayed by mere words. *Such as my words to our Lord*, he thought, *his ways are a mystery even unto himself*. And so he sat himself down next to Mariano and spoke to him as if he could be heard.

"Of all the things you have done in your life, this is the worst you could have done to those that considered you a friend. It will go badly especially for Rodrigo, as I know he thought of you as a brother. The rest of us will look on your passing with dismay and anguish. They will look on in fear of their own demise, their hope and faith diminished unfairly. Rest ye well, Mariano. I pray you are at peace." He shifted his gaze to the boy, who he knew to be named Gilberto. "I knew you not well, young man, orphaned as you were by the shipwreck. For better or worse, your circle had been closed, and there was no one there to witness it save poor Mariano. Take his hand and guide each other to eternal life in the Kingdom of Heaven." Spent, he rose and found himself a drier spot among the trees and lay down as if one also bereft of life. He dared not sleep, however. His fear of meeting the terrible Tsewa again was greater than his fear of death, and so he began to recite the rosary.

Rosa had watched him from a distance, yet when he finally lay himself down, she did not go to him. *He fights more than the rest of us and with less weaponry*, she mused. *Yet, he is just a man. A man of strength and conviction, but a man nonetheless.*

Despite himself, Ignacio *did* fall asleep, but it was dreamless and he awoke hours later feeling much refreshed. The rain had abated and now a mere sprinkle was falling. As he stretched his aching limbs, a shout rang out. The scouts had returned. Ignacio leapt to his feet and ran toward them. De Cuellar was at forefront and immediately began accosting them.

"What news do you bring? Is there a way before us." He gave no notice of the men's condition. They were bedraggled, muddied and bleeding from a score of scratches on their arms and faces. They had not come out of the forest at a run. They came with a shuffling numbness that only physical expenditure can bring. De Cuellar fumed as the men took water from those that offered it and remained silent. "Well? Speak! What have you found?"

Rodrigo glared at him a moment and then replied, "There *is* a trail. Several actually. Who or what has made them is not for me to say, but yes, there is a trail that seems to go in the direction we seek."

"So, you did not take it to the end to be sure?"

"No Captain," replied Rodrigo wearily, "The return climb would have been grueling and we would not be standing here before you until the morrow."

"I have no thanks to give you for a task half done. Get thee on the way again and find out for true!"

Despite his fatigue, Rodrigo bristled and soldiers in his retinue looked on in disbelief. Ignacio chose this moment to intervene saying, "Captain, these men have done what you have asked and more. If there is a way forward, however imprecise, we should *all* go. We accomplish nothing sitting here and waiting."

De Cuellar looked at Ignacio the same way he would look at a weevil on his breakfast biscuit. Yet, to his credit, he did not explode into the stubborn rage that had become his hallmark. Instead, he calmed himself and said, "You speak truth, Father. My passion has gotten away from me. Forgive me." He looked about at the others and then at the landscape in general. "The day has gotten away from us. We shall pass the night and enter the jungle at first light. We will see then where this trail truly goes." Ignacio breathed a sigh of relief and nodded, grateful that the confrontation he had feared did not come to pass. "Get what rest and nourishment you can," de Cuellar said, addressing the group. "On the morrow, we move."

One of the soldiers then stepped forward with a bulging bag. "We were fortunate, Captain. It is not much but we managed to snare some game along the way."

"Start a fire then," responded de Cuellar, "If there is any dry tinder to be found in this waterlogged hole. At least our bellies with have something to gnaw on." He paused a moment and added, "Thank you, men. You have done well." This alone went far in mollifying the demeanor of Rodrigo and the soldiers and they visibly relaxed.

As they set about to prepare a meager meal, Ignacio managed to catch Rodrigo's eye and motioned him over. He led him to a relatively secluded space and said, "Rodrigo, I appreciate what you have gone through this day, and we are all grateful for the trials you have faced. You are no doubt tired, but there is something I must tell you." Rodrigo frowned, causing Ignacio to lose some of his composure. "Nay," he said haltingly, "it is perhaps better if you see for yourself." He led Rodrigo to where Mariano and the young boy lay, and stood by saying nothing else. Rodrigo looked on the scene, his face dropping. His shoulders slumped and he fell to his knees by Mariano's side.

"Were you with him at the end?"

"Alas no. I was not witness to his passing, or that of Gilberto, the boy. I do not know what their final moments entailed, but I have faith they went in peace.

"Aye, so it appears. In many ways, I lost my friend many days ago," he said, glancing at Ignacio. "Strange that he would wait until I was away to go on his own journey."

"It was perhaps a blessing, Rodrigo. Do not blame yourself for things you cannot control. Had you been here, it may have gone worse for him, and no doubt yourself."

Rodrigo stood and wiped his face. "Yes, I believe you are right. The end would have come were I here or not. It was, I suppose, a matter of time and we have spent far too much time pursuing the inevitable."

"Have hope, Rodrigo. All is not in vain."

"So you are obligated to say, Father." He turned to Ignacio and continued. "Thank you for telling me about Mariano straight away. I will handle things from here."

Ignacio, confused, said, "What is it you plan to do?"

"I will tend to the bodies. I will inter them myself. No, no...," he said as Ignacio made to protest. "This is something I have to do. Something I *need* to do. You go tend to the living, I will do one last favor for my friend."

Ignacio stepped back a pace and bowed his head. "Peace be with you, Rodrigo." The big man made no reply and set about his task.

* * *

In a relatively short amount of time, a fire had been started and the smell of roasted meat drifted through the air. There was not much to go around, as the scouts had returned with only three small beasts, but everyone was at least afforded a taste. Many continued gnawing on bones long after the meat had been stripped away. By then, full dark had fallen and the sky began to clear. Stars sparkled in the newly washed sky like precious gems affixed to the dome of Heaven. The sight gave Ignacio no comfort. He had experienced more today than he had in many days, and although he was rested in body, his mind, his soul, were in turmoil. Against his own will, he replayed the events of the day; from his initial nightmare to the one that followed, he found no relief. He stared into the fire, which having been small to begin with, was now sputtering into a mass of embers and ashes.

Rosa had, wisely, stayed away from Ignacio throughout the day. She had watched him as he dealt with his struggles, but resolutely vowed to give him the space he obviously needed. As she watched him sit by the fire, she could no longer hold back. He had been her only source of comfort and friendship since their arrival on the beach. She felt safer by his side. She walked over to the dying fire and tumbled down next to him. He made no sign that he was aware of her, so she picked up a nearby stick and began prodding the embers with it. Finally, he turned to her and gave her a wan smile.

"It is good to see you," he said anemically.

"Forgive me, Father, for I have sinned," she said, with a touch of drama.

"Oh, is it time for the Confessional?" he replied, somewhat more animated. And what, pray tell, is this egregious sin you speak of?"

"I have a friend, who was clearly in need of comfort and relief, and through my own selfishness, denied him what he needed."

He chuckled and some of his old self began to come through. "I see plainly what you are driving at. You are not the only conspirator to this misdeed." He took her hand at looked at her. "I too, am guilty of selfishness. I take all the burdens of the world and make them my own, eschewing all help that is freely given, thinking wrongly I have the means to fix them."

"You speak from despair because that is not how you truly perceive yourself. You care, yes, but never do you place yourself ahead of others. There are things you cannot control."

Ignacio laughed. "Truly, I said those very words to Rodrigo not long ago. I should heed my own advice."

"Indeed you should." She was quiet for a moment, then, "It was terrible what happened. Mariano, that young boy."

"Gilberto. His name was Gilberto. Very shy boy. Lost both his parents in the wreck. Trauma atop trauma for that young soul. I am afraid I never spoke more than two words to him in his short life."

Rosa saw immediately that he was once again slipping into introspection and so tried her best to change the subject. "The fire was a nice touch after all that rain. And what was that we ate? Do you know what kind of animal that was?"

"Ha, I am not quite sure. Some kind of rodent, no doubt. That is what we are reduced to, eating rats." He chuckled again and added, "And it was the best thing I have tasted in a long time. I plan to make it a regular part of my diet from now on." Rosa laughed.

"We have reached a point in life where, not only are we eating rats, but complaining that there are not enough of them!" She grabbed Ignacio's arm and mused, "There is such beauty here and because of our own plight, we never take the time to look and take it all in. Look at those stars, Nacho. Listen to the sea crashing against the cliff. There is beauty and music if we would just look and listen."

"You are right. There is a rich tapestry all around us, right there beyond our noses. We are the ones bringing chaos and discord to a new land. I hope we prove ourselves worthy of such a gift."

"Time will tell, Nacho. I, for one, am looking forward to our excursion into the forest tomorrow. I cannot help but wonder what lies beyond that canopy of trees. Adventure aside, it will be nice to get away from all this sand for a while."

"I know of what you speak," he said playfully. "It has become quite abrasive." Rosa groaned.

Chapter Ten

South America's northern coast along the boundary of Ecuador and Peru is a living tapestry. Dense mangroves meet the vibrant rainforests, creating an extraordinary convergence of ecosystems. Capuchin monkeys swing through the tropical canopies while panthers prowl beneath. Herons and caimans navigate the mangrove swamps, and meanwhile the nutrient-rich waters invite a wealth of marine life, sustaining the coastal communities and the entire web of life that depends on the seamless interplay between land and sea."

-Valeria Torres-Castillo, Ecologist and Expert on Ecuadorian Coastal Biodiversity

They had no choice but to walk in single file. The trail through the jungle was so overgrown in many places that it was near impossible to keep it in view. The men who had led the previous sortie were at the forefront, now acting as guides. The path was a narrow channel between brambles, bushes and broad leaves and they were all soon covered in scratches on their arms and faces. Scratches that attracted insects in droves. Their time was split between swatting at branches and swatting bugs whose only purpose in life seemed to be getting in eyes and mouths.

The going was slow. The canopy above them hid the sun and they were in an eerie gloom. They had long ago lost all sense of direction, and if it were not for scouts, they would have soon become hopelessly lost. The group gave no thought to going quietly as they crashed through the boskage, but the jungle was even louder. The incessant whining of flying things, monkeys chattering in the trees and calls of exotic birds, had them all on tattered nerves. Ignacio walked ahead of Rosa, clearing the path for her as well and as often as he could, but it was impossible to shield her completely.

He helped her over a fallen log and quipped, "Are you missing the sand yet, dear Rosalilly?"

"Not yet, Father Ignacio," she responded in kind, "nor do I miss the sun baking me like bread."

A few more steps brought them to a small ravine, filled with brambles, that Ignacio had to jump over. He held Rosa's hand when it was her turn to hurdle the obstacle. "Watch yourself. There you go." The ground suddenly leveled off and they made some haste to catch up to those in front of them. "We certainly do not want to become separated in this confusion. It is a wonder that Rodrigo and his men did as well as they did."

"Yes," said Rosa panting, "and he is sailor not a woodsman."

"Well, he had help, but there is no denying he is a smart man when it counts. That man has depths no one has plumbed."

Abruptly, the road became very steep and treacherous. There now stones and rocks of various sizes to contend with and they became silent as all their efforts went into the climb. An indeterminate amount of time passed and still they moved upward. Rosa, winded, said to no one in particular, "Is there no end to this? I am not a mountain goat!"

"I think we are coming to the backside of the cliff we saw from the beach. I did not appreciate how much higher it was at the time." All at once Rosa slipped on a loose stone and slid back down the slope, nearly bowling over those that followed. They helped her up as Ignacio made his way back to her. "Are you hurt?" he asked when he reached her.

"No," she said, dusting herself off. "I think I must have offended a mountain goat somewhere and it taught me a lesson. Do not fret about me, we are losing the others. Let us make haste."

Finally, they came to a place where, if not the top of the incline then quite near it, they caught up with the leaders who were laying or sitting about, exhausted. Ignacio and Rosa took this as an unspoken invitation to do the same as the last of the troupe filed in behind them. Ignacio looked at Rosa who was reclined and panting.

"You have scraped your legs in the fall. Do you have any other injuries?"

"I am well, thank you. It looks worse than it is. There is nothing to be done for it at any rate, except shoo away these nasty creatures who seem to have taken quite an interest."

"We should perhaps try to cover them or bind them to keep the insects away."

"With what, Nacho?" she asked huffily. "All that we have is what we wear."

"I could give you my shirt. Tear it into strips and..."

"Do not be foolish. As I said, I am fine. I will be ready to travel as soon as the time comes."

In what seemed mere moments, de Cuellar was on his feet, gesturing for the others to rise. "We cannot tarry here at will," he announced. "We burn what little daylight we have and I have no intention of spending the night here if it can be avoided." With that, the line began to move once more. The path was still as treacherous but the incline was less severe. In a while, the travelers came again to a halt. They had come to a fork in the trail.

"Which way?" he asked of the scouts. The Lieutenant spoke up. "We encountered this yesterday. Going to the right leads to the cliff's edge and stops. The other is our road."

"Then we will go to the cliff face. I would like to take a measure of how far we have come and see perhaps what lies ahead."

It was not a long detour and they soon found themselves coming into daylight. Reaching the edge, they reached a very narrow ledge overlooking the sea. To the right, far below, was the beach they had started from. To the left was unbroken jungle right to the water's edge. Further away, they espied their next challenge. A bright ribbon of water cleaved the jungle at the limits of sight. A river cut across from some hidden source and poured itself into the sea.

De Cuellar studied the scene and frowned. He then looked to the sun. "It is clear we yet have a long way to go and we are all tired. Moreover we will lose the sun in another hour. We will make camp here, such at it is and make way in the morning."

"At least we will be going downhill," said the Lieutenant. "We will make better time."

Rodrigo who, shielding his eyes against the sun, suddenly pointed toward the distant river's mouth and said, "Wait! Are those boats?"

* * *

They settled in along the cliff, well away from the edge, and made camp. Some were sent to hunt for game, others set about making a fire. There was rampant speculation about what Rodrigo had seen to the south. Not everyone had the sailor's eyesight that Rodrigo had and even de Cuellar expressed his doubts. 'We could be seeing pods of whales or dolphins. It is too far to tell," he offered. While boats were the general consensus, there were those that were not totally convinced. True, they had no alternate explanation, but they remembered de Cuellar's claim of seeing a city wall when it had in fact, turned out to be the escarpment upon which they now rested. But there *had* been something on the sea, many somethings in fact, that were slowly making their way up the river. The light had quickly failed and now all they had was conjecture. Morning might bring confirmation or it might not.

Ignacio took this time to retrieve his journal. It amazed him that he had managed to retain his pouch throughout their ordeals, and that the contents we relatively unscathed. He found himself a spot away from the general bustle and gathered his thoughts. His last entry was more than a week ago, and so it took him little time to start scribbling words onto his pages, straining his eyes to see in the gathering gloom. Behind him, the sounds of the nocturnal forest were beginning their clamor and, struggling, he managed to bring tonight's entry to a close. The fire was just being lit and he made his way over to it.

"Perhaps someone will see our little fire now that we are on higher ground," he said to no one in particular.

"If what I saw were indeed boats," intoned Rodrigo's gruff voice, "They were heading home for the night. There is too much vegetation between here and where they might dwell. This cliff faces the wrong way."

Ignacio mused on this and took his seat next to Rosa. The hunters had had little success in bringing game to the table and sat nearby, bemoaning that they had no weapons and were reduced to using sharpened sticks and rocks to bring down their prey. Be that as it may, the offering was a little larger than the night before, but they still grumbled as they set about skinning their spoils.

Before long, the smell of cooking meat wafted through the air and everyone soon fell in to their repast. The meat seemed a little gamier and less palatable, but no one complained too loudly, at the same time wondering when, if ever, they would they would again enjoy a decent meal. In time, they fell off to sleep, one by one, as the exertions of the day caught up with them. Soon, there was gentle snoring all about save for the two sentries posted to keep watch. The jungle sounds continued unabated, but the sleepers had become accustomed to the ruckus and slept on. A few hours later the sentries were relieved by their comrades and the night went on.

Morning came all too quickly for some as the prospect of another long trek weighed on their minds. Those that were hoping for another view of the purported boats were disappointed. The air was quite cool and the view to the south was obscured by a dense fog. They would be well on their way before the morning sun managed to burn it off. A quick repast of fruit was had before the camp was struck and the troop was made ready to continue the journey. Ignacio gathered his meager belongings, making sure the contents of his pouch were all accounted for. Satisfied, he joined the queue on the trail, falling in behind Rosa as usual.

"I am quite cold," she said to Ignacio over her shoulder. "I was shivering when I woke up."

"We were very exposed on that cliff," he replied. "I fear that soon you will be protesting that it is too hot." He looked around at the surrounding foliage and added, "Although it may take some time before the sun warms us in here." They soon reached the fork in the trail and followed it to the right. They again encountered a slope, although not as steep as the previous day's, and this time it was going down instead of up. As they made their way down, the forest seemed to close in on the them. The scouts at the front of the line found it increasingly difficult to follow the trail.

One of the scouts turned around and said to de Cuellar, "This is as far as we were able to make it previously. Any farther and we would been forced to spend the night." De Cuellar frowned slightly but made no reply. He instead gestured to keep going. The day was young and they had many miles to go. The pace slowed in places as the trail often disappeared. Sometimes it would be long moments before it was rediscovered. As a result, those following had no trouble keeping up and they occasionally jostled against each other.

As Ignacio predicted, the temperature began to rise and soon they we all drenched in sweat. The forest floor began to rise and fall although the tendency was generally downward. As before, they could not see the sun or landmarks to keep track of their heading. All they had was the barest hint of a trail, upon which their lives depended. The day wore on and the unchanging forest seemed to go on forever. At length they came upon a small clearing that barely had room for them all and a stop was called. De Cuellar stood, staring up through the trees, hoping get a glimpse of the sun but its rays could not penetrate the roof of branches and leaves.

"I judge to the sun to be about there," de Cuellar said pointing, "but that tells me nothing about which direction we are headed, how far we have come or how far we have yet to go. The accursed trail has been winding and I have lost my sense of direction."

"My sense is that we travel more or less in a southward direction," said the Lieutenant in response. "We have also been moving generally downward. It stands to reason that we are approaching sea level."

"I do not hear the ocean, nor the cry of gulls. We are perhaps too far inland. We are committed to follow the path to its end, wherever that may be."

"The end may be ours," quipped de Arobe, who up to now had kept his calm and been mostly silent while decisions were made around him.

"You can stay here if you like, Sirrah," de Cuellar shot back. "or follow the path back to the beach, I care not. If you *do* intend to follow, then follow and keep your tongue within your head." De Arobe hung his head while his sons glared.

The mood became sullen after that, and everyone remained silent. Partly because they were all tired, but mostly no one was willing to become part of de Cuellar's next tirade. After an hour or so, the signal was given to move on. There was some grumbling at this, but nothing loud enough to reach de Cuellar's ears.

Their path became somewhat easier as the ground leveled out and the trees abruptly became sparser. They were now able to walk together in small groups instead of single file and the inevitable chatter began once more. A few times they were loud enough for de Cuellar to have to wave at them and admonish them to dampen their continued racket. The trees continued to thin out and they were able to hasten their pace but then they were faced with another downward incline strewn with loose rocks and gravel. Although many managed to stay on their feet, others were forced to slide down on their bottoms, while a few flat out fell and rolled down the hill. Surprisingly, when they had all gathered at the bottom, there were no major casualties other than abrasions and bruises.

A few more minutes of walking brought them to a stream some ten feet wide. It was not very deep but flowed swiftly. Where the trail ended at the bank, several large stones had been placed, by someone apparently, that spanned the stream, easily crossed by hopping from one to another. Several people ran forward to slake their thirst and wash their wounds. De Cuellar called a stop to the march.

"We have had a long road today," he said. "We will make camp here and forget about our toils until the morrow." This was met with hearty approval from everyone as they waded into the water and began washing themselves of days of accumulated grit and dirt. It soon became apparent that the stream was populated with scores of fish and the men set themselves to catch as many as they could. By the time evening came, they had a bounty of food as they had not had since their days shipboard. Soon the fire was going and a feast began in earnest.

"That was the most I have eaten in a long time," said Rosa after her second helping.

Rodrigo, who was probably on his fourth helping, grunted in assent, adding, "Aye, same here. I had forgotten how good it feels to not have hunger constantly gnawing at you." He licked his fingers as he contemplated another helping. "Although it would have been nice to have a little salt for seasoning."

"Too much and never enough, eh Rodrigo?" asked Ignacio jokingly.

"You are the priest, Señor. Get us some loaves to go with the fishes!"

Ignacio laughed and was about to reply but Rosa interrupted him. "He is right, you know. When was the last time you did something priestly? Apart from blessing our meal just now, I mean." She looked around in the gathering gloom. "This is a wonderful place for a service, is it not?"

Ignacio sobered and nodded. "It is indeed. Now that bellies are full, it may be time to fill souls as well." He rose and added, "I should get going then. After a hearty meal, many are sure to start falling asleep. I must get to them before they do." With a laugh, he joked, "Although people tend to fall asleep at my sermons on the best of days."

As the fire crackled softly in the night, the weary group gathered around Ignacio. His face, illuminated by the dancing flames, reflected a sense of both relief and reverence. He stood slowly, wiping his hands on his tattered robes, his voice calm but strong, filled with the weight of their shared trials.

* * *

"My dear brothers and sisters," Ignacio began, "tonight, we have been given a blessing that none among us can deny. After days of hunger, of wandering through the wilderness, God has seen fit to provide for us. This stream and its bounty are a gift, a reminder that even in the harshest moments of our journey, we are never abandoned. He has heard our cries, He has seen our suffering, and in His mercy, He has laid before us a feast. We walk through this wilderness, not merely as travelers, but as pilgrims. Our journey is not only one of survival, but of faith. And it is faith that sustains us in moments like these, when all seems lost, when our bodies are weak and our hearts burdened. It is faith that reminds us that every step we take, every hardship we endure, brings us closer to God's embrace.

"We must remember the trials of our Lord Jesus Christ. Did He not wander in the desert for forty days, with neither food nor water? Did He not face hunger, temptation, and suffering? Yet, through it all, He remained steadfast in His trust in the Father."

Ignacio spread his arms wide, as though to embrace the entire forest that surrounded them. "Just as Christ was sustained by His faith, so too must we be. The fish we caught today are not simply nourishment for our bodies, they are a symbol of God's providence, a sign that we are not forgotten in this wilderness. The Lord provides, in His time, and we must trust in His plan for us."

His tone grew softer, more introspective. "We do not know what tomorrow will bring. We may face more trials, more hunger, more dangers in this land. But let us carry this moment of grace with us, in our hearts. Let us be reminded that even when all seems dark, God's light shines before us, guiding our way."

Ignacio clasped his hands together, his gaze falling to the ground. "And so, let us pray. Let us give thanks for the gift of life, for the food we have been given, and for the strength to continue on this path. Let us ask for the courage to face what lies ahead, with faith and love in our hearts. And let us remember that we do not walk alone, for God walks with us."

The group bowed their heads, the sounds of the forest quieting around them as Ignacio's words settled over them like a blanket of peace.

"Amen," Ignacio said softly, looking around at the faces of his companions. "Now, let us rest, and tomorrow we shall rise, renewed in spirit and body. For we walk together in the grace of God."

Ignacio held up his hands one more time. "Before you go off to your well-deserved rest, I have but one more announcement. Captain de Cuellar has informed me that we will spend the next several days here, to stock up on fish and game and whatever else we may be fortunate enough to find. It is his hope, and mine, that when we do set out again, hunger will not be one of the hardships we face. In the intervening days, people will be assigned tasks to facilitate this venture." This was greeted with some applause and cheers.

"Enough from me," he concluded, "go get some sleep. You have earned it."

Chapter Eleven

The spear of twilight is coming, son, my son
Quick dodge it!
The hollow spear is coming, son, my son
Son, my son, the spear of twilight is coming for you
Quick, dodge it!
The emesak, as it is called
Let it not lie in wait for you, son, my son
Let it not behold you with the clear vision of natem trances
As they gradually bear you away
Let each of your steps be disguised as a chonta palm

-Traditional

They quickly settled into something of a routine. Rudimentary baskets and nets were fashioned to help with fishing while, the de Arobe sons surprised everyone by creating simple snares to trap small animals. They were not always successful but did provide the occasional treat. The fish in the stream, however, were noticeably reduced in number after the group's first feast and that led to another problem. The caiman, whose home was the stream, came out more readily in search of food. To them, the travelers were just another source of sustenance, and quickly became a nuisance that could not be ignored. They seemed to ignore diurnal cycles and were a threat at all times of day or night. By some miracle, no one was injured in these encounters, but it was a constant reminder to not become complacent. It was evident that the survivors time here would be shorter rather than longer. Still, they managed to restock their larders and, after assembling a pair of bags made from the animal skins they had trapped, they were well set to leave their impromptu settlement.

After three days, the decision was made to continue their journey and find a more permanent solution to their situation. On the morning of their departure, Ignacio performed a short mass and bestowed blessings on them all. He did not have a sermon to offer them other than to thank God for their all too brief respite. With that, they gathered what they had and started out. The stepping stones in the stream turned out to be quite slippery and more than one person had to be pulled out of the water before the ever-present caiman could make a move on them. There were several close calls.

Eventually, they had all made their way across, more or less intact. The forest on this side of the stream was nearly the same as before, but before long the vegetation began to once again encroach on the path and strangely, the ground itself was becoming spongier until after some miles, it was actually wet and began sucking at their feet. The path itself, never really clear to begin with, had disappeared as they moved into the deepening morass.

De Cuellar called a stop and conferred with Lieutenant Martinez. "It is clear we are approaching the river," de Cuellar said to him, "but whether it is a matter of feet or miles is a question that cannot be answered."

"I have no better sense of it than you do," responded Martinez. "However, I seem to think that moving inland will help us find a way to circumvent this bog and offer us drier land to walk on."

"And not towards the ocean?"

"Well, it is toward the river we want to go. That is where we are most likely to encountered the boats we saw from the cliff. Remember, that view showed us the forest going right up to the edge of the sea. I fear it is all swamp between here and there."

"With more caiman, snakes and who knows what other horrors." He paused and heaved a sigh. "Very well, we will go eastward until we find a better way around this marsh."

The terrain eastward rose slightly, confirming that they had been traveling through the lowlands near the shore. They were back in the jungle proper and it was mainly by dead reckoning that they maintained their course. No paths or game trails were to be found and as the sun again began to set, they resigned themselves to finding a clearing in order to hole up for the night.

Thoughts of their days by the stream weigh on them as they settled in for a long night in the jungle. At least it was drier here and kindling and wood was easily gathered, and so a fire was lit to ward off the dark and any creatures that might have taken an interest in them. De Cuellar ordered food to be distributed, but for the first time in many days, rationed as they had no idea when they would once again come across such bounty as they had by the stream.

"Why is it, that the more you eat, the hungrier you get?" Rosa wondered aloud.

"We had food aplenty without the expected toil," answered Ignacio. "In a matter of days we apparently fell into old habits. Now we sit here once again with aching feet and rumbling stomachs."

"Are we going the right way? I fear de Cuellar and Martinez are just guessing at this point. We all are. We do not know for true where we are, where we are going...I do not even know what day it is."

"I do not intend to mock, but the day is today and tomorrow comes next. I have come to not think beyond that."

"That," she replied tartly, "is not very helpful at all. Your sermons seek to fill us with hope and resolve, yet here you are espousing that you yourself have no hope at all."

"I have not said that. I just know that what I imagine our destination to be, it is a mere fantasy compared to the truth that will present itself. I will accept it when it comes."

"As I said, hopeless." She laid down and turned away from him. Evidently the conversation was over and Ignacio was left to ponder his own words.

I have confidence that we will, in the end, be delivered from this trial of faith, he thought to himself. *Yet I accept that the world is large and we are merely dust specks upon it. We have traveled far, yet at a snail's pace for much of it. An eagle could have flown the distance in a day.* He lay down as well, wishing he could see more above him than the few twinkling stars that shone between the leaves above him. *Can you see us, Lord? Can you hear me when I call to you from under this endless canopy?* There was no answer forthcoming and he was left only with his roiling thoughts as his companion.

* * *

You come closer, son, my son. Closer to Nunkui Nampet. Its shadow is upon you. Soon, we will meet, and you will know the truth that binds this land. Do not stray from your path. The spirits guide your steps, but now, you must turn south. Bear south, toward the river. The earth will speak, the river will show the way. When you reach Nunkui Nampet, you will find what you seek. But beware, son, my son. Not all journeys lead to salvation. Some paths must be walked in shadow. Bear south. You will soon be with Tsewa. The earth is calling you. Now, Awake!

Ignacio woke with a jolt, feeling as if he had not slept at all. The echo of Tsewa's voice reverberated through his head, which he shook to try and clear his mind. It was early morning with just a hint of the dawn that was to come. Around him, others were beginning to stir. He felt somewhat reassured that at least this time he had not cried out. He stood and brushed absently at the debris he had acquired during the night and saw that de Cuellar and Martinez were also awake and conversing quietly. He stepped over Rosa's slumbering form and made his way to them.

"Good morning, Captain. Lieutenant," he said quietly. "How do you fare this morning?"

"Fair enough, Father," replied Martinez. "I trust you slept well."

"Well enough," he replied, pausing slightly to gather his thoughts. "Not to seem impertinent gentlemen, but I spent a good portion of the night thinking about our plan for the day. We have traveled several leagues eastward. Should we not now attempt to turn south and strike the river?"

"That is, in fact, what we were discussing ere you joined us," said de Cuellar in response. "The land rises as we progress east and if that continues we will be far above the river. It is hard to assess precisely in this low light, but we seem to have cleared the worst of the bog."

"Your judgment this morning," added Martinez, "only served to sway the vote. I was arguing for another day eastward, but now I feel that perhaps you have provided a bit of divine intervention. We will scout the area once it is light enough."

Not precisely divine, thought Ignacio, *these visions of Tsewa may turn out to be misleading, but compelling nonetheless.* "Thank you for your time, sirs. I will begin to gather the others." De Cuellar and Martinez nodded and continued with their business.

He made his way back to where Rosa still lay in repose, thinking to wake her gently, when Rodrigo stopped him. "Nay, let her sleep," said the Pilot. "She was a little out of sorts last evening. Let her body tell her when it is time to wake."

"I too, was 'out of sorts' last night, my friend, and I am afraid I am not much clearer on things since then. Still," he said looking at Rosa, "She did seem somewhat fatalistic, which I did not think was in her character. We will see what the day brings."

"Hopefully, something less sharp edged."

They turned then to rouse the others when a voice said, "I can hear you, you know."

* * *

De Cuellar and Martinez had reached a compromise, it seemed. The troupe began the day again in an easterly direction while scouts were sent ahead to find a path to the south. They had not been walking long when these same scouts came running back to them with excitement. "There is a path," they cried, "running down from the hills before us. It curves and goes south."

De Cuellar looked at Ignacio critically. "It seems your midnight epiphany has borne out, Señor. Any further clue as to where this path leads?"

"I do not claim to know more than has been presented, Captain, yet it seems that the course is laid before us. I feel it to best to follow a path that leads in the direction we already want to go."

"I spoke in jest, Father," de Cuellar said unapologetically. Turning to scouts, he asked, "How much farther to the trail?"

"Less than a mile, Captain," came the reply. "It lays straight across our course, well worn and clearly defined. We cannot miss it."

"Then let us get to it."

It may have been less than a mile, but the going was arduous. There was no clear way ahead and they were often hindered by vegetation that was nearly impassable, but, step by step, they made their way through and were soon rewarded with the appearance of the trail. It was indeed well defined. This was no animal trail, and although there were no footprints, it was clear that it had been made by man. The jungle growth had obviously been cut back to afford access and some of the trimmings could still be seen.

"This road is well maintained," observed Martinez, "and well traveled by the looks of it, although not since the last rain it seems."

De Cuellar dispatched the scouts. "Run on ahead. If there be others on the trail, I should not like to come upon them unawares." They hurried off as de Cuellar called after them. "Not too far ahead, but far enough to give us warning."

"Is this a road the savages use?" Martinez asked.

"There is no reason to assume it is not. I do not want to come upon a circle of their huts unannounced, lest we end up as dried heads on spikes."

"Encouraging words as always, Captain. We have little choice in the matter. I will take the lead."

They walked much more easily now, if not much more uneasily. De Cuellar's words had them on heightened alert and, with eyes darting left and right, they went on. There was no evidence of any danger and the jungle made its usual cacophony. After a while everyone relaxed and began to walk more confidently. Yet they *were* being watched. Not only by the monkeys in the trees, but by the supposed 'savages' of which they were so fearful. In places they walked within feet of them without ever knowing. They moved like ghosts among the underbrush without a rustle to give away their presence or position. Unknown to Ignacio, they were mostly flanking *him,* as if he were the sole object of their attention. Yet they were more curious observer than threat.

Rosa had been several paces behind Ignacio, but now she quickened her pace and sidled up to him.

"It looks as if we are finally going somewhere."

Ignacio looked down at her and replied, "Oh, so now we are talking again, Señora?"

"Nacho, I do not want to go down that road again. Nothing hurtful was said, we merely spoke what was on our minds. What has *been* on our minds for a long time. I did not take offense, I was exasperated by your fatalistic attitude."

"*That,*" he said coldly, "did not sound like an apology to me."

"Because it was not intended to be. I was merely..."

Behind them, Rodrigo grumbled, "Please, not this again." Abashed, Rosa fell silent. For his part Ignacio felt no rancor toward Rosa's comments the night before and had been looking forward to patching the differences between them.

"Today is a new day and a new path with a new promise. What is past is past. We learn as we go and so we will not linger on what went on before." He looked at her and added, "Let us walk now, with eyes, minds, and hearts open. Let us be prepared and take each new step as it comes."

Rosa smiled and said, "That was rather priestly. Composing your next sermon?"

Ignacio sighed, "I cannot help what I am but I will endeavor to be more a friend than your pastor."

"Amen to that," Rodrigo chimed in. They walked on then in the gloom of the forest making occasional but friendly comments as they went. The path was no longer straight but meandered this way and that. It was clear that this was meant to avoid certain hazards, such as fingers of the bog to the west intruding into the forest, great patches of mud that could possibly swallow a man whole, and dense copses of trees. But around each bend of the path nothing truly new was revealed and some obstacles could not be avoided. Once, they had to come to a halt to deal with a giant snake, as big around as a man's waist that had decided to lay across their trail. It hissed and threatened but finally, perhaps reasoning that the odds were against it, slunk off to a darker patch of ground under dark foliage. It had disappeared but everyone gave that area a wide berth as they passed. They had been looking into the trees for signs of danger, but now they had to be careful of where they placed their next step.

On and on they tramped as the day burned away. Twice they stopped briefly to take water and regain their breath. Twice they went on on with less enthusiasm than before. But no one was willing to stay in one spot for very long. The jungle became gloomier indicating that they were soon to lose even the meager rays of the sun that managed to penetrate the leafy ceiling. Without having to be told, they quickened their pace as no one was relishing the prospect of a night on the trail. As if to whip them along, a soft growl came from somewhere nearby.

At the front of the line, de Cuellar and Martinez were beginning to grow concerned.

"Where are the scouts?" asked de Cuellar rhetorically. "I commanded them to not stray too far ahead and report when they could. Certainly before dark."

"And that is nigh upon us," observed Martinez. "Perhaps they found a pond full of alluring mermaids and lost track of time."

"I have no time for flippancy, Lieutenant. Their sole purpose was to clear the road for us and warn us of impending dangers."

"I know this well, Captain. Forgive me. All I can conclude then is that they have not reported because they cannot."

"That is becoming increasingly apparent. Whatever has befallen them waits for us as well." He took a moment to scan the trees, turning in a circle as he did so. "Of late. I have had glimpses out of the corners of my eyes of movement or an odd shadow, but when I look there is nothing there."

"It could be naught but those insufferable monkeys that infest the trees and mock us."

"Those have not shown a capacity for stealth, in fact, they chatter incessantly. No, I think there is something else lurking here."

"An animal perhaps?"

"That may well be, but my senses tell me it is something more sinister."

"You believe there are savages here then?" said Martinez, now looking intently into the foliage. "Why then have they not shown themselves?"

"What civilized man can look into the mind of savages? Their intent is foreign to me and I will not waste time trying to explain it away. All that I know," he said grimly, "is that we are not alone."

* * *

In spite of their brief burst after the snake encounter, they were now flagging and realizing they would not be out of the jungle before full dark descended on them. Almost as if nature decided to relent, a clearing opened up before them and seemed to welcome them to stay the night.

"We can do no more today," de Cuellar said, addressing the group. "We will do well to stay here and weather the jungle as best we can." At this point, he had considerable reservations about this course of action but there was nothing to be done about it. It would do them no good to continue on, stumbling in the dark, falling prey to almost anything.

It was while they were gathering fuel for the night's fire that someone yelped loudly in fear. Rushing over they saw what had caused the commotion. There at the edge of the clearing was a large pool of blood and a man's leg. The leg, fortunately, was still attached to the man himself, whose body was hidden by a large bush. After their moment of surprise, the man was dragged out and turned over. It was one of the two scouts. Of the other there was no trace. Relieved, they saw the scout was not dead, merely unconscious and beginning to moan as he was manhandled into the clearing. He was not dead but perhaps that moment was not far off, for his body exhibited long gashes on his arms and torso which bled profusely.

Martinez held the man's head in his hands and tried to rouse him. "Vasquez! Vasquez, who did this to you? Where is Lorenzo?" Turning to the others, he cried, "Water! Someone bring water!"

Martinez dribbled water onto the man's lips, but instead of drinking, he sputtered it out convulsively. His eyes briefly focused on Martinez who repeated the question. "Vasquez, what happened? Tell me!"

Vasquez's eyes were beginning to glaze, but he managed to force out three words.

"Panther...gone...dead." He closed his eyes and said no more. His breathing was shallow and his moaning ceased. The end was not far. Martinez put the man's head down and rocked back on his heels, bowing his head.

"No one here can help him," he said quietly. "Get the Priest here. Only he can do something worthwhile ere the end." Ignacio was already there and, taking the dying man's hand in his own began murmuring the last rites.

De Cuellar helped Martinez to his feet and said to those around him, "Get that fire going. There is no telling if that creature will return to claim his second victim."

"No," said Martinez regaining his composure. "I am sure its belly is being filled as we speak. It will not be hungry again for a good while."

Moments later, Ignacio joined them. "It is over," he said solemnly. "He is gone."

"Did he say anything else?" asked de Cuellar.

"No. He went as peacefully as could be allowed."

"God rest his soul."

"It is clear that the panther attacked Lorenzo and Vasquez tried to fight it off," said Martinez. "No braver end for a soldier of his standing. A true shame he did not succeed. Or survive"

"His wounds were too grievous even for one so stout such as he." said de Cuellar. "Yet we learn from this. No longer shall we split our forces and give our enemies advantage. We go as one or not at all."

"A very wise decision, Captain."

The fire had been made, perhaps a larger one than they had made in previous nights, and set themselves to having a small dinner before bed. No one seemed very hungry, or very talkative. And if some preferred to sit with their backs to the fire and stare into the jungle gloom, well, who could blame them. The body was covered as best as it could be. They would dig a grave in the morning as exhaustion and despair had taken its toll.

But by morning, the body was gone.

Chapter Twelve

"See, I am doing a new thing! Now it springs up; do you not perceive it? I am making a way in the wilderness and streams in the wasteland."
Isaiah 43:19

There was panic when it was discovered that their camp had been invaded during the night. All that was left was a bloody smear where the body had been dragged away. De Cuellar's leadership was openly questioned and they cornered him with insults and complaints.

"If the body had been properly buried, this would have never happened!" shouted Domingo de Arobe. "Why was that poor man left in the open like that? Where were the sentries?"

De Cuellar raised his hands defensively. "The sentries were keeping *you* safe! Had we buried Vasquez, one of *you* might have been the one to be dragged away in your sleep! And for the record, who among you volunteered to dig a grave? Who among you offered to stand guard over him?" He stomped off away from the crowd and added, "While you stand here and babble like children, alerting every creature and savage within earshot to our presence, there is plenty of work to be done ere we abandon this camp. I suggest you get to it!"

Ignacio did his best to quell the fury that had been unleashed by, what was now, a mob. "People, please! Please quiet down!" he yelled above the tumult. Hearing his voice, they turned from staring at de Cuellar's back and gave heed. "I understand what you are feeling. I know your fears. We have been wandering endlessly with no end in sight while our fellows fall around us." As the survivors quieted down, Ignacio lowered his voice. "I too, have openly questioned the methods of the Captain. At one time, and perhaps deservedly so, I thought him to have gone mad. But very little of what we have endured is his fault." At this, accusations again started, and Ignacio waved them down. "We are in a situation he did not choose. We are on a trail he did not choose. But he has led us as best he could on a journey that was laid before us, through misfortune or providence. We will not know until the end, which again, *he* will not choose. By default, he is our leader and there is no alternative but to follow him. There is no other way forward, only the way back whence we came." The crowd's hostile temperature lessened and they began to disperse. "Now, do as was bid and gather your things."

There was not much to be gathered and they were soon on their way. It had been Ignacio's intent to give a convocation and blessing before this next leg of their trek, but he thought better of it. *Let their anger give them strength,* he thought. *Hard work has a way of quieting the heart and mind better than the idle prattling of a priest who has no more hope than they do.*

Walking beside him was Rodrigo, who muttered, "He is only the leader because he is at the front of the line."

"Rodrigo, you are testing even *my* patience," replied Ignacio. He pointed ahead. "Go you then. Quicken your pace and set yourself ahead of the Captain. Then we will all follow you instead." Chastised, Rodrigo pursed his lips and kept to his pace. "You were of his crew," Ignacio continued. "You have spent years following his every command until the wreck. Where is your loyalty?"

"Aye, I followed his every command and where did that land us? On a rock that tore our ship out from under us. Had I not, we would be in Callao by now."

"You cannot dwell on what might have been. This is here and now. Do your duty, Sailor."

* * *

The trail stopped its meandering and was now running straight and true. The jungle, however, began the hem them in creating a dark tunnel that became increasingly claustrophobic. The temperature increased dramatically, the air becoming thick and moist. The group trudged on, covered in sweat and mosquitoes, each step they took was heavier than the one before. Further on, the trail seemed to give way to the unrelenting advance of the jungle. Their way was now strewn with creeping vines and mosses than clung to what scant clothing they still had.

Rosa was leaning on Rodrigo for support. Her strength was quickly leaving and she took her breaths in big gulps. "This jungle is evil, Rodrigo," she panted. "I cannot believe Hell would be worse than this. How did the first settlers ever gain a foothold here?"

"Were we Conquistadors with armor, muskets and swords then things would be different. We have none of those things."

"Savages do not have those things as well, yet they survive here."

"I have no answer for that, Señora. In some way, they are part of the jungle, like the snakes and monkeys."

"Yes, I suppose they must know things we could never comprehend." She stumbled and Rodrigo quickly snatched her up and set her on her feet. "Can we not stop? My legs feel as though they have no bones."

Rodrigo paused and made room to let those behind him by. "Only for a moment, Señora, else we will be left behind. Here, drink some water." Rosa sat on a log and drank greedily.

"I would pour this over my head but I am already soaking wet." She slumped slightly, her head bowed. "Rodrigo, I do not think I can go on. I need to lie down." With that, she fell forward like a limp rag. Rodrigo shook his head as looked on her prostrate form. With a grunt, he picked her up and slung her over his shoulder.

"Forgive the indignity, Señora, but this is not a safe place. You will thank me later." With his new burden, he quickly caught up to the rest of the group. Ignacio had stepped aside to wait for them. When he saw what had happened, he rushed to them.

"Is she alright?" he asked with great concern.

"She lives, she breathes, but she has no more to give."

"And you? Carrying her will exhaust you as well."

"What else can I do, Father? At any rate, she has the weight of a feather, and is no great inconvenience."

"Thank you, Rodrigo. You are a great asset and good friend."

"Do you still question my loyalty?"

"Not even a little bit, my friend. I hope someday to be able to repay you in kind."

"Good," said Rodrigo with a chuckle, "then perhaps you can carry *me* for awhile." Ignacio laughed.

"If I could, I would, but I think you would smother me before I could ever lift you."

"Calling me fat now?"

"Heaven forbid."

As it turned out, there was not much further for Rodrigo to carry his charge. The group had come to a halt ahead and when they joined them they found themselves out of the jungle with nothing but blue sky in front of them. They were on a rocky ledge overlooking the most beautiful thing Ignacio had ever seen. There, shimmering softly, perhaps a yard beneath their feet, was the broad river they had seen from afar.

* * *

Below the rocky ledge, the river had carved a small cove where there was a narrow band of sand. On either side, as far as they could see, the dense forest came right to the waterline. There were no paths or embankments they could follow. They made camp here and waited, unsure what to do next.

De Cuellar stood at the water's edge, small waves lapping at his feet, and scanned the southern shore. Turning to Rodrigo, he asked, "How wide is this river, Pilot?"

"The river's mouth stretches nearly as far as the eye can see," he replied, "about two or three musket shots across, or perhaps a good half-mile wide. A *ship* would need time to cross from one bank to the other." Rodrigo wondered why the Captain would ask such a question in the first place. "Wait, you are not thinking about swimming to the other shore..." he said incredulously.

"No, you cannot be seriously considering such a thing!" Ignacio interjected.

"I am merely assessing the challenge here should the Pilot's boats be revealed to be imaginary. There are certainly no boats on the water now."

"I am certain of what I saw, Captain," said Rodrigo in a measured tone. "We are certainly not going to see someone taking a pleasure cruise, but if they are fishermen, as I suspect, then they will go out in the early morn and return as the sun sets."

"We will wait then," responded de Cuellar. "It now just past midday. It will be some hours before we learn the truth."

Ignacio turned to Rodrigo. "The river is wide here," he said. "We must devise a signal of sorts should these boats pass closer to the other shore."

"Aye, although at such a distance we may yet be passed unnoticed. We will start a fire, even though it is not yet dark. The smoke alone should alert them." He thought a moment. "We could also tie some white garments to poles. These we can wave and draw their attention nigh."

"Rodrigo," asked Ignacio conspiratorially, "*will* there be boats?"

"Most assuredly, Father. That does not mean you should stop praying."

Rodrigo had placed Rosa gently on the sand of the cove and she now began to stir. The elder de Arobe was near and helped her to a sitting position. He gave her some water, which she gulped down. She sat for a moment, blinking, momentarily confused about what she saw before her.

"What happened? Where are we?"

"You are safe. Señora," said de Arobe. "The last leg through the jungle overwhelmed you. Our friend Rodrigo carried you the rest of the way."

"I do not recall...," she said, her voice trailing.

"Do not be concerned. In reality, you have missed nothing save that we are finally out of that accursed forest."

"I feel so weak."

"I will get you something to eat, then you must rest. There is not much else to be done for the moment."

"Thank you, Señor." She looked out across the water and said, "So beautiful. Our prayers are being answered."

"So it would seem, Señora. So it would seem."

The sun continued its slow march across the cloudless sky while everyone sat and waited for something to happen. The dark jungle loomed above them like a predator whose prey was just out of reach. The chatter of the monkeys and birds that had haunted them for days still filled the air around them and lent no comfort to their relative safety. When Ignacio had finished his small chores, he came to her and found her sitting on the sand, hugging her knees.

"Rosa, how fare you? You appear to have recovered from your swoon."

"Uh huh," she replied distantly. "Señor de Arobe saw fit to attend to me, as he has others." She shielded her eyes from the sun and looked at him. "Ignacio, where is your shirt? It is unseemly for you to go bare-chested."

"My shirt has been sacrificed to serve the greater good. It has been torn to make flags that can be waved at passing vessels."

"Just yours, or did you lose a wager?"

"Not just mine, as you can readily see," he said, waving toward some of the other men on the beach. "Mine was just the whitest."

"Savages wear more than you do."

"And you know this how? For the moment, we need to discard our notions of prudishness. Frankly, I am surprised that our clothing has lasted this long. Anyhow, I wear the mantle of God as my cloak."

Rosa chuckled at this and said, "You have lost your clothes but not your sense of humor." She patted the sand next to her and said, "Come. Sit with me. Tell me what plan you rugged men have devised."

Ignacio sat with a grunt. "The plan is quite simple, actually. We sit and wait for someone to rescue us."

"I see."

"We are trusting that Rodrigo did in fact spy boats from the cliff. No one among us has his eyesight. I, for one, could not make out more than the wind blown waves shining in the distance. We should know more by sundown. It may be folly, I know, but de Cuellar has more than half a mind to swim across the river."

"Half a mind indeed! No, I would not even *consider* such a thing. Leave me here, I would sooner build my own boat with sticks and leaves than make such an attempt. Remember, I cannot swim."

"You would build your own boat," Ignacio mused. "That is not such a bad idea at that. I think that someone like Rodrigo could assemble rafts to get us across."

"To what end? To continue de Cuellar's folly of traveling further south? Take a look around you, Nacho. Look at the people. We are depleted and many more will die if such an ordeal is thrust upon them. Only de Cuellar would survive. He is too stubborn to die."

"Let us not think more on that until we are forced to. I do not relish the prospect any more than you do. Let us see what evening brings."

* * *

To call them boats was generous in the extreme. The small flotilla returning upriver from the sea were little more than rafts cobbled together with discarded planks and crudely sawn logs. Most had masts and tattered sails but a few relied strictly on rowing as a means of propulsion. As had been feared, the boats were closer to the far shore than hoped for and so there was a sudden frenzy to pile more fuel on the fire. They began brandishing their flags and yelling at the top of their lungs, some wading into the water as if to get closer.

It seemed to have worked as one of the boats tacked a new course toward them. Loud cheering erupted from the survivors as the boat edged its way closer. The cheers became wails of frustration when the boat reached mid-river and then executed a lazy circle to make its way back to the other boats and continue upriver. The boats soon disappeared around a bend farther on. There was no doubt that they had been seen, but for some reason they were left stranded.

Furious and dejected, they dropped their flags with disgust and collapsed on the beach.

"We were so close," moaned Rodrigo. "So close to getting off this God-forsaken beach. Why did they leave us here?"

"We appear as half-dressed screaming savages," Ignacio responded. "Life in the wild encourages one to be suspicious of anything out of the ordinary."

De Cuellar, who had been within earshot said, "For better or worse, we can say but one thing. I had had my doubts, but Rodrigo here was right about seeing boats, and being right about that surely means that they will come by again in the early morning. Whether they will again hug the southern shore and ignore us will be a discussion to be had then."

"They were obviously fisher-folk. If they travel this water course on a regular basis, then there must be a village or town around the bend that we cannot see. We may be closer to salvation than we think," Ignacio postulated.

"Time will tell, Father, and time is one thing we have in abundance."

"I plan to die of extreme old age," offered Rodrigo, "but I do not plan to spend it all here."

"Perhaps, Father," de Cuellar said to Ignacio, "you should prepare a sermon about the merits of patience."

"I do not know if you say that in jest, but overall it is not a bad notion."

* * *

Later, when most of the people were beginning to drowse by the fire, Ignacio stood and called for their attention.

"Before we all drift off into, what may be for many, a troubled slumber,

I would like say a few words. Do not fret," he said to some who rolled their eyes, "I will keep it short.

"Friends, I know the weight of this journey presses heavily upon each of you, and we have been tried by hunger, thirst, and the ever-present fear of the unknown. Yet, it is in times like these, when the path ahead is uncertain, and the promises of tomorrow shimmer like air over this fire, that we are most in need of patience.

"Patience, I say, is not a mere waiting. It is the quiet endurance of our trials. It is the stillness of the heart when the world around us is in turmoil. To be patient is not to be passive, but to trust in the wisdom of Providence, which guides us, even when the way is unclear.

"Look around you. Nature itself teaches us patience. The tree does not bear fruit overnight, and the river does not carve its way to the sea in a single day. The wind, though fierce, takes time to carry the clouds across the sky. And so it must be with us.

"If we act in haste, driven by fear or frustration, we risk stumbling into greater peril. But if we remain steady, if we trust that each step brings us closer to the path set for us, then we shall find our way. Patience is the handmaiden of faith. It reminds us that though we cannot see the full plan, we are a part of it

"Do not be dismayed by uncertainty. The Lord has not abandoned us to the wilderness, nor has He forgotten our suffering. He tests our spirits, yes, but only to strengthen them, to prepare us for what lies ahead. In patience, there is strength, and in faith, there is hope.

"Hold fast, my friends. Let us walk this path together with hearts full of patience, knowing that every trial endured with grace brings us closer to our salvation." There was a smattering of amens and Ignacio smiled. "That is all I have. Now, go to sleep."

* * *

In the early dawn, many were already awake and alert in anticipation of the arrival of the fishermen. Those that were not awake were soon roused out of their slumber by the excited hoots and calls of their fellows. The flock of fishing boats were once again heading out to sea for their daily labor and, instead of staying near the southern bank, they rode the middle of the river. There was truly no doubt now that the fishermen knew of their plight, for as they went by, many of the fishermen waved and shouted back to those on shore. However, it was apparent that they had no intention of stopping at the cove and kept sailing by the survivors. When the Spaniards realized this, they redoubled their shouts and pleading, but to no avail. Most of the fishermen ignored them at this point, but some on the nearest boat began shouting something incomprehensible and pointed up the river from where they had come.

Their attention diverted, the castaways looked in the direction offered and spied another vessel heading their way. This was not a ramshackle assembly of spare parts that floated, but a well made Spanish caravel, its triangular sails bellying in the wind. Cheers went up as the vessel drew near and the Royal Standard came into view, fluttering proudly off the main mast. Spanish, though the ship clearly was, the faces that appeared at the rail were obviously of mixed race, looking more like Francisco de Arobe and his sons.

The caravel dropped anchor in deep water and shortly a longboat was lowered for the excursion to shore. The survivors were beyond ecstatic, rushing out into the water to help the boat to shore. When it was near enough, a tall, dark man jumped out and walked up to the group, arms outstretched in greeting. "I am don Juan Ephraim de Yllescas," he said. "On behalf of my father, don Alonso Sebastian de Yllescas, chief of Santa Maria del Oro, I bid you welcome. Have I permission to join you?"

De Cuellar extended his hand in greeting. "I am Captain Alonso Sanchez de Cuellar, late of the *San Felipe y Santiago,* shipwrecked on your shores while enroute to Callao. You are most welcome to our little enclave." Turning to the others he added, "This is Lieutenant Diego Martinez, Pilot Rodrigo Silva, and our esteemed Father Ignacio de Montemayor." Hands were dutifully shaken all around, de Cuellar adding, "There will be time to meet the others as we go."

Yllescas signaled to his men and they began unloading provisions from the longboat. "We have brought such viands, breads and meats as we could on short notice." Glancing at Ignacio and some of the others, he added, "We have even brought some clothing as the messengers said some of you were lacking. Perhaps we may break bread together. I would know more about you and your intentions going forward."

Chapter Thirteen

"Remember that at that time you were separate from Christ, excluded from citizenship in Israel and foreigners to the covenants of the promise, without hope and without God in the world. But now in Christ Jesus, you who once were far away have been brought near by the blood of Christ. For he himself is our peace, who has made the two groups one and has destroyed the barrier, the dividing wall of hostility, by setting aside in his flesh the law with its commands and regulations. His purpose was to create in himself one new humanity out of the two, thus making peace, and in one body to reconcile both of them to God through the cross, by which he put to death their hostility. He came and preached peace to you who were far away and peace to those who were near. For through him we both have access to the Father by one Spirit. Consequently, you are no longer foreigners and strangers, but fellow citizens with God's people and also members of his household."

Ephesians 2:12-19

To Rodrigo's delight, the rescuers had also brought casks of wine and he set to resetting his quota to pre-shipwreck levels. There was much merry making that day on the beach between the castaways and the caravel's crew, but there was also some serious talk taking place a little ways away from the revelers. Yllescas sat with de Cuellar, Martinez and Ignacio while also inviting don Francisco to join them. Yllescas had taken an interest in de Arobe, perhaps it was just a sensed commonality in their heritage, but Yllescas deferred to him more often than not in their conversations.

"Tell me Señor," said Yllescas, "What was your intent on going to Callao?"

"Mainly my two sons. I want them to become proper Spanish noblemen. One was great potential within him while the other, well, he has some growing up to do."

"He seems to be fully enjoying his prolonged boyhood at the moment," interjected de Cuellar, recalling the younger de Arobe scion's conduct aboard his ship.

"Relax Captain," Yllescas rebuffed, "It is a day of celebration for you, is it not? He can grow up tomorrow. Provided, of course," he said with a laugh, "that he survives the devil's price for indulgence!" Turning back to de Arobe, he continued. "In all seriousness, Santa Maria is a Protectorate of the Kingdom of Quito. Consider establishing yourself here, and when all is in readiness, present your sons to the Governor."

"Then Quito is not far?" asked Ignacio.

"Everything is far in this land, Father, but really it is a trip up the river, a jungle road and zip, zip! You are there," said, gesticulating to make his point."

"We thought the same for Portoviejo, which was our immediate destination," said Ignacio, aware of an unhappy glare from de Cuellar.

"Porto...," started Yllescas with a sputter and then breaking into laughter. "You might as well walk to Callao for all the difference it would make. No, Portoviejo is much farther than the distance you have already come. Including the sailing part."

De Cuellar quickly changed the subject. "So, this road to Quito...is it safe?"

"Safety is a relative term in this part of the world, Captain. Our land borders on land held by various factions and tribes, some of which can be quite unpredictable and volatile at times. We have good relations with some while others change depending on mood, but with a proper escort, the trip can be made in relative safety."

"That is not very reassuring," Martinez chimed in.

"Oh, come now, Lieutenant, you have already traveled that very distance, if not more, without provisions or arms, with disease dogging your heels. As I said, with a proper escort, survival is all but guaranteed."

He paused to drink from his cup, noting the trepidation of his companions. "Tomorrow, we will board the *Santa Estrella* and make our way to Santa Maria. There you will rest from your efforts and in time you come to see how simple life is here on the frontier."

A shadow seemed to cross de Cuellar's face as he listened to Yllesca's declamation. He withdrew into his own thoughts, the voices of his group fading out of hearing. He did not like Yllescas. His flippant and casual tone irritated de Cuellar to no end. And then there was the issue of Yllescas' heritage. *These people prattle on about being Spaniards and noblemen, while true Spaniards are forced to listen and accept these professions as true? I think not. The conquest of these lands was not made on their backs but by the toil, blood and sweat of those like me, who have professed fealty to the Crown itself.*

Abruptly, de Cuellar excused himself and walked away. He wanted to be alone with his thoughts. Walking to the water's edge, he stared at the caravel lying at anchor. *Mongrels flying the Royal Standard! Spanish ships under their command! What is next, savages at the dinner table? I was not bred to subjugate myself to one such as he. We must change course in this new world else the very notion of the Empire will be lost!* He had to consciously relax his fists which had been clenched white and took a long breath. Somewhat calmer, he continued to stare at the ship. As he stood there brooding, a dark thought began to creep into his mind.

At the fire, Yllescas was still holding court. "A sailor once brought a parrot aboard the *Santa Estrella*, a gift from a certain chieftain in the jungle. The parrot was smart, but there was one problem: it repeated everything the sailor said, no matter how rude. One evening, while the crew was eating, the sailor said, 'This soup tastes like it was boiled in the captain's boots!' The parrot, without hesitation, squawked loudly, 'Boiled in the captain's boots! Boiled in the captain's boots!' The captain, hearing this, marched over with a scowl. 'Who said that?!' The sailor pointed at the parrot and said, 'Captain, I would never! But you know how these birds are, you cannot trust a word they say!' The crew erupted in laughter, while the parrot wisely kept silent for the rest of the voyage."

Laughing, Ignacio said, "When I said 'tell me about your ship' that is not what I meant. What I wanted to know was, where do you sail her to, how often? Things like that."

"The short answer is nowhere and never. We use it to ferry visitors upriver to the jungle trail and back. For example, when the Governor visits next month we will use her, otherwise she sits at berth. In any event, I would not trust her on the open sea. She may look good on the outside, but the inside is a different story. Constant leaks, constant maintenance. And there are no real sailors to crew her, just some men who have learned a thing or two." He paused, taking another drink. "We have no charts or navigation skills. There are plenty of landmarks on the river, fewer on the ocean."

"I ask only because our Captain seems to have taken a profound interest in her," he said, glancing in de Cuellar's direction.

Yllescas followed his gaze. "As well he should," he said. "He is a professional seaman, after all. Once he boards, he will have a different assessment. Now then," he addressed Ignacio, "There is a Mercedarian friar, Burgos is his name, that makes his way to us every so often, but his visits are irregular at best. Add to that the fact that we have a church with no pastor..."

Ignacio smiled. "I would be happy to be of service, for however long or short I am here."

* * *

The next day dawned with a dreary drizzle, with a light fog rolling in from the sea. Many revelers were still strewn on the beach, their insentient snores marring the stillness of the morning. Yllescas and his men had spent the night on the *Santa Estrella* and were now busy preparing for the trip back to Santa Maria. Although Yllescas had partaken as much as anyone the previous night, he was busy ordering his men about without any signs of encumbrance. Ignacio looked on his fallen comrades with a lighthearted smile on his lips.

No doubt the bacchanal was well deserved, he thought, *but I must prepare the confessional in Santa Maria quickly once their senses are slowly restored.*

"That was quite the night, no? Even the monkeys were out-performed." Ignacio turned and saw Rosa looking about in amazement. "The beach looks more like the aftermath of battle than a social event."

"It *was* a battle, Rosa. These men were fighting to reach the bottom of the bottle."

"Well, it looks like there were no winners. She looked at Ignacio. "You seem to be managing well."

"I was never one given to excess. Even in my younger years I knew when I had reached my limit."

"Just one sacramental wine per Mass, eh? You were always overly pious, even as a young boy."

"Piety has little to do with it, yet here I am, one of the few still able to stand."

Rosa shook head with resignation and walked down to the water's edge. There she began to wash her face and arms. Ignacio watched her for a moment, then his eyes drifted to the waiting caravel. There he saw Yllescas watching Rosa in a quite different manner. The man was obviously fixated on Rosa in a way that disquieted Ignacio's sense of propriety. *That could be a bit of a problem,* he thought. *Rosa would be quite the catch out here on the frontier.* Yllescas suddenly noticed Ignacio watching him. He flashed Ignacio a wide grin and turned away to his duties. *Yes, a problem, to be sure.*

A short time later, Yllescas boarded the tender and made his way to shore. He was met by de Cuellar and Martinez who, like Ignacio, had tempered their baser instincts the night before.

"Ho there, Captain," cried Yllescas, bounding ankle deep into the water. "How fare your people this fine morning?"

"That, you can see for yourself, Sirrah," de Cuellar fairly growled. "Though generous in intent, your gifts were abused to the extent of incapacity."

"You sound a bit under the weather yourself. *Someone* is grouchy after a night of merriment," Yllescas said with a wink.

"Enough," spat de Cuellar, "when are we to board?"

If Yllescas was taken aback by de Cuellar's venom, he did not show it.

"The tender is here at your disposal," he said with a casual smile. "Those of you who are still upright may board at any time."

"That will be enough to fill the tender for now. It will take several trips to gather us all."

"Those that you are able to rouse will be welcome to join us. The rest can sleep off their inebriation and be rescued later."

"You will *not* leave any of my people behind, you...you...," de Cuellar cried, struggling to say something other than he meant. He paused, caught his breath and stated flatly, "I will not leave them here."

"As you wish, Captain, but our time is short. The tidal current will soon reverse and we have need to make use of it. I suggest you get moving."

De Cuellar stomped off and began kicking sleepers unlucky enough to be in his path.

Yllescas watched him in amusement. "Your Captain is quite the character."

"He has his flaws, like any of us," replied Martinez. "Yet he is quite resolute in his desire to not lose any more of our company. You would do well not to goad him."

"I can see that. Well, you should begin to round up the first load, perhaps beginning with that young lady," he said, tipping his head in Rosa's direction. "And the Priest, of course."

It was mid-morning before everyone was loaded onto the caravel and anchor was hoisted. Yllescas pointedly placed all those that were not quite sober near the railing, stating, "The deck was just swabbed this morning. If any see fit to defile it rather than going over the rail, a pail and mop will be handed to you." The sails were then unfurled and began to billow in the stiff breeze. The ship rocked a bit until they reached the main current and there were more than a few green faces among the afflicted.

Yllescas had been honest about the condition of the Santa Estrella. Upkeep on the aging vessel had been poor. Many areas of the exposed wood had cracks and splinters that were to be avoided, some of the brass work meant to decorate posts and pole ends were missing altogether. Ignacio hoped fervently that this condition did not extend below the waterline.

"How old is this vessel, don Alonso?" Ignacio asked the next time Yllescas was near.

"In truth, I do not know, Father. She has been at Santa Maria my entire life. I never thought ask, but she is obviously ancient. It would do well to have a total refit but alas, we do not have the skill."

"There are some among us with knowledge of ships and ship-craft. Perhaps they could be persuaded to share their skills."

"That would be greatly appreciated, Father. I would like to see the *Santa Estrella* regain some of her former glory."

"It would be the least we could do to repay you for our rescue and your generosity."

"Then it is just a matter of convincing your Captain de Cuellar," said Yllescas, leaning against the mast. "He does not seem to like me much, that one."

"I will admit he is an acquired taste, even among his own men. Yet when you are by trade, a sailor, seldom do you have choice of a master."

"Well said, but you are not a sailor. What is your assessment?"

"I too, have sometimes come to be at odds with him, but in the wilderness there was really not much his eccentricities could affect, as there was only the road before us. It could be argued that our initial shipwreck came about because his ego got in the way, but I cannot speak on that for true. My interactions with him before the wreck were limited."

"A very noncommittal answer," said Yllescas with a laugh. "You are to be commended. I suppose it is within the clergy's purview to not be openly critical of another above their station."

"Think what you will, don Juan. In time, you will reach your own assessment." Ignacio glanced at the jungle passing by on both sides. "How far is it to Santa Maria?"

"At this pace, I would say some two hours. My father will meet us at the dock and no doubt there will be a mighty reception for you. Not as raucous as last night, for my father is not as tolerant or free with his wines, but a reception just the same."

As the ship rounded a bend in the river, the jungle on the southern bank abruptly came to an end. It was replaced by farmland that was nestled in a wide valley surrounded by mountain ranges to the south and east that cradled the largely flat landscape

Yllescas saw Ignacio staring at the scene in wonder. "You cannot see it from here," he said, pointing eastward, "but this part of the forest was cleared generations ago and the wood used for the building of Santa Maria. It lies just out of view near the foothills of those mountains."

"It is astonishing that you have carved out such a niche. Tell me, what sort of crops do you grow here?"

"Oh, the usual things. The land is parceled out to many farmers and they grow everything from maize, cocoa and potatoes to cassava, plantains and cotton. Not much of what you see is held over for livestock, although we do have some. We subsist mainly on what is grown here...oh, and grapes, a good many grapes for our small winery. You must try it, yes?"

"I suppose I must. How long has your family been here?"

"Oh, since the beginning, many generations as I have said." He flashed his grin at Ignacio and said, "We are very much like you in that regard. The original settlers of Santa Maria were also survivors of a shipwreck, although the difference was that most of them survived their wreck and were able to recover most of their stores. Santa Maria was not built overnight. It took many long years and intense labor to get to where we are today." Ignacio nodded and continued watching the passing landscape. Yllescas took this as his cue to move on. "I will leave you now, as I have duties to perform ere we land. My father can provide you with more insight as he is the historian, not I."

"Thank you, Señor. I will not keep you." Ignacio watched Yllescas take his leave and then turned back to the passing view. It was inspiring to see such a wealth of agriculture. His experience with townships in the New World and he only had coastal ports like Perico to compare it to. These relied on the constant trade with incoming and outbound ships and as such had no farmland to speak of. Ignacio was anxious to see the settlement that had this many resources at hand. *They must be very isolated for Santa Maria to not be on the shipping routes. Their distance from the sea may be a factor but the farmland alone is truly a hidden gem.*

Ignacio turned and looked at the opposite bank. There the jungle seemed impenetrable and ominous. He had an idea of what may lay behind that dark wall, and his thoughts went involuntarily to the spectre that haunted his dreams. *Tsewa, are you there, perhaps laying in wait, to pounce on us like a panther in the night?* The jungle gave no answer and Ignacio began to feel uneasy.

In the meantime, de Cuellar was putting the voyage time to good use. He roamed the vessel, inspecting every part of it that he had access to with a sharp eye. He longed to go below decks and inspect further, but had been rebuffed by the crew when he tried to gain access. He meticulously noted the condition of every spar, mast and sail and what was needed to bring them up to standard. Of course, he could not be sure until he inspected the inner hull, but he had no doubt the Santa Estrella could be refit with minimal effort. After he saw everything he could see, he sought out Rodrigo, who was leaning over the rail, looking decidedly bleary.

"Pilot, what are your thoughts on this vessel?"

Rodrigo turned a bloodshot eye at his captain and replied, "She is garbage and should be scuttled. I am surprised we are not already swimming."

"Why do you say that, sailor?"

"She moves like a garbage scow. The hull is clearly shipping water. They must be pumping it out on a daily basis to keep her afloat."

De Cuellar said nothing else and Rodrigo returned to his self-imposed misery at the rail.

At last the town of Santa Maria came into view. If anyone had been expecting a collection of mud huts they severely underestimated what was now presented. While not a sprawling metropolis, the town was populated by stately buildings that were obviously patterned from European influence. Several two and three story edifices fronted the waterfront, while behind them a large plaza was surrounded by what seemed to be homes and official buildings. At the far end of the plaza stood a modest church, but the largest Ignacio had seen in the New World.

As Yllescas had intimated, there was a sizable crowd by the dock awaiting their arrival. De Cuellar looked out among the faces, and felt dismay. In spite of the European style of the town, it was not reflected in its inhabitants who clearly represented a mix of black and native races. As soon as the *Santa Estrella* reached her berth and secured, a gangplank was brought ship side and the survivors began to debark. At the front of the crowd, a man of imposing heft and girth, his curly white hair gleaming in the sun, came forward with his arms outstretched in greeting.

"Welcome friends, welcome," he cried as the crowd cheered. "I am don Alonso Sebastian de Yllescas, chief of Santa Maria. We have been awaiting your arrival with great anticipation." As the passengers came off the dock onto the town proper, the crowd began to disperse. Obviously they had been required to attend as a show of community and, while some did stay to shake hands with the new arrivals, most went off to do what they would have been doing otherwise.

Introductions were made between the survivors and the elder Yllescas, including prominent members of the community. They were quickly whisked off the river-front and herded toward the plaza where indeed, a banquet had been prepared in their honor. Small groups shortly formed as the people of Santa Maria plied them with questions. The passengers of the doomed *San Felipe y Santiago* were all too willing to give voice to their tragic story as well as expressing a myriad of their own questions about Santa Maria and life on the frontier. Except for de Cuellar, who remained aloof and reticent as the conversations swelled around him.

Midway through the banquet, the hum of conversation quieted as Don Alonso Sebastian de Yllescas rose from his seat. His imposing figure, a beacon of authority and charisma, commanded the attention of all in attendance. With a warm smile, he raised his cup and cleared his throat, preparing to address the gathered survivors and townspeople.

"Friends, both old and new," he began, his voice booming but friendly, "it fills my heart with joy to stand before you all today, to welcome you to Santa Maria. Our town may lie at the frontier of this vast land, but our hearts are as open as the seas you have crossed to reach us."

He paused for a moment, glancing at the newcomers, his eyes filled with genuine compassion. "I know the journey that brought you here was fraught with hardship, danger, and great loss. But now, you are among friends. Santa Maria may be small, but we are a strong community. We will take care of you as though you were born of this very soil."

There were murmurs of gratitude from the travelers, their exhaustion momentarily lifted by Yllescas' welcoming words. Ignacio, seated nearby, exchanged a glance with one of the elders of the town, sensing a deep sense of community in the people here.

"As for the days ahead," Yllescas continued, "we have prepared quarters for each of you. The women will be housed with families in town, while the men will stay in a nearby lodging house we've readied for such an occasion. You will find food, warmth, and a bed to ease the weariness from your bones. If any of you have questions or concerns, do not hesitate to seek me out personally. I am at your service."

The crowd offered polite applause as Yllescas acknowledged the gestures of appreciation. He lowered his cup but then, with a twinkle in his eye, raised it again as he turned his attention toward Ignacio.

"And now," Yllescas said, his voice slightly more reverent, "I wish to share some wonderful news. Father Ignacio," he gestured toward the priest, "has graciously agreed to take over the vicarage here in Santa Maria. We have been without a priest for some time, and the people of this town are in need of his spiritual guidance. His arrival could not have been more timely."

Ignacio rose from his seat with humility, offering a slight bow to Yllescas and the crowd. The applause that followed was warm and sincere, an outpouring of relief from the faithful of Santa Maria who had long awaited such a figure.

"We are blessed," Yllescas continued, "to have him among us. And I know that under his care, the spiritual life of our town will flourish. So, let us raise our cups once more—to new friends, to survival, and to the enduring spirit that binds us all."

As the guests raised their cups, the air was filled with a renewed sense of hope and camaraderie. The clinking of mugs echoed across the plaza, and for a brief moment, the pain of the past weeks seemed to dissipate. Ignacio smiled softly, feeling the weight of his new role settle upon him. There was much to be done in Santa Maria, but for tonight, they would celebrate the gift of life and the bonds of community.

Chapter Fourteen

Field Entry:
Date: May 10, 1973
Location: Ruins of Santa María del Oro, Spanish town near Shuar territory
Description of Discovery:

As we arrived at the site that local histories had named Santa Maria, it was immediately clear we were standing on ground untouched by modern archaeology for centuries. The surrounding jungle has done its work, with dense vines crawling over the remnants of what must have once been an imposing colonial town. Among the ruins, we found evidence of what had been a central plaza, mirroring the design of other Spanish settlements of the time, with crumbling foundations marking the positions of long-forgotten buildings.

The presence of a large structure, undoubtedly the remains of a church or mission, solidifies the historical references we've studied. Scattered remnants of bricks and stones indicate a settlement that once had the means for relatively advanced architecture for the region. It's eerily silent now, but the stories these ruins hold seem to whisper with every step we take.

What remains of the town layout suggests it was designed as a central trading post, perhaps even a crucial settlement for expeditions deeper into the jungle.

We expect further excavations to reveal more about the daily lives of these settlers and the challenges they faced, perhaps ecological, perhaps indigenous resistance.

Dr. Elena Ramirez

While the church itself was in good repair, the quarters Ignacio would be using were less than appealing. There were thick layers of dust in the cramped space as well as the remnants of a long forgotten meal, not to mention that there was something living in the space behind the moldering settee.

Ignacio and Rosa held their noses as they inspected the area but don Juan, while profoundly apologetic, seemed nonplussed.

"I am truly sorry," began Yllescas. "Brother Burgos was the last to use this room some two months ago. Obviously it was not cleaned of maintained since. I will see to it that it is made ready for you."

Rosa began sneezing uncontrollably and the three of them made haste to get outside where the air was decidedly cleaner. "Dios mio," she said between sneezes, "that was the vilest place I have ever seen!" Yllescas handed her a handkerchief while Ignacio brushed himself off. At length, Rosa's fit subsided. "You must get rid of everything. I mean it, down to the bare walls, the furniture...everything."

"It will be done as you say, Señora. I will have them start immediately, and we will have it ready for Father by nightfall."

"No," Rosa countered, "you will not. Ignacio will stay in the men's lodge one more night at least. That room needs to be aired out and all traces of that rat, or whatever it is, must be cleaned and scrubbed, not just swept."

"I will oversee it myself. You will not recognize it when we are done."

"I had better not. And put some flowers in there to dispel the odor." She blew her nose. "I will never get that smell out. How did that Brother of yours live in that?"

Ignacio smiled at the exchange. *Rosa is truly in her element here,* he thought. *Woe be to the Brother when he returns.* This prompted another thought that had been on Ignacio's mind.

"This Brother," he asked Yllescas, "Burgos, I believe you said his name was, what can you tell me about him?"

"As I mentioned previously, he is a Brother of the Mercedarian order who visits whenever he is in the area. He has no set schedule and appears as quickly as he disappears."

Ignacio pressed him further. "And where is he when he is not here?"

"I cannot say for surety for he has never offered that information. To me, at least. I am of the mind that he wanders the wilderness, seeking to convert natives wherever and whenever he encounters them."

"Well, that explains much," said Rosa. "He lives with savages, and acts like one when he is here."

"Those are harsh words for a man you have never met, Señora," Yllescas replied. "He is as pleasant and kind as a man of the cloth can be. Do not rush to judge him."

Rosa pointed back to the room they had vacated. "I can judge him by what he left in there. He is kind to animals, I will grant him that. Letting them live behind his furniture."

"It is not entirely his fault. We should have cleaned it when he last left. Again, I apologize."

"Hmmph," was Rosa's response, clearly not mollified, arms crossed.

Ignacio, not wanting to pursue this line of thought further asked, "The natives of the area, do they ever come into Santa Maria?"

"It is not uncommon. They often come to trade for cassava, from which they make a drink that is a staple for them. Sometimes, some will accompany Burgos when he comes."

"Why am I not surprised?" Rosa said with a pout.

Rosa and Ignacio walked back into the church proper, leaving Yllescas to deal with rounding up a cleaning crew. It was a large place with a high ceiling that had several windows near the roof. Shafts of sunlight filled the space, illuminating all but the furthest corners.

"This at least is usable," observed Rosa. "When do you expect to resume services?"

"I expect that by Sunday I will be able to preside officially. There are some minor things I would like to take care of before then but nothing that would hinder that first service. I would like to confer with don Alonso about a re-dedication ceremony as this church has not had a priest assigned to it in many years."

"You should think about renaming it as well. 'the church' leaves much to be desired."

"Well," Ignacio said with a laugh, "I am told the name of the church is...The Church of Santa Maria."

"Not very imaginative."

"No, not very. I have given some thoughts along those lines. I want something that conveys a sense of renewal, for us as well as for the town. I was thinking of Nuestra Señora de la Nueva Esperanza or La Iglesia de la Resurrección as both names evoke themes of spiritual rejuvenation."

"Oh, I like the first one," she exclaimed. "It would be named after your sister and no one would know save the two of us."

"Yes, that had crossed my mind, although it seems rather self serving."

"Do it for her then, not for yourself. In all likelihood, you will never see her again. Nor will I, for that matter. That alone should justify it." She looked at Ignacio who was nodding his head slowly. "Pray on it, if needs be, but do not reject it out of hand. You would be honoring her." Ignacio made no further reply and she thought to change tack slightly. "So, it seems that between the re-dedication and renaming that you plan to stay here.

"If I had indeed made it to Callao, I would be a minor functionary in a large cathedral. The people of this town have nothing and no one at all. I feel I have been brought here for a reason and that this is what God wants of me. I have no desire but to serve so, yes, unless there is another sign, I will stay." Ignacio looked at Rosa expectantly. "And you? What do you think you will do?"

Rosa hesitated a moment before answering. "I have not been here long enough to truly think about it. I left Spain and my widowhood to strike out and find my own path, which to be honest, was more impulsive than planned. As it stands at this moment, I have nowhere else to go." She paused again and added sheepishly, "At least here, I have some friends."

"Rosa, I have no doubt that you would have friends anywhere you go. You must, of course, follow your own counsel and in time you will know. For whatever it is worth, I have grown fond of you and would regret your leaving, but do not let that be a consideration should your aspirations take you elsewhere. I am sorry for pressing you on the matter so soon."

Rosa laid a hand on his arm. "Nacho, I have nothing but time, it seems. You will not be rid of me so quickly. Besides, we have a re-dedication to plan."

* * *

De Cuellar awoke early as was his habit. He sat on the edge of his bunk listening unhappily to the men who shared the lodge. No one else seemed close to waking and that suited him just fine. The last thing he wanted to hear was the interminable chorus of 'Good Morning, Captain' that he was routinely subjected to. He dressed quietly, slipping on his boots and walked out of the lodge into the early dawn. There were few people about at this time of day and for a few moments, de Cuellar allowed himself to enjoy the solitude.

He stretched, working out the kinks he had accumulated on the hard pallet that served as his bed, and reflected on the nights he had spent recently on sandy beaches and jungle floors. He could not decide which was worse, missing his billet on the *San Felipe y Santiago* all the more. Having spent most of his life at sea, he was becoming increasingly uncomfortable on dry land, and so, he found himself drawn to the dock that at least had some semblance to his old life.

The fishermen had already left for their day of labor and all that was left was a collection of ancient barges and rafts, and of course, the *Santa Estrella*. *What a vessel she must have been in her day,* he thought, wondering how long ago that might have been. *Rodrigo has written her off as unsalvageable but she still holds some promise.* While he was admiring the vessel's lines, he couldn't help but notice that there was perhaps some truth in the pilot's appraisal. The ship was riding lower in the water than an empty vessel should. Still, he could not tear his eyes away as a deep nostalgia for the sea came over him. Never did he think that he would be stranded while being rescued. Stranded on land for the foreseeable future. *I was mistaken about Portoviejo,* he admitted to himself, *but any seaside port would have been better than landing here.*

Abruptly, he had had enough of this line of thought and turning, walked back into the town. His feet lead him to the broad plaza and he decided to circumnavigate it around its edge. He turned to the left, behind the buildings that bordered the riverbank and came to the first turn. Here, the plaza was flanked by homes, presumably the homes of Santa Maria's elite, for they were well made and maintained and larger than the other homes he had seen around the town. Certainly larger than the lodge he had been forced into.

As he came to the next corner, he encountered a house that was even larger with decorative foliage adorning the front. He realized immediately whose house this must be and quicken his steps to pass it by, but it was too late. A figure came out the front door with a shock of white hair that de Cuellar recognized instantly as don Alonso. He was trapped.

"Good morning, Captain," the elder Yllescas called out. "Another early riser I see."

"Yes, I am just stretching my legs before the day begins," he replied and kept walking past the house.

"We are just setting the table for breakfast, and I doubt you have had yours yet. Please join us and meet the rest of my household."

"Thank you, but I..."

"I insist, Captain," said Yllescas firmly. "We shall have a pleasant conversation about your future with us. Come."

Resigned, de Cuellar turned back to the house. *Damn*, he thought.

The inside of the house was even more opulent than the outside. Large rooms, tastefully decorated with a distinct European flavor. The wooden floors that gleamed, reflecting the early morning sun. De Cuellar allowed himself to be led into a sitting room with overstuffed divans and couches. The clatter of dishes could be heard from an adjacent room, presumably the dining room.

"Please sit, Captain. It will be a moment yet before the board is laid," said Yllescas. De Cuellar picked a seat that had the least cushion and sat heavily. "I was planning to meet with you later today," began Yllescas. "The council would like an opportunity to confer with you and your compatriots. Find out a little more about your backgrounds and what your expectations are."

"An interrogation, then?"

"Nothing of the sort, my good man. It was thought that one meeting, with everyone present, would be better than approaching you individually. We can make a meal of it, friends getting to know one another. Does that sound unreasonable?"

"No, of course not, Señor," replied de Cuellar. "Please forgive my suspicious nature. We are, of course, grateful for the help and generosity you have afforded us, but perhaps you will allow us a few days to come to grips with our current situation."

"That is no problem at all, Captain, although sooner is better than later. People tend to make all sorts of judgments about people they do not know well, and we do not want all sorts of conjecture flying about."

"I understand, Señor. That is a common practice among sailors, although I have tempered myself against such things."

"Very good," Yllescas said with finality. "Then we shall revisit the matter another day, but do not be surprised if there are awkward looks and pointed questions in the meantime."

De Cuellar smile wanly and spread his hands. "It is all part and parcel in a new place." He shifted his weight on the deep cushion and added, "There are, however, some things I would like to discuss in private."

At that moment, a woman's voice cried out from the dining room. "A comer!"

"Ah," said Yllescas, lifting his bulk from his settee, "the breakfast table is ready. We will have our private session after we eat. Come! Come!"

By the time they entered the dining room the spacious table was fully occupied and another chair had to be brought in to accommodate de Cuellar. Yllescas introduced the members of his household and de Cuellar forgot them as soon as he heard them. The conversation around him was lively, but he made his best effort not to engage, answering only what was asked directly, never expounding more than necessary. The food itself was good, if not typical of diets in the New World. There was an emphasis on corn and fish, as well as breads and fruits. De Cuellar had to politely turn away requests from, he assumed, Yllescas' wife, to help himself to additional servings. Don Alonso set himself under no such restriction and ate until de Cuellar was afraid the man might burst.

Finally, the meal ended and Yllescas, sensing de Cuellar's impatience, rose and motioned for the Captain to follow him. Shortly, they settled in Yllescas' study where the large man offered de Cuellar a wooden box.

"Would you like cigar, Captain?"

De Cuellar, who had not had a smoke in weeks, readily agreed and soon there were billows of blue grey smoke filling the room. He settled back in his chair, rolling the cigar between his fingers and inspecting it. "This is actually quite good," he said. "Do you have them imported?"

"Certainly not," Yllescas replied proudly. "We grow our own tobacco here in our own fields and I believe it rivals the best the formal colonies can offer."

"I am impressed," said de Cuellar, and in truth he was. The cigars he was accustomed to purchasing at his ports of call were often bitter and mixed with other leaves that were not necessarily tobacco.

"Then say no more, I will see to it that a supply makes its way to you.

Here, take what is left of the box as I have have plenty in store."

"That is most gracious of you, Señor. I shall truly enjoy them."

Yllescas chuckled and leaned back in his chair, taking another long puff. He blew some smoke rings into the air which promptly disappeared into the growing haze above their heads. "So Captain," he said at length, "tell me of these private matters you wish to discuss."

De Cuellar hesitated a moment and took another pull at the cigar. "I pray you do not think me too forward, after all, you and your townsfolk have gone out of your way to provide us aid and comfort when it was most desperately needed. However, there is a matter I would like to address." De Cuellar leaned forward slightly in his chair. "It is unseemly that I be asked to share bed and board with those serving under me. It leads to a familiarity that is counter to a chain of command. Therefore, I would respectfully ask that private quarters be made available to me."

"Ah. Well, on its face, that is not an unreasonable request, but in truth we build what we need as we need it. At the moment, there are nothing that can be offered for you to take up residence."

"Yes, I had anticipated that might be the case. That leads me to the next thing I would like to discuss." De Cuellar paused for effect. "The caravel. The *Santa Estrella*."

"What of it?"

"I am a man of the sea, Señor. I would be most at home in the vessel's cabin, even if there is need for its occasional use."

"Captain, that boat is a hazard. It creeps lower into the river day by day and we bail more water out her day by day. Soon her keel will rest on the river's bottom. If it were not for the Governor's impending visit, I would have had it dismantled long ago. In fact," he said pensively, "once his visit is concluded and he is ferried back safely, its dismantlement could provide enough salvageable timber to build you a new home."

"It need not be so. With respect, Señor, there are those with me that possess such skills as to bring her back to form. I would have my residence and she would once again be seaworthy."

"Seaworthy? It would be a fight to make her river worthy." Now it was Yllescas who leaned forward. "That ship presents another problem. The fishermen have such limited space for docking at the end of the day and that boat takes up valuable room that could be used more wisely, given its condition. "It would be far easier for us to dismantle it than build a new dock."

"As I said, we have the skill and willing labor to accomplish both."

"And you have discussed this with your people?"

"Not as such, but I have no doubt there will be compliance."

Yllescas sat back and pondered the situation. After a long minute he seemed to have reached a verdict. "Very well. We will compromise. For the time being, make use of the ship's cabin and do your due diligence with those under your command. We will discuss this further after the Governor leaves."

De Cuellar found his mind to be unsettled. One the one hand, he had gained a victory with the *Santa Estrella,* but now he gave some thought to what Yllescas had just said.

"Your pardon, Señor, you have mentioned several times of the Governor's imminent arrival. What is the purpose of his visit? Is he coming to avail himself of your cigars?"

"Ah, I see now the confusion in your mind. You think of Santa Maria as strictly an agricultural center, and while that is true to some extent, our real value is in mining. In the beginning, yes, we were primarily focused on farming, but some years ago gold and silver lodes were discovered in the foothills to the east, and mining operations were commenced. Mining on its own has its own hazards, but mining here is particularly perilous. The more we mine, the more we encroach on the land of the Shuar, the natives that live just beyond our borders. They do not care for our presence there and there are occasionally skirmishes, sometimes deadly ones.

"The reason for the Governor's interest is twofold. Firstly he means to assess our operations himself, as to production and yield, and of course, this assessment will be forwarded to the Crown. With luck, this would result in better equipment to process the ore and speed up production."

"And secondly?"

"He will be arriving with a full complement of soldiers to quell the Shuar and safeguard the operation. After that it will be a matter of time before a coastal shipping route is established to move the ingots with more efficiency. That, Captain, is why I intended to scrap the *Santa Estrella.*"

De Cuellar fairly stammered. "I...I had no idea."

"And how would you know? The mining camp is some miles from here. You might see an occasional wisp of smoke from the smelters, but nothing more." Yllescas reached into a cabinet behind him and pulled out two rectangular ingots. One gold, one silver. He placed them on the desk. "What do you think of those?"

De Cuellar stared at them intently and smiled. The missing pieces of his dark plan were moving into place. He knew now what he had to do. He picked up the silver bar, turned it over in his hands, then looked at Yllescas and said, "Absolutely wonderful!"

* * *

Rodrigo was not a morning person. It took him quite a while to get to the point where he could tolerate the presence of another person, let alone speak to them. Thus it was, that when Martinez sat across from him at breakfast, he neither acknowledged him or made room for him. Martinez, for his part, knew something of this facet of Rodrigo's personality and kept looking at at Rodrigo's face, goading him while he ate his meal in silence. Rodrigo noticed this and was not happy.

"What?" he growled at Martinez.

Martinez smiled at kept his gaze. "Nothing."

Rodrigo glared at Martinez. "Then eat your breakfast and leave me be."

"I have not said anything. I am just here, enjoying a wonderful breakfast, on a beautiful day, enjoying the company of friends. The sun is shining, the birds are singing, and I do not have anything to worry about. We are safe, comfortable with nary a care in the world.

"I thought you had nothing to say."

"I do not. I have absolutely nothing to expound on," said Martinez with a grin.

"And yet you prattle on."

"I? Prattle? You have me confused with someone else. When I have nothing to say, well, I say nothing at all. Is it my fault that the Lord has granted us another day in this marvelous world that he has created? Is it my fault that He has seen to see to our comfort in our time of need? Is it my fault that you snore like a wounded bear? No, that is not my fault."

"My snoring? Is that why you have chosen to torment me?"

"The furthest thing from my mind, my friend. I quite enjoyed seeing all the wild animals emerging from the forest to hear your love songs. They must have come from miles around."

Rodrigo banged his hand on the table. "Enough of that! I swear I will tear you limb from limb if you do not..."

His outburst was interrupted by the sudden appearance of Captain de Cuellar at the table.

"Martinez! Rodrigo! I would have words with you!"

Chapter Fifteen

"They will throw their silver into the streets, and their gold will be treated as an unclean thing. Their silver and gold will not be able to deliver them in the day of the wrath of the Lord. They will not satisfy their hunger or fill their stomachs with it, for it has caused them to stumble into sin."

Ezekiel 7:19

De Cuellar was not the only one with thoughts of Santa Maria's mine. From the safety of the trees beyond the mining camp, a pair of dark eyes looked upon the scene with disdain.

I used to hunt here when I was a young Kakáram, thought the warrior, whose name was Pinchu. His settlement was not far away and the constant hustle and bustle of the mining camp was becoming a great concern among the Pacháka, or clan elders.

There was major controversy among them as to what to do about the encroaching invaders. Some of the elders advocated for moving deeper into the forest, but the majority were of the mind that the interlopers must be eradicated, a move that Pinchu wholeheartedly agreed with. They argued that the clan's access to the river had been severely limited, and that the situation was bound to get worse if these foreigners were allowed to continue their expansion at the current rate. How far would they have to retreat? To

Pinchu, the answer was clear. The clan must show these people no mercy. Show them they had no place here.

How could Tsunki, the spirit of the river, allow such a thing to happen? *Tsunki, do you not miss the People who bathed and fished in your waters since the beginning of the world while these demons befoul everything they touch? The very air around them cries for cleansing. Do you not hear it?*

Pinchu continued to observe the camp. He noted the number of men, both slave and free, the number of animals cruelly made to walk endlessly in circles for the mere crushing of stone, the billows of black smoke coming from the melting pits. It was all too much and his soul cried in anguish. Anguish that was fueled by a growing anger. He wanted to jump out and kill them all himself but he knew that, in the end, that would be a fruitless gesture. One that would have severe consequences for his people. *Or it could push them to do the right thing,* he thought. He made himself relax and took some deep breaths. *I must calm my mind, report what I see and what I feel. Perhaps Tsewa can show me the way.*

* * *

Tsewa was old. Older than he had a right to be. In his being, he still thought himself a young man and he longed to roam the forest again, spear in hand, feeling the thrill of the hunt once more. But it was not to be. Too long had he been Uwishin. As the spiritual leader of the clan, he felt a closer relationship to the forest world than any of his fellows could ever experience. But that time was becoming short. It would soon be time to move on. This did not trouble him greatly but he knew things were about to happen. Things that would need a strong Uwishin to guide the people, a strength that was waning day by day.

He was no longer able to take the deep trance as often as he had in the past. When he did, the visions were often cloudy and vague. And it was exhausting, sometimes taking him several days to recover from the effects of the potent ayahuasca potion.

Nantá Iwia, he thought, *the Wandering Spirit I have seen in my dreams. He may be our only hope.*

Tsewa settle on his chimpui, the stool of the master of the house and waited. He sensed that his son, Wajari was near although he had not seen or heard him approaching. Presently, Wajari entered the house with a white-lipped peccary draped across his shoulder. This he dropped unceremoniously at the feet of Tsewa's second wife and went to sit as his father's side. Wajari was everything Tsewa had been, tall and broad shouldered, with straight jet black hair that hung to his shoulder. Tsewa looked on his son with pride and not a little bit of envy. *Without doubt he is a fearsome warrior and hunter. It is a shame he does not have aspirations beyond that.* Tsewa had hoped to groom Wajari to succeed him, but it was not to be. Wajari was too headstrong to be a passive link between the seen and unseen.

"The hunt went well, I see," said Tsewa. "I hope you did not have to give chase too far."

"It was hardly a challenge," replied Wajari. "I spied it feeding on roots. One dart blow and it was over."

Tsewa nodded. "A gift from Nunkui then. I know game is harder and harder to find."

"There is plenty if one knows where to look, and this one knows. Yet it *is* becoming more difficult with the devils at our doorway creating such a racket with their rock smashing."

"Rest now, son, my son. You have done well, challenge or no."

Tsewa turned his head to where his wives had begun to prepare the peccary.

"Nijiamanch! Wari, jiamanch, jiamanch, jiamanch!" he cried loudly. Moments later his youngest wife came bearing two pininkia, bowls brimming with manioc beer. Manioc was a staple of the forest people. Cultivated from the roots of the yucca plant, it was used in a variety of forms in their diet, but the fermented version was their favorite.

Out of deference, Wajari waited for his father to take the first sip from his pininkia, then he raised his own bowl and drained half of it in one long gulp. He burped loudly and wiped his lips on his arm. Tsewa chuckled at the sight and took another sip of his own. His days of excess were far behind him and he reserved the intoxication of his mind for ayahuasca. Still, he enjoyed the flavor of the beer and allowed himself a bowl at least once a day. Not so with Wajari, who drained his pininkia and loudly demanded another.

After completing the same ritual as before, Wajari put his bowl aside and looked at Tsewa.

"What have you heard from the Pacháka?" he asked his father.

"Nothing of consequence. I keep myself apart from the elders as much as I can and do not concern myself with such trivialities."

"Yet, you are most elder of all. To you they would listen. You will not think it so trivial when the devils kick you off your chimpui and drag you away."

"It will not come to that. Anyway, the counsel I have is contrary to the options they debate."

"Which is to do nothing," said Wajari bitterly. "I long to spill their blood on my spear, to see their heads as tsantsa and adorn my house with them."

"Well do I know this, son, my son, and that may yet come to pass. I do not see a future without bloodshed. Any path chosen will have its consequences."

"Whose blood will it be then, ours or theirs? Have your visions told you that?"

Tsewa sighed and took another sip of beer. *This is why I could not have him train as Uwishin. I love him above all, but he is reckless and impatient. He will be a leader of men, never a follower.*

"Should Arutam himself appear to me, you would not take his advice."

"Arutam provides us with strength, protection, and immortality," Wajari rebutted. "He would not have us sit by and accept our doom."

"So now you would give the spirits counsel?"

"Bah," exclaimed Wajari, rising from his stool. "It is pointless to argue this with you. I have many things to do. I will see you at the evening meal."

Tsewa watched his son leave and a stone of sadness was in his heart.

* * *

Bahati had been in Santa Maria since he was a boy. He was a quiet and resilient man, but with great stamina and strength, which was exactly what his overseers wanted of him. What they did not know was that Bahati was also equipped with a sharp intellect that he employed discreetly, even among his peers, who looked on him as their de facto chief.

The sweat gleamed on his skin as he loaded his master's precious ingots onto a cart. They were still hot from the smelter and Bahati had not been afforded gloves. In early days, the ingots had burned his hands fiercely but after years of toil, he barely felt any discomfort. His hands were calloused and rough, like the hands of so many others. He thought of his grandfather, who made fishing nets in his long lost village. He would not have been able to tie a simple knot if he had Bahati's hands.

Bahati looked at the sun, seeing that it was to set soon. Not that it mattered much as they were often worked into the night. As long as there was fuel for the smelter, there would be work for Bahati.

He stole another glance at the nearby jungle and wondered if his forest friend was lurking there. Tonight was the night they were to meet, but Bahati was not sure when that would be nor how he would sneak out of the barracks unseen. The good thing about the forest dwellers, they were incredibly patient. They had only met twice before and both only had a smattering of the master's language between them, but they held a common trait. The oppressors must go.

The first time they met was quite accidental, although Bahati suspected he had been watched for just such an opportunity. His overseer had sent him to gather more wood for the fire and the forest man stepped out of nowhere in front of him. Bahati had not been fearful. He knew people lived beyond that barrier of leaves and that sooner or later he would see one. That first meeting was short. Bahati learned that the man's name was Pinchu and that he was often watching when he was not hunting.

The second time, Pinchu had brazenly entered the slave's barracks in the darkest hours before dawn and roused Bahati from his sleep. There were no guards as their overlords thought it impossible for them to escape into the jungle where certain death awaited. Bahati had followed Pinchu outside and another halting conversation was had. That night he learned that he and his people had allies tied to a common purpose. The time would be soon, he was told, but not now. Bahati was not sure what the forest people had in mind, but perhaps he would learn more. Tonight.

It came as a surprise when the call to stop working came. It was barely past sunset and there was plainly more work to be done, but Bahati did not complain. He would take advantage of another few hours of sleep after his meal and use that extra energy conversing with Pinchu.

To his amazement, Bahati could not sleep. His body was resting, but his mind was awhirl as he waited for Pinchu to make his appearance. His thoughts drifted, as they often did in the long hours of the night, to Amina.

Amina had been in the mining crew and had quickly caught Bahati's eye. She worked the kitchen for the workers and had daily contact with them, but none like Bahati. She clearly had taken a liking to Bahati, batting her eyes and making little flirtatious comments. She was young, with bronze-like unblemished skin and Bahati wanted her. During the day, the camp was supervised, but on nights like this, the two had found each other in the dark and let their feelings be known.

Then the unimaginable had happened. A townsman had visited the camp. A fat man with a crown of white hair. He had caught sight of Amina's beauty and promptly whisked her away to serve in his household. Bahati had not seen her in two years. He wondered if his dealings with Pinchu might not only change his fortunes, but bring Amina back to his arms.

It was during this reverie that he heard a soft scuff on the dirt floor. He looked up and saw a figure, silhouetted in the doorway, that could only be Pinchu. He rose quietly from his cot and made his way outside. Looking up he gathered the night still had many hours to go. The night was quiet with only the chirruping of night insects to disturb it. Pinchu was sitting with his back against a tree waiting for him.

"Friend Bahati," said Pinchu in a low voice.

"Friend Pinchu," he replied in the same tone.

Pinchu held out something he held in his hand. "You like?" It was a cigar. Cigars were not something readily made available to slaves. They were a forbidden pleasure. Bahati smile broadly as he took the cigar and said, "I like."

The warrior pulled out a little pouch with flint and tinder and lit both their cigars. Bahati took a long drag and held it in. When he let out his breath, great billows filled the air. He took a seat next to Pinchu and they both smoked a bit in silence. Finally, Pinchu turned toward him.

"Friend Bahati. Talk of men." Bahati was a moment in deciphering what he meant. They had no common language in order to talk plainly. Bahati knew what Spanish he needed to do his work and not much beyond that, while Pinchu had learned some words from the traveling priest that sometimes wandered among the clans.

"Men with me?"

"Yes, friend with Bahati," said Pinchu, pointing at the barracks. "Many? Talk with Pinchu?"

Bahati pondered this. He had not told anyone of his meetings with Pinchu and did not know how they would react. But he did know they hated their existence and might be open to change.

"Some, others, *no se*."

"You make talk with men. Make talk with Pinchu. Make talk war."

Pinchu gestured toward the mine. "No work for Bahati. No work for men." Pinchu rose and walked toward the forest. "Men here," he said and held up two fingers on hand, pointing to the sky with his other. "You bring. I come. Make talk." Bahati nodded and his friend melted into the jungle. *Two nights. I have two nights to gather followers.*

Pinchu walked just a few feet into the jungle where Wajari was waiting.

"Well, what did he say?"

"I think I was able to make my point. We will know soon if he understood."

"He cannot be a man and not understand. His life and the lives of the others like him have been taken from them. How can one give of themselves with nothing in return? You see allies here while I see nothing but weak cowards. Why have they not yet fought back?"

"You see weak cowards everywhere. You have as much, openly, about the elders."

"I only speak what is truth. The elders would have us run and hide, but that is not the right path. We need something to wake them out of their slumber."

"What does Tsewa say?"

Wajari spat and said, "That old fool is the worst of them. He refuses to give them counsel one way or another. He is too deep in the world of spirits to give heed to the real world around him."

"Yet the spirits *do* talk to us. They are all around us at all times. Their words come through Tsewa's mouth."

Wajari took a breath and sighed. "I argued this with my father earlier. I am still hot from it, but enough. Do you think there is a way forward here?"

"I believe there is, but this must be cultivated," said Pinchu. "We need more information if we are to have a plan."

"When there is strife between clans, we have no plans. We go and take as many heads as we can."

"But these invaders are not like the clans. They have weapons we cannot match, reinforcements willing to help because of the greed they all share. Those people over there," Pinchu said waving to the slave barracks, "they are not allowed to share in their greed. They have everything to gain in helping us reclaim what is ours."

"When will you meet them again?

"Two nights from now."

"Good. I will come with you this time. I want to see for myself what they have to offer." Wajari started walking up the path to the village. "Come now and eat the morning meal with me. I have lost a night of sleep and my stomach is not happy."

Pinchu followed him. "There is one more thing, Wajari. The work at the mine was halted earlier than usual yesterday. They most often work until the darkness is complete."

"What of it? Perhaps their little hole in the ground has run out of shiny stones."

"I think not. They would just start digging another hole. No, a group of men came from the town. They were looking at everything very carefully, counting all the stones. They were not like the town people we have seen. They were white men."

Wajari turned and looked at him closely. "You are sure? You saw this all by torchlight."

"I have no doubt. I think some new invaders have arrived."

Wajari gave this some thought. "It may mean nothing, they all have the same goals of raping the land and the people who live in it. But we will keep a close eye."

* * *

Earlier in the night, Tsewa had his wives prepare another portion of the dream drink. He knew *Nantá Iwia* had made it safely to Santa Maria. He had watched him carefully ever since *Nantá Iwia* was revealed to him long ago on the ill-fated ship that sank. Through the ayahuasca and the Uwishin of the northern clans, *Nantá Iwia* had been followed closely as he trekked through the wilderness to Tsewa. But now Tsewa felt he had to see him again, now that he was so close. Whether the ayahuasca would take him to *Nantá Iwia* or some other matter, he did not know, but he had to try.

He admitted to himself that he knew almost nothing of the strange white man and his even stranger beliefs. *Yet there is a reason the spirits have revealed him to me. He is a crucial part of some grand scheme of which I have only seen the edges. Yes, he is a crucial part, and I, in my turn, must play my part as well. Has he seen me in dreams? Does he know anything of what lies ahead? I must know. Somehow I must make him take those few last steps to me.*

Finally, the potion was ready and his wife Wari brought it to him in his bowl. He settled onto his worn mat on the floor and cleared his mind. He tried to focus on *Nantá Iwia* and him alone. He slowed his breathing and relaxed his muscles. When he felt ready, he picked up the bowl and drained it in one long gulp. Almost immediately, the familiar waves of nausea engulfed him and he smiled, knowing that the drink had been made especially well. The world began to melt away and he redoubled his focus on his goal. *Nantá Iwia, Nantá Iwia.*

As the potion took him, he began to slump. Wari signaled Tsewa's other wives that it was time. They carefully lifted Tsewa's frail frame onto his cot and covered him with a blanket. He would be chilled after traveling the world of spirits. Their duties complete, they left the hut and Tsewa alone.

At first there was nothing. For a long time he drifted in limbo with no thoughts of his own, no feeling in his limbs. Then there was a rush of colors and a sense of motion. The colors streamed by him with increasing speed and suddenly he could see. He was high above the village looking down. It was not day. It was not not night. It simply was and he could see his world in incredible detail. Looking to the horizon, he could sense other Uwishin who had taken flight this night, but he gave them no mind. He looked down again and saw the vast crescent of unlife that bordered the broad river. It was as if a great bite had been taken out of the jungle and this was where the invaders had staked their claim.

Seeing this made him sicker than the ayahuasca had. The land was defiled with their buildings and filth. How anyone could consider this a home was beyond his comprehension. Yet this was where he needed to send his spirit if he was to accomplish his goal. He could see sparks where every living creature was but he could not find the one he sought. He floated, ethereal, unbound and with no idea which of those sparks was the one he needed. He forced himself to calm down and soon the spark he was looking for revealed itself.

Nantá Iwia, I come to you.

Chapter Sixteen

Ayahuasca, known for its profound spiritual and hallucinogenic effects, is carefully crafted by indigenous shamans of the Amazon basin, including the Shuar people. The brew is made by combining the vine Banisteriopsis caapi with leaves from the Psychotria viridis plant. These two plants, each with distinct properties, are boiled together in large pots for hours, sometimes even days. The vine contains harmala alkaloids, which act as MAO inhibitors, allowing the psychoactive component of Psychotria viridis, DMT (dimethyltryptamine), to take effect. The preparation process is deeply ritualistic. Shamans may chant or perform invocations to infuse the brew with spiritual energy, guiding the transformative experience it is meant to provide. What's remarkable is the indigenous knowledge behind its creation. Without modern chemistry, these peoples have understood that combining these two specific plants produces a visionary state. It is said that the plants themselves 'taught' the shamans how to make ayahuasca. The resulting brew serves as a bridge to other realms, used for healing, guidance, and connecting with spiritual entities.

Dr. Marcos Jara, Cultural Anthropologist, University of Mexico City

Pedro de Arobe was walking through the town square when he saw her. She was, to his mind, the most beautiful woman he had ever seen. Not since his night with the African slave women on the *San Felipe y Santiago* had he felt such desire and he changed his direction and stride to match hers. She was clearly a household servant on her way to market, with an armful of cloth bags ready to be filled with foodstuffs. He kept a safe distance from her, stealing glances whenever he could. Whenever she stopped at a stall, he was at another nearby, pretending to look at the various wares.

When she approached a fruit stand, the vendor called out to her amiably.

"Good morning, Amina. What is your pleasure today?"

"Hello, Mateo. As usual, some plantains and perhaps something a little special. How are these pineapples?"

Pedro did not hear anything beyond the initial exchange after hearing her name. *Amina. A wondrous name for a wondrous creature.* Her fruit purchase complete, she made her way around the other stalls, placing orders for grain, flour and fish, then finally a stop for spices. By this time, her bags were bulging and she kept switching them arm to arm as they tired. She started to leave the market when she was distracted by a vendor who sold oils and candles. She did a quick mental calculation and decided, yes, the household did need a few more candles. She stuffed them into one of the bags, hoisted them up awkwardly and began her journey home. It was the moment Pedro had waited for and he made his move.

"Excuse me, Señorita," he said bowing slightly. "I see you have quite a load to carry. Would you like some assistance?"

She looked him up and down as if he were some exotic specimen of insect. There was something about him that mildly repulsed her and that wide white-toothed grin did nothing to change her impression. Moreover, it was unseemly for her, as a slave, to accept help from someone above her station. What would they say at the estate? She might be beaten for her lack of judgment.

"No thank you, Señor," she said meekly. "I do not have far to go."

"Please, I insist. I must know more about..."

She left him there mid-sentence and hustled back toward her home. Pedro stood there stunned for a moment by her abrupt departure. He followed her with his eyes and after a moment he began to follow her. Looking over her shoulder, Amina saw his intent and redoubled her pace, the large bags bouncing off her thighs, impeding her progress. Finally she approached the Yllescas estate. As she expected, there was someone watching out for her return, the head housekeeper, Estefania. Amina slipped into the kitchen between the door jamb and Estefania, who was still at the doorway looking toward the square.

"Who is that?"

"I do not know, Doña. He has followed me since the market."

"Did you provoke him in some way?"

Amina felt Estefania's suspicious glare. "I swear, Doña. I have never seen him before."

Estefania maintain her glare a moment longer. All she said was "Hmmph," and went back to the doorway. She saw Pedro just standing there looking at the house and decided to get to the bottom of things. She came down the steps and approached Pedro.

"Señor," she called out. "Is there something you need?"

Pedro was startled out of his musings. When he realized he had been seen, he turned tail and ran back to the square like a frightened rabbit.

Estefania put her hands on her hips as she watched him go.

"Hmmph."

* * *

The first meeting of the conspiracy took place in the Captain's cabin on the *Santa Estrella*. De Cuellar looked on each of the assembled, taking stock of each of them. Martinez, with four of his remaining soldiers, Ordoñez, Ruiz, Galindo and Medina, de Cuellar's Harquebusiers, Salazar and Mendoza, as well as some of the men who had survived the shipwreck with them.

De Cuellar had spent the day approaching each of the men, urging them to come to the caravel to discuss matters of urgency. De Cuellar did not divulge much more than this, although Martinez and his men had more of an inkling about what would be presented here. Of all the men here, only one gave the Captain some concern. Rodrigo. *He needs to be handled with care*, he thought, *but we cannot go forward without him. He is the only one among us with knowledge to refit this vessel.*

Detecting a touch of restlessness among the assembled, he addressed the cohort.

"I have invited all of you here, tonight, because of three things. Firstly, we are all survivors of the *San Felipe y Santiago* and thus comrades in arms. Secondly, I know that many of you stand much to lose now that you are stranded in this backwater town instead of where you meant to be, Callao" He paused for effect and said, "Thirdly and lastly, because you are all true

Spaniards." His meaning was not lost on them. It was plainly evident that none of the de Arobes were in attendance. The soldier, Galindo, spoke up.

"What of the Priest, Ignacio? Surely he meets with the criteria you have set, moreover, he has been a great asset and friend to us all." Many heads nodded in agreement.

"I value Ignacio as well," replied de Cuellar. "However, in his case, it is a matter of loyalty. The Church is his uppermost focus. He has found here what would take a lifetime to achieve in Callao. A parish of his very own, answering to no one but himself."

"You slander him too easily, Captain," said Miguel Ordoñez. "Only he can speak for himself in such matters, but I understand your concern, no matter how inelegantly you have expressed it. Be that as it may, why have you brought us here?"

De Cuellar gave the man a hard stare until Ordoñez averted his gaze.

"It was revealed to me, among other things, that the chief of this town, Yllescas, has planned to scuttle this vessel when the Governor completes his visit and returns to Quito. I had asked him to allow me to take residence here and see to her refit. His answer was noncommittal at best, but he has allowed me to stay here until such a time as he sees fit to revisit the situation."

"And what would you have of us?" asked Galindo. "Few of us have skills for shipbuilding. We sail on them, sometimes we swim from them as they sink, but that is all." There was a spatter of chuckles at this, but de Cuellar ignored the jibe.

"There are more skills among us than you think. For example," he said referring to a list he had compiled, "Señor Rios is a carpenter by trade, are you not?" Rios nodded in assent. "And Rafael Serrano, you are a blacksmith, and Antonio Vega, fisherman. Rodrigo will lead the refit crew and you three will assist him, unless you have something else in mind."

"Pardon me, Captain," said Vega, "All this to afford you a personal yacht?"

"No, this is to the benefit of us all, as you will see. You my word that you will be rewarded appropriately for your effort. Are there any objections?" There were no dissenters. "Very well. Rodrigo, take them below and create a list of what needs to be done and assign the necessary tasks. As for you soldiers and military men, stay behind for there is more I would have you know about the project before us."

After the civilians had made their exit, de Cuellar addressed the remaining men.

"This town of Santa Maria is more than what it appears to be. Lieutenant Martinez can attest to what I am about to tell you as he was with me as I conducted a tour that was quite revealing. As you have heard, the Governor of Quito is making an unprecedented journey to this flyspeck in the middle of nowhere. It was not until I asked why, that an answer was afforded to me. As it happens, Santa Maria is not an idyllic little farming community but a mining site that extracts several tons of gold and silver ore every year. In addition, they have the facilities to process on site and thus have piles of ingots waiting on hand. That is why this Governor makes his way here. To take possession of a shipment bound for the Crown."

The soldiers looked one to another in amazement, and then to Martinez.

"You knew this?" asked Galindo. Martinez smiled and nodded.

"I only learned this recently. Everything the Captain says is true. I have seen it with my own eyes."

"That is why I need this boat repaired and ready to sail before this Governor makes his appearance. The time is short and it will be on your backs that it is all completed in time."

"Your pardon again, Captain," said Ordoñez. "What is this to do with ingots? Are we to escort the shipment?"

"No, dolt. I mean to steal it. And the boat." He watched as Ordoñez and the others seemed to digest this. He fully expected to hear objections to committing an act of piracy but that was not the case. Ordoñez looked to his fellows who were nodding in agreement.

"When is this to happen?"

"The very moment that this caravel is able to hold more silver and gold than water, we shall be at the ready."

"And these ingots," asked Ruiz, "where are they now?"

"Ah, that information was not given to me by Yllescas, but I have asked discreet questions here and there and have found where they are stored. The younger Yllescas can be quite loquacious when wine has been bought for him. It is not guarded very well, after all, who is to steal it?" de Cuellar said with a smile. "Pirates? No, in their infinite wisdom they have warehoused the ingots in a nondescript building right here on the waterfront. In fact, you walked by it on your way here. It is literally at our doorstep."

Someone let out a low whistle in sheer amazement. Ruiz clasped his hands together and turned to de Cuellar.

"Assuming this goes to plan, what happens then?"

"We make haste for Callao, as originally intended. Once there, any story can be concocted to explain our appearance and then we divide the spoils, going our separate ways. Until then, we speak to no one about this, and that includes the work crew I have sent below. And especially not the priest. No confessionals for any of you."

"So the work crew does not have a share?"

"I promised them adequate compensation and they will receive it. Rodrigo has too honest of a heart beating in his chest and I do not trust him with the full details, but I need him most to get this ship ready. He will no doubt divine the plot, but by then we should be at sea."

"And should he betray us at Callao?"

"We will convince him otherwise, of course. Failing that, well, the *Santa Estrella* would not be the first ship to come into port without her pilot."

"Piracy is one thing, Captain," said Martinez. "Murder is quite another."

"And I have suggested no such thing, Lieutenant. There are plenty of beaches between here and Callao to strand him and any others of the work crew that voice objection."

"Adequate compensation, then."

"Look," said de Cuellar with exasperation, "let us not quibble about things that may or may not come to happen. Let us focus on the task at hand, which is to get this vessel seaworthy. To that end you will work alongside the others until it is time to load our cargo." Some of the men moaned at this. "What, you expect the work to be done for you? Go! Help and learn what you can about sailing. I have no doubt you will come to need it."

* * *

Ignacio sat at his table, writing in his journal by candlelight. He paused for a moment to collect his thoughts, his eyes straying around the small room. Don Juan had been true to his word. His quarters had not only been cleaned and aired out, but the walls had been freshly painted and new furniture had been brought in. And, thanks to Rosa, there were fresh flowers in every corner and on every shelf. Ignacio smiled and returned to his writing.

The Lord has provided me more than I deserve, more than I expected. I am reminded, in the peace of this space, that even in the wilderness, beauty can flourish when one opens his heart to the gifts He bestows. The flowers Rosa has brought remind me of the love and care we must show to each other, as they soften the harshness of our trials. I feel comforted knowing that, despite the hardships ahead, God's grace surrounds us even in the smallest acts of kindness.

Ignacio set his quill aside and closed the book. *There are not many pages left in my journal. It is fitting, I suppose, to close one book and begin another as well as a new life. This old one has been through so much with me. I pray the next will take longer to fill with far fewer challenges to populate its pages.* He rose from his chair, stretching his back from the kinks he had acquired hunched over his desk. It was late. The light of the moon shone softly from his solitary window and he yawned. Turning toward his bed, he knelt before the crucifix Yllescas had thoughtfully hung over it. It was crude, crafted from reeds and twigs, but Ignacio thought it beautiful. It truly captured the essence of this new place. Yes, even in the wilderness, beauty can flourish.

He crossed himself and began his nightly routine, speaking softly to himself. He had barely begun the Confiteor when something interrupted his thoughts. Unsure as to whether he had heard something or if he had imagined it, he looked about. He could hear nothing but there was a feeling in his gut that something was amiss. There was nothing to which he could ascribe it, but he was overwhelmed by a need to enter the church proper.

Sitting back on his heels, he took a few deep breaths, but the feeling did not go away. Hastily crossing himself, he rose and turned to the door that connected with the church. Opening it, he was met with darkness, save for the sparse moonlight from the high windows. Waiting for his eyes to adjust, he waited in the doorway, listening intently. He was ready to retreat back into his quarters when he noticed it. There was a soft glow by the altar that was not caused by moonlight or reflection. Almost involuntarily, he walked toward it. Slowly, by degrees, an image seemed to be taking shape, and then there it was. A man sitting cross-legged upon the altar.

Ignacio was prepared to demand the figure's identification, but he caught himself. He knew full well who this was. A nearly breathless whisper escaped his lips.

"Tsewa!"

The apparition nodded gravely and beckoned to Ignacio. He took a few halting steps forward. The encounters he had experienced in his dreams were vague and poorly remembered, but what he now saw before him was exactly as he had first seen when he first boarded the *San Felipe y Santiago.* A young Native, black haired, with painted stripes on his face.

As he approached, Ignacio realized he could see through Tsewa, as if he were composed of mist. Ignacio stopped in his tracks and came no closer. *This is an illusion...a dream...a vision.* Ignacio was terrified and wanted nothing more than to run from this place, but he was fixated and could not move, helplessly staring into Tsewa's eyes.

Tsewa began to speak. His lips were clearly making words but there was no sound to be heard. Ignacio broke from his stupor and tried to make sense of what he was seeing. Finally he shook his head and pointed to his ears. Tsewa seemed to understand and mouthed 'Ah'. He then began gesturing with his hands, pointing to himself, then to Ignacio. It was like watching through a haze, but Ignacio got the sense that the gestures were trying to convey friendship and he allowed himself to relax. Tsewa appeared frustrated, gesticulating wildly but Ignacio could make no sense it. Finally Tsewa pointed to Ignacio, walked his fingers across the palm of his other hand and then pointed to himself. The meaning was clear.

"You want me to come to you."

Tsewa smiled, nodded, and then faded away like smoke on the breeze.

How long Ignacio stood there staring at the altar, he could not say. He was trying to process what he had just witnessed and considering whether he might just be going mad.

* * *

The water in the hold was less than a foot deep, but it had been there a long time and it reeked. Rodrigo inspected the beams and fittings while Rios held the lantern aloft.

"It is not as bad as I had first thought," said Rodrigo. "I do not think the hull is actually leaking. All this water could have come from the boat sitting out in the rain for years and no one caring enough to pump it out occasionally. I will know better once this filth is pumped out. Here, bring that light closer. See those fittings? They are still doing what they are meant to, but they are heavily corroded."

Rios took a closer look where Rodrigo indicated.

"I will have Serrano take a look at those and see what his opinion is," said Rios. "Metal work is beyond my purview."

"Well, do not despair, my carpenter friend. These boards here are rotted through and through. If they are not a problem now, they will be very shortly. I suspect there will be more problems below the waterline. Pitch at the very least."

"So how do we get the water out?"

"Follow me. We will inspect the bilge pump and see if it still functions. My hopes are not high." They came to a contraption near the stern, a hand crank that fed a chain through a wooden pipe. Attached to the chain were a series of discs that moved the water out when cranked. "Rusted as I expected, but let us see if we cannot give it a turn." Rodrigo pulled on the crank with all his might but it was not enough. "Here now, give me a hand with this." The two wrestled the crank and with a loud scream of protest from the chain, it began to turn. Rodrigo stepped back and mopped his brow with his shirt.

"A bucket of oil will take care of that. I think it will actually work and one of our problems will be solved."

"Rodrigo, what does de Cuellar really want with this vessel?"

"I have my suspicions, to be sure. He is, after all, a man of the sea, as am I. If I were to hazard a guess, I would say he wants to sail her out of here and leave Santa Maria far behind him."

"It does not belong to him."

"I am sure that in his mind, it does. Why should that matter to you?"

"It is a matter of my own conscience. I would not have a hand in anything untoward."

"I would not give that any further thought. Yllescas had plans to dismantle this vessel. In that case, this is a salvage operation and nothing else. Come, let us go find that oil and pump this filth out."

They climbed out of the hold and into the sunlight. Rodrigo expanded his chest, taking in a lungful of air.

"Ah, that is better. That stink below was unbearable."

Rios tugged on Rodrigo's sleeve and nodded toward the soldiers across the deck who were smoking and having a laugh.

"See? That is what I mean. If this is a salvage operation, then why the soldiers? They are not the ones pumping water."

Rodrigo looked over and began to wonder that himself. Nearly as one, the soldiers turned and glared at Rodrigo and Rios. Rodrigo was not one to be easily intimidated and so he walked over to them.

"Hey," he said amiably, "have you another one of those smokes?"

Ordoñez silently handed him a cigar and then lit it from his own.

Whatever conversation they were having ended abruptly when Rodrigo joined them. He swirled the smoke around in his mouth and blew out a large ring that blew away over the railing.

"Beautiful day, is it not?" The soldiers nodded quietly. Rodrigo, seeing that any conversation they wanted to have did not include him. "Well, thank you for the cigar. We are off to find some oil for the bilge pump."

Rejoining Rios, he muttered under his breath, "I think you are right to have questions."

Chapter Seventeen

"Then the mystery was revealed to Daniel in a vision of the night. Then Daniel blessed the God of heaven."

Daniel 2:19

In the forest, Tsewa slowly came back from the spiritual realm. His first reaction was anger. He had assumed that *Nantá Iwia* would himself be in a dream state and that they would be able to converse freely. *Nantá Iwia* was clearly frightened by Tsewa's appearance. That was unexpected and unacceptable. Because of the toll ayahuasca took on his body, he would be unable to attempt another spiritual journey for several days. There had to be some way to meet in the flesh. Tsewa himself was not up for such a journey, even though it was just a matter of a few miles. That left kidnapping, which was totally out of the question. *Nantá Iwia* must come of his own volition, as the wandering spirit he embodies.

Tsewa stared at the thatched roof above his head as he lay on his cot. *My time is short, I can feel it in my bones. If I die before my time, the clan will be left without an Uwishin, or worse, the wrong Uwishin. Would that I had more sons. The spirits saw to give me one and no more. Even my daughters have only daughters.*

His second wife, Namoch, broke his reverie. Seeing him awake, she brought him a bowl of water, which he slurped noisily.

"Help me up, wife. I tire of counting the reeds in our roof."

Namoch barely exerted herself, lifting Tsewa's back and swinging his legs around, sitting him on the edge of his cot.

"You must not drink so much ayahuasca," she admonished. "You are like a drunkard and no good to me for days on end."

Tsewa laughed. "I have been no good to you for a long time. Soon you will need a new husband."

"I am not finished with the one I have. Now stop being so foolish. I will get you something to eat."

She is right, as always. I dwell too much on the day I join the spirits when there are other matters that need my attention. Yet it seems that the answer to all these matters always lead back to one thing. Nantá Iwia.

At that time, Wajari entered the hut. Namoch scolded him saying, "Whenever there is food around, that is where you can find Wajari, but when his father is getting himself drunk, Wajari is nowhere to be found."

Wajari waved her off, grinning as he did so. "Quiet woman, learn your place."

"Your place will be across my knees, if you are not careful."

Wajari patted her on the bottom. "Yes, mother," he said, continuing on to Tsewa.

"Father. I have news. The scouts say that that demon, Burgos, approaches from the south. I beg your permission to bring his head to adorn my hut."

"Wajari, you know I have forbidden this. Demon he may be, but I know he can still be of use." *And I think I know exactly how to use him.* "Bring him to me," and with stern look added, "Unharmed! I would have words with him."

* * *

Fray Burgos had come to the New World with the best of intentions. He subscribed to the mission of the Mercedarian order to ransom Christian captives from Moorish lands. Of course that did not strictly apply here. The were no Moors, nor were there any captives. But there were potential Christians held captive by their ignorance of the Word and it was his intent to correct that.

His naivety on arriving on these shores had not prepared him for the struggles he encountered, beginning with the harshness of life in the wilderness. His initial encounters with the native peoples were marked with genuine attempts to convert them to Christianity, but eventually, Burgos' methods began to shift. The natives he encountered were not the only ones who influenced his life. He saw the pressures of colonial survival firsthand and came to realize these people had to only be converted, but conquered. Outwardly maintaining the appearance of a devout missionary, he slowly became more manipulative, driven by a sense of superiority and the demands of Spanish colonial interests.

He followed the worn path unafraid. His escort had left him at the borders of their land and there was only a short distance until he reached the borders of Nunkui Nampet, or, as he translated in his head, Crown of Spears. He had no doubt that they were already aware of his approach and he eyed the foliage with mild apprehension. Although he had come to Crown of Spears before, one could never be too sure of their receptiveness until the moment of encounter.

Burgos had come to this land a much younger man, but corpulent and inexperienced in hard labor. Times like these always made him reflect on how far he had come physically. His younger self would have been sweating and panting by now, but now, as he approached middle age, this was just another day. He trudged on, and after an hour began to wonder why his presence had not been acknowledged. When the encounter came, he was unprepared for it.

As if by magic, five warriors were suddenly surrounding him. As they closed the circle, Burgos noticed with dismay that they wore face and body paints as well as feathered headdresses. Most notable were the spears and shields. This was, beyond a doubt, a war party.

Burgos scanned the faces around him and found he recognized at least two of them. His mind could not come up with the name of one, but the other's sprang forward.

"Wajari! Friend," he said, slipping into the Jivaroan language effortlessly. "You have surprised me. Do you go to war? Are there enemy warriors about?"

"Only you, demon," spat Wajari. "For you we must prepare as if for battle to strengthen us against your evil."

"Wajari, you know me. I have no evil in my heart."

"Do not use my name. You seek to bind me with your demon ways. My spear will find your heart and show the truth of my words."

Burgos, in spite of his determination to show no fear, began to sweat.

"Waja...uh, warrior. What are your intentions here? I have ever been a friend to your people."

"You will be silent. I am forbidden from killing you but I will not hesitate if you utter one more word. If I had my way, you would now be laying in a pool of your own blood, never knowing when the blow came. You will come with us now. One word, one misstep and you will not reach Crown of Spears. Now run!"

With that, they raced down the path, with the occasional poke of a spear to Burgos' backside prodding him along. It was not long before Burgos began reassessing his state of physical fitness.

* * *

It took most of the day, but between Rodrigo and Rios taking turns at the crank, most of the water had been pumped out. No new water seemed to be coming in and what was left was a matter of mops and buckets.

"Well, that went better than I thought," said Rodrigo, sitting on an old barrel. "The pump did very well for having been abandoned for who knows how long."

"It is in better shape than my arms at the moment," replied Rios. "At the very least we have something to show for our efforts."

"Aye, while revealing the other things that have gone wrong on this boat, still it is better than my initial assessment. I will send Serrano down and the two of you can further take stock of what is needed."

"Where is Serrano anyway? I have not seen him all day and he certainly did not help with the pumping."

"I sent him into town ere we started to seek out the local blacksmith. He is probably there already forging the initial pieces."

Rodrigo rubbed his arms which were still cramping from the efforts at the crank.

"I will go see him and then make a quick stop at La Posada. I will return after that."

"What about me? I could use a quick drink myself."

"You can go after you have made your list of woodwork and have brought down the pitch. I will not be long and will relieve you when I get back."

Rios grumbled a bit but set about his tasks as Rodrigo started his climb out of the hold.

As Rodrigo's head reached the level of the main deck, he heard voices near the opening and halted his climb. Recognizing the voices as Ordoñez and Galindo, he felt a sudden compulsion to not reveal himself and listen to their conversation. After the strange way the soldiers had responded to his presence earlier, his curiosity got the better of him.

"It is right there," he heard Ordoñez say. "The squat one with the thatched roof."

"Then the job is as good as done, although the load will be a heavy one," replied Galindo.

"Our backs are as strong as they ever were and the reward will be great enough to offset any strain they might incur. It is just a question of when, not how."

Galindo said something that Rodrigo could not make out, but Ordoñez replied, "That is not an issue. When the time comes, we will attend to it." Their voices started fading and Rodrigo could hear their footfalls moving away from him, but he could not make out any more of the conversation. As he stepped onto the main deck, he was greeted with the same sudden silence he had been subjected to before. Ordoñez and Galindo turned at his approach, nodded to acknowledge his presence, but said nothing else, not even a greeting. Rodrigo did the same, offering a quick salute and heading to the gangplank. He felt that they were staring at his retreated back but a quick look over his shoulder showed they were once again into their conversation.

Rodrigo tried very hard not to look at the buildings on the waterfront with any interest, as the pair might still be watching him. He could not help but notice the structure of which they spoke, indeed he had to pass it by on his way to the square. *What is in there that is of such interest to them?* The building itself had no windows, a pair of barn-like doors marked the only entrance. Nor were there any signs or markings to announce its purpose, just a plain, nondescript edifice that he had walked by every day without noticing.

Now was not the time to linger and so he passed it by without another glance. Crossing the square, he turned on a side street and walked to the end where the blacksmith's stall was located. There, he found Serrano as he had expected. He quickly relayed to the man everything he could think of in regards to the progress of repairs on the Santa Estrella and confirmed that Serrano had completed many of the fittings needed for the refit. They could begin installation later today, the man told him, and Rodrigo congratulated him on a job well done. Satisfied that everything was progressing well,

Rodrigo took his leave and headed toward his true destination.

La Posada del Viento was the premier, if not only, tavern in Santa Maria. Supporting a population of just over eleven hundred residents, it was the only establishment serving the community that served food as well as drink. Rodrigo needed both.

He found himself a table near the door where he could watch the patrons as they entered. He desperately wanted aguardiente, a strong alcoholic spirit distilled from sugarcane, but he needed to keep a clear head, at least for the moment. Instead, he ordered wine along with a plate of grilled meat and bread. He had barely taken his first mouthful when Don Juan Yllescas entered the establishment. Spotting Rodrigo, Yllescas flashed a toothy grin and took the seat across from him.

"Good day, my friend. Rodrigo, am I right? Do you mind if I join you? Tables are always at a premium here." Rodrigo grunted and shrugged his shoulders. Yllescas took this as an invitation. A servant soon arrived and Yllescas said, "I will have the same as my friend here, but chicha rather than wine." Chicha was a fermented beverage made from maize and a staple drink for the locals.

"So then, how are you finding Santa Maria?"

"It is there when I open my eyes in the morning," replied Rodrigo sarcastically.

Yllescas laughed. "Oh, that is some good sailor humor if ever I have heard it. Seriously, are your needs being addressed?" Rodrigo shrugged again and shoved another piece of meat into his mouth. Yllescas looked at him a moment expectantly. Seeing no verbal answer was forthcoming, he changed tact.

"I see your people have taken over my pleasure boat."

"You can have it back with merely your say so."

"Oh, I care not. Calling it my pleasure boat was merely a jest. If your Captain finds pleasure in making his residence there, who am I to deny him?"

Again there was silence from Rodrigo. Yllescas did not seem to notice and he went on.

"That vessel was ancient before I was born. It has been moored here a very long time."

That seemed to perk up Rodrigo's interest.

"How did the ship come to be here then?"

"Well, that is a good question," said Yllescas as his order arrived. "It is a small mystery that no one has ever been able to decipher. The *Santa Estrella* was found listing at the mouth of the river. No crew or passengers were ever found. It is unclear if they ever made the shore or were lost at sea. There was not so much as a captain's log or any such records."

"Cargo?" asked Rodrigo around another mouthful.

"A hold full of rotted fruit and textiles. Nothing salvageable but the ship itself, adding more to the mystery of how it got there. It was then towed. You have seen our little fleet of fishing boats. It was no easy task, I assure you."

"That I can believe." Rodrigo fell silent once more. The information Yllescas gave of the Santa Estrella was interesting but Rodrigo's current thoughts lay elsewhere. After a moment he decided to change the subject.

"Tell me, Señor Yllescas, what use are the buildings along the waterfront?"

Yllescas looked at him strangely. "What an odd question," he said after a moment. "Why do you ask?"

"Idle curiosity. Nothing more. I pass by them everyday, but aside from the administrative building, I know not what is there."

"Yes," Yllescas said slowly, "the administration center certainly. There are some offices for minor officials and the rest are just storage."

"Oh?"

"Supplies and equipment for the fishermen, no great mystery there. Storage for anything coming in from the river."

Or going out to the river, no doubt, thought Rodrigo.

He drained the last of his wine and stood.

"Forgive me, Señor. I must get back to my duties. It has been a pleasure."

Yllescas followed Rodrigo with his eyes as the sailor exited the tavern. A curious look was on his face.

* * *

Rosa entered the church and crossed herself at the altar. Looking around, she spied Ignacio sweeping between the chairs near the back. She walked toward him, noting the plumes of dust swirling in the air.

My word," she said, as she waved the dust away. "I thought Yllescas was going to take care of this."

"My quarters," replied Ignacio, his back turned to her. "In that regard, he did exceptionally well." As he turned toward her, he added, "Apparently the church proper is my purview." When Rosa saw his face, she gasped.

"Nacho! Did something happen? Are you ill?" There were large dark circles under his eyes and his hair, full of dust, looked like a bird's nest."

Ignacio rested the broom against the wall and sat in a nearby chair.

"No, I am fine. I am just tired. I did not sleep well."

"More like you have not slept in a week!" She sat in a chair next to him and studied his face. There were lines that had not been there before and he looked not just tired, but haggard.

"Did you have another one of your dreams?"

"What? No," he lied, though in truth he had not been plagued by dream, but by a nightmare of a different sort. "The re-dedication has been weighing on my mind, that is all."

"I am finding it hard to believe you. You look terrible."

"I assure you, there is nothing to worry about. Now, are you here for something or just here to nag at me like my mother used to do?"

Rosa crossed her arms and frowned at him. "You are clearly not yourself and so I will forgive your little jab. I came to invite you dinner at the home of Señora Fernandez. She was kind enough to give me and Maria Delgado refuge after our rescue and has offered to host a small gathering so that she can meet the new vicar of Santa Maria."

"When is this?"

"Tonight. And I will not have you refusing," she said sternly when he started to shake his head. "You have a few hours. Get some sleep and for God's sake, clean up and do something with your hair. You need to make a good impression and I will not have you looking like a vagabond."

"Very well," he said wearily. "I cannot win a battle against you and the dust will patiently await my return. I will be there as you wish."

* * *

Back at the caravel, Rodrigo watched as Rios and Serrano install the newly crafted fittings and boards. The last of the water in the hold had been cleared out and the space had begun to dry. The smell of mold and stagnant water had been reduced greatly, although it still lingered in the air. He looked about and asked, "Where is Vega?" Although the man was not a craftsman, he was another pair of needed hands.

"The man is worse than useless," said Serrano. "Does not know a hammer from a carrot, that one. I got tired of him getting in the way, so I sent him topside to inspect the rigging and replace what needed replacing."

"Is he as bad as that?"

"Not as such. He is not witless, he is just mystified as to what we need to do down here."

"He is as ignorant to carpentry and metalwork as we are to rigging lines on a mast," added Rios. "I cannot blame him for what he does not know. I suppose it was our fault to try and enlist his help."

Rios looked at Rodrigo with hope in his eyes.

"Did you bring us any food or drink? I know you had yours."

"I did," said Rodrigo as he handed over a bag. "I made a stop at the market on the way back. Not much, bread, cheese, some fruit. Enough to tide you over."

Rios took the bag from him.

"You are truly a prince among men, Rodrigo. I thank you."

"Think nothing of it," said Rodrigo, as the men began dividing up the treats. "I think I will go up and check on Vega. Here, give me some of that for him."

Rodrigo gained the deck without encountering any of the soldiers, which of late, was unusual. There were most often to be found on deck these days, smoking and holding little conferences among themselves. But never working on the refit. *Oh no, that is quite beneath them, it seems.* He cast about, looking for Vega and finally sighted him high on the main mast. *I guess I will will just wait for him to come down. My days of clambering like a monkey are over.* As he waited for Vega, he stood by the railing and looked toward the buildings facing him. There were many questions still unanswered and he started having more related to Don Juan Yllescas.

As he stood there, he noticed Captain de Cuellar and his constant companion Martinez coming up the path to the riverfront. It was evident they had just indulged in some time at La Posada as they joked to each other with a slight sway to their steps. *And where have you been, you old pirate,* he thought, never realizing how close he was to the truth. *One way or another I will find out what is swirling around in your head, and when I do...* With that thought unfinished, another came to the forefront. *This, no doubt, has something to do with that storage building. The building so conveniently close to the vessel you have claimed as your own.* He thought back to Yllescas' guarded and vague answers to his questions. *Somehow I must learn what lies there and how this all connects. Yes, Rodrigo, what will you do?*

how this all connects. Yes, Rodrigo, what will you do?

Chapter Eighteen

"Fearing that we would be dashed against the rocks, they dropped four anchors from the stern and prayed for daylight. In an attempt to escape from the ship, the sailors let the lifeboat down into the sea, pretending they were going to lower some anchors from the bow. Then Paul said to the centurion and the soldiers, 'Unless these men stay with the ship, you cannot be saved.'"

Acts 27:29-31

"Good evening, Señora Fernandez. I hope I am not too late," said Ignacio as the matron of the house opened the door. She was a portly woman with a shock of grey hair that surrounded her head like a halo. Ignacio liked her from her reputation alone. Childless and recently widowed, she had been among the first to open her home to the newly arrived refugees, taking in not only Rosa but the three other women as well. The house that was suddenly too large for one person finally had a purpose.

"Nonsense, Father. The evening is just underway and there are guests yet to arrive. Please, come in and make yourself comfortable."

Ignacio looked around as he made his entry noting the typical Spanish flavor that dominated this frontier town. Roomy, with arched ceilings that reminded him of his own home in Seville. He was immediately distracted by the greetings of his erstwhile travel companions and he took a moment to acknowledge and embrace each one in turn.

"Maria, Inéz...," He fumbled for a moment before he recalled the third woman's name. "And Carmen! How wonderful it is to see you all once again, and under much better circumstances."

"Please, Father," said Inéz, "do not remind us. You helped us and saw us at our worst. Now is a time to celebrate and put that all behind us."

Ignacio followed them to the parlor where he was ushered to the finest chair in the house.

"May I provide you with something to drink? A wine perhaps?" asked Carmen.

"Wine would be lovely. Thank you."

Señora Fernandez sat across from him. "These girls have been a Godsend," she said with obvious affection. "I have no relations here in Santa Maria, and when my husband passed away, I found myself in an awkward position. I could not keep the house staff and so I was left rattling around by myself in this overlarge house. Suddenly, I have family again and I thank the Lord for showing me his grace."

"I am truly sorry for your loss, Señora," said Ignacio, accepting a goblet from Carmen. "If I may be so bold, how did he pass?"

"Oh, it was a sudden thing. He went in his sleep, it must have been that his heart gave out in his old age."

Ignacio took an appraising look at her face.

"Again, forgive my indulgence, but you seem...well, quite young."

"Were that that were true, Father," she said with a laugh. "I am well into middle age, but you are right. My husband was twenty years my senior."

Taking a sip from his wine, he said, "You mentioned there were to be other guests." At that moment Rosa emerged from the kitchen, wiping her hands on a towel.

"I took the liberty of inviting the de Arobes," she said. "I am surprised they are not yet here." She looked at Ignacio approvingly. "You look much better, Nacho. And cleaner."

Ignacio caught the wide-eyed look on Señora Fernandez's face.

"I was sweeping out the dust in the church today. Rosa caught me when I was quite covered with it."

"Yes, but *Nacho*?" Fernandez asked, eyebrows still arched.

"Ah, yes, well," he began, "my given name is Ignacio. Nacho is a name that Rosa and my sister imposed on me when I was a young boy."

"I had no idea that you shared a common history. I thought that the two of you had been thrown together by your mishaps." She looked at Rosa reproachfully. "Rosa has not shared this with me."

"It was a long time ago, in a land far away, and with many years in between. We only discovered our mutual history when we boarded the *San Felipe y Santiago*. It was quite the surprise."

"Well, I can see that there will be much to uncover during dinner," Señora Fernandez said with a whimsical smirk. "I look forward to tales of the young Father."

Thankfully, before Ignacio could reply, a knock came on the door. The de Arobes had arrived.

Maria greeted them at the door and showed them into the entryway. As Ignacio rose, he saw that Señor de Arobe bore a large bouquet of colorful flowers, and felt a pang of unease. He had given no thought to such a gesture and had arrived empty handed.

"What beautiful flowers!" exclaimed Maria. "They will make a lovely centerpiece. Thank you."

"They are no more beautiful than what I see before me, Señora and Señoritas," he said smoothly, eliciting several giggles from the women. "No offense, Father, but I cannot say the same for you."

"I am not offended, Señor. Apparently, my beauty is not as obvious." As he shook hands with de Arobe's son Domingo, he asked, "And Pedro? Did he not come with you?"

"Ah," said Don Francisco with a frown, "I was hoping no one would notice. No, Pedro insisted, without elaboration, that he had a prior engagement that could not be missed. I suspect it has to do with a curvaceous new bottle at La Posada del Viento that has caught his eye. I will deal with that later."

"I am sorry to have mentioned it," he said sheepishly. "I feel I have let you down in that regard, as I was never able to counsel him as I had promised on the ship. And then later, well..."

"Not to worry, Father. What is done is done. Or undone, as the case may be. Pedro is his own man now, and free to leave my household when he wishes. Do not pin his shortcomings on yourself."

Señora Fernandez clapped her hands to get everyone's attention.

"Now that we are all here, follow me into the dining room. Let us enjoy each other's company."

* * *

De Arobe was not far off the mark. Pedro was indeed at La Posada, drinking himself to oblivion. He was not just enamored by one bottle, he was doing his best to drink them all. He became drunker as he drank. Louder as he became drunker. Belligerent as he became louder. Soon even the patrons of La Posada had had enough and the call was made to remove him from the premises. This led to punches being thrown and tables overturned. Finally, a group of men grappled with Pedro and forcefully pushed him out the door. As Pedro made to reenter the tavern, one of the men clocked him on the chin and put him to sleep. Laughing, these men then picked up Pedro's limp form and threw him in some nearby bushes. Morning would be worse than a mere punch to the face.

Rodrigo watched all this with some amusement. He had been in the tavern when Pedro had first come in. When he saw how things were bound to progress, he went outside to have a smoke and watch the inevitable unfold. He was not disappointed.

Grinding the last of his cigar with his heel, he turned to return to the barracks and get some sleep. A sudden thought came to him. He turned around and went back the way he had come. It was full dark now and most people were in their homes or at La Posada. Now might be a good time to take a look at those storage buildings by the riverfront unobserved. He knew no one would see him from the Santa Estrella. They were all at the tavern. Even Captain de Cuellar.

He kept a sharp eye out as he rounded the corner of the building and stood before the intriguing barn doors. He was sure it would be locked, but thought there was no harm in trying. He reached out to grasp the door handle and nearly jumped out of his skin. A figure stepped out from the shadows.

"I thought I might find you here," the figure said calmly.

Rodrigo peered through the darkness trying to make out the man's face.

"Yllescas?" he said, "Is that you?"

The figure stepped out into the light. It was indeed the younger Yllescas.

"I saw you at the tavern," stammered Rodrigo. "I thought you were still there."

"I saw you there as well, my friend, and after our talk earlier, I thought to keep an eye on you. Come now, do not be so surprised. You gained my interest with your questions about this very storage shed," he said, gesturing at the building with a nod of his head.

"It meant nothing, just..."

"Idle curiosity. Yes, I remember well. And now that curiosity has brought us here." Yllescas went to the door and rattled the handle. "It is, as you thought, locked, but had you opened the door and snuck in, you would have seen naught. It is quite dark in there."

"Stop bandying about. Are you going to tell me what lies beyond those doors or not?"

"I *will* tell you, else your curiosity become a stronger thing, but I must caution you. Do not reveal what I am about to tell you to anyone, although there are many that already know."

"Fine, fine. I seek only to satisfy my own mind. You have my word I shall speak naught of it."

"Well then, as strange as it seems, I trust you and so I will tell you." He again nodded his head toward the doors. "In that shed are crates. Crates filled with bars of gold and silver."

Rodrigo gave him a look that made it clear he thought Yllescas was lying to him.

"I see your doubt, my friend, but it is true. It was not something I could spout in the middle of a tavern. As you are new here, you may not know that Santa Maria has become a mining town of late and *that*," he said pointing to the shed, "represents the fruits of our labors thus far."

Rodrigo scratched his chin in thought.

"Why is it here then, and not somewhere safer?"

"Oh, it is safe enough. Where would it go? It is here to make it easier for the Governor to inspect, which is the whole purpose of his coming here."

Rodrigo stared into the distance, lost in thought.

"Does that satisfy your inquisitiveness?"

"Yes it does," said Rodrigo, snapping back to the here and now. "I thank you for telling me and rest assured, I will keep it to myself."

"I do not doubt that you will. Come, let us return to La Posada, now that that de Arobe lout has been removed, and I will buy you a drink."

As they walked back to the tavern, Rodrigo could feel the puzzle pieces clicking together.

* * *

The meal was sumptuous and in far more abundance than they could eat in one sitting. In addition to the basic breads and cheeses, there were platters of game fowl and one particularly good dish made with wild boar.

Ignacio wiped his mouth and leaned back in his chair. He had not eaten a meal this hearty in along time. Glancing at the de Arobes, he could see that they too had been enjoying leaner meals of late.

"Señora Fernandez," he started, suppressing a burp, "That was all very wonderful. I thank you for being such a gracious hostess, but I fear you may have depleted your household budget with such lavishness. Although grateful, we poor refugees may be undeserving of such a bounty."

"It is mine to deplete, Father," she replied. "But now that you bring it up, I must let you in on a little secret. Since admitting these fine young women into my home, there has been a surge of interest among the potential suitors of the town, and they have not been shy in their intentions, bringing gifts in an attempt to garner attention it seems." She gestured over the much depleted table. "Gifts that have been used to nourish our guests."

"And so these fine ladies have been a boon to the local economy," said Ignacio with a laugh.

"And may they continue to be," said Don Francisco, raising his glass. "A toast then, to the most beautiful boarding house in Santa Maria, and to our most compassionate and benevolent hostess."

A cheer went around the table, causing Señora Fernandez to blush. She recovered quickly however, and addressed Ignacio.

"I may be able to provide you with yet another boon, Father."

"Oh? And what might that be?"

"Tell me," she said with a twinkle in her eye, "how go the plans for the re-dedication of our little church?"

"They go well, albeit slowly. I have been of the thought lately of postponing the ceremony until the Governor's arrival, as there is yet much to be done. In the meantime, the Mass services will continue as they have been."

"Splendid!" she exclaimed, clapping her hands. "Then this is what I propose. Beginning tomorrow, the members of this table," here she nodded toward the de Arobes, "will descend upon the church and prepare it for the ceremony. And I am sure," she said with a wink, "that many of the admirers we have accumulated of late, would be more than willing to lend their efforts to such a noble cause."

"I cannot speak for my father," said Domingo de Arobe, "but I for one will help in any way that I can."

Don Francisco let out a short laugh that was more like a bark. "My back is not what it once was, but I too shall be at hand, even if only to supervise."

Ignacio was now the one on the verge of blushing.

"My friends, I cannot tell you what this means to me. When we first arrived in Santa Maria, we were diluted into the community, several going their separate ways. But now I see we are still together, with a common purpose and goal. What more can I say beyond 'Thank you'."

Rosa spoke up, saying, "You can offer us a blessing for our success in this venture we have agreed to."

"So be it," said Ignacio, gesturing for everyone to stand and join hands.

"Lord," he began, his voice steady and calm, "we gather here, grateful for the opportunity You have placed before us. We are blessed with fellowship and a shared purpose, one that brings us together in Your name. We ask for Your strength and wisdom as we work to restore Your house, to prepare it as a place where we can honor You and seek Your guidance. Grant us success, O Lord, in our labors, and let our efforts serve as a testament to the faith we carry in our hearts. May this church stand as a beacon of hope and renewal for all who enter its doors. Bless each hand that contributes to this sacred task, and bless the community that has welcomed us with such grace and generosity. May we grow closer to one another through this work, just as we grow closer to You. In Your holy name, we pray. Amen."

The circle around the table responded with a resounding, "Amen!"

* * *

De Cuellar and Martinez sat in the Captain's cabin aboard the *Santa Estrella*. The soft glow of a single lantern illuminated just enough to allow them the task at hand. The consumption of a bottle of wine. De Cuellar took a sip from his goblet and made a face.

"How they can even *call* this wine is beyond me. It burns a hole in my gut and insults my tongue. What I would do for a fine Castilian Rioja."

"Patience, Captain," said Martinez, "that time is coming." He swirled a mouthful of wine before swallowing. "It is not that bad once you get past the flavor."

"Surely you jest. The flavor is the most important part, and if anything, the aftertaste is worse."

"Still, it gets the job done. Speaking of jobs, how are we in regards to this tub?"

De Cuellar opened the wooden box on the sideboard and extracted two cigars.

"I have to admit, however, that I have had no finer cigar in the New World. These rival the best the Empire has to offer." He proceeded to light the cigars, then leaned back in his chair, blowing plumes of smoke toward the ceiling. Martinez tried again.

"Captain, the ship?"

"Oh, yes, yes. It all goes well. Apparently she was not as neglected as the pilot would have us believe. It should all be completed within the week."

"That is good news. We should be on our way before the delegation from Quito gets here."

"Yes, but before that, I have noticed that your men are doing nothing to learn anything about sailing a ship. We are stretched thin with those who have any experience, yet anytime I see your men, they are lazing about, smoking cigars and playing cards. You need to get a fire under them and quickly. I will not load my ship to the brim with ingots and then wallow mid river."

"Very well. I will fill them with hellfire on the morn. Speaking of the ingots, how is it that they are not guarded. Can it be as easy as walking in and taking what we will?"

"It is. Without transportation, the ingots could sit on the dock uncovered. They are of no use to anyone residing in this backwater. I have observed that once every morning someone comes and takes a quick tally of the storage shed's contents, but other than that, there is nothing."

"Never suspecting that the thieves are a little more than a hundred feet away."

"Correctly, yet crudely put. I do not think of it as thievery. These half-breed colonists are undeserving of such wealth, even if the seat in Quito be deemed an outpost of the Crown. I think of it more as a redistribution that will benefit the Empire more than some fat Governor miles away in the jungle."

"You have told me, I remember, that you mean to purchase your own vessel. Discover new lands, new riches, what have you. An explorer of wealth and fame."

"At least I have a plan, whereas I suspect you will drown yourself in women and other debaucheries."

Martinez laughed. "Of course, there will be some of that to begin with, but my ultimate desires I will keep close to my heart for now."

They both continued smoking in silence. After a bit, de Cuellar refilled both their goblets.

"This wine reminds me of something," said Martinez. "I saw Juan Yllescas twice today at La Posada. I did not talk to him of course, but I did see him."

"And what of it, Lieutenant? A town small as this would have you walking into everyone you know multiple times a day."

"You are right, but what caught my eye was that he was with your man Rodrigo both times."

De Cuellar's eyes narrowed. "Really? And of what did they speak?"

"Alas, I was never near enough to know, but perhaps we should keep a tighter leash on our pilot until we are to depart."

De Cuellar pursed his lips and thought.

"I cannot keep him from his drink. He becomes insufferable if deprived, but I can make sure he spends more time at his duties. In any event, we will keep a closer eye on him."

"Remove him from the barracks at least. Quarter him here on the ship and keep him out of trouble."

"Not a bad idea, Lieutenant. Not a bad idea at all."

* * *

Rodrigo was not drunk but his head throbbed anyway. As he made his way back to the barracks, he looked at the sky. The stars were bright and glittering, but he felt as if they were mocking him somehow. The events of the day rolled around in his head, threatening to overwhelm him. He had learn a lot, but the bigger question was what would he do with that knowledge? He had always been a working man, never having to consider plots and schemes. He did not know if there was anyone he confide in, or even if it was wise to do so. Suddenly he remembered Mariano and he felt his heart break a little. Mariano would have listened to him, and while not a criminal genius, would have been able to counsel Rodrigo as to what to do next.

He saw the lights of the barracks ahead, but he also heard the commotion of the men that had returned from La Posada before him. Wonderful, he thought, and here I was thinking I would get some rest tonight. Something made him look to the right. In the middle distance was the church, dark and quiet. He turned his feet in that direction and soon came to the door. It was unlocked, but he peered inside cautiously just the same. *Why not?*, he thought. *I am sure the good Father will not mind.* He curled up behind the altar and almost instantly fell asleep. His last conscious thought was, *Thank you, Mariano. This was a good idea.*

Chapter Nineteen

Woe to those who go to great depths to hide their plans from the Lord, who do their work in darkness and think, 'Who sees us? Who will know?'

Isaiah 29:15

Pedro awoke with a start the next morning, when a bucket of cold water was poured over his head. He sputtered, shaking his head and trying to see who had thrust this indignity upon him. He tried to get up but his legs were tangled in the upper branches of a bush and therefore above him and not where he needed them. He was then dragged by his collar and dragged out of the bush entirely. He sat there, wiping the water out of his eyes and hair, becoming, as usual, very angry.

"Give him another bucketful," said a voice he did not recognize. "He is is covered in vomit and who knows what else." Before Pedro could protest, another deluge crashed into his face. Once again sputtering, he jumped to his feet, which were under him this time, and attempted to lunge at his tormentors. Several hands gripped him and, unable to complete his charge, he once again vigorously shook the water from his head.

"What is happening?" he shouted. "Cannot a man get some peaceful sleep around here?"

"A peaceful man can indeed get peaceful sleep, in his own bed. But you are neither peaceful nor was your sleep which was more stupor than anything else," said the voice.

Pedro's eyes finally managed to gain some focus as he looked on his perceived attackers. The hands dropped from their grip upon him, leaving him to stand unsteadily. He mopped his hair with his hands, glaring at those arrayed before him. He recognized Matías García, the proprietor of Las Posada del Viento, and his son Santiago. The rest were members of the tavern's staff. Pedro half-heartedly brushed some leaves and detritus from his clothes and glared at them.

"What is the meaning of this? Is this how you treat your patrons?"

"Patrons pay for their drinks and the privilege of sleeping on the premises," said Matías, "and you will now pay what is owed before I eject you from my property."

"For treatment such as this, I will pay you what you deserve. Nothing!" spat Pedro. "Now get out of my way and give me another drink!"

"Empty his pockets, boys," Matías ordered. Immediately, a struggling Pedro was forced to the ground, screaming at the top of his lungs as his opponents forcibly took their due. They handed Matías their findings which he counted in the palm of his hand.

"This will more than do," he said. "The extra funds will go toward the special service we have just provided you."

"Robbery! Robbery! These men have just robbed me!"

The spectacle had attracted several of the townsfolk who stood at the edge of the conflict, shaking their heads in disbelief and dismay. It was an embarrassing spectacle for all involved, none more so than Pedro, of whom the residents of Santa Maria had quickly lost their patience and respect. Pedro shook his fist at them in frustration.

"Did you not see? These men robbed me! I demand justice!" The bystanders merely shook their heads all the more and started to disband. Seeing this, Pedro calmed somewhat and his shoulders slumped. He looked at his feet and said much more civilly, "Fine, I will go. One more drink and you will be rid of me." He started to stagger toward La Posada's door.

Matías quickly barred his way.

"Oh no, you will not! Nor will you ever again enter through those doors! If you do, you will receive the same treatment you have just experienced. You are lucky I choose not to have you beaten. Begone lest you sully your father's honor and he will hear of this, you have my word."

Pedro glared at Matías for a moment, then spat at his feet.

"Fine," he said, "I will go and to Hell with you and yours!" With that, he stomped off.

Matías watched him as he left. He was not angry with the young man, really, but he was concerned what kind of man Pedro would become.

"It is a shame that Don Francisco's love for his son blinds him so," he said to Santiago. He has been aught but a respected and honorable man since he arrived, but this is a stain that will follow him unless he does something soon."

* * *

Rodrigo had a similar, albeit drier, awakening of his own. He felt the prodding of a booted foot in his rib cage and lurched up to a sitting position, momentarily unclear about where he was and how he had gotten there.

"Wake up, you lout! This is not some lodging for drunkards!"

Rodrigo looked up and saw Ignacio towering over him. He awkwardly got to his feet and faced him with a good amount of shame on his face.

"I am sorry, Father. I meant to awaken before you discovered my presence but, well..."

"Your snoring was shaking the walls. I thought a wild boar had gotten in here. At any rate, this is not the place to sleep off your excesses. And in the sanctuary, no less."

Rodrigo wiped the crust away from one eye, then hung his head contritely

"Your pardon, Father. I meant no disrespect and I swear to you I have not been drinking. It is just that the barracks were so loud, and I was so tired, and I had a thousand thoughts fighting in my head, and the church was so dark and quiet that..."

"Enough of your rambling, Rodrigo. Here is another thought to add to those thousands in your head: Get out." He steered Rodrigo toward the door by his elbow. "Go back to the barracks, clean up and get some food. You look terrible." As he said this, Ignacio painfully remembered being the object of the same criticism the previous day. His tone softened. "If you so desire, you can come back later and I will help whittle those thousand thoughts down to a few hundred."

"I do not think you will be able to help me, but I will consider it."

"Very good. Now, be on your way. I will have visitors shortly and I do not want them to see you this way." He waved as Rodrigo exited the church with a backward glance. He felt a deep affection for the big man, and he smiled, chuckling to himself.

As promised, at mid-morning, Señora Fernandez and her retinue of refugees descended upon the church. In tow were an assortment of men eager to do whatever was asked of them in order to gain a measure of favor in the young women's eyes. Don Francisco and Domingo were also on hand as they had pledged. Rosa came bounding through the door wielding a large basket.

"Good morning, Ignacio," she said, giving him a peck on the cheek. "I have brought you some breakfast. It should provide the energy you will need to deal with this gaggle of hens."

"And speaking as a hen yourself, you would know," he said with a laugh and taking the basket. Rosa gave him an exaggerated pout and then laughed merrily.

"We will have such fun today. You will get to boss people around, no one will listen of course, and when the day is over, you will not recognize the place."

"That is what I am afraid of," he said with a groan. This gained him a slap on the arm and another pout. Putting the basket down, he gestured for everyone to gather around.

"I want to thank everyone for giving of your time to this endeavor. I remind you that you are not doing this for me but for yourselves. This is *your* place of worship, *your* church, and I am merely the caretaker. With that said, I now hand over authority to Señora Fernandez, who no doubt has a plan already in mind." He raised his hands over them. "Go then, get to work and may God bless you."

Ignacio was not wrong about Señora Fernandez. Within moments, she had everyone scurrying about the church following her commands. There was, apparently, no stone to be unturned. The church quickly lost the quiet it had acquired over many years of neglect and became a hive of activity.

Ignacio peered into the basket Rosa had brought, picking out a choice morsel. He sat and, as he took the first bite, caught Señora Fernandez looking at him. She quickly hustled over to him.

"And what do you think you are doing, young man? Put that down and get to work. There will be time for treats later when the work is done." Ignacio swallowed hastily, covering his mouth as he laughed.

"I go now with haste, Señora. Pardon me for my momentary idleness." He pushed the basket away and hustled off to find a broom or a rag.

Señora Fernandez called after him, "And you preach to *us* about the Devil's hands?"

In a very short time, it was apparent that the church was undergoing a much needed transformation. The floors were clean, the railing at the sanctuary gleamed, the hangings and banners had been taken down and beaten free of dust. As he cleaned and dusted yet another chair, Ignacio looked about and marveled at the changes his crew had wrought. Or rather, Señora Fernandez's crew. She was clearly in her element and he wondered what life was like under her roof. Clearly she was amiable, else Rosa would have warned him, but it was also clear that she was a woman who was used to getting what she wanted and knew how to get it.

At length there was a break, and Ignacio sat with Rosa out in the sun, the infamous basket between them.

"Señora Fernandez is quite the taskmaster," he observed between bites.

"I am loathe to break it to you, Nacho, but that is a trait *all* women share."

"I have never gotten that impression from *you*."

"And I can forgive you that ignorance as you have chosen a profession that limits contact with females, but I will ask you this: who do you think gave Señora Fernandez the hint that help was needed here?"

Ignacio arched his eyebrows. "You? Really?"

"None other. And I will tell you something else. We have made plans to install gardens out here, flowers and other beautiful things. Perhaps we can enlist someone to carve statues of Saints or make a decent cross for the entry, there are a whole host of things we have planned. We intend to make this church the centerpiece of the town."

"Rather than La Posada," said Ignacio. "But wait. Plans? When did you make plans? Last night?"

"Of course not! We, and I mean myself and the others, have been thinking about this ever since you announced you intended to stay."

"And I thought God moved in mysterious ways. I had no idea."

"That is not surprising. You have a tendency to be oblivious to the most obvious things. And there is no mystery, I have told you all there is to know. About the church, anyway."

Ignacio looked at her sharply. "And what do you mean by that?"

Rosa wiped her hands and stood. Grabbing the basket's handle, she walked back to the church.

"Do not concern yourself, Nacho," she said over her shoulder. "Just another obvious thing."

Ignacio sat there dumbfounded for a moment, then he felt a pang of, not horror, but of something he never expected to consider.

No, She cannot mean that!

* * *

The sight of canoes on the river was not an uncommon sight. Santa Maria was neighbor to a large indigenous population that used the wide river as much as the town did. Usually these canoes hugged the northern shore and were thus of limited concern, but when one was spotted coming downriver mere feet from the southern shore, on which Santa Maria lay, the townspeople came to full alert.

Such encounters were rare, but not unheard of, and as proved the case, this was revealed itself to be a welcome event. It marked the return of one Fray Daniel Burgos. Still, they had learned to be cautious and thus the canoe was greeted by a contingent of armed men, just in case.

It was a small threat, to be sure. Fray Burgos was accompanied by only two Shuar warrior, and though their demeanor was daunting, they posed no real danger.

The canoe pulled into the beach next to the wharf and the occupants disembarked. As Burgos stepped ashore, he spotted Don Juan, who had joined the onlookers, and embraced him heartily.

"It is good to see you again, my friend," he cried, ignoring the men with muskets at the ready.

"It has been a long time indeed, Fray," Yllescas replied. "If not for your bald pate, I may have mistaken you for a native."

Burgos laughed and replied, "Little chance of that, although I must admit my tonsure is in need of a trim." Looking to the armed men, he added, "There is no need for these, they only serve to make my friends nervous." He then called out to the warriors, who were securing the canoe, in the own tongue. They seemed unhappy, but nodded their assent.

"What was that all about?" asked Yllescas.

"I told them to leave their weapons behind. Clearly they were reluctant, they view them as extensions of their own bodies, but in good faith, they have complied." He waved again toward the group of armed men. "Now, if you would just..."

"Certainly," said Yllescas, dismissing the men with a wave of his hand. "My father will be well pleased to see you. There have been some small excitements in the town since you were last here, let us go to the tavern, have a small libation, and I will fill you in on what you have missed before you see him."

They walked into town, the two warriors trailing them warily, garnering more than their share of circumspect looks from the townspeople they passed. The warriors gave hard looks in return. When they reached La Posada, Burgos bade them to wait outside, to which they readily complied. Being indoors with nervous patrons was not something they were willing to do. At any rate, García would not tolerate their presence.

Yllescas and Burgos settled at a table with a good line of view to the warriors outside. When their drinks arrived, Burgos drained his immediately. Yllescas looked at him with an arched eyebrow.

"You must have been yearning for a drink these many months."

"Yearning, but not necessarily needing," he said as he burped and wiped his mouth on his sleeve. "The Shuar are not lacking for fermented beverages. The manioc beer is a bit of an acquired taste but they also have several juices that provide quite a punch. Distillation, however, is a different matter. The best of their drinks cannot compare with the lowliest one provided here."

"And you have sampled all of them in your time," Yllescas said with a wink.

"A necessary evil in these environs. Now, tell me of these 'excitements' as you put it."

"We have had the good fortune of a group of strangers washing up on our shores, survivors of a galleon that met with disaster while at sea. On their way to Callao, if memory serves me. By and large, they are good people and a much needed infusion of new blood. One of them, by the hand of Providence it seems, is a young priest."

"Really?" said Burgos with interest. "Tell me about him."

"Well, as I said, he is young. I do not know his order precisely, Jesuit I believe. He took a liking to to Santa Maria almost immediately and has decided to stay. He has, of course, taken residence at the church, with grand plans of renovation and re-dedication. The town is very excited. I like him."

"Well then, I cannot wait to meet him," said Burgos with the knowledge that this was the very man Tsewa had instructed him to meet. "What is his name?"

"Ignacio de Montemayor. Do you know of him?"

Burgos shook his head. "No, of course not. I have been in the wilds too long. I cannot recall the names of the members of my own order," he said with a chuckle. *But I will know all about him soon enough.* He raised his hand, signaling for another drink.

* * *

When Burgos had arrived in Tsewa's village, he was so winded that the prospect of being skewered by Wajari's spear started to seem like a good idea. He stumbled into Tsewa's hut and fell to the ground.

"Get up, you worthless slug," Wajari had growled. "You grovel like an old woman."

Tsewa put up his hands and admonished him. "Leave him be, Wajari. It is clear you have mistreated him to the point of death, which I told you not to do."

"You told me not to kill him, and I have not, sorely tempted as I was."

"You banter with words that mean nothing. Go now! Go back to your house and cool your head."

Wajari turned to leave but not before administering a kick to Burgos' ribs. Tsewa let him lie there for a while, to allow him to recover his wits and his strength. At length, Burgos struggled up to a sitting position and took stock of his surroundings. Tsewa waved his hand and Namoch brought Burgos a bowl of water. Burgos gulped the water down hungrily and asked for more. After the second bowl, he addressed Tsewa.

"What now, O great chieftain? A beating?"

"I am not chief, as you well know. At the moment, I am the only barrier between you and certain death."

"But why, Tsewa? What have I done to merit such a fate?"

"You must search within yourself for such answers. I will not provide them nor engage in such a discussion. I have need of you and Wajari brought you to me. Now you are here. That is all I care about."

"I was on my way here anyway."

"And you would have been killed on sight if not for my intervention."

"I do not understand why that should be. I have been here before, I have drank manioc with you here in this very hut."

"And in many ways you have sought to corrupt those who you claim to call friends. But enough of that. I have a task for you that will allow you to live a while longer. Refuse and Wajari will have his trophy."

"I am a man of God. I will not not do anything against His will."

"Bah! What do you know of gods and spirits? Anything you seek, you seek only for your own benefit, and it will cost you greatly in the end. You are no different than those white skinned invaders who desire our deaths and our lands. You share that skin with them as well as their desires. I do not trust you to bring me my bowl. If there were another way this task could be done, I would not hesitate to allow Wajari to have his way with you. And it would not be painless or quick."

"Then speak, old man. What would you have of me?"

"Choose your words with more care, lest you find yourself pleading for your life without a tongue."

Burgos hung his head in defeat.

"I beg your forgiveness, Tsewa. I am sorry if I have offended you. I am yours to command."

"Better, if not entirely sincere. The task before you is simple, even for someone like you with limited talents. I want you to find a certain man who dwells among the invaders. His name, I know not, yet you will find him and talk to him. This is what I want you to say."

And Tsewa told him.

* * *

The work crew had finally departed. Ignacio sat wearily at the desk in his quarters and looked at his journal. He did not really feel like writing just yet, however. His mind was still sorting out the events of the day. About the church itself, Ignacio was immensely pleased. It had probably not looked as good since it was first erected, although the exterior was still wanting for a good coat of paint. This, he had been promised, would be accomplished on the morrow and Ignacio looked forward to it with great anticipation. The church would finally gleam like the jewel it was.

On the matter of Rosa, his thoughts and feelings were less clear. Certainly he loved the woman. The trials and hardships they had experienced together, as well as their relationship to his sister, had forged a bond between the two, but never did he think that Rosa take that as anything else. After her thinly veiled admission to him earlier, he had found himself avoiding her. For her part, Rosa continued acting as she always had, ignoring the turmoil she had set in Ignacio's heart. *I must not allow this matter to fester*, he thought. *She knows full well what my duties require of me. I cannot allow such things to keep me from my calling.* He was flattered, of course, but that was as far as he could allow himself to go.

With a sigh, he opened his journal to his last entry and began to write. He methodically detailed the events of the day, but was hesitant to put his thoughts about Rosa to paper. He was really unsure what to write. Perhaps in the morning his thoughts would be clearer after a night of introspection and prayer. He pushed the book away and stood. Yes, perhaps prayer was the best option. He crossed himself and prepared to begin the Litany when a knock came upon the door. Fearing, and also somewhat hoping, that Rosa had returned, he timidly opened the door, preparing himself for an encounter he was not ready for.

Instead, he found himself facing a man he did not know.

"Father Montemayor," the man said, "I am Fray Daniel Burgos. May I have a moment of your time?"

Chapter Twenty

"The encounters between the Shuar and Spanish settlers reveal a complex interplay of resistance, diplomacy, and mutual adaptation. While the Spanish came with the intent of conversion and control, many Shuar communities approached these newcomers with both caution and curiosity, often testing their intentions before fully engaging. Trade goods, especially metal tools, textiles, and occasionally glass beads, facilitated exchanges, but the Spanish encroachment was met with swift resistance whenever Shuar autonomy felt threatened. The Shuar, with deep ties to their territory and keen survival instincts, were particularly wary of forced labor and foreign diseases, which disrupted social structures. Yet, notable figures among the Shuar occasionally pursued tentative alliances to defend against common threats or achieve favorable terms, navigating an era of escalating pressures with shrewd pragmatism."

Dr. Esteban Cárdenas, Anthropologist, 1978

"Thank you, Father Montemayor," said Burgos as he drained the cup of wine he had been offered. He looked about the room and added. "I am pleased you were able to make a home for yourself here. As you are no doubt aware, I was not the best in terms of housekeeping."

"Ignacio will do, Fray," said Ignacio. "I myself cannot claim to have restored what you see here. The people of this town have gone well out of their way to make me feel welcome here and these quarters are a mere fraction of their generosity."

"I am pleased to hear that. I was too much of a wandering nomad, too much time spent away to be the recipient of such attention. I do not fault them for this, of course. Much of the neglect of the church and its grounds fall squarely on my shoulders. Yet I am glad."

"I have not been here long," said Ignacio slowly, "yet already I owe much more than mere gratitude."

"Yes, I have heard about the unfortunate circumstances that brought you to these shores. I am appalled by the number of your people that did not survive the ordeal."

"It was indeed a trauma, and I grieve their loss every day, yet somehow I feel that I was meant to be here, as much as I regret the method."

"I must agree that it *does* seem that you are meant to be here. By now you must be wondering why I have come to you at this time."

"It was my understanding that you roamed these lands and that your arrival was inevitable, given that you did not fall prey to mishap. I, for one, have been hoping for your arrival with the anticipation of meeting my predecessor, as it were. However, if you come seeking lodging..." Ignacio left the statement hanging between them, hoping that this was not the case.

"To be sure," replied Burgos, "I have no such expectation nor do I request such a thing from you. Do not concern yourself about my accommodations, I assure you, the matter is in hand." Burgos took a moment, seemingly to collect his thoughts and continued. "I come to speak to you tonight on behalf of another. Someone who is an unlikely mutual acquaintance."

"Everyone in Santa Maria fits that descriptor, Fray. Please come to the point."

"Very well, Father. I speak of Tsewa."

Ignacio was not prepared for this and the pronouncement rocked him visibly. He paled, a knot beginning to form in his belly. Burgos quickly poured another measure of wine into Ignacio's cup and handed it to him. Ignacio ignored the offering forcing Burgos to place it on the table.

"I see that you were not expecting me to utter that name," said Burgos, with care. "And it is not without some trepidation that I allow it to spill from my lips." Burgos took another sip of wine before leaning forward and looking into Ignacio's blank stare. "Yet he has conscripted me to convey a message to you." Ignacio's reply was barely above a whisper.

"What is his message?" Before Burgos could say anything, he came back to himself and blurted out, "Wait! You mean to tell me that Tsewa is a real man and not the product of a fevered mind that is recovering from weeks of untold trauma?"

"You have seen him, then," said Burgos cautiously, "in your dreams?"

"Yes, there and in other ways," Ignacio said said quietly, his eyes cast downward. "How is this possible? Is this yet another fit of madness?" He looked at Burgos sharply. "Are you truly here or is this yet another dream from which I will awaken, shaken and chilled to the bone?"

"I am real, Father. And Tsewa is real. A man like you and I, made of flesh and bone. The same and yet profoundly different."

"I ask again then," said Ignacio, "how is this possible?"

"There are things that happen here in the wilderness that cannot be reconciled in the civilized world. I do not pretend to comprehend how these things happen, I can only accept that they do. I myself have been witness to events that, if I tried to understand, would leave me questioning my mind and, at the least, shake the foundations of my faith."

Ignacio stood and began pacing the small room. Burgos looked on him with no small amount of concern.

"I have been where you are now, Father. The sooner you accept these truths, the sooner you regain your composure."

"I seriously doubt will be the case, as once you have delivered your missive, my mind will no doubt reject it out of hand." Ignacio stopped his pacing and faced Burgos. "Very well then, tell me what Tsewa wishes me to know."

"I must paraphrase, as this was relayed to my in his native tongue, yet he warned me not to change his words. The message is thus: 'I regret my words should come to you from the mouth of a demon, yet it must be so. I cannot come to you for reasons that the demon will explain. I have found that you, among all your race, have in you that which I seek. You alone have a spirit that will allow you to see the world as I do. I will take the blindness from your eyes and in doing so, you shall be reborn as a true spirit of creation and my son of sons. My time in the green world grows short and we must meet before the end comes. Come to me, Wandering Spirit.' That is the whole of it and yes, before you ask, I am the demon."

"And what is it the demon has yet to explain?"

Burgos ignored Ignacio's use of Tsewa's character reference.

"Tsewa is ancient. Older in years than many of his kind and ours. He is frail, hardly leaving his hut other than for the removal of bodily waste. He has weakened as he nears death. His wives struggle to meet his every need. He cannot travel save in spirit."

Ignacio shook his head.

"I have seen him, Burgos. He is young and hale, a strong man."

"That is no doubt how he sees himself, and his spirit *is* strong and hale, but I assure you, his body betrays him, subject to the passage of time of which there remains little."

Ignacio sat on his bed, elbows on his knees, his hands over his face.

"Where is he then?" his voice muffled through his fingers. "Where is it I am to meet him?"

"He resides in a village called 'Crown of Spears', which is apt, since that is all I have been shown when I go there. It is some miles from here. Perhaps a day's walk through the forest."

Ignacio sighed and dropped his hands.

"There is much to consider, Fray. I have much to think about, much to pray about. I cannot here say aye or nay."

"As I said, time is short, Father," Burgos said, his hand on the door, "but not so short that you cannot take days to settle your mind." Burgos rose and turned toward the door. "I thank you for your hospitality and your wine, but I have yet another meeting to attend and must now leave you. I will be near, should you need me. Good evening, Father."

With Burgos gone, Ignacio laid back on his bed, staring at the ceiling. A small spider was weaving its web in the corner. *Are these trials to come by the day now, Lord? No sooner am I confronted with one that another raises its head. I beg of you, Lord, what is thy bidding?* There was no answer forthcoming and Ignacio rose. He considered his journal, whose last entry was interrupted by the arrival of Burgos. *What could I write that would make any sense, when I cannot make sense of it in my own mind?*

Burgos closed the door to the vicarage behind him, and before he had managed to take a dozen steps, his two guardian warriors appeared at his side out of nowhere. Far from being surprised, Burgos only wondered where they had been.

"Hello boys," he said mirthlessly, "What took you so long?"

Wajari and Pinchu were not amused. Wajari shoved Burgos so hard that he almost fell over.

"You are the one wasting time. Why did it take so long for you to deliver a simple message? Did you attempt to corrupt the Wanderer will your demon ways? Answer me, you pile of dung!"

Burgos stumbled to get his feet beneath him, glaring back at his tormentors with disdain.

"I did as was I was bidden. No more, no less."

"You lie! You were in there for a long time."

"I could not just deliver the message and leave. He does not know me. I had to show him I was sincere."

Wajari scoffed. "Sincere?" Wajari glanced at Pinchu who smiled.

"Pinchu, did you know a demon could be sincere? Come along, you," he growled, grabbing Burgos by the collar and shoving him ahead of himself. "We have miles to go before the dawn and you will not waste any more of our time. Get moving!"

* * *

Aboard the *Santa Estrella*, Rodrigo was preparing to close up for the day. The repairs were near complete, and though he had misgivings about the intended use of the vessel, took pride in the completion of the task that had been set before him. After wishing Rios and Serrano a good evening, he made his way toward the gangplank, thoughts of dinner and a drink at La Posada swimming in his head. Before he could step off the ship, however, he heard his name called. Turning, he saw Ordoñez waving him back

"Ho, Pilot! The Captain wants to speak with you ere you depart." His visions of La Posada evaporating like wisps of smoke, he grumbled under his breath and made an about face. The door to the cabin was closed and so knocked politely and waited.

"Come," came the Captain's voice through the door. Reluctant to enter, Rodrigo opened the door and leaned in.

"You wanted to see me, Captain?"

De Cuellar looked up from his desk. "Ah yes, yes. Rodrigo, please come in," he said, motioning for Rodrigo to take a seat across from him. "I wanted to take an appraisal of your progress," he said, as Rodrigo took the proffered seat. "I know you have been hard at work and have much to show for it, but you have been rather lax in reporting your advances."

Rodrigo could not help but notice that although the Captain had a goblet of wine at his elbow, none was being offered. He licked his lips before he replied.

"The ship is ready, Captain. The last of the rotted boards have been replaced and tarred. The cordage and sails have been mended or replaced, and every fitting that was needed is now in place."

"Excellent!" exclaimed de Cuellar. "And what of the swivel guns fore and aft?"

Rodrigo was taken aback. "The swivel guns, Sir? What need have we of those?"

"Did you misunderstand me, Pilot," said de Cuellar, eyes narrowed and leaning forward, "when I said that this vessel was to be *fully* operational?"

"No, Captain," replied Rodrigo carefully, "but I respectfully submit to you that I am a sailor, not an armorer. My knowledge of the maintenance of those weapons is severely limited. Would not the soldiers..."

"And they have not done so," de Cuellar snapped. "You are in charge of the refit. All of it. You will make full inspection of those guns on the morrow. Enlist whomever you need to assist you, but get it done."

"Yes Sir, but forgive my asking, who will you fire upon?"

"Do you not see where you are, Pilot? We are in the middle of the wilderness, savages skulking behind every tree, planning God knows what. I will have them at the ready even if they are never used. Do you understand me?"

"Completely, Captain. If that is all...?"

"It is. You are dismissed." Rodrigo got up and put his hand on the door. "One more thing," said de Cuellar before he could make his escape. "I want all crew quartered on the ship. Find a cabin and make it your own. The galley has been fully stocked. You will dine with us tonight."

Rodrigo was torn. He did not relish the thought of returning to the barracks, but inside he mourned his plans regarding La Posada. He bit his lip to hide his dismay.

"As you wish, Captain. Good evening."

* * *

Bahati was made to work well into dark. He grimaced knowing he would not get much sleep before he was once again forced into labor. The labor itself did not bother him. He had worked hard his entire life and, without a miracle, would work until he breathed his last. He looked up at the moon. Tonight was the night he was to meet the men of the forest. He glanced over at Obadele, laboring nearby. Although he had talked to several others about the forest men, it was Obadele who was instrumental in gaining their interest. While Bahati had the superior intellect, it was Obadele who possessed the charisma necessary for recruitment. Obadele would be with Bahati tonight if tonight ever came to a close.

At last, the bell was rung and another day at the mine ended. After a quick meal of thick corn porridge and dried fish, Bahati stood in the doorway of the barracks peering intently into the darkness. His vigil turned into hours, by which time his eyes lost their focus and his head began to nod. Catching himself several times, he began to pinch himself to stay awake. Finally, his efforts were rewarded. Out there in the darkness, the lit end of a cigar was making slow circles in the air. Bahati kicked Obadele's cot, where Obadele had been snoring away the day's labor.

The pair made their way toward the signal and stopped short. Obadele was already apprehensive about meeting the forest men, but it was the sight of a third man with them that caused them pause. A white man. Was this some sort of trap? Wajari and Pinchu came forward to reassure them, and soon they were all seated passing the cigar to one another. Pinchu said something to the white man who then looked at the slaves.

"Pinchu extends his greetings," he said in Spanish. "The man with us is Wajari. They are happy that you have joined us."

Bahati struggled to understand and only caught a fraction of what was said. Obadele, fortunately, had a good grasp of the language and relayed the information to Bahati, who nodded and smiled. Soon, a conversation began that required two translations for every sentence before it was understood by all. One of the first questions Bahati asked was regarding the white man. Burgos was immediately apprehensive about how to reply. He turned to the warriors.

"He wants to know who I am," he said in Jivaro. "He wants to know why I am here, a white man."

"Tell them you are a demon we captured in the forest," said Wajari.

"You cannot tell them that," chided Pinchu. "You will frighten them and they are already nervous about us as it is." Turning to Burgos, he said, "Tell them that you are a friend to us and to them. You are here so that we can talk freely."

This was conveyed to the Africans and they seemed to accept it.

Bahati, fearing that dawn was not far off, got right to the point.

"My friends, what is it that we can do for you? How will you help us?"

"These people who enslave you, these people that are destroying our homes, they must be stopped and sent back to their own lands. With your help, we, and you will be free of them," said Wajari. When he did not hear Burgos begin translation, he glared at him menacingly. Burgos swallowed in a dry throat and repeated Wajari's words.

"This is our wish as well," replied Bahati. "Long have we labored for those who have torn us from our homes, supplying riches we can never enjoy. How will this be done?"

"First we will take from them this hole in the ground they cherish so much. It will be soon, and when the time comes, you will know it. When you see our spears, you will join us. You will be spared and free." Again Burgos hesitated, garnering another glare from Wajari.

"Why do you not speak?"

"I cannot. What you are proposing will result in many deaths. I cannot be a part of this."

"Your refusal will result in *your* death, here and now, demon. Of a sudden, you care for others as long as they are of your own race. You will tell them what I have said or I will kill you, and you know I very much want to."

With great reluctance, Burgos did as he was bid, sweat breaking on his brow, revealing his trepidation. The Africans noted the effect these words had on Burgos but did not address it. Instead Bahati asked, "And what of us? What happens to us afterward?"

"Live here, live with us, it does not matter as long as we live in peace and you do not despoil the land."

"We come from a forest land," said Obadele, after conferring with Bahati. "We know well what it means to live in peace with the forest."

The meeting ended before the rays of the sun tinged the sky. Bahati and Obadele returned to the barracks with the hope of gaining an hour or so of sleep before beginning their day of toil. As soon as the pair had departed, Wajari looked hard at Burgos who visibly perturbed by the revelations he had heard this night. Without warning, Wajari landed a blow on Burgos' chin, sprawling him on the ground. Pinchu had to hold him back from continuing his attack.

"Stop, Wajari," he cried. "The demon has been rendered senseless and can no longer feel your wrath. It was hard for him to hear plans that would betray his people, you cannot fault him for that."

Wajari turned on him and said, "I can and I do. He has no thoughts for others, his kind or not. This worm has outlived his usefulness."

Pinchu kept his hand on Wajari's arm. "I feel your anger, brother, but he cannot be killed. At least not yet."

"Why not?" asked Wajari, shrugging off Pinchu's hand. "There is no further need for him to speak our words for us. We have said what we needed."

"You speak truth, but remember, Tsewa alone holds this demon's life in his hands, he will have need of him when the Wanderer comes to Nunkui Nampet. He is to interpret their words. After that, *then* he is useless."

"What are we to do with him, then? He will speak of what he has heard here at the first opportunity."

"We will not give him the opportunity. We must leave this place, Wajari. Take the demon ere he can cry out for help, toss him in the canoe and return home. But we must go now, before the sun rises and we are seen by the whites."

Wajari looked on Burgos' limp form and sighed. Then, with seeming ease, he threw the unconscious man over his shoulder.

"I would prefer to make him run before us, but you are right. We must make haste. Forget the canoe, we will return through the forest."

"Surely we can make it back to the canoe without being seen," Pinchu protested. "I have been without my weapons for far too long, and the trek is long through this part of the forest."

"We dare not risk it. You said it yourself, we must depart and soon. We will send someone back to retrieve our belongings next nightfall, before anyone even misses this fool." Pinchu nodded his assent thoughtfully, acknowledging the uncharacteristic wisdom in Wajari's words. With that, they ran toward the forest. As they passed by the mine itself, Wajari slowed his pace and took a long, last look.

When I return, you will burn.

Burgos was jostled to wakefulness on Wajari's shoulder and began to cry out. Wajari quickly threw the man to the ground and held him there with a foot to his chest.

"Quiet, demon," he said softly. "Another sound will be your last." Burgos looked back at him fearfully. Wajari lifted his foot and allowed the man to rise. "The spirits have granted me a boon. You shall indeed run before me this night."

"Run? Run where?" asked Burgos nervously.

"We return to Nunkui Nampet with haste," said Pinchu. "Cry out and it will go ill for you."

"But what of Ignacio...the Wanderer. He will want to have words with me, I am sure."

"That is no longer your concern. Now turn and run like the demon you are."

Wajari laughed. "Perhaps we *should* have gone back for our spears, Pinchu. I would greatly enjoy pricking the demon's ass all the way back."

Burgos took that as his cue. He turned to the forest and ran like a madman. The warriors were close on his heels.

Chapter Twenty One

A man's path may look clear beneath the trees, but when the river shifts, only the forest knows the way.

-Shuar proverb

Rodrigo ran his eyes over the aft swivel gun. Even without experience with weapons, he could see that the wooden mounts of the gun carriage had some rot and wood need Rios' attention. If sufficiently weakened over time, they would need to be checked for stability, to prevent the gun from falling off its mount. After inspecting the fore gun, he found the mounts to be in even more need of repair. In this humid environment, the wood had swollen and cracked, allowing mold to grow in the fissures.

One of the soldiers, Carlos Galindo, saw Rodrigo making his inspection and wandered over, an already lit cigar in his hand. This prompted him to stop and light one of his own. He was fishing around in his pocket for his flint and steel when Galindo stopped him.

"Do not spark a flame so near to the gun! If there is any leftover gunpowder in it, it would be degraded and unstable. You could blow us all to pieces. Come over by the rail if you want a smoke. I will light you from my own." The pair walked away from the gun and Rodrigo's cigar was lit.

"What is of such interest that you would risk your life and mine?"

"I myself have little interest and even less knowledge in regards to the guns, this one and the one aft, yet the Captain has ordered that they be inspected and assure their functionality should the need arise. I was also ordered to enlist those who have such expertise," said Rodrigo, taking another drag. "I know wood, however, and I can see there is some work to be done there. But as to the workings of the weapon itself, I must defer to you or one of your compatriots."

"Alas then, it falls upon me," said Galindo. "I have some experience with weapons." He tossed the remains of his cigar into the river and said, "Come, let us take a look together and I will tell you what I see."

"I have to ask, and please do not take offense at this, I am not accusing anyone of anything, but it seems to me that, as military men, you and yours would have already inspected them, given the needs the Captain has expressed."

"No apologies are necessary," Galindo said with a laugh. "We did, in fact, inspect them but found there was much work necessary and we put it off. Lieutenant Martinez berated us about it just moments ago and I was on my way here when I saw you attempting to kill us. It seems our idleness must now come to an end and we must confront what we have been avoiding."

Rodrigo disposed of his cigar and followed Galindo back to the gun.

"As you can see," Galindo said pointing, "there is a fair amount of rust, but that is not a major problem. Both of the guns actually, are in comparable condition."

"And so what needs doing?"

"Firstly we need to clean the barrel. Rust and debris have built up over years of exposure and lack of maintenance. The barrels need to be scrubbed with brushes and oil to restore smoothness. If there is any pitting, it could affect accuracy, but these are short-range guns, much less critical. The bore needs to be reamed to remove any blockages or build-up of powder residue. The trunnion," he said pointing to the mechanism that allowed the gun to pivot, "works well enough, although with some protest. There is some chipping here and there that needs to be looked at by your blacksmith."

He stood and faced Rodrigo.

"It is not, fortunately, any major repairs that are needed," he continued, "but what I have listed is labor intensive. That, and a generous application of grease to the trunnion, will get these guns to the next stage."

"Which is?"

"Securing fresh ammunition and powder. Any to be found onboard would be too old and unsafe. After that, we can attempt some test firings."

"I will get Serrano and Rios up here to get their opinions," said Rodrigo, scratching his chin, "but the rest of it must fall to you, I am afraid. I can only do so much."

"As I said, we are now under orders as well. We will do what we must."

* * *

To Bahati, it seemed that the closing of his eyes had triggered the bell announcing the start of a new day. He hated that bell with all his being. One day, he mused, he would take that bell and insert it in the overseer in a very uncomfortable place. Rising, he was surprised to find that he was not suffering from lack of sleep. Indeed, he felt strangely invigorated even if not totally refreshed. His meeting with Wajari and Pinchu was uppermost in his mind, a mind that now had a glimmer of hope, a goal that promised a profound change in his life. He had not felt this way in years.

After a quick breakfast of yet another bowl of *atole*, the watery porridge made from ground corn, he hustled over to his work position. As usual, Obadele was his work partner, which was why he had been the first that Bahati had approached and brought into the conspiracy. Today, Bahati and Obadele were to shovel a large mound of dirt that had been deposited near the mouth of the mine by the excavation crew. They nodded to each other and picked up their shovels. Once the overseer was satisfied that his charges were hard at work, he drifted over to other workers under his command, leaving the pair with the ability for some limited conversation.

"Did you get any sleep?" asked Obadele in a low voice. "You look like you were trampled by a mule."

"If I did, it was only for an instant. But it was all well worth the trouble of missing a night to gain something else. And you?"

"Much the same," Obadele replied. In an even quieter tone he added, "After the bell tonight, we will speak with the others in the barracks."

"All of them?"

"Many already know, but yes, all of them."

"Are there any who are resistant? There are those that are in good standing with the overseers."

"We all want the same thing, Bahati, to free ourselves of this yoke, but you are right. Some are more to be trusted than others. There is a risk but I think we already have enough allies among us to convince the rest."

"If I felt we had more time, I would say we should be more careful, but this could happen at any time. We must be prepared and unified."

"It will happen, brother. It will happen. Quiet now, that fat oaf with the whip returns."

The overseer thought he had heard them talking and came over to strike their backs and silence them, but when he got there, Bahati and Obadele were quiet as mice, except of the sound of their shovels striking dirt. Bahati risked a sidelong glance.

Very soon, you dullard, very soon that whip will be in other hands.

Smugly assuaged for the moment, the overseer walked away a short distance but kept an eye on the pair hoping for an excuse to exercise his authority, to mete out punishment. Bahati was not about to give him the satisfaction and worked all the more diligently, but he smiled to himself. *Yes, very soon, but not now.*

Bahati repeated this in his mind over and over in his mind until it became a silent battle cry, repeating it every time he lifted a shovelful. At his side, Obadele worked just as hard. Bahati had no idea what thoughts Obadele might hold in his own head, but he knew they would be similar to his own.

* * *

Pedro was in a foul mood. Not only did he have to contend with the humiliation he suffered at La Posada, he had become a laughing stock and generally referred to as the town drunkard. He could not walk through town without sidelong glances and snickering directed at him. His own father regarded him that way. When he learned of Pedro's debacle at the tavern, Don Francisco had hauled him over the coals. Don Francisco was a prideful man and ambitious. He had scolded Pedro sharply, expressing deep disappointment in his son's actions.

"Do you think it is easy to build a name, a place of respect in this town?" he had shouted. "I have labored to rise from nothing, to become a man of standing and since arriving in Santa Maria, I have had to prove myself and our family's name anew. Now you drag our name through the mud with that deplorable spectacle at La Posada, letting others see you as nothing but a common drunkard!"

Pedro took it all without objection, his eyes focused on the floor while his father stormed around him much like a hurricane.

"There are consequences to your actions, Pedro. Not just for you but your family. Even if you were to reform yourself today, it will be years before our name is free of this stigma you have imposed on us through your wanton lusts and recklessness. You embarrassed me greatly on the *San Felipe y Santiago* in front of the Captain. And also the Priest, no less. Not once, but twice! I will not tolerate any further shame, do you hear me? You *will* alter your behavior immediately! You *will* make yourself worthy to be my son and to carry the de Arobe name. This ends now!"

Pedro did not move or meet his father's eyes until the older man had exhausted himself and left the room in disgust. He felt the rage growing within him until he felt he was ready to explode. His mind was swirling with resentment and no small measure of shame. Don Francisco's words had cut deep, adding fuel to his fury. Feeling trapped in the shadow of his father's unreasonable expectations, he vowed then to rebel against his father's authority altogether. With a burst of energy, born of determination, he turned on his heel and left.

He stepped outside and tried to calm himself. One thought suddenly came unbidden. *God, I need a drink.*

He was barred from La Posada. No amount of apologizing or begging would alter Matías García's edict. But there were other places a drink could be had and Pedro knew them all. The closest was a little hole in the wall aptly dubbed El Trago. He set his feet in that direction. So focused was he on his goal, that he did not see a woman cross his path as he rounded a large shrubbed corner of the walkway.. He plowed into her and she went sprawling to the ground. Pedro's senses came back in an instant and he stooped to assist the victim of his carelessness. His eyes widened when he saw her face. It was Amina, the slave girl.

Everything he had been holding in suddenly exploded forth in a volcanic burst. Here was the perfect vessel for him to express his rage. Rather than help the woman to her feet, he instead clubbed her on the side of her head, stunning her. He firmly clamped his hand over her mouth and began to drag her into the shrubbery. As soon as Amina felt his hand on her face, she began to try to bite the offending palm, only to be rewarded with another powerful cuff that filled her eyes with sparks. She struggled as she was manhandled into the foliage, but to no effect. Her attacker was fueled and strengthened by a force she could not overcome. She felt her clothes being ripped from her and began to struggle all the more. Suddenly the hand was removed from her lips and she attempted to scream, but it was cut off, for now the hand was around her throat squeezing out her breath. Her sight began to dim and after a moment, Amina knew no more.

* * *

"Where are you off to in such a hurry?"

Don Juan Yllescas looked at his father and shrugged.

"Estefania bade me to go to the market. There was something that she forgot to tell the house girl to get, and I thought since I was going into town I would get my breakfast there."

"Any opportunity to start your day early at La Posada, eh? You *do* know we have a full larder here and Estefania works hard to provide meals for you?"

"I do, and yet it was she who burdened me with this errand." He laughed and patted his father's ample belly. "In any case, I am sure that you will make up for any leftovers caused by my absence."

Don Alonso regarded his son with a frown. "I had rather hoped that I might impose on you to help me with the ledgers. They are in a bit of disarray and with the Governor's impending arrival, well, you never know what he might want to inspect."

"Do not worry yourself, old man," said Don Juan, now patting his father on the shoulder. "I will not take long and will return to set your mind at ease."

"Unless you are distracted by a skirt or a bottle of rum."

"Well, there *is* that," he replied with a chuckle, "but you have my word I will make my best effort to hasten home."

"Hmmph. I have been the victim of your 'best efforts' before," said Don Alonso without a trace of sarcasm. "Well, be on your way and I will hope for the best."

"You wound me, father. For that insult alone I shall return post haste and seek my retribution." With that, he bowed comically making an exaggerated gesture and left.

He bounded past Estefania, who was sweeping the stoop, and walked briskly on the path leading to the square. The sun felt good on his face and he raised his head to feel it more fully. Soon he was humming to himself, interjecting little dance steps as he went.

As he rounded a tall shrubbery, he came to an abrupt stop. There on the path he spied a large bag on the ground with comestibles spilling out of it. As he stood pondering the meaning of the scene, he became aware of strange sounds coming from within the shrubbery itself. He parted the branches and was stunned into disbelief by what lay within.

He yanked Pedro out by the collar and threw him on the ground. Pedro began to protest but was cut short when Yllescas silenced him with a strike to his chin. Forcing his way into the hedge, he carefully pulled out Amina's limp form. Her face was beaten and bloody, her clothes torn from the waist down. Yllescas looked about frantically and began shouting.

"Help! Come quickly! I need help!"

Several people within earshot came at a run, immediately stunned by what they saw. Pedro struggled to get up, his trousers still about his ankles, looking at the growing crowd with fearful eyes. Yllescas was kneeling, cradling Amina's head in his lap and calling her name, but he could not rouse her. He gently laid her down on the sward and stood. He looked at his hands which were now covered in her blood.

"She is dead," he proclaimed softly. Then, with murder in his eyes and the greatest fury he had ever felt, he lunged at Pedro, stopped only by the men who now held his arms. Pedro backed up in fear but the trousers at his feet caused him to fall on his backside.

"She asked for it!" he cried from his awkward position. "She begged me for it!"

Yllescas made a renewed effort to lunge at the boy and was again restrained.

"She did not asked to be killed, you scoundrel! Let me go! I will tear you limb from limb! You have indeed asked for it!"

Now hands were on Pedro and they hauled him up roughly to his feet, his trousers still far below his waist. Yllescas, somewhat calmer, nodded to the men holding his arms and they released their hold. He brushed himself off and looked at the limp form at his feet. He was deeply saddened. A member of his own household had been needlessly brutalized and killed. Slave or no, this would not go unanswered.

"Take him," he said to the men holding Pedro. Take him and lock him up somewhere, I care not where. Walk him through the town with his shameful manhood displayed before him, for all to see the heinous crime he has committed. My father will impose the appropriate punishment."

As Pedro was led away, his feet still encumbered by his garment, Yllescas again knelt by Amina's side. He covered her bareness as best he could. He signaled the remaining men closer.

"Take her to my house. Don Alonso will be witness to her demise, as she was one of his favorites. He will not look on this kindly."

Amina was lifted gently and the men carrying her began the short journey that would mark her final return to her home. Yllescas watched them go, then stooped to refill the spilled market bag Amina had carried. Following the procession back to the manor, he was hit with a combination of fury, grief and sadness. A single tear ran down his cheek.

* * *

From the deck of the *Santa Estrella*, Rodrigo could see something was happening in the town. What it could be was a mystery, as nothing ever seemed to happen in this sleepy little town and he yearned to find out what it was. He also yearned for a visit back to La Posada, and while he was not forbidden, de Cuellar seemed to be making sure that Rodrigo had enough work to keep him aboard.

The guns had been brought up to specification and tomorrow they could attempt some test firings, assuming Ordoñez returned with the necessary ammunition. Ordoñez had been compelled to go to the mine to obtain the requisite gunpowder and was not expected before morning. In the meantime, the various parts of the swivel mechanism had been cleaned and greased and the barrels had been reamed. The woodwork itself had been a simple matter. The replacements had been rough-cut but perfectly suitable for the task they were meant to perform. Very soon, Rodrigo thought, he might have some time to himself.

As he watched the happenings in town, he spied Rios returning from some errand the Captain had set him on. He carried only a small box that Rodrigo, quite correctly, took to be a box of cigars.

"The Captain seems to be loathe to leave the ship himself, it seems," he said to Rios as he came aboard, "and must send his minions to do his bidding."

"That is what minions are for," replied Rios. "Have we been anything but since we procured this ship? And I am not even part of the crew."

"You are now," said Rodrigo with a chuckle. "So tell me, what is happening that has the town stirring like a hive of bees?"

"That troublesome son of Don Francisco. Apparently he has murdered a slave girl."

"What? A drunkard for sure, but a killer? I would not picture him knowing which end of a knife to hold."

"I do not think he used a knife. From what I have been told, he forced himself on her and in the course of his attack, killed her."

"So it was a knife of a different sort that got him into trouble. What will happen to him?"

"I do not know. It was not just any slave girl, mind you, but one of the household of Chief don Alonso. Right there at the edge of the square on her way back from market."

Rodrigo whistled. "That was a bit of daring, I must say. In plain daylight, no less."

"There is quite the commotion right now. No matter how it turns out, I doubt you will be seeing Pedro at La Posada again. His shame will be too great. Everyone will shun him."

"I never liked that boy. Something wrong with him. He does not strike me as one to feel shame," said Rodrigo. "As for the tavern, he has already been banned." He paused and then added wistfully, "The only person I would like to see at La Posada again is myself."

"You will get there ere long, my friend," said Rios. "As for myself, I had better get this box to the Captain before he turns his eye on me."

Rodrigo watched Rios make his way to the Captain's cabin, then fished in his pocket for his own cigars. He only had two left. Perhaps he should have cajoled Rios into sneaking him a couple from the Captain's box. Sighing at this errant thought, he lit up.

Chapter Twenty Two

This is what the Lord says: 'Cursed is the one who trusts in man, who draws strength from mere flesh and whose heart turns away from the Lord. That person will be like a bush in the wastelands; they will not see prosperity when it comes. They will dwell in the parched places of the desert, in a salt land where no one lives.'

Jeremiah 17:5-6:

Outside of Sunday, daily Mass in Santa Maria did not have high attendance, so it was only a handful of people that came this morning to observe it. The expected hour came and went by without an appearance by the Vicar. As time wore on, the church goers became restless and began drifting out the door, as it became apparent no service was forthcoming. There was one, however, who refused to leave and she was becoming increasingly incensed. When she was finally the only one remaining, Rosa got up from her seat, crossed herself, and marched off in the direction of the vicarage.

Reaching Ignacio's door, she knocked on it politely. There was no response and after moment she knocked more strenuously. Again, there was no response or sound coming from within Ignacio's chambers. She tried the door and it opened easily under her hand.

It was dark within, but she clearly saw Ignacio, laying on his bed, dead to the world in slumber. She tried to rouse him, but he just mumbled at her and made a feeble attempt to push her away.

She called to him, rubbing his shoulder. "Ignacio, wake up! Are you ill?" He merely rolled over and continued his sleep

Stymied, she looked around and saw a vase with flowers she had placed there herself. Removing the now wilting blossoms, she poured the remaining water on his face. He came up with a lurch, blubbering like a man abruptly saved from drowning.

"What in the world?" he cried wiping his face of the offending water. "Cannot a man be left in peace in his own bed?" He sat up and saw that it was Rosa, vase still in hand, that had been object of his ire. "Oh. Rosa. I am sorry to snap at you. I did not know what to expect."

"What you *should* have expected," she said with a little stomp of her feet, "was to be at morning services! Unless you are deathly ill, you have no excuse. *Are* you sick?"

"Nay," he said rising. He looked at Rosa and continued, "I am not ill, at least not in body."

Rosa sniffed and made a grimace.

"Wait...are you drunk? Have you been drinking? You stink like the bottom of a wine barrel!"

"Please, not so loud. I had some wine before bed and that is all."

"Unless you went to bed ten minutes ago, I cannot believe you. And look at you!" she exclaimed. "You look like you lost a battle with a bear!" Ignacio made a half-hearted attempt to smooth his hair, avoiding contact with her eyes.

"I had a late night in prayer," he mumbled. "It may have gotten out of hand."

"Out of your head, more like. So you drank yourself into oblivion forgetting the rest of us rely on you to set a moral example?"

"Perhaps that burden is misplaced."

"Is that all you have to say?" She opened his one small window and the door. "I am going outside. You clean yourself up and then join me. I cannot stay another minute breathing this foul air."

It was many long minutes before Ignacio came out of his quarters. To Rosa's eyes, he looked only marginally better even though he had brushed his hair and put on fresh clothing. She looked in his face and saw bloodshot eyes that looked painful as he shielded them from the bright sun.

"Have you eaten?" she asked with concern.

"No, nor do I think I can at the moment. Look," he said, "I know how this must appear to you, but I beg you not to be unduly worried. I am troubled by many quandaries for which I sought answers through prayer and, unfortunately, wine. It is not likely to happen again."

She studied his face and saw a modicum of shame there.

"And you find yourself this morning no closer to the answers you sought." She said this rhetorically, a statement rather than a query. "But you have learned something nonetheless."

"Undoubtedly," he replied. "Listen, can we sit? I am still a bit unsteady." He led her over to a pair of sawed off stumps where they sat facing each other. "Wine, as you say, does not provide much clarity, in fact, the opposite. But it does, in time, dull the senses enough that the questions are quieted and not so incessant." He paused, composing himself for a moment before continuing. "Yet prayer did not provide clarity either, and I am left wondering which is the better solution."

Rosa did not know how to respond. Ignacio was clearly struggling with something that was taxing his ability to cope. She began to wonder if she had played a part in his difficulties.

"Is it because of me?" she asked softly.

Ignacio smiled at her. "Only partly," he replied. "The greater part is causing me a profound scrutiny of my Faith. I cannot feel God at the moment I need Him most. My prayers are becoming just words and I am becoming lost."

Rosa leaned forward. "Tell me, Nacho. Tell me what has you so distraught. Perhaps some of God's voice will come through."

Ignacio rubbed his face with both hands and drew in a big breath.

"A man came to see me," he started slowly, "His name is Burgos. Fray Daniel Burgos."

"The wandering monk?"

"The same. We talked, he and I, and the things he said left me reeling. He had knowledge that only I knew. He knew more about me than I knew for certain for myself. The implications of his message exposed my naive confidence in the workings of the world and spirituality. Everything I knew in my heart has been turned on its head."

"Message? What message did he give you and from who?"

"To answer that I must first relate all the things that I have experienced prior. Things that I kept secret because embracing them or relating them would mark me as descending into madness. After meeting with Burgos, I have come to realize it is not a madness within myself but in the very fabric we call reality. Everything I have claimed to know has fallen into question."

"Ignacio, I have no idea what you are talking about. It seems to me your head is still full of drink."

"I know how it must seem, yet I am in full possession of my faculties, or so I believe. I will start from the beginning, which was when I first boarded the *San Felipe y Santiago* those many weeks ago."

He told her then, about the dreams, about the visions, about Tsewa and the confirming message that Burgos had brought so soon after his last encounter with the apparition in the church. As he told his story, he felt a great weight lifting much as he had felt during confession. The mere act of saying these things aloud gave him comfort, even though he was now unloading his encumbrance onto some one else.

Rosa, for her part, listened attentively without interjecting questions or commentary. Nor did her face betray anything other than her rapt attention.

"And so it seem," said Ignacio as he reached the end of his tale, "that this Tsewa awaits me in the forest. That meeting with him will free me of all doubt."

"How can you be sure of his intent? How do you know this is not some elaborate attempt to ensnare you in some way?"

"I cannot be sure of anything. When I first experienced these encounters, I must admit I was terrified, but of late it seems less a nightmare yet still a mystery."

"Where is this Burgos now? We should talk to him. He is a man of God, in his own fashion. He has the insight you lack."

"I do not know where he might be. He did not cover his words under the cloak of Christianity but spoke for Tsewa alone. It was clear he did not necessarily want to speak such things to me but rather he was compelled to do so."

"And so now what? Shall you wander into yon forest and seek out this heathen savage?"

"In truth, I know not. But I do know this state of unease in my soul will persist if I do not."

Rosa turned her head and looked at the line of forest trees not far away as if she could see through them to the source of Ignacio's predicament.

Something or someone in there has reached out made its presence known but not its aim. Rosa came to a decision then and turned back to Ignacio.

"Fine. Then I shall go with you."

"What? No, you cannot. I myself have not made such a pronouncement and I would do so with much trepidation. Who knows what dangers would await you out there."

"I traveled that forest, as you did, for days at a time and no harm came to me."

"Surrounded as you were by many others. And even then we sustained our losses. No, I forbid you even contemplating such a thing."

"You forbid...Who are you to stop me? I will follow you if needs be,"

"You must not."

"Why?"

Ignacio sighed and looked away.

"Because I love you."

Rosa stiffened as if shot. Stunned into silence, she sat, her eyes unfocused. This was not was she had expected to hear and did not know how to reply. Ignacio also did not say anything and kept his eyes averted. It became an uncomfortable tableau that persisted for long minutes. When Rosa was finally ready to make a reply through a tightened throat, she was unexpectedly, and perhaps mercifully, interrupted.

"There you are! I looked for you in the church but you were nowhere to be found."

It was Don Juan Yllescas, fresh from his confrontation with Pedro. Ignacio turned in surprise. He had not heard the man approach, so absorbed he was in his own thoughts. Rosa discreetly wiped tears from her face, but Yllescas did not seem to notice the tension between the two.

"Don Juan!" said Ignacio, his voice strained. "How can I be of service?"

"I am sorry to interrupt," said Yllescas, appearing to finally notice Rosa. "Señora Alvarez, I hope you are well." Rosa nodded but did not greet him in return. Yllescas turned his attention back to Ignacio. "It is not you that I need so much as ask you for the use of your church."

"Of course. The church is yours as much as it is mine. What is the need?"

"There is to be a town meeting this evening, and as there is a threat of rain, there is need of a space large enough to accommodate the anticipated crowd." Ignacio looked at the sky and noticed that indeed dark clouds were moving in and would soon blanket the sun.

"I sense some urgency in you. Has something transpired that requires the meeting of the town entire?"

"Alas, there has, Father. You are no doubt aware that Don Francisco's youngest son has been somewhat of a nuisance since his arrival. Public drunkenness and fistfights are his hallmark, it seems, but now the matter has risen to a new level that must be addressed forthwith."

"Yes, I am aware of Pedro's...ah...deficiencies. There was some trouble on our ship as well. Have his transgressions resulted in his arrest?"

"They have, and now we must come to some consensus about what should be done. He has gone from nuisance to dangerous, and that cannot be tolerated."

"Señor de Arobe must be beside himself. That boy has ever been a thorn in his side."

"Yes, yes, de Arobe is angry but not as much as my father, who is livid. You have not heard, I see, that his son has raped and murdered a member of our house staff. Even though she was a slave, she was well liked, even loved, within our household and out. My father has taken this as a personal affront, and not even Señor de Arobe will escape his wrath."

"That is terrible," said Rosa, aghast at hearing the news. "I would have never thought that he was so far gone."

"I believe the death was accidental and not his intent. An unfortunate ramification of his unbridled lust, but one does not forgive the other. This one happened to be indentured, but who knows what would happen if he were to be left unchecked."

Ignacio shook his head in disbelief.

"This is truly incredulous," he said. "Where is he? I must speak with Pedro."

"You seek his confession? He was caught in the act. By me."

"If he wants to cleanse himself with confession, that is his prerogative, but no, I seek some understanding of his thoughts and motives. There may something that can presented on his behalf at tonight's gathering that may shed some light on, not his crime, but the motive behind his actions overall."

"I believe the case is clear," said Yllescas, unmoved, "but have it your way. I will take you to him."

Ignacio reached out and took Rosa's hand.

"Forgive me, Rosa," he said with a serious tone. "I must take your leave and administer such help as I can. We will talk soon."

* * *

Santa Maria is a small town, and as such, news travels faster than one would deem possible. The account of Pedro's misdeeds was the biggest story the town had had in many years and it reached far and wide, reaching even the semi-cloistered crew of the *Santa Estrella*. Captain de Cuellar was not one overly given to gossip, but even he entertained the revelations with interest. He had not had much of a liking of the de Arobes, particularly of Don Francisco, who he viewed as a pretender to Spanish nobility, and he thought even less of his sons. That such as these would be the face of the New Spain of the frontier left him with a sour taste that no amount of wine could dispel. He reveled in any humiliation that the de Arobes suffered without shame.

And yet, his pleasure at Don Francisco's dishonor held another facet that delighted him as well. Here was an opportunity that, if timed correctly, would see him with the ability to shed the stench of this little town once and for all. He opened his cabin door and looked out. Seeing Alonso Medina, one of Martinez's soldiers, he bade him to summon the lieutenant to his cabin. Going back to his desk, he lit a cigar and waited. Several minutes passed, but eventually a knock came at his door.

"Enter," he said loudly.

"Captain de Cuellar," said Martinez as he entered the smoke filled room. "You have need of me?"

"Indeed I do. Please," he said with a gesture, "have a seat and give me a status report."

"The *Santa Estrella* is at the ready and awaiting your command. It is the same report I gave you earlier today when you last asked."

"Yes, I did not forget. Tell me, have you heard the salacious stories emanating from the town?"

"One could not avoid it, Captain. An entertaining state of affairs, to be sure. There is almost a feel of festival in the air, though many are fraught with fear and apprehension."

"Mixed with shame and humiliation, no doubt. What is being done with the boy?"

"There is to be a meeting tonight at the church, presumably to mete out some form of justice that will appease the town's chief, whose property and honor has been defiled. Why? Do you plan on attending?"

"Certainly not! I believe it may rain tonight."

Martinez looked at him with puzzlement. "It may, but I do not see why that would sway you yea or nay, and I do not see why you are giving these proceedings such thought."

"Only because of the opportunity they present. Think, Lieutenant! The majority of the town will be at the church, it will be dark and it will be raining. Tonight we will relieve Santa Maria of its burden of ingots and there will be none to witness it. We will fill the hold and be on our way before the sun rises or anyone knows what has befallen."

Martinez nodded his head with a sudden glint in his eyes. "I agree. This particular set of circumstances will not present itself again and it comes to us without the asking. However," he added, "there is one problem."

"Oh?" said de Cuellar. "And what is that?"

"Those of the crew that are not privy to our plans. They will be curious if not an outright hindrance, yet we cannot afford to put them ashore just yet."

"Nor shall we. Tonight after dinner, they are to be secured to their quarters while we work. Make up any story you like, but keep them locked up until we are ready to sail, well, at least until the cargo is safely below decks."

"And if there is resistance?"

"There will not be. You will see to that. Make sure they have a larger than normal allotment of wine and then manhandle them into their cabins if you must. Keep them happy. Keep them quiet."

The night was indeed dark and the town was seemingly uninhabited as the meeting at the church began. Moreover, it began to rain in earnest, buckets of water pounded Santa Maria unrelentingly. Thus the work of the soldiers began with no impediment other than the weather. Rodrigo and his crew had been successfully wrangled into their cabins with very little effort, if not a lot of questions. These were mostly quelled by locking each man up with a full jug of wine. In a short while, even Rodrigo had stopped pounding on the door and shouting slurred obscenities.

The storage hut was breached and even the grumbling soldiers took great pleasure in the task that was set before them. Once they saw the gold and silver ingots for themselves, they found the strength in their backs that they needed. It was slow going but they went on unimpeded. Two by two, the soldiers made innumerable trips from the hut to the hold carrying the heavy pallets between them. They knew that every pound they carried was another small fortune to put in their pockets.

On the deck of the *Santa Estrella*, de Cuellar and Martinez supervised the operation, each man seeing more than just their minions hard at work. Here were their very futures being laboriously transferred from one account to their own. In spite of their greed, the soldiers began to tire about halfway through the operation but de Cuellar was having none of it. He berated each team as they passed him on their way to the hold.

"My grandmother would have finished by now," he rebuked them, shouting over the torrent. "And she is blind and bent with age. Get moving, you dogs! There will be time to rest later."

"God forbid you should put your own back to it," said Ordoñez under his breath to his partner Carlos Galindo who laughed quietly.

"Soon you will look back on this and laugh as beautiful women fill your mouth with grapes."

"Why? Will your mother be there? If I make it through this night I will give her an extra kiss."

"I am sure she would want more than that yet you are not man enough to please her."

"You talk about your own mother that way?"

"Why not? Yours said much the same."

In time, the work was done. Everything that could be taken from the storage hut had been taken. The doors were shut as they had been found and no one from the town was any wiser. The soldiers lay on the deck, exhausted from the unaccustomed labor. Mercifully, the rain had diminished to a mere annoying drizzle that felt good to the bone-weary men. Yet not for long would they lie in repose. De Cuellar took to kicking each of the men to get them on their feet.

"Get up," he cried, "there is yet much to be done. It will be light within the hour and we must be away. Roust those drunkards out of their cabins and prepare to push off." There was much grumbling, but the men rose and began to do as they were bid. They quickly found that this was much harder to do than they had realized. Rodrigo and his men were asleep in a drunken stupor and several attempts had to be made just to get them on their feet.

Yet, besotted as the sailing crew was, the *Santa Estrella* pushed off from the dock just as the first light of the new day began to tinge the sky. Few there were to witness her departure and even fewer to know what it meant. Before long, the ship had drifted to the middle of the river, quietly and without fanfare, and unfurled her sails to gather the morning breeze.

Chapter Twenty Three

Long ago, two Shuar tribes, the People of the Rising Sun and the People of the Setting Moon, lived on opposite banks of the great Forked River. They often quarreled over fishing rights, hunting grounds, and the spirits of the land. Their disputes led to small skirmishes that cost lives and sowed bitterness. One season, the eldest Uwishin of each tribe had a vision. In their dreams, Nunkui, the mother of the earth, spoke: "The river gives to all who respect it. Meet on the river's heart and speak as kin. Only through words can you honor me." Heeding this, the tribes agreed to meet on a narrow island at the center of the river. Each side prepared offerings of fish, fruit, and sacred tobacco, seeking to show their goodwill. Yet, in the shadow of the meeting, both secretly doubted the other's intentions. Warriors kept their spears nearby, hidden but ready. As the talks began, suspicion crept into the words exchanged. A careless remark about the river's ownership sparked old grievances. Raised voices gave way to accusations. Within moments, a warrior from one side, feeling his pride slighted, threw a stone. The gathering dissolved into chaos, and the blood of both tribes soaked the island. When the survivors returned to their camps, Nunkui appeared again in their dreams, her voice heavy with sorrow: "You spoke not with the tongue of peace, but with the teeth of distrust. Now the river flows red, and the earth mourns. Until your hearts learn humility, the river will turn its back on you." The next season, the river's fish dwindled, and the land grew barren, forcing the tribes to wander far from their home.

-The Tribes of the Forked River, Shuar parable

In spite of the weather, the church was filled to capacity and beyond. All the seats had been taken and the remainder of those in attendance stood two deep against the walls. For a small town like Santa Maria, this was the biggest event in a long time, surpassing even the recent Christmas holiday. Many of the spectators had brought their own candles and thus the church was well illuminated, long shadows were cast along the back wall and crucifix behind the altar as those that would decide Pedro's fate settled in at a table at the front. There was a cacophony of chatter and speculation among the crowd that came to an abrupt end when the meeting was called to order.

"We are gathered here tonight," said Don Rafael Esteban Montoya, the chief magistrate of the town, "to determine what punishment, if any, will be leveled against one Pedro de Arobe." Montoya was a respected figure in the community, known for his strict adherence to colonial law. Don Rafael was a pragmatic man and, while he was occasionally at odds with both the ruling class and labor groups, he was deemed to be a fair man. He gestured at two men at the back of the church who held Pedro between them. They quickly brought Pedro to stand a few paces before Montoya.

"Pedro de Arobe," Montoya said gravely, "it is not the stature of a man that determines his worth, but his deeds and how he carries the name he bears. Your actions, whatever the charges may be, not only reflect upon you but upon your father and this community. I will ensure that justice is fair and impartial, but you must consider how your conduct affects those around you. If you are guilty, restitution or punishment will be determined; if innocent, your honor will be restored. But heed my words, every man must learn to master himself before he can rightly judge others or act with integrity."

Montoya turned to his clerk. "You will now read the charges." The clerk cleared his throat and, held out a document and commenced reading.

"The accusations are as follow: multiple instances of public drunkenness, multiple instances of violence in the form of repeated fights at La Posada, multiple verbal outbursts including but not limited to threats of violence and insults of a derogatory and malicious manner. Further accusations are one instance of public indecency and finally the destruction of property in the form of the assault, rape and consequent murder of a house servant owned by don Alonso Sebastian de Yllescas, chief of Santa Maria del Oro."

The clerk then rolled up the document and returned to his seat.

Montoya fixed a grave look on his face and paused, taking a deep breath to steady himself. The weight of the accusations made against Pedro de Arobe was significant, particularly the final charge, which carried the gravest implications. He leaned forward slightly, his voice steady and clear, addressing Pedro directly.

"Pedro de Arobe, the charges brought before this court are numerous and grave, culminating in one that shakes the very foundation of justice and morality in this town. Each accusation, whether it be of disorder, violence, or indecency, is a stain not only on your name but on the integrity of this community. Yet, it is the final charge, the taking of a life, albeit one of a slave and therefore falls under the clause of destruction of property, that cannot and will not be ignored. If these allegations are proven true, they represent a violation of divine law, human decency, and the trust we seek to foster among all who live here. You will have your opportunity to respond to these charges, for justice must be fair, even when the weight of evidence appears damning." Montoya then turned to the others seated around him and continued, "Let the evidence be presented with clarity and impartiality, for this matter affects not just the accused, but the very soul of Santa Maria. Present your first witness."

What followed then was a string of complainants, mostly ordinary citizens who had experienced unfortunate encounters with the accused including Matías García, the proprietor of Las Posada del Viento and his son. Montoya listened to them all passively, his face betraying no emotion. As García finished his testimony, don Alonso rose to give his, but Montoya waved him back.

"A moment, don Alonso, if you please. Your declaration and that of your son, don Juan will be the culmination of this hearing, but first I would like to hear from someone without complaint who can perhaps shed some light on other aspects of the accused that we have not heard. Father Ignacio, would you be so kind as to approach us?"

Ignacio made his way before the magistrate and bowed slightly.

"If I may be of help to your inquiry, I will freely answer any question you may have."

"Thank you, Father," said Montoya. "It is my understanding that you met with young Pedro shortly after his arrest. Moreover you were on the ill-fated voyage and trek that brought you here. You have spent more time with him than any of the witnesses. Is there something you could tell us that might bring a measure of leniency?"

Ignacio clasped his hands thoughtfully before beginning. His voice was calm, his words measured.

"Don Rafael, I will not deny that Pedro de Arobe is a young man who has stumbled, often and seriously, in his conduct. His actions, as recounted by the witnesses today, reflect a troubled soul in need of guidance and correction. However, during the time I have spent with him, I have seen another side. One that perhaps does not absolve him but might explain some of his behavior.

"When we first arrived in Santa Maria, after enduring shipwreck and the harrowing journey that followed, Pedro was among those who bore the strain with strength, even if he did so in silence. He did not quarrel then, nor did he shirk his responsibilities. I saw in him a spirit that could persevere, though he carries a great deal of anger Anger I suspect arises from wounds unseen, wounds of the heart and mind.

"When I spoke with him in the jail, I did not find a man who denied his faults or sought excuses for them. He expressed shame for how far he had fallen, though he struggled to articulate why he acted as he did. I believe there is in him a flicker of goodness, buried beneath his transgressions. If that light can be nurtured, through firm but fair discipline, it might yet shine brighter. I ask you to consider that possibility, even as justice is served." Ignacio paused, looking briefly at Pedro before addressing Montoya directly.

"It is not for me to excuse him or to determine his fate, but I pray that the punishment rendered today leaves room for repentance and redemption, for the sake of his soul and for the good of our community."

"Thank you, Father Ignacio," said Montoya, "I will give your words weight when it comes down to present my judgment. Now, don Alonso, I will listen to your statement."

Ignacio made his way back to where he had been watching the proceedings, as don Alonso rose from his seat with a measured but visible intensity. His imposing frame, usually a symbol of paternal authority and command, now bore the weight of grief and indignation. Addressing the magistrate and assembled townsfolk, his voice resonated with equal parts sorrow and anger.

"Señor Montoya, esteemed council, and good people of Santa Maria," he began, his tone calm but charged with emotion. "I speak today not only as the master of my household but as a man whose heart has been deeply wounded. Amina was indeed my servant, a member of my house, and according to the law, my property. Yet to call her only that would be to diminish her entirely, and I cannot abide such dismissal. She was more than a servant. She was a part of my family, a young woman of grace, diligence, and spirit. She was cherished by all who knew her and brought light to our home."

Don Alonso's voice faltered momentarily as he collected himself. "But that light was extinguished in a manner so brutal, so dishonorable, that it shakes the very foundation of my household. The crime committed against her is not only an affront to her memory but an insult to my house and to this town. If we cannot protect the innocent within our walls, then what does that say of our society?"

He turned slightly toward Pedro de Arobe, his expression hardening. "And you, Pedro. Your actions have not only destroyed an innocent life but have sullied your own soul and brought shame to your father's name. Your drunken rages, your lack of discipline, and your callousness have led you here, but it is Amina who paid the ultimate price."

Returning his gaze to Montoya, don Alonso continued. "I understand the law, and I know that Amina will be judged as property in the eyes of the court. Yet I beg you, as a man of conscience, to consider the gravity of what has been lost. Not just in my household but in the moral fabric of this community. Justice demands that Pedro answer for his actions, not simply as a thief who has stolen from me, but as a man who has taken what can never be restored: a life."

Don Alonso's voice softened slightly as he concluded. "I leave the matter of justice in your capable hands, but I ask this: let this judgment serve as a warning to all. Let it remind us that we cannot permit the darkness of cruelty and lawlessness to go unpunished, lest it consume us all." He bowed slightly to Montoya before returning to his seat, his face a mask of barely restrained fury and sorrow.

"Thank you, don Alonso," said Montoya. "It is evident that to you this is much more than a dispute about property, and that you do indeed grieve for the life that was lost more than the work she provided, yet we must adhere to the law as much at it may pain us." Montoya then gestured to Yllesca's son, who had been sitting quietly but with a dour look on his face.

"I would now here from don Juan, the witness to this heinous act perpetrated on the young girl."

Don Juan Yllescas stood before the court, his demeanor a blend of control and sorrow, unwilling to even look in Pedro's direction. His voice, when he began, was steady, though underpinned by unmistakable anger and grief.

"Señor Montoya and the good people of Santa Maria, I come before you to recount the events of that day, though it pains me to do so. I speak not only as a witness to an unspeakable act but as one who deeply valued the life so cruelly taken.

"On that fateful day, I was coming from my household on an errand when I came across a scene I shall never forget. I saw Amina's market bag lying abandoned on the ground, its contents scattered. Suspecting something amiss, I investigated further and discovered the accused, Pedro de Arobe, in the hedge, straddling Amina, his hands about her throat. his clothing disheveled and his manner frantic. I pulled him out by his collar. He resisted and I struck him.

"But it was what lay within the shrubbery that struck me to my core. Amina, my household servant, lay motionless, her face beaten, her clothes in tatters. She was utterly unresponsive. I called out for help, and townsfolk arrived swiftly, witnessing the horror I had found."

Don Juan paused, taking a deep breath before continuing. "In that moment, I was overcome with rage at the sight of Pedro, who offered no explanation but to malign Amina further with vile lies, claiming that she had invited such treatment. His words, 'She begged me for it', shocked me almost as much as his actions. Even now, they burn in my memory.

"I tried to restrain myself, Señor Montoya. Truly, I did. But I could not contain my fury at the monstrous crime committed against her. When I calmed myself, I ordered that Pedro be marched through the town for all to witness his shame and that he be confined until this court could mete out justice.

"Amina was more than a servant to my household...she was a kind soul, diligent and cherished by all who knew her. To see her life stolen in such a manner fills me with profound grief and righteous anger. Her death is not just a crime against my household but against decency and humanity itself.

"I trust, Señor Montoya, that this court will deliver justice, not merely for the property stolen from us, but for the young woman whose life and dignity were so violently taken. It is my sincerest hope that this case will send a message: that such heinous acts will not be tolerated in Santa Maria."

Don Juan stepped back, his hands trembling slightly, and resumed his seat, his face a portrait of restrained emotion.

"I believe that is the last of the accusers and witnesses," said Montoya. "Are there any others who have something to say?" He looked over the assembled crowd but no one came forward. "Very well. Then it is time to hear from the accused and bring these proceedings to an end. Pedro de Arobe, do you have something you would like to say before the verdict is delivered?"

Pedro stood before the magistrate, his shoulders slumped and his face ashen. His voice, though trembling, carried a tone of sincerity as he began to speak.

"Señor Montoya, noble citizens of Santa Maria, and Don Alonso... I stand before you in complete acknowledgment of my crimes. I will not attempt to deny the accusations brought against me, for they are true. My actions were abhorrent and without excuse, and I am filled with shame and remorse for the suffering I have caused.

"The girl, Amina... she was an innocent soul. I stole her life and her dignity, and in doing so, I have stained my own soul beyond redemption. I cannot begin to imagine the pain and grief I have inflicted upon her household and upon Don Alonso, who trusted me to live as an honorable man within this community.

"I have no defense, for there is none. My actions were not those of a man but of a beast, overcome by drink and sin. I acted in anger, in selfishness, and in lust, and for that, I deserve your scorn. There is no punishment this court could impose upon me that I do not already impose upon myself every moment.

"Yet, I humbly throw myself upon the mercy of this court. I plead for leniency. Not for my own sake but in the hope that I may one day find a way to make amends, though I know I never can truly atone for what I have done. If it is to be my life that is taken, then so be it. If it is imprisonment or labor until my dying breath, I will accept that judgment.

"I ask only for the chance to live long enough to beg God for forgiveness and to perhaps bring some small measure of good to this world before my time ends. For now, I leave my fate in your hands and in the hands of our Lord."

Pedro stepped back, his head bowed, tears streaking his face. He made no effort to wipe them away as he awaited the magistrate's judgment.

Don Montoya, leaned forward, his hands steepled thoughtfully as the tension in the church grew palpable. He glanced at Pedro, whose head remained bowed in shame, and then surveyed the assembly, allowing a heavy silence to fill the air before he spoke.

"This matter before us is grave indeed," he began, his voice solemn. "The evidence and testimony presented today have revealed acts of unimaginable cruelty and malice, but they have also shown us the deep remorse of the accused. Justice is a heavy burden, and it is not to be carried lightly."

He shifted his gaze to Don Alonso Yllescas and his household. "To you, Don Alonso, and to all who mourn the loss of Amina, I extend my deepest sympathies. This crime has not only claimed the life of a cherished member of your household but has also scarred the heart of our community. No judgment can truly heal such wounds."

Turning back to Pedro, Montoya continued, "The court has heard your plea for mercy and has taken note of your confession and remorse. However, the heinous nature of your actions demands careful consideration of justice, not only for the punishment of your crimes but also for the preservation of order in Santa Maria."

He straightened in his chair, his expression unreadable. "I will require a short time to deliberate and weigh the evidence, the testimonies, and the cries for justice against your plea for leniency. During this time, I urge all present to reflect on the gravity of this situation. This will not take long and given the present weather conditions, I ask that everyone remain where they are and be patient."

"If it please you, don Rafael," said Ignacio, "I offer you the use of my quarters in order to provide you some privacy in your deliberations."

"That is more than kind, Father and I appreciate the gesture." He then marched down the central aisle with his clerk in tow as Ignacio led him to the door connecting the church to the vicarage. The cacophony in the church rose gradually as the magistrate departed, opinions and postulations tossed haphazardly to and fro. Ignacio was accosted almost immediately once he had ushered the magistrate out of the church, but he refused to succumb to speculation, telling those surrounding him that the matter was out of his hands. He made his way back to his original place near Rosa, who questioned him by merely raising her eyebrows. Ignacio returned her gaze and shook his head.

"I have nothing to add, Rosa. God's will, in one way or another, will be done. I have no doubt that whatever verdict don Raphael delivers it will be free of malice and just."

"I have that feeling as well," she replied. "I still fear for Pedro. He had done terrible things but he is not a terrible person. Does that make sense?"

"Two opposite facts can exist at the same time. That is why we rely on arbitration to resolve matters. It will not always be the outcome we hope for but it is the best that we, as mere mortals, can provide."

"I *do* believe that Pedro should face some consequence for his actions but I am fearful of what that might entail, now and in the long run. He will bear that scar forever."

"All we can do is wait," said Ignacio taking her hands in his. "Wait and pray."

The voices in the church swelled and waned around them as they stood in silent prayer oblivious to all else. After what seemed an interminable time, but was actually a little more than an hour, don Rafael re-entered the church. The room came to a sudden silence as the magistrate made his way back to the altar.

The magistrate, Don Rafael Montoya, stood before the assembly, the gravity of his decision evident in his expression. The church fell silent, every ear straining to hear his words as he rendered his judgment on Pedro de Arobe.

"Pedro de Arobe," he began, his voice steady but filled with the weight of authority. "You have admitted your guilt, and the evidence against you is overwhelming. Your actions, heinous and despicable, have brought suffering to an innocent and dishonor to this community. Amina, a member of Don Alonso's household, was not merely property as our laws might define her, but a living being whose life was extinguished in the most brutal fashion. Justice must be served, and yet, as a magistrate, I must temper justice with wisdom and understanding."

Montoya's gaze swept the room, addressing not only Pedro but also the gathered onlookers.

"Some may call for your life as the only fitting recompense for the life you have taken. And indeed, under the strictest interpretations of the law, such punishment would be within reason. Yet, as much as your crime calls for retribution, I cannot ignore the possibility of redemption, even for one who has committed such grievous wrongs. Punishment must be corrective as well as punitive, and thus, I have sought a sentence that reflects both the enormity of your offense and the faint glimmer of potential for atonement."

Turning his full attention to Pedro, Montoya's voice softened slightly, though it remained firm.

"You will not die, Pedro de Arobe. Instead, for the duration of one year, you will live the life of the oppressed. You will labor in the mines alongside the slaves of this town. You will rise when they rise, work as they work, and retire when they retire. You will eat their meager rations, endure their brutal conditions, and share in their suffering. In essence, you will be a slave."

The room stirred, some gasping, others murmuring their reactions. Montoya raised a hand for silence.

"This sentence is not borne of cruelty or caprice, but of a deliberate effort to teach you the value of the humanity you disregarded. You must understand the pain, humiliation, and despair your actions have inflicted, not only on your victim but on those around you. The labor you will undertake will be arduous, and the conditions harsh, but they will serve as a mirror to your soul. Should you survive this year, it is my hope that you will emerge as a man reborn, humbled and deeply aware of the consequences of your actions."

Montoya paused, letting the weight of his words settle. Then, addressing the crowd, he continued: "Let this be a lesson to all who hear it. Justice is not only about punishment but also about restoration. Pedro's sentence is severe, yet it offers him a path to redemption. It reflects the balance this court seeks to uphold: fairness to the victim, accountability for the perpetrator, and the preservation of order in our town." Finally, he fixed Pedro with a piercing gaze.

"Pedro, the year ahead will test your body and your soul. What you choose to make of this sentence will define the man you are when you walk free. May you use this time to reflect, repent, and rebuild."

After delivering Pedro's primary sentence, Magistrate Montoya turned his attention to the financial repercussions of the crime.

"Before this court is adjourned, there remains one additional matter. While Amina was more than mere property to Don Alonso's household, the law in its current form considers her so. Therefore, to address the tangible loss inflicted upon Don Alonso de Yllescas, I levy a fine upon the accused. As Pedro de Arobe has neither the means nor the capacity to pay, this burden shall fall to his father, Don Francisco de Arobe, who bears responsibility as the head of his household." Montoya paused, allowing the murmurs in the courtroom to subside.

"The sum of this fine shall be two hundred pesos. It is a considerable amount, reflecting not only the value of the labor and presence that Amina brought to the Yllescas household but also the irreparable damage to the esteem and harmony of their home. This compensation, though inadequate to truly atone for the loss, seeks to recognize the profound injustice perpetrated."

Montoya looked toward Don Francisco with a stern expression.

"Don Francisco, the prompt payment of this fine will not only serve as restitution but also stand as a reminder of the obligation that those with privilege bear to ensure the proper conduct of their kin. I trust you will see to its fulfillment without delay."

He then addressed Don Alonso.

"Don Alonso de Yllescas, while no amount of silver or gold can replace what has been taken from you and your household, I hope this token will at least offer some measure of reparation. Know that this court recognizes and shares in your grief, even as it struggles to render a justice that can never be complete."

With that, Montoya strode back down the aisle, signaling the end of the proceedings. The crowd erupted into a mix of reactions, some satisfied with the magistrate's measured judgment, others calling for harsher penalties, but the law had spoken.

Chapter Twenty Four

Anyone who has been stealing must steal no longer, but must work, doing something useful with their own hands, that they may have something to share with those in need.

Ephesians 4:28

Captain don Rodolfo de Salazar of the *Santa Victoria* stood on the deck and swept the coastline with his glass. The last of the night's rain had faded to mere intermittent spits that occasionally spattered on the already wet deck. The journey from Puerto de Guayaquil had been uneventful but unique to the ship and its captain. The usual route would take them from Guayaquil to the southernmost outpost on South America's western coast, Valdivia, but orders had come down from the Governor of Quito himself to make this stop in the largely unsettled area of the Esmeraldas River. Thus the *Santa Victoria* left port with half its usual cargo with instructions to pick up a shipment of gold and silver from a frontier town the captain had never heard of.

Salazar put down his spyglass and turned to his first officer, Martín Pérez de Velasco.

"I see the river but naught else," said Salazar with disdain. "Where is this damnable town we are looking for?"

"Our charts, of course, have no information on that," replied Pérez, "but from what the Governor's advisor said, the town is inland and not on the coast itself. We must make our way up the river some miles."

"I doubt any galleon has been on that river before. We will proceed, but slowly. And I want constant depth readings as we go. I will not have us stranded on some backward beachhead, orders or no."

"Aye Captain," said Pérez. "I will tell the pilot to make for the river's mouth and have someone man the sounding stations."

Captain Salazar was proud of his ship, as most captains are. He had sailed on her decks for nearly twenty years now, transporting gold, silver, slaves and goods along a good portion of the western coast and had no thought of ever relinquishing the role. He held no fantasies about retiring to a cozy villa and enjoying the fruits of his earnings. The *Santa Victoria* was his villa, his home, and his one true passion.

His new orders had added this new stop, the town of Santa Maria to his route, both on the way to Valdivia and on the way back. Apparently, there had been a discovery of precious metals there and mining efforts had been quite successful. Now the fruits of their labors would make its way back to the empire. The town itself would also benefit from the new goods they would have available from being added to the shipping routes. Perhaps in a few years Santa Maria might be as important a port as Callao or Valdivia, but Salazar had his doubts. He expected Santa Maria to be no more than a collection of half-breed colonists in mud huts eking out a meager existence on the frontier.

The ship turned its considerable bulk and entered the river proper. Almost immediately, they encountered a flotilla of ramshackle fishing boats heading out to sea. The fishermen hooted and whistled at the sight of the *Santa Victoria* as they passed her on either side. The sight of the fishing fleet gave heart to Salazar that there was indeed a town to be found but did not improve his expectations of what he would find there.

The *Santa Victoria* made its way slowly up the river. In spite of Captain Salazar's misgivings, the soundings showed that the river was nearly as deep as it was wide, more than enough for a vessel of its size. Still, the soundings continued, with sailors calling the depths to each other across the ship. In the course of a few hours, they came to a bend in the river which held an unexpected sight. A caravel was rounding the bend just ahead of them.

Captain Salazar called for a stop as he picked up his spyglass for a better look. Pérez came to his side at a run.

"Captain, what do you see? Are they pirates?"

"I cannot be sure at this distance but they are running the Royal

Standard. It is doubtful pirates would do such a thing, yet see how low she rides in the water and how slow their progress is. Their holds are full of something to be sure."

"We have come to a stop, Captain. What would you like to do?"

"Belay the stop order! Bring me alongside that vessel. I want to know who they are and what they are doing."

The sails unfurled once more and the Santa Victoria, now freed, leapt forward and closed the distance. The caravel tried its best to turn and make a run but she wallowed and made little headway.

"Bring us alongside her on the windward side," shouted Salazar. "Have the soldiers ready themselves for boarding!" Salazar went to the railing where the caravel was now only a few feet away. "I, Captain Salazar of the Imperial ship *Santa Victoria*, order you to heave to and prepare for boarding!"

The caravel made no effort to stop. Slow as she was, her captain was still determined to make an escape. Captain Salazar was not a man of patience.

"Set the grappling hooks and bring her to a stop!" he barked. "Prepare the boarding planks! Soldiers be ready to board!"

In very short order, the caravel was seized by the grappling hooks and soon a contingent of soldiers, far greater in number to the *Santa Estrella's* crew, were on board.

Once the ships were secured, Salazar himself strode onto the deck of the Santa Estrella. De Cuellar wriggled himself free from the soldiers holding him and came before Salazar, wagging a finger in his face.

"Who are you to stop and board a ship of the line? We are on a vital mission for the Empire!"

Nonplussed, Salazar studied de Cuellar's face for a moment, saw the anger and disdain, and also the fear and sweat on the man's brow.

"Were that true, you would not have attempted your escape." He gestured to a squad of soldiers. "Go below. Bring up anyone hiding below decks and find out what is in the hold."

As the soldiers went to do his bidding, Salazar turned his attention back to de Cuellar. "Identify yourself."

"I am Captain Alonso Sanchez de Cuellar, late of the *San Felipe y Santiago,* now Captain of the *Santa Estrella*. Who might you be?"

"I know you not, Captain," said Salazar coolly. "I am Captain don Rodolfo de Salazar commanding the *Santa Victoria*. I trust you have documentation regarding your status?"

"Not as such. I was forced to commandeer this vessel after the loss of my own."

"Forced? That seems like a story worth hearing. Is this part of your 'vital mission'?"

De Cuellar stood there and said nothing. Salazar looked him up and down, walking around him. As he finished his inspection a soldier ran up to him.

"Sir, there is no one else below, the others are inspecting the hold."

Salazar sniffed at the news and turned his attention back to de Cuellar.

"And so, Captain, where did this ship come from? Did it perhaps come from the small town of Santa Maria further up the river where I myself am bound? Whatever your destination, you would hard pressed to make the voyage with a meager ten men, most of whom," he said gesturing at de Cuellar's crew, "have no experience at sea except perhaps as passengers. Am I correct in my assessment?"

"It seems you already have all the answers you want," said de Cuellar defiantly. "Again, I protest your misguided boarding of my ship. You have no right to so impugn an active captain, your peer, while he is in the service of the Empire."

"So you say Captain, yet you lack any sort of proof to ascertain your claims other than your say so. In my position, would you do anything less? It may be that it is as you say, but I am duty bound to establish that to my satisfaction." Again de Cuellar fell silent, staring ahead blankly. At this moment, the squad of soldiers emerged from the hold. The sergeant, Gomez, approached Salazar with a solemn look on his face.

"Well, what have you found, Sergeant?" asked Salazar.

"The hold contains several crates, my Captain," replied Gomez with a short bow, "all of which are filled with bars of gold and silver. There is nothing else."

Salazar turned on his heel and cried out to Pérez who was at the galleon's rail.

"Get the assessor over to this vessel immediately! I have work for him." He turned his attention back to de Cuellar who was still betraying no emotion other than the line of sweat on his brow.

"Now then, Captain, this becomes a curious matter. You may be wondering why we have an assessor among our compliment. I will solve that mystery for you. The *Santa Victoria* and I were dispatched from Guayaquil, under orders from the Governor, to come to Santa Maria, *assess* their mining operation, and take shipment of whatever had been produced thus far. Now we find you, in your battered caravel, your hull well below the waterline and moving like a slug. Moreover you have in your hold the very thing I was sent to inspect. How do you explain that?"

"I took it upon myself to make delivery. I felt it my duty to provide the bounty rather than wait."

"How noble of you. And now to get back to a previous point in my inquiry, you do, no doubt, have such a mandate signed by an of official of Santa Maria. Such treasure would not be left unaccounted. I ask again, where is your documentation? Your inability to produce official shipping documents or an authorization letter raises alarms I cannot ignore. An Imperial officer is well-versed in naval protocols. Do you have such authority or not?"

"As you surmise, I do not," said de Cuellar in a low growl, "but that does not change the veracity of my position or intentions."

"I am disinclined to believe you, given the meager evidence presented." He turned to the soldiers and said, "Take the Captain and his men to the Santa Victoria. Put them in the brig and in chains." Turning back to de Cuellar, he added, "We will tow this vessel back to Santa Maria and then we will know the truth of all this."

Hours later, the *Santa Victoria* was still at anchor while the Santa Estrella was being prepared for the journey back to Santa Maria. On the bridge, Pérez was giving Salazar a status report.

"Aside from the ingots in the hold," Pérez began, "there is nothing else of value on the caravel. Even the crew quarters held nothing of value barring the captain's cabin. There we found an excess of wines, cigars and fine linens, and in contrast to other quarters, looked quite lived in."

"I cannot fault him there. I too, would rather live on a ship than a house no matter how splendid. Once a sailor always a sailor. What is the condition of the ship itself?"

"It is apparent some repairs were recently made, however the ship is old. There is not much life left in her. Still, rather than towing her, might I suggest manning her under her own power with a crew of our own? It is, after all, just a short trip up the river."

"That will be fine, Pérez. Make the necessary assignments. Before you go, have the assessor meet me in my cabin."

"Aye, Captain." Pérez turned on his heel and went to do the Captain's bidding.

Captain Salazar found the assessor, Domingo Luján, a man of corpulent proportions and diminished height, to be somewhat repellent. He was bureaucrat, one of those self indulgent and self absorbed parasites that infested the offices of governance, seeking to ingratiate themselves wherever they could in a quest for power and influence. Yet he was a necessary evil for the completion of this mission.

"Ah, Señor Luján," said Salazar as the man entered the cabin. "Please, have a seat and tell me about what you found in the hold."

"The hold has twelve crates and each one appears to be the standard *carga* in weight," a carga being approximately 297 pounds. The man sat, twisting his fingers as if he were in front of a lavish dinner. He was clearly enthralled by the size of the treasure. Salazar noticed this and his revulsion of the man increased. He found himself watching Luján's jowls bouncing up and down as he spoke. "I cannot be certain of the weight, of course, nor can I testify to the purity of the bars but so far," he said with a chuckle, "I am quite impressed."

"Is there a stamp on the bars?"

"Yes, yes. One quite unfamiliar to me. I assume it is a family crest of some sort but the name Santa Maria is clearly marked. I cannot wait to see the mine itself. Then I can make a better judgment as to purity."

"Well, be patient Señor Luján," said Salazar amiably now that the session was almost over. "You will be there shortly as we will be under way as soon as we can."

As Luján exited the cabin Pérez entered.

"Captain?"

"Yes, what is it Pérez?"

"All is in order and we are ready to depart on your order."

"Very well, get us on our way."

"Yes, Captain," said Pérez. "There is one thing you should know. The caravel, laden as she is, will be much slower than us. Shall we keep pace or let her fall astern?"

"Let her fall. With our crew in command, I have no fear of the ship's safety. She will not be far behind." He saw that Pérez made no move to leave, and so he asked, "Is there something else?"

"There is, Captain. De Cuellar, the captain of the other ship, has been raising a commotion below. He insists that he talk with you once more. Shall we let him vent until he has exhausted himself?"

"No," replied Salazar in a weary voice. "Have him brought up and get yourself to the *Santa Estrella*. Get us underway."

"Aye, Captain."

After long moments, Salazar felt his ship stir to life around him as the *Santa Victoria* resumed its course. Several long moments after that, a knock came on his door. It was de Cuellar flanked by two soldiers. Salazar admitted de Cuellar and bade the soldiers to stand guard outside.

De Cuellar, still chained, shuffled his way to the chair in front of Salazar's table and fell into it. Salazar eyed him cautiously and sat across from him.

"I understand you are fond of wine and cigars, are you not?"

"I am indeed, Captain," de Cuellar said with the beginnings of a smile.

"Sadly, I have none to offer as neither is a habit of mine. Tell me, why are you making such an outcry in the brig? Do you wish now to make a confession?"

De Cuellar scowled. "I will make no admissions to you as I deem you to have no authority over me."

"Then why are we here?"

"You may brand me however you wish, thief, pirate, scoundrel, but I take full responsibility for any and all charges you lay against me. I have my circle of allies that will ultimately be charged, that is, until we are all cleared, but there are others in the brig who do not deserve to be there."

"Oh? How so?"

"There are four among us who had no knowledge of our cargo nor of our destination. They are workers who enacted the refit of the caravel and were still onboard at our departure. Only one, Rodrigo, is a sailor by trade but he too was ignorant of our undertaking."

"How can that be if they were on the ship? They surely saw everything."

De Cuellar bowed his head, his eyes fixed on the table.

"They were plied with an excess of wine after their labors were complete. They were quite incapacitated when the final preparations took place. They witnessed nothing."

Salazar stared at de Cuellar and drummed his fingers on the tabletop.

"You strike me as a stubborn and ruthless man," he said after several silent seconds. "Why would you care about those under your command?"

"You know nothing about me! I am not without honor. I am a Captain of the line! I care because they are undeserving of any contrived charges they will face."

"And you *are*. Interesting. Strange that you would cite honor as one of your qualities given the circumstances of your apprehension."

"Again, Sirrah, you do not know me. My men follow me because of those very attributes."

"Be that as it may. We will not determine anything until our arrival in Santa Maria. There the investigation will begin in earnest. Until that time, all of you, including your 'innocents' will remain where they are. I will not be moved merely on your assertion."

Salazar sat back and appraised de Cuellar. The man was an enigma. Full of bluster one moment and sheepish the next.

Leaning forward, he asked, "Tell me something to satisfy my idle curiosity. Where were you bound?"

"Callao," replied de Cuellar, his head bowed again.

"Callao?" Salazar burst out with a laugh. "Why, you could barely make it down the river! What did you expect when upon the open sea and a thousand leagues before you?"

"I expected to persevere."

"I see. You rely on your stubbornness to pull you through. That is no doubt how you lost your first ship."

"We struck a rock, an outcrop from the floor of the sea. It was no one's fault."

"As Captain, anything that happens on *your* ship is *your* fault. You know that."

"And you know that God puts obstacles in our path to challenge us. In spite of it, I have persevered, to use that word again, and have come out the better for it."

"As you sit here in chains. Look, Captain de Cuellar, I am not at present going to sit in judgment on you, and I assure you that when the time comes I, and whomever is the presiding magistrate, will look at the evidence before us and make a fair determination. I have to say, however, that it does not look good and your compatriots will be subject to the same scrutiny. I warn you that postulating it was all somehow God's will, is not a good defense. I ask you now to reserve anything else you may have to say until such a time as it is appropriate."

He stood and opened the door. Motioning to the guards he said, "Take this man back to the brig. Make sure he and his men are properly fed and watered but do nothing else without my consent. If he persists in making a commotion, you are at liberty to douse him with a bucket of water."

The men hustled de Cuellar out of the cabin, and while he resisted, it was not an attempt to escape his fate but rather a show of indignation at being man-handled by subordinates. Salazar was not impressed. *Where is your dignity, man?* He shook his head cheerlessly and stepped out onto the deck. At the rail, he watched as the dense landscape drifted by. Looking back, he saw the *Santa Estrella* struggling to keep up with the larger ship, but steadily falling behind. *It would have taken de Cuellar a year to reach Callao in that old bucket, if he made it at all.* He chuckled to himself as he pictured de Cuellar swimming the rest of the way with the ore on his back. *But that is what perseverance is all about.* His reverie was broken by a shout. Looking ahead, he could see the plowed farmland that marked the beginning of Santa Maria's border. *Perhaps there will be more than mud huts after all.*

Presently, the town came into view and Salazar felt a wave of relief. Here was something more than the mud huts he had expected. Here was a modicum of civilization that stood proudly against the mysterious might of the surrounding jungle. The white buildings shone in the sun and most of Salazar's misgivings melted away. There was already a line of people at the shoreline as if they had anticipated the *Santa Victoria's* arrival, although the truth would turn out to be more serendipitous than expected. As he watched through his glass, he could see the people's surprise as they noticed the galleon draw near. There were sudden shouts and waving. They were clearly joyous at the ship's imminent arrival. There were even more cheers as the *Santa Estrella* rounded the bend behind them. The dock was not large enough for the *Santa Victoria* to berth, so Salazar ordered the anchor to be dropped and the tenders were readied for the excursion to land. Meanwhile the *Santa Estrella* had no problem with the dock and those on board arrived at Santa Maria first.

This has been a day of surprises, thought Salazar. *Some better than others, but in the end, hopeful.*

Chapter Twenty Five

But whatever were gains to me I now consider loss for the sake of Christ. What is more, I consider everything a loss because of the surpassing worth of knowing Christ Jesus my Lord, for whose sake I have lost all things. I consider them garbage, that I may gain Christ.

Philippians 3:7-8

"What do you means it is all gone!" bellowed don Alonso Yllescas to his son, Juan.

"Exactly what I stated," said the younger Yllescas. "When the storage shed was checked this morning, everything within it was gone. They found the lock broken and every single crate of ingots is nowhere to be found."

"This is a disaster!" continued don Alonso. "I will look a fool before the Governor! It took months of correspondence to convince him that we have a viable, productive mine and now there is nothing to show for it. He will have me in chains for this! Or worse!"

"There is something else that is missing as well. The *Santa Estrella* has left her berth. There is no sign of her anywhere, but I believe it, and the ingots, are in the same place."

"De Cuellar! That bastard! He led me to believe that he merely wanted the ship to feel the rolling of the water on the deck beneath his feet, when he had this planned from the very beginning."

Don Alonso sat down heavily in his chair, taking great gulps of air caused by his outburst. After a moment his breath began to come more easily. "I should never told him about the mine. I should have never shown him that ingot." He buried his face in his hands as if to shut out the world. "First the tragedy with Amina, now this. Oh, this is terrible."

"You could not have kept the mine from him. He would have found out eventually. It is not a secret. Anyone in town could have told him or any of the new arrivals."

"Why could that have not happened after the Governor's arrival? What am I to do?"

The younger Yllescas put a hand on his father's shoulder

"An answer will present itself, you must have faith. You cannot blame yourself so harshly. A seed was planted and de Cuellar wasted no time in exploiting the opportunity. The fishermen will have seen their departure and which direction they took."

"What will that accomplish? They are gone. Everything is gone." Don Alonso jumped up from his chair and shook a fist in the air. "That scoundrel! If I ever see him again I will send him to the mines myself, the hell with the magistrate. I will see that he works until his dying breath!"

Don Juan gently pushed his father back onto his chair.

"Please Papa, do not exert yourself so. There is still a mine, as you say, and more ingots as well. Perhaps we have yet a little time and can still make a good showing."

"Perhaps I will only lose my title and my lands," don Alonso said sourly. He sighed deeply and looked at his son.

"It could be that there is some truth in what you say. Today they are taking the young de Arobe to the mines to begin his sentence. Go with them. See what progress they have made and report back. I will not rest until I know."

* * *

"Where are you bound at such a pace?"

"Ah, Rosa," said Ignacio, shifting his bag from one shoulder to the other. He had entered the plaza at a little less than a run and had not noticed her until he was nearly upon her. "Forgive me, but I am running late and they will not wait for me."

"Who and what are you talking about? Surely you have minute or so."

"I am sorry. They are escorting Pedro to the mine and I want to make sure he arrives safely. I will surely confer my blessings on him before he is set loose among the slaves, that he may survive his sentence and find the redemption he so desperately needs. The journey will take the better part of a day, meaning that I will spend the night there and return on the morrow."

"That is quite the undertaking. For a priest. Surely you could bless him without having to make the trip yourself."

"I could indeed, but I want to go and see this mine and the conditions there for myself. I only learned of the facility at Pedro's trial. I can pray for him better if I can picture where he is and the challenges he will face. Please, I must go if I am to join them."

"Then I will walk with you." At this Ignacio raised his brow questioningly "Ay, Ignacio, eres un tonto. Not to the mine, Heaven forbid, but to not delay you further. Come, let us go." Ignacio picked up the pace again with Rosa fairly sprinting to keep up.

"Thank you, Rosa, for being so understanding and a good friend."

"Yes, I suppose I am 'a good friend'. Nacho, we have much to talk about. We were about to talk when this whole Pedro fiasco exploded. There are some things I need to say to you and perhaps give clarity to your misgivings, your apprehensions."

"That much is true, my dear Rosa. I promise we will have that talk but it will have to wait until my return. Until then, you must seek clarity within yourself. Gather your thoughts, your feelings and the implications of where they may lead. I myself will be doing very much the same while I am on this expedition, and of course, I will continue to pray for guidance. Ah, good! They have not left yet!"

They came up to a small group of men who were loading Pedro, who was still shackled, onto a horse drawn cart. Among them were don Francisco, his son Domingo and don Juan Yllescas who smiled as he saw Ignacio approach.

"I was not sure if you were serious about joining us, Father. It was such a last minute declaration of your intent and then you ran off."

"Yes, I had to get some things I thought I might need. I hope I have not caused you delay."

"Not at all, in fact we are right on schedule. Leaving now will get us there just about night fall."

Yllescas turned his attention to Rosa. "Señora Alvarez, how pleasant it is to see you again. Are you perhaps coming with us?"

"No, I am afraid that I have had my fill of wandering through the wilds. Enough to last a lifetime. I am merely here to see the good Father off. It is up to you t make sure he returns safely."

"That he will, Señora, I assure you. The way is long but not difficult. We have a well maintained road that a blind man could follow. There will be no wandering, as you put it. We will have him safely back tomorrow near sunset."

"I will hold you to that. Pray you do not disappoint me."

"I shall not, Señora." Yllescas bowed slightly to her and went back to the cart and the assembled men.

Rosa turned to Ignacio and said softly, "I suppose this is goodbye, then."

Ignacio cupped her face in his hands and looked at her directly. "It is just for a day. We often go a day without seeing each other. This is one of those days. Have no fear. I am in the company of stout men who are already familiar with the dangers and I have been assured there are none. I will return as promised and when I do we shall sup together. I will regale you with tales of my adventure and then we will talk, You and I."

Rosa nodded her head, but said nothing. She smiled a weak smile that could have, just as easily, been a frown. Ignacio turned and trotted to join the group that was already underway, heading down the road toward the distant forest. She watched them until they were swallowed by the wall of foliage, hoping all the time that Ignacio would turn and wave before disappearing. He did not, but she raised her arm and waved back anyway.

She stood there in silence for a while until she realized there was some sort of commotion going on behind her. Turning, she saw several people running toward the waterfront. She set her feet in that direction to see what was going on. She did not run and eventually got there at her own pace. What she saw was a marvelous sight: a Spanish galleon with its flags and pennants waving proudly in the breeze.

There was a mixed reaction from the people at the dock. Some hooted enthusiastically and waved, while some stood there somewhat mesmerized. Few people in Santa Maria had ever seen such a thing with their own eyes. A new cheer came from the crowd as another vessel came into view, a smaller ship and familiar. The *Santa Estrella* was returning to her home.

As the smaller ship docked at its berth, don Alonso pushed his way to the front of the assemblage as lines were thrown to secure the mooring. When the gangplank had been placed, he made to board the ship but was rebuffed by several armed soldiers that he did not recognize. He struggled against them, determined to have his way, but to no avail. He was pushed, none too gently away from the gangplank.

"De Cuellar!" he cried to the boat in general. "De Cuellar, get out here and explain yourself! I will have you thrown in irons! I will..."

"Please, Señor, calm yourself. Do not make such an outcry. Captain de Cuellar is not on board," said a voice beside him, calmly yet firmly. Don Alonso stepped back and appraised the new man standing before him.

"Then where is is he? I will have an accounting or I will have his blood!"

"Again, Señor, all will be explained in a short time if you will allow."

"Who are you then?" asked Yllescas impatiently.

"My name is Martín Pérez de Velasco, First Officer of the Santa Victoria, the ship you see at anchor yonder. I am under the command of Captain don Rodolfo de Salazar. We have seized this ship and all aboard. More, I cannot tell you until Captain Salazar has come ashore. In the meantime, please direct me to the proper authority of this township that I can prepare the way."

"I *am* the proper authority here, you half-wit. I am don Alonso Sebastian de Yllescas, the chief of Santa Maria del Oro. I demand you set de Cuellar before me this minute. He has committed an atrocious crime against this town!"

"That may well be true, however I cannot accede to your wishes as Captain de Cuellar is being held aboard the *Santa Victoria* and will remain so until Captain Salazar deems it otherwise. Until that time, it would be wise for you to dispel this troupe of onlookers so that the Captain will be unhindered, and then arrange for a private meeting room away from idle ears."

Grumbling, yet knowing it was the proper thing to do, Yllescas set about dispersing the spectators, urging them to go about their business. As the last of the stragglers wandered away, Yllescas turned back to the dock and saw that a long boat full of sailors had come ashore.

Out came a tall man, who Yllescas, quite rightly, deemed to be Captain Salazar. Salazar and the First Officer were having a discussion as he approached them, then quickened his step as Velasco pointed at him discreetly. He nodded at the tall man and shook his hand.

"Captain Salazar, I presume."

"Ah, yes, Señor Ybarra..."

"Yllescas," Velasco interjected.

"Of course, Señor Yllescas," said Salazar without missing a beat. "A pleasure to make your acquaintance. I must admit, Santa Maria is much more than what I was led to expect, being somewhat off the map as it were. The Governor himself had no clear knowledge of your settlement. He will be please to know that Santa Maria is a thriving community."

"The Governor?" exclaimed don Alonso. "Is he here? Did you bring him from Quito?"

"Sadly, no. He is consumed by matters of state and he sends his regards. I was commissioned to come in his stead with the assumption that there was cargo to be transported." He held up a hand as Yllescas was about make a reply. "Before you state your grievances against Captain de Cuellar, I will have you know that we intercepted him and the *Santa Estrella* with what appears to be the shipment in question. It is all onboard the caravel and will be moved to the *Santa Victoria* over the next few days for transport to Quito. We retrieved twelve cargas of ingots bearing your stamp. Is this the extent of the consignment?"

"I...I do not have the exact figures," stammered Yllescas, "but that seems to be correct. There may, of course, be more as more ore comes from the mine weekly but to be completely honest, I do not know the schedule. My son will be able to tell you more."

"That is quite alright, Señor. Twelve cargas is more than sufficient for a beginning. Santa Maria has been officially added to my route and will be visited regularly. As it is, I do not plan on staying here long, just long enough to conclude this transaction. There is the matter of discussion about Captain de Cuellar, but I deem it need some sensitivity and discretion. Is there some place we can pursue this further?"

"Certainly. I have an office here in the administrative building." Yllescas gestured for them to follow him. "It is not far. Just at the edge of the plaza."

Later, behind closed doors, Yllescas and Salazar faced each other across the Chief's rough hewn desk. Velasco had gone to secure the landing site and see to the quartering of those coming ashore.

"Perhaps I can interest you in some of our local wine," Yllescas offered. "It is quite good in spite of its plebeian origins. We, of course, grow the grapes here, a unique strain found only in these regions. That scoundrel de Cuellar helped himself to several cases, which I reluctantly gave him, along with cigars that are among the finest in the New World."

"Thank you, but no. I neither imbibe nor smoke when I am on duty which, I must admit, is every moment of every day. But your generosity does not go unnoticed. I am sure there are many among my crew that will readily take your offer, although I hope not to excess. No, let us instead pivot to the matter at hand, that being the erstwhile captain of your caravel."

"It was not his nor was he her captain. He begged me to use it as a residence, and nothing more. If I had any inkling of what he was planning, I would have burnt the thing down to the waterline myself!"

"Then you readily concur that no papers of transit, official shipping documents or an authorization letter was issued by you or any of your subordinates?"

"Certainly not," Yllescas replied hotly. "If any such documents exist, they are surely forgeries. We have been patiently awaiting the Governor's arrival, never with the intention of transporting any goods ourselves, and certainly never with a ship such as the *Santa Estrella*. The boat is ancient and uncared for. It is fine for a jaunt on the river, but the open sea? Pha! You have no doubt seen our fishing fleet. Little more than logs with sails. In matters maritime, we have very little knowledge or skill. Before de Cuellar's arrival, I was strongly considering dismantling it and using the timber for homes or something else."

"Thank you for confirming what I already suspected. In my mind there is no doubt that Captain de Cuellar is guilty of thievery, in essence, piracy, both of your vessel and the consignment of ingots. I also acknowledge that he did not act alone."

"Of course he did not. His little band of mercenaries are just as guilty as he is."

"That may well be. What can you tell me about his crew?"

"Very little. I truly do not know them. They all arrived when he did, after trekking through the jungle following their shipwreck. None of them are native to Santa Maria. There are others of that group that have become citizens of note and very well regarded. In particular, a priest, who has taken over the reins of our church and revived our spiritual community, as well as a nobleman and his sons. It is my belief that de Cuellar rounded up all the undesirable to himself and pressed them into his service with promises of riches and fame."

"I am not sure that 'pressed' is the correct word. No doubt, many of them were willing participants. However, de Cuellar, while not admitting to any guilt, impressed upon me that some among his crew were indeed unwilling and free of any ill intentions."

"A liar as well as a thief, then. How can they be with him and not be part of the scheme?"

"I asked him that very question. Apparently there was some kind of subterfuge that kept them from the details of the plot. I do not entirely believe him, yet why would he create such myth if there were not some element of truth? With your permission, I would like to bring the suspects ashore and conduct an informal inquiry to ascertain the guilt or innocence of these men. For my part, I would much rather transport a few prisoners than many. As it is, they are housed three to a cell."

"Why can you not conduct your investigation on your ship? Surely you have enough room."

"I do not want de Cuellar anywhere near the treasure. It is bad enough he is on the ship and will be upon our departure. I have no doubt he is already trying to coerce his guards into freeing him and rising up in mutiny."

* * *

Ignacio had some vague, idealistic notion about what the mine site would be like but he was completely unprepared for the reality of what lay before him. Instead of an orderly work camp, what he saw was a desolate, barren landscape strewn with rocks and boulders. Aside from one well constructed building, which was obviously where the overseers were housed, the encampment consisted of a few ramshackle hovels to house the slaves and a corral for the mules.

He was struck most profoundly by the slaves themselves. Nearly all were men, all gaunt and under nourished, sweating and toiling under the merciless gaze of the foremen, who rode around on horses and extolling the slaves to work ever harder. It was, to Ignacio's eyes, the very image of Hell.

He looked fearfully at Pedro, who was observing the scene and trembling. Pedro's face had gone pale when he realized what was in store for him, and tears sprang from his eyes. Ignacio began to understand that this may well be a death sentence for the young man. Pedro began to struggle as he was taken from the cart but to no avail. Many rough hands gripped him and fairly threw him from the relative safety of the cart.

On his knees and sobbing, he began to plead for clemency. Don Juan Yllescas looked at him in disdain but did not reply to his cries. This moment always comes when the damned are face with the inevitable.

The chief overseer rode up and dismounted before Yllescas. A large, powerful man with a face that had never had a smile invade his face, towered over them. His name was Severino Almagro, a man who saw the mine as his personal dominion, ruling it with an iron fist. Little patience had he for insubordination, showing no mercy to those who fell behind in their grueling work or attempt to resist. His cruelty was legendary. He was, in effect, the Devil of this small portion of Hell.

"So, this is the whelp they send me?" said Almagro in a sharp and derisive tone. "A boy accustomed to comfort and drink, now thrust among men who toil and bleed. You think this will be a respite from your sentence? Think again. In my mine, you will find neither pity nor reprieve. Fall behind, and you'll feel the lash. Step out of line, and you'll wish the magistrate had condemned you to the gallows instead." Ignacio felt it necessary to step in.

"Señor, I beg you to temper justice with mercy. Young Pedro stands before you not as a hardened criminal, but as a broken man seeking redemption. His sentence is not merely to toil in the mines but to learn humility and atone for his sins. If you crush his spirit, you will destroy any hope of his reformation. Treat him with the firmness required, yes, but do not deny him the dignity of a second chance. As scripture says, 'Blessed are the merciful, for they shall receive mercy.' Let us not forget that even the hardest stone can be shaped by patience and purpose."

Almagro looked at Ignacio as if the priest had suddenly sprouted a second head. Yllescas came between them then and took Ignacio by the arm.

"Now, now, Father. Almagro knows his role here and the time of pleading for leniency has passed. Please do not make matters worse by making Pedro an object of contempt among the overseers. Your compassion is admirable, but it is misplaced in this instance. The magistrate's decree is clear: Pedro is to serve his sentence as a slave for the span of one year, no more, no less. He is to be treated with neither greater nor lesser regard than the others who labor here. To do otherwise would mock the justice we sought in court."

Turning to Almagro, he said, "Don Almagro, you are charged with ensuring this punishment is carried out fairly but with full weight. Pedro is not a guest in this place nor a man with privileges. He is here to work, to toil, to understand the suffering he has inflicted. Let his hands blister, his back ache, and his spirit wrestle with the lessons he must learn. Only then will his debt begin to be repaid. Treat him as you would any other under your rule."

It was only then that a smile crossed Almagro's face, but it was a smile of pure maliciousness and cruelty. He gestured to the men holding Pedro and they dragged him away to the slaves' barracks. Don Francisco had held back until now. When he saw his son being taken, he called out after him.

"Pedro! You have shamed yourself, your family, and our name, but you are still my son! Bear this punishment as a man, and if there is any hope for redemption, find it in this suffering. Do not let this break you!"

Yllescas looked at don Francisco with a frown. "Don Francisco," he said coldly, his voice laced with scorn, "your words will be the heaviest chain your son bears. Not the lashes, nor the stones he must carry, but the sound of your voice. You have provided no comfort, only the reminder of everything he has lost and the disgrace he has wrought upon you and your name. If cruelty has a sharper edge than regret, then you have just wielded it."

Chapter Twenty Six

"The crucible for silver and the furnace for gold, but the Lord tests the heart."

Proverbs 17:3

Don Alonso provided Captain Salazar a temporary office in the administrative building for his use while in Santa Maria. Here he would conduct the implementation of the policies and procedures necessary for any port along the trade route as well as manage the resources required by ships, primarily the *Santa Victoria*, to house troops and passengers as well as provisions and the trade of goods. The town square had already been requisitioned as temporary housing for the ships soldiers and tents to accommodate them were being erected.

It was only Salazar's first day in Santa Maria and already he was inundated with the minutia of logistics, sending messengers hither and thither to procure what was needed. He was no stranger to these obligations, as a ship's captain was little more than an administrator, yet he sometimes found the obligation tedious and sought to expedite things as quickly as he could to be on his way to his next port of call. With any luck, he might be able to conclude his responsibility within a day or so and get to the matter of interrogating the prisoners and conclude which of them, if any, should be left in Santa Maria.

De Cuellar and his men had been removed from the *Santa Victoria,* where accommodations were tight, and placed under heavy guard in a building adjacent to the square. Here, at least, the prisoners could be housed and fed without depleting the ship's stores and resources.

Don Alonso and his lieutenants had provided the necessary documentation for the transfer of the ingots and other goods, and it was while he was counter signing the certificates that Luján, the mineral assessor and assayer, entered the office.

"I am sorry to intrude," began Luján, "but I would like to make my report about the gold and silver found on the *Santa Estrella.*"

Salazar put his quill aside and stacked the documents.

"And what conclusion have you come to?"

"I do not yet have a formal written report, you shall have it as soon as it is drafted, but it will be no different than what I tell you now. Upon careful inspection and assessment of the ingots recovered from the caravel, I can confirm the following: The gold is of remarkable purity, measured at approximately 22 karats. It shows minimal impurities. Its sheen and density are consistent with gold mined from the Potosí region, known for its high-quality deposits.

"The silver ingots exhibit a purity level of around ninety three percent, aligning closely with the standard of silver extracted from the Andes. Traces of lead and other base metals are minimal.

"Both the gold and silver ingots bear identifiable marks as being produced in Santa Maria, indicating that these were smelted and marked with the explicit intent of transportation to Spain and the Crown authority. These ingots were undoubtedly destined for royal coffers. Their presence aboard the caravel, without proper documentation or seal, strongly suggests theft or unauthorized possession. I recommend holding the accused until further verification from the Viceroy's office."

"I have already anticipated your recommendation, Señor Luján, and while I may not hold some of the men under his command, pending a review I will soon conduct, I have no intention of releasing de Cuellar until we reach Valdivia where he will face a tribunal. In the meantime, I have assigned a squad of soldiers to secure the mine site. You will accompany them. You will leave in the morning."

"Captain, that is not in my purview. I was only to assess the quality of the ore and supervise its transport back to Guayaquil. I have no obligation or desire to enter the wilderness."

"Perhaps the Governor was clearer in his orders to me than he was to you. Your service is what I deem it to be and at this time your desires are less than secondary than the needs of this mission. You will go, observe the techniques used, improve what you can to make sure that everything is up to Imperial standards. You will nominally be in charge and I have the documents ready that proclaim you as such. Upon my return from Valdivia you will have a full report ready for me and then we can talk about your return to Guayaquil."

"Captain, I must object! It will be months before you return from Valdivia! I am a civilized man not some adventurer with a gun in one hand and a sword in the other. What you ask for can be accomplished in a few days!"

"In a few days, I, and the *Santa Victoria* will depart. Whether you go to mine on your own feet or dragged there by soldiers matters not to me. You will do as ordered. You can complain to the Governor when or if you see him again."

"When or if? That is a threat if ever I heard one."

"You know well Señor Luján, that circumstances can quickly change any plan. Take for example our encounter with the *Santa Estrella*, who was carrying your precious cargo. If we had delayed, even a little bit at sea, there would have been no treasure nor any sign as to where it went. But take it as a threat if you like. There is no threat in commanding you to do your duty. Only in your refusal. The way I see it," Salazar added with a chuckle, "you will be among the only things you truly love in life: gold and silver."

* * *

"What do you think will become of us?"

Rios paced the room that he currently shared with Rodrigo as they awaited news of their fate. They had been moved from the holding cells on the *Santa Victoria* to a building fronting the town square. Outside, a village of soldiers had erected their tents, and many others had been posted around the premises. Inside, the prisoners had been quartered two to each room, locked and guarded by men patrolling the hallway connecting them.

"For the love of God," growled Rodrigo, "sit down and be quiet."

"But you must be wondering," said Rios, completely ignoring the request. "We are not really sure of what we are accused of, and yet here we are...accused and imprisoned. I should have known that de Cuellar was being far too generous with his wine. Here I was, thinking we were being rewarded for a job well done and instead we find ourselves complicit in some nefarious scheme. Go to sleep in a blissful state of inebriation and wake up in chains." He continued pacing while Rodrigo glowered.

"The guards refer to us as pirates. Why? We have done nothing wrong. We were used by de Cuellar and Martinez. And those self-important soldiers. They had something going on all along, did they not? But what was it? And why were we so far from shore when they released us from our cabins? Oh, I should have never listened to you and helped with the repairs. I could be at La Posada right now without a care in the world."

"Rios, shut up or I will shut you up. And stop that infernal pacing! You are driving me mad. The answers you seek are in the questions you ask, if you just think about them. De Cuellar stole something, something very important and was fleeing with us drunkards still on board."

"Stole something? What did he steal?" asked Rios, finally taking a seat opposite Rodrigo.

"I have my suspicions, but better that I do not tell you, lest it compromise your innocence. It is just a supposition, and I am probably wrong."

"But I *am* innocent, as are you. We can prove that by ignorance alone.

"You, at least, are ignorant of the fact that I asked you to be quiet." With a sigh, he continued, "I do not know what awaits us. It is clear we are guilty by association, but if we maintain our innocence and give only the truth when asked, then we are closer to vindication."

The tranquility Rodrigo sought was granted for a time as they both sat in silence. Outside, the sound of soldiers in the plaza came through clearly but not loud enough to disturb the pair. Rodrigo was beginning to nod off when the door to their room was suddenly opened.

Two soldiers entered with plates of food which they set on the table. It was a meager meal of watery maize porridge and beans, a meal not different than was provided slaves at the mine, and a meal that was very familiar to Rios and Rodrigo during their interment. Rodrigo sniffed the air in disgust and, hungry as he was, made no move toward the food. The soldiers noticed this and laughed to each other.

"Eat up, boys," one of them said, "You will need your energy tonight when you face Captain Salazar and meet your fate. He has interrogated several of your friends and not one has come out again without chains and a look of doom on their faces."

"I would prefer that over this miserable gruel," said Rodrigo.

"You are lucky to have even that," replied the soldier. "If it were put to me, all you pirates would already be swinging from trees, like monkeys unable to tell their heads from their tails."

"Very much like you with your head and your ass."

The soldier went from laughing to sneering in an instant, landing a blow on the back of Rodrigo's head with as much force as he could muster.

"I will remember this moment when the rope is about your neck, then I will laugh as your face turns purple." With that the soldiers left, slamming the door behind them.

Rodrigo glared at the closed door, then turned to Rios. Sensing the man was about to say something, Rodrigo said sternly, "Do. Not. Say. A. Word."

Sooner than expected, the door was thrown open again. It was the same two soldiers, but this time they carried chains and shackles instead of food. They took Rios and bound him, marching him out of the room. Rodrigo watched this impassively, banking his ire for a hoped-for future where an opportunity for redress for his friend and himself might present itself.

Hours went by. The sun set and Rodrigo was left in darkness with only his thoughts as company. Rios had not been returned and Rodrigo was beginning to feel some concern regarding the fellow's fate. Resigning himself to providence, he threw himself on the floor and tried to sleep. *What more can I do but worry? Only time will provide the final answer.*

He had just begun to drift when the door was once again rudely and noisily opened. Soldiers again, but they were not returning with Rios. Instead, the chains they bore were empty, ready for another to fill their void.

"Get up, you fat oaf!" said the soldier. "It is your turn now to pay for your crimes!"

* * *

"I must warn you. Yours is the last in a long line of interminable interviews I have conducted today. I am weary and my patience is nonexistent. Any half-truths or duplicity from you will not go unnoticed or unpunished. I have heard everything I need to hear from your compatriots to have garnered a full understanding of the events leading up to the capture of the *Santa Estrella* and the offenses against the people of Santa Maria del Oro as well as the Crown. Anything you say will be considered truth only by me.

This is not a trial or tribunal and, as such, you are afforded no rights or considerations at this time. In any event, at the end of this discussion you will be taken back to the *Santa Victoria* and transported to Valdivia. Whether that will be as a prisoner confined below decks or as a member of the crew is entirely for you to decide. You will be truthful. I will not accept less. Do you understand?"

Rodrigo stood before Salazar, still encumbered by his shackles, his defiant manner subdued in the presence of authority.

"Yes, Captain Salazar. I understand," he said, bowing his head.

"Very well then. Let is begin. What is your name?"

"Rodrigo Silva. Yes, I know that is a Portuguese name, but I want to hereby state that my upbringing and loyalty to the Crown is unclouded by my heritage and I live my life in service to Spain and the Empire."

"I will take that into consideration as it seems that is a stance you need to take often, but from now on, please only answer the questions in a concise manner. Now, what was your role upon the *Santa Estrella*?"

"I had no established role on that ship other than to conduct certain repairs under the instruction of Captain de Cuellar."

"And before that you served with him on the *San Felipe y Santiago* which unfortunately ran aground some time ago stranding you here. I am well acquainted with the details of that event, so you may discount that in your attestation. What was your role on the *San Felipe y Santiago?*"

"Pilot, Sir, although on our last voyage, I was made to assume some of the duties of First Officer."

"Why is that?"

"Our First Officer was let off at Perico, I do not know the reasoning behind that. We were to take on his replacement at Callao."

"Now to the present. What know you of the contents of the hold on the caravel?"

"At the time, Captain, nothing, although I now have a good suspicion of what it is you found."

"Oh? And what might that be?" asked Salazar with sudden interest.

"Ingots of gold and silver," replied Rodrigo quietly.

"You realize, Pilot, that your knowledge of the seized contraband puts you in the same category as the conspirators, yet you say you only know of it now. Explain yourself."

"As I related, Captain de Cuellar enlisted me to effect some repairs on the *Santa Estrella*, yet I became puzzled when he ordered me to see to the restorations of the ship's deck guns. If the vessel was to be only his residence, then the repairs made sense. Restoring the guns did not. Yet I did as I was told and the guns were repaired."

"I do not see how this relates to your knowledge of the cargo."

"If I may, Captain. The night before our capture, I was involved in a conversation with don Juan Yllescas. It was he who told me of the mine and the ingots stored by the waterfront, saying it was no great mystery as it was common knowledge in the town. Apparently, Captain de Cuellar knew of it as well, but it was not until my confinement, when I had time to reflect, that his concern over the guns was made clear. He needed to protect his ill-gotten cargo. Up until now, I had not put two and two together."

"Did you assist in the loading of the cargo?"

"No, Captain, I did not. I was unaware such a transfer took place."

"How can that be? You were aboard the vessel."

Rodrigo bowed his head further and mumbled a barely audible reply.

"What was that, Pilot? Speak up!"

Rodrigo raised his head and looked at the Captain shamefully, his eyes brimming with moisture.

"I was in my cabin. Drunk and insensate to the world." He shook his head to clear his eyes and added, "I thought the Captain was being free with his wine to celebrate the completion of repairs and we indulged heartily. As a result, I saw and heard nothing."

"And when you say 'we', to whom do you refer?"

Rodrigo thought for a moment, then a look of realization came upon him.

"Why, just the repair crew!"

"None of the soldiers or officers?"

"No. It was Rios, Serrano, myself and some others, but all of us were involved in repairs." Rodrigo chuckled to himself then. "The old fox got us drunk to keep us out of the way. So much for 'a job well done', eh?"

"Thank you, Pilot Silva. I have everything I need." Salazar gestured to the soldier at the door. "Take this man to the *Santa Victoria*. Release him from his chains and assign him to the Boatswain as a crew member." Turning back to Rodrigo, he said, "Welcome to the *Santa Victoria*."

Shortly after Rodrigo was led away, Salazar blew out the candles and left the office. It was time to quench his hunger and get some much needed rest.

It had been a day that had taxed the usually indefatigable Captain to the utmost. As he exited the administrative building, he was unexpectedly accosted by don Alonso.

"Captain! I see that you have concluded your business for the day. Are you returning to the ship?"

Salazar turned to face him, intentionally feigning more fatigue than he actually felt. "My men have erected a tent for me in the square. I intend to grab a bit of sustenance and then some sleep."

"Nonsense!" exclaimed Yllescas. "A fine man such as yourself should not be relegated to sleeping on the ground. I insist you come with me to my home. A fine feast awaits as well as a soft bed to ease your bones."

"I thank you, don Alonso, but I am unused to such exuberance. I am more accustomed to a simpler solution to my needs."

"I will not accept that as reason enough to decline my offer. Come! The household awaits. I promise you will not be inconvenienced overlong and we will get you to your bed as soon as possible."

Salazar sighed and accepted his defeat, turning his feet to follow don Alonso.

"Tell me, did you offer such hospitality to Captain de Cuellar?"

"To a degree. He is not as convivial as you, and in hindsight, I am glad not to have overly wasted such efforts on him. In any case, he did not swoop in from nowhere and save me from a crushing humiliation, rather he was the cause of it. I owe you much, Captain. Thank you for allowing me to convey my gratitude in such a small way."

"Señor, I merely conduct my duties as required. I do not expect, or want, any compensation for my actions."

"Well, at least I did not invite you for drinks at the tavern. This will be a much more subdued event as befits a man of your standing. Ah! Here we are."

As promised, the meal was a restrained affair that did not intrude much on Salazar's sensibilities. Afterwards, he allowed himself to be led into Yllescas' study for a cigar before bed.

"Are you sure I cannot entice you with a drink? It need not be wine, a hot cup of chicha perhaps?"

"Again, thank you, but no. I am breaking my own rules in partaking in this cigar with you. I rarely smoke, but I must admit this is one of the better cigars I have had."

"I take great pride in telling you that the leaves are grown right here in Santa Maria and I take even greater pride in your appreciation of it."

"As well you should, don Alonso. It was gold and silver that put you on the Imperial maps, but it seems a greater treasure was overlooked for a long time. These will make an exceptional addition to the goods we bear bound for Valdivia."

"I will see to it that a few crates make their way to your hold." Yllescas took a moment to pull on his cigar and then said, "How long will you be in Santa Maria, Captain?"

"Not long. Tomorrow we will begin transferring the contents of the *Santa Estrella* to the *Santa Victoria* and I will overseeing the implementation of some of the infrastructure needed if Santa Maria is to be a productive hub along our root. For instance, the waterfront must be reconfigured to accept larger vessels like my ship, and the construction of barracks and such to accommodate soldiers and passengers from such vessels when they are in port. All in all, perhaps two days before we raise anchor, but you can expect our return in a few months."

"I do not know that all of that will be completed before your return. Our resources and manpower are meager at best."

"Oh, it need not be all completed in that time frame, yet these things must be done. I have already given much thought to the task at hand. We carry a contingent of African slaves and I will provide you with a good portion of them to act as your workforce. I am also deploying a number of soldiers, two squads to be exact. One to the mines for additional security and one here in town to maintain order. I realize this will put a strain on your resources, but judging from what I have seen of your farmlands, perhaps it will not be so bad. In any event, you will be supplemented on our return journey."

"I am sure it will not come cheaply."

"Don Alonso, you are already paying your tithe in precious minerals, and the Empire is making a substantial investment in Santa Maria to assure that it remains so. Your standard of living, as well as everyone in town, will increase tenfold. In a few years, Santa Maria will be markedly different from what you have now. On that, you have my word."

Chapter Twenty Seven

Field Note: May 15, 1973
Site: Santa Maria Mine

Today's examination of the Santa Maria mine revealed fascinating insights into the brutal and exploitative nature of 16th-century colonial mining operations. The mine itself, situated on a steep hillside some miles outside the main settlement, shows clear signs of prolonged use, with tunnels carved deep into the rock, supported by deteriorating wooden beams. These beams, cut from native hardwoods, speak to the engineering acumen of the period but also highlight the environmental toll such operations inflicted on the local ecosystem.

The conditions faced by workers were abhorrent. The presence of crude ventilation shafts and poorly constructed drainage systems implies that the miners worked in stifling, wet environments. Artifacts found near the entrance, broken tools, fragments of ceramic water jars, and remnants of coarse textiles, suggest the harsh reality of life for the enslaved individuals forced into this labor.

Of particular interest is a carved wooden tablet bearing inscriptions that appear to document production yields. This may provide critical data on the economic impact of the mine. However, one haunting detail remains: evidence of a collapse, likely fatal for those trapped within. Skeletal remains found near the entrance, hastily buried, indicate the lack of value placed on the lives of these laborers.

The mine serves as a grim reminder of the intersections of greed, exploitation, and human suffering during the colonial era. It is essential to preserve and study such sites to ensure that the stories of those who endured such hardships are not forgotten.

Dr. Elena Ramirez

Pedro strained against the rope harness with all his might, but his exertions were for naught. The ore cart, laden to the brim with ore, refused to budge. This was a task usually reserved for mules, but the overseer, Severino Almagro, relished in the thought of presenting Pedro with an impossible task.

"Pull, you miserable son of a whore!" shouted Almagro. "You are very lucky that your dear papa is still in the camp else I would flay the flesh from your back! Once he leaves, you will feel the full might of my lash if you fail in your tasks. Pull, I tell you!"

Finally, Pedro could take no more and he collapsed into heap in front of the immovable cart. Almagro, with a sadistic grin on his face, signaled to a nearby slave.

"Get him out of there. Get him on his feet and give him a shovel. If he cannot pull, he will dig. And if he falls again, I will see to it he never gets up again."

To Almagro, Pedro was a gift brought to him by God. The scion of one of the poorest families in Santa Maria, he had long resented the so-called Nobility of Santa Maria who strutted around with their noses in the air because they could claim some small percentage of Spanish blood. But they were all a mixed breed. Every resident of the town, apart from the slaves, had some measure of Spanish blood distilled into their bodies, yet Almagro's father and family had toiled in the fields, growing food for the aristocrats, while they themselves often went hungry. Now Almagro had been given the chance to vent his long brewing anger and he planned to enjoy himself immensely. He was going to be Pedro's personal devil.

Pedro, newly revived and teetering on his feet, had a shovel thrust into his hands which he looked at with a stunned look. Almagro grabbed Pedro by the shoulders and spun him around. With a forceful boot to his backside, he thrust Pedro toward a pile of rubble.

"If you cannot pull the cart, then fill it!" as Pedro sprawled once more onto the dirt. "Get up and get to work, boy! You're no nobleman here. Here, you are dirt. Less than dirt. You think your *noble* blood makes you better? It will be the same color as the rest of these slaves when it is dripping into the ground. If you're too soft to pull a cart, you will shovel rubble until your arms fall off."

Almagro leaned in closer, his voice dripping with venom. "And let me make one thing clear, Pedro de Arobe. There is no mercy here. Not from me. I will decide if you will eat, sleep, rest or shit, if you have earned it. And if you think you can do as you please, you will find my whip has a long reach. Now move!"

Almagro was known for his cruelty and his ability to produce results, not for his oratory skills. He was a man of few words, using them only to bark orders, yet he felt strangely prideful of his diatribe toward Pedro. *Perhaps I have touch of nobility within myself after all!*

Not far away, Ignacio and don Francisco viewed the activity in the camp. Disgusted by what he saw, Ignacio said, "This place is an altar to the worst of human desires, a monument to avarice and the lust for power. The earth is torn asunder, not for sustenance or survival, but for greed, and the cost is paid in the suffering of souls. Look at them, don Francisco, beaten down, not by the work itself, but by the cruelty that feeds on them like a parasite. There is no dignity here, no semblance of humanity. These men who sponsor this camp do not seek to enrich lives or better the world; they seek only to feed their insatiable hunger for gold. This camp, this entire endeavor, reeks of sin, and the weight of it will drag us all into darkness if we do not stand against it." His voice softened as he looked away, the fire in his eyes giving way to sorrow. "How far we have fallen to allow such iniquity to thrive in the name of progress."

Yllescas, who was within earshot, interjected.

"Yet you wear around your own neck a crucifix made of gold, as well as many of the trappings of your priesthood which are made of things dug from the earth. Where do you think it all comes from if not from places such as these? You speak of sin and darkness, Father, yet you wear its fruits on your very body. That crucifix, those robes, the holy vessels in your church. How do you think they came to be? From the toil of hands just like those you pity, from places just like this. The gold and silver you decry fund the very missions you preach from. It is easy to condemn the greed of others while reaping the benefits of their labor."

Yllescas sighed deeply, realizing that, while he himself was distraught by the conditions of the camp, he felt compelled to defend its use. "Do not speak to me of cruelty when your faith itself depends on the work of these mines. If this place is a monument to avarice, then the altars of your churches are no less complicit. Tell me, Father, will you cast aside your golden relics and call them unworthy of God?"

Ignacio had no reply. The truth of it was before him. It was easy to not give a thought to where things came from, whether it be the food on your table, the wine in your cup or the sandals on your feet, someone, somewhere made them for someone else's benefit, and not always because they wanted to. While Ignacio processed these thoughts, don Francisco, his voice steady and resolute, stepped forward to address Yllescas.

"That is true enough, don Alonso," he began, "the fruits of labor, be they honest or cruel, often reach hands that neither see nor question their origins. But do not lay the burden of every injustice at this man's feet," he said nodded toward Ignacio. "He may wear a crucifix of gold, but he does so to serve a calling higher than material wealth. His life is not one of indulgence or luxury; it is one of sacrifice and service. He cannot undo the sins of this world, but he can speak to its conscience, as he does now."

Don Francisco gestured broadly at the mine. "If we are to condemn those who benefit indirectly, then let us all stand guilty. For who here wears no cloth that others have sewn, eats no bread that others have baked? The question is not what we take, but what we do to make the taking just."

Settling his gaze on Yllescas, he added, "Blame does not absolve blame, don Juan. If you would criticize the priest, then also reckon with your own role. For every man here, noble or not, contributes to the conditions you see before you. But let us not deflect from the truth, there is nothing moral about this place. It is built on greed, yes, but also on the backs of men who have been robbed of their humanity. That is the true sin."

"I am not defending anything don Francisco," replied Yllescas, "and my apologies to you, Father Ignacio, if my words have stung you inadvertently. I am as stricken by this as much as you are. Yet, here is a fact of life, and it would do us well to recognize the hypocrisy inherent in our world."

Ignacio inclined his head slightly, a gesture of humility as he absorbed Yllescas' words. "Don Juan," he began gently, "your apology is not necessary, although I appreciate it. The truth of your statement cannot be denied. Hypocrisy weaves itself through the fabric of our lives, as much a part of us as our breath. Yet, it is in recognizing this that we have a chance to change, to do better."

He clasped his hands together, his tone softening further. "I do not pretend to be free from guilt, nor do I claim my calling exempts me from the stains of the world. But I believe, however small, that each step toward compassion and justice, each word spoken to challenge cruelty, can ripple outward. Even if our efforts are flawed, they are not meaningless. We are both stricken by this place, but perhaps being stricken is a beginning. If we do not lose sight of the human faces amid the stone and gold, then there may still be hope for redemption, however distant it seems."

"Well said, Father," replied Yllescas. "It seems we are like in mind, if not in experience. I have lived my entire life in Santa Maria and under the shadow of the mine. I am accustomed to this and our arrival here did not shock me as much as you who are seeing it with fresh eyes. Yet that familiarity does not dull its brutality. It only makes it harder to imagine life without it. This is the reality we inherit, and though it sickens me, I have not the luxury to look away. But perhaps your fresh eyes see what we cannot, or choose not to. Perhaps you and others like you can remind us that this does not have to be our fate forever." He turned and started to walk away. "I think it is time we take our leave of this place."

Those were not the only eyes watching the scene. Surrounded by dense foliage, Wajari and Pinchu crouched unseen, developing tactics for their impending raid.

"Look at them, Pinchu. They are no different than the peccaries, scrabbling in the dirt for more and more morsels to ease their never-ending hunger. At least the peccaries dig for themselves and do not enslave others to do the work for them. They have no regard for the spirits of this land, digging here and there, felling trees that have stood since time began and carry the spirits of our ancestors. The sooner we drive these demons from our land, the better it will be for all."

"Time is growing short, Wajari," whispered Pinchu. "That ship that arrived yesterday carries more of their foul kind. More hungry mouths to fill from the labors of the oppressed. If we do not act soon they will send many soldiers to protect their precious feast and then what will we do against them? We will be pushed back further into the forest."

Almost as if it had been orchestrated, a group of men suddenly appeared at the end of the road leading into the camp. Six of them wore metal skins which clanked as they moves and sparkled like waves on the river. In their midst was another man, not a soldier but clearly someone they were protecting.

"See! I told you we have waited too long," said Pinchu. "Already they send armed men. An attack from our clan's warrior will not be enough."

"I am not afraid of six men who can barely walk with all the rattling shells on their bodies. They are like birds strutting with shiny feathers, making them slow and heavy, stiff as broken branches. Their feathers may shine, but they will not save them from a true warrior's spear." Wajari stared more intently at the group.

"Who is the little fat man? Is he their chief?"

"I do not know, and it does not matter. We cannot accomplish the raid on our own. We need more warriors than just the slaves we set free."

"Look at him!" exclaimed Wajari, apparently ignoring Pinchu. "He goes straight for the gold without talking to anyone else. It is all he cares about! Ha! I will call him Gold-Chief." Wajari rose from his crouch. "You are right, Pinchu, things have changed. We must meet with the other clans at the island in the Forked River. Come, let us send out the word."

Unlike the others toiling near him, Bahati knew where to look and he saw the warriors hiding in the nearby jungle. He gave no sign that he had seen them and continued at his work unabated, but his mind began to fill with questions that he had no way of asking but to himself. *When will the signal be given? When can we shed ourselves of the shackles that bind us?* He was distracted from his musings when he heard a sudden clatter. He looked to see what it was and his heart fell into his bowels. The sight of the soldiers rooted him to the spot, his shovel frozen mid-arc. *All is lost! There will never be an uprising now.*

"What are you gawking at?" said a nearby overseer. "This is not a pageant for your amusement! Get back to your work lest you prefer the lash!"

Luján was exhausted from the trek up the mining road from Santa Maria, but the sight of the mine and its product re-invigorated him, making him feel like a child at Christmas. The first thing that drew his eye were the piles of raw ore and neatly stacked gold and silver ingots being made ready for transport. Their glitter was a powerful visceral delight to his senses. He had assumed that the cache found in de Cuellar's possession had been the product of many years of production, yet here was a trove nearly as large in a timescale of months rather than years.

Yet he was oblivious to the constant movement of the slaves hauling carts, smelting ore, and pouring molten metal. All he saw was the end product. He was, of course, obligated to inspect the smelters and forges, to verify the purity of the ore, but for the moment he allowed himself to be enthralled by the wealth that surrounded him.

"You there!" came a sudden voice that shocked Luján out of his reverie. "Who are you and what are you doing here?" He turned and saw the mountain of a man that was Almagro. Luján adjusted his composure, brushing off the dust of the road and meeting Almagro's imposing figure with a steady gaze.

"I am don Domingo Luján, the appointed assessor of His Majesty's treasury," he said, his voice tinged with both pride and irritation at the rough welcome. "I have been sent here to evaluate the quality and quantity of this mine's production, to ensure its proper contribution to the Crown's wealth." He extended a hand, indicating the wealth around them. "This... impressive operation appears to be producing extraordinary results. I trust you will provide me with the information I need to perform my duties efficiently, as I will need full access to every stage of production."

"We already have assessor," growled Almagro. "It is to him than you should direct your attentions. You show up here unexpected and unannounced, with armed men, no less! Go to the forge for the man you seek and stay out of my way. I have much to do without prostrating myself to the likes of you!"

Ignacio, Yllescas and the de Arobes followed the new arrivals at a discreet distance. They had been preparing to leave the camp when Luján and his men appeared. Curious, they wanted to find the meaning behind the sudden materialization of Spanish troops in the camp.

"It is most odd," said Yllescas. "There have never been soldiers, actual Imperial soldiers, here before. The Governor must have arrived while we have been away, but usually there are heralds announcing an imminent arrival from Quito. Why would the mine now be fortified?"

"There are many questions here to be asked," replied Ignacio, "but surely the Governor's arrival is the simplest answer. Perhaps we can ask our questions of one of the soldiers once we catch up to them." They watched as Luján had his brief encounter with Almagro and then stomp off, leaving the soldiers watching him go.

"Good soldiers," called Yllescas as they approached the knot of armored men, "Who among you can tell us how you have come to be here. I am don Juan Yllescas, noble of Santa Maria, from which you have undoubtedly just come. Has the Governor arrived?"

"Greetings, Señor," said one of the men. "I am Sergeant Vargas. I and my men were assigned to escort the Court's assessor to this mine...that man who just walked away. We arrived yesterday on the *Santa Victoria*, a galleon out of Puerto de Guayaquil. I know not of the Governor but can assure you that he is not with us."

"A galleon, you say? That is passing strange. Santa Maria is far from the shipping lanes. What brought you here?"

"I am not privy to such orders, Señor," replied Vargas. "Your inquiries would be better handled by our captain, Captain Salazar. But if I were to guess, I would say that this mine has much to do with our arrival here. That and the capture of a vessel laden with gold that was fleeing your town."

"What! Someone was stealing our gold? We have never been attacked by pirates! I doubt they know of our existence."

"Again, I cannot speak to that. All I know is that it was a small vessel, a caravel with the name *Santa Estrella* painted on its stern. The ship was captured and all aboard arrested. Your gold is probably even now being loaded into the *Santa Victoria's* hold."

"My boat!" Yllescas exclaimed. "This has de Cuellar's fingers all over it, I warrant. We must return to Santa Maria quickly. Come gentlemen, it is time to go. Thank you, Sergeant." Yllescas took off at a trot, leaving Ignacio and the de Arobes running to keep up.

"I am sure everything is safe now," said Ignacio. "Whatever de Cuellar was attempting has been thwarted, at least according to the Sergeant."

"Yes, he said much while claiming to know nothing at all. I will not rest until I know the whole of it. After years of peace, we are suddenly beleaguered by theft, murder and an armed invasion. We were better off before you people emerged from the jungle!"

"I know you speak out of anger and frustration, the sheer ignorance of what has transpired, but you cannot lay the blame of it at our feet. The gold and your production of it are the root cause. Something like this was bound to happen given enough time."

"Already, I regret my words, Father, but suddenly everything is spinning out of control. I can already see that the idyllic Santa Maria that I love will change overnight and, not seemingly, for the better."

"If I may say something," said don Francisco. "Señor Yllescas, change is inevitable, especially when wealth of this magnitude is involved. However, it is not the gold itself that brings ruin, but the greed and power it incites in men's hearts. Santa Maria may indeed face transformations, but it is within our power to guide that change for good. You are a man of influence here, and if you take a stand with wisdom and justice, the soul of Santa Maria need not be lost to these recent troubles." He turned to Ignacio and added, "Father Ignacio, your guidance and faith can help temper the passions of the people and remind them of higher virtues. Together, you both hold the means to preserve the spirit of this town."

"Although I acknowledge your sentiment, don Francisco," replied Ignacio, "what you have just described may be an insurmountable task. More people will be flooding into Santa Maria. More people with more voices, some of them with authority behind them. More voices does not mean more consensus. You yourself, as a nobleman, stand poised to benefit from this transformation. When the time comes, will you turn your back?"

"My son, who we have left behind, is a slave. I am forever tied to the lowest echelon of society. I, for one, will only look to the immediate future, when my son is returned to me. All this talk is hypothetical. We cannot know the future until we can look back from that very future. Let us learn what we can, of the present, yet be mindful of its meaning."

Like a kettle, whose lid is removed to release steam, the foursome allowed their own thoughts to simmer quietly. They walked along the road at a much less frantic pace but swiftly nonetheless. Several long minutes passed, until Domingo, who had been silent throughout the heated exchange suddenly piped up.

"Already I miss him."

Chapter Twenty Eight

Long ago, when the Earth was young, the rivers had no path, and the water roamed freely across the land. The spirit Nunkui, guardian of the Earth, wished to give the people a place of unity. She struck the ground at the fork of two mighty rivers, and from the clash of water and stone rose Kuntui, a verdant island surrounded by flowing waters.

Kuntui was a gift to the Shuar. It was said that the trees on the island could hear the voices of those who walked beneath their canopy, carrying their words to the spirits above. When two clans quarreled, they were to meet on Kuntui to speak their truths, for on the island, deception turned to silence, and only the honest could be heard.

The Place of Voices, Shuar legend

Bahati was puzzled over the newest addition to the team of slaves. He was clearly not African and he was clearly unused to any kind of physical labor. Moreover, he seemed to be a target of malice from the overseers, who went out of their way to inflict as much pain and humiliation as they could without actually whipping him. Bahati stole glances at him whenever he could, feeling sympathy toward him with each insult and punishment that came his way. The life of a slave was not easy, but every slave knew how to *be* a slave. Knowing your place was the surest way of survival. Keep your head down, keep your mouth shut, do as you are told and you will avoid the harshest of treatments. It seemed to Bahati that the youth would be dead before he learned any of those lessons.

Toward the end of the work day, the overseers, most notably the brute Almagro, changed their tactics toward the youth. They began kicking and punching the boy for the slightest perceived infraction and those actions were followed most often with a sting from the lash. By the time the evening bell rang, the boy seemed near death, and as the camp was cleared, he was left lying in the dirt, near naked and bleeding. None of the slaves, Bahati included, were willing to jeopardize their own well-being by offering help and so the youth was left to suffer on his own.

After the evening meal, Bahati sought out Obadele and pulled him aside.

"It is not good to talk about this," said Obadele preemptively. "Our revenge on these bastards may never happen. I too, saw them peering at us from the trees but no signal was given."

"No, not that. The time will come or it will not. No, tell me of the overseers. You have a better ear for the vulgar language they speak. Have they spoken of the boy thrust into our midst?"

"Ah yes, the boy. Most of what I heard was directed at him and more vile and depraved than anything they say to us. Clearly they bear some resentment toward him." Obadele looked around to make sure there were no eavesdroppers, then leaned toward Bahati and said in conspiratorial tone, "I did hear a conversation between bosses. Apparently, the boy is some kind of criminal. He is to be here for a year as punishment for his crime."

"He was barely able to survive a day. He will never survive a year. Do you know anything of his crime?"

"No, but you know me. I keep my ears open while my hands are busy. I will learn more soon enough, but it must have been a crime so monstrous that they would send one of their own here to suffer at the hands of Almagro."

"They could have just put him to death."

"The laws and morals of the whites are incomprehensible. They use them arbitrarily depending who is affected. For us, the laws are clear, but the worst offense we may commit might be nothing more than a mild insult between whites, while to you and me, it might mean death."

"So his crime then, is somewhere between monstrous and insulting. Let me know if you hear anything else, but there is nothing to be done for him. We have our own lives to think of." Bahati jerked his head up as he heard footsteps approaching. He hissed at Obadele, "Quiet now. The overseers!"

Two of them came, dragging Pedro between them. The boy was bruised and covered with welts, a thin line of drool hanging from his lips. The overseers dumped him at Bahati and Obadele's feet and gave him a kick for good measure.

"Feed him, water him, get him ready to work at first light. If he dies, bury him but that had better be the only reason he is not working at first light." Laughing, the two bosses walked away into the darkness.

"And now his problem has become ours," said Bahati. "That may be us laying on the dirt tomorrow if we do not at least get him on his feet."

They wrestled Pedro onto a cot, propping him up into a sitting position, although his head wobbled limply and his body threatened to collapse.

"Do not let him lie down," said Bahati. "He needs water above all and we cannot risk him drowning." Pedro looked at them through bloodshot eyes that had no focus. He mumbled something incoherently through his blistered lips.

"Go and fetch water, plenty of it." said Obadele, holding Pedro upright. "We need to cleanse his wounds and lower the heat of his flesh. Oh, and chicha. Perhaps it will clear his confusion."

When Bahati returned, they did their best to clean Pedro's skin and forced water down his throat. After a while Pedro seemed to come to some of his senses. He was now able to hold himself up without support. He abruptly put his face in his hands and began sobbing.

"I am sorry...I am so sorry."

"What is he saying?" asked Bahati.

"He is sorry for something, but I do not know what. Get some of that chicha in him."

They pried Pedro's hands away from his face and forced the crude cup to his lips. At first he sputtered, but then took the cup from Bahati and drained it hungrily. His eyes were still unfocused, his stare distant, but he already seemed better. Suddenly the sobs racked his body again.

"I didn't mean... I didn't know it would be like this..." His voice cracked as he gasped for breath between sobs. "Please, forgive me... Forgive me, Father... I failed, I failed everyone..." He rocked slightly, his trembling hands clutching at his dirt-streaked face. "She is gone... gone because of me... I can still hear her screaming... Don't leave me here... Please, God, not here..."

Pedro's words became a mixture of frantic whispers and incoherent cries, his eyes wide and haunted as if reliving something terrible. Bahati exchanged a look with Obadele, their expressions grim.

"He is rambling," said Obadele. "Nothing he says makes much sense other than..."

"Other than what? What does he speak of?"

"Mostly he is begging for forgiveness, probably of the crime he committed."

"She... she screamed, but it did not matter," Pedro muttered through cracked lips, his gaze unfocused. "Amina... just a slave... nothing. They do not count, do they? They are nothing, nothing at all..." He shook his head violently, his voice trembling. "She would not stop... would not listen... had to make her stop... but it was not wrong! It was not wrong, was it? She was nothing... worthless... worthless..." His voice broke into a choked sob, the words tumbling out with increasing desperation. "It does not matter, it does not matter! Why should it? No one cared... no one ever cares..."

"Obadele," gasped Bahati, "I grasp little of what he says, but Amina comes from his lips. Did he hurt her in some way? Is that his crime?"

"Bahati, I think it is best if you step away. I will tend to him. Right now his mind is untethered from his body. I doubt even *he* knows what he is saying. Yes, he speaks of Amina but I do not know why. I will tell you all when I can, but for now our task is clear; to get this one somewhat ready for the morning. If he falls then, we will be blameless."

"If he did anything..."

"Go, my friend. Have someone take your place and get your rest."

Bahati stepped back, glaring hard at Pedro, then turned away.

Monstrous or an insult?

Obadele watched his friend walk away. He regretted treating him that way, but his first concern was getting the boy out of his care and back in the hands of the overseers. For his own safety, and Bahati's, he could not have Bahati jump to a conclusion that might harm all of them. He remembered Amina, of course, and had become quite fond of her as had all the men in the camp. He had felt some small jealousy when she and Bahati had become intimate, but had learned to deal with it. He too had grieved when Amina was taken from the camp, but when it comes to slaves, he realized it would be a good thing for the girl. Serving as a household slave was worlds better than life in the camp.

He looked at his charge and wondered what could have happened to bring him so low. If he had indeed hurt Amina...well, that was a concern for another time. Pedro had calmed down quite a bit and his breathing was calm and regular.

Obadele took a risk and asked him, "What is your name?"

"Pedro de Arobe," he replied mechanically.

"Pedro, my name is Obadele. You have been placed in my care. How are you feeling?"

"Hurts...all over. And I am tired...so tired."

"Yes, I can see that. Pedro, why are you here? Why have you been sent to us?"

"I am being punished...something not even a crime. I am sorry she died, but she was property, you know?"

"You speak of Amina?"

"That was her name. She should have been grateful. I am the son of a nobleman. I would have bought her had I the money." Pedro closed his eyes and said, "I am so tired. Please let me sleep." Obadele helped him lie down and, for the first time, Pedro looked at him directly and mouthed 'Thank you' before drifting off to a sleep that was not the product of a beating, but a natural repose.

Obadele looked at Pedro with sadness. Not for the boy's plight, but for the fate that surely awaited him. *I am not sure he does not deserve it, but who am I to say?* Then his thoughts went to Bahati. He would have to lie to his friend and keep the knowledge of the boy's crime to himself. At least until the inevitable happened. He took one last look at Pedro's face.

You will be alright, at least for now. Tomorrow will be a different story, perhaps with a terrible ending, but alright for now. You had better hope the bosses kill you before Bahati does.

* * *

The four men walked along the road in silence. Their squabble at the beginning at of the trip home had set the tone and now they were all locked in their own heads with their own thoughts. Ignacio, in particular, was deeply troubled. It seemed that at every turn there was something to challenge, and even shake, his faith. Pedro, the slaves at the mine, the mysterious Tsewa and even dear, sweet Rosa burdened his soul with doubt.

Lord, I have followed Your commandments, and I have worn my faith like armor. But where is Your justice now? I see suffering all around me...the innocent crushed beneath the weight of greed and cruelty. I watch as people suffer, and I wonder, do You even care? How can You allow such things to happen? How can You let a boy like Pedro, so young and misguided, fall so far? And Amina, her life snuffed out as if she were nothing but a shadow. What are we to do when the world You created seems so broken?

I have loved, Lord. I have loved with all my heart, and yet I am lost. You tell me to turn the other cheek, but what good is it when the world itself slaps us at every turn? You tell me to trust, but in what, exactly? Where is Your guidance when all I see are contradictions and pain?

I feel Your silence more than Your presence, and the weight of my own doubts presses heavier on me than any burden of sin. If You are truly all-powerful, then where is Your intervention? Where is Your mercy? Show me, Lord, because I cannot see it. I cannot feel it anymore. Are You even listening?

Lord, You know my heart...how it is torn between the love I feel for You and the love I feel for Rosa. But I wonder, Lord, is this love I feel a gift from You, or is it a snare? I have vowed to serve You, and yet my heart pulls me in a different direction. Is it right to love someone so, to desire someone who is not meant for me? She is of a different world, a different station, her heart should not be for me, and yet I am consumed by thoughts of her.

What will become of me, Lord, if I allow this love to grow unchecked? How can I be Your servant when I cannot even control the desires of my own heart? How can I be a man of faith when every day I am drawn to something I cannot have? I fear, Lord, that I may fall further into temptation, that my love for her may blind me to You, to Your purpose in my life.

And what if I fail her, too? What if this love is nothing more than foolishness, a fleeting desire that will only end in pain and regret? Should I not love You above all else? Yet, my heart betrays me.

Do You hear me, Lord? Do You see the conflict that tears at my soul? I fear I am losing my way, not just with You, but with everything. My love for her... my uncertainty... it all feels like a storm, swirling around me, threatening to drown me.

Help me, Lord, for I am lost.

The road finally came to an end and they entered Santa Maria. Everyone had said what they needed to say and so they went their separate ways with nothing more than a nod and a word of parting.

Ignacio took in the new sights of the town, the galleon at rest offshore, the city of tents that had sprung up in the square, the doubling of people milling about. Soldiers and slaves as well as locals. He looked about as he made his way back to his own abode. He had seen no sign of Rosa and he was not sure whether he was relieved or anxious about it. She had seemed so stressed about his leaving that he was sure she would be awaiting his return, but of course, she had no idea when that would be. Knowing her, she probably waited at the rectory and the thought made Ignacio frown. He was not ready to confront the day's events again, as he would have to, no doubt, recount the details of his journey to Rosa. She was unrelenting to say the least.

Reaching his door, he braced himself, expecting to be greeted by her. Instead, as he stepped within, he saw nothing. There was a sudden sting at his neck and before he could react, the nothingness became all-encompassing.

* * *

The island was named *Kuntui,* and Wajari was convinced it was the same island from the old tales. *It must have been a long time ago,* he reasoned, as the jungle here was lush and not barren as in the stories told by the elders.

He stepped into the center of the ring next to the Speaking Stone. All around him were members of not only his tribe but those of other clans who had heeded the call to meet.

"Brothers, warriors of the forest, listen to my words. We gather here, under the protection of Kuntui, where our ancestors once stood to decide matters of survival. The stories of this place tell of barren soil, of a scar upon the earth. Yet today, the jungle has reclaimed it. The forest and its people always fight back. This is the lesson of Kuntui. It is a sign, that we too must fight back.

"Too long have we tolerated the outsiders who claim our land their own. Too many times have we stepped back and allowed them to take what they want. Look around you! Their greed as insatiable as the flames they use to burn our lands. They carve into the mountains, they poison our rivers, they enslave the innocent. Now, a ship has arrived, carrying more soldiers, more tools to destroy, more chains to bind.

"This ship, it is the first but it will not be the last. We must ensure they have no reason to return. When this ship is full with all the gold it can carry, it will leave and that is when we will take away their reason for returning. This mine is a wound upon the earth. Its destruction will send a message, not only to those in their village but to all demons who dare to trespass on our lands. Let them know that we are not weak, that we will not stand idle as they strip our forests, desecrate our sacred places, and enslave those who cannot defend themselves.

"I call on each of you! Join me in this fight! For every tree they cut, plant ten more in your heart. For every drop of blood they spill, let it feed the fire of your anger. Together, we will destroy their mine and show them that the clans of the forest are united, strong, and unyielding."

His speech stirred those attending and soon the hubbub of voices filled the glen. Wajari stood impatiently. He had expected his speech to be greeted with approval and not endless discussion. Finally he could control himself no longer.

"This is like dealing with the elders! Where are the warriors?"

At this, a warrior from the clan north of the river stepped into the ring.

"Wajari, your words are powerful, and your heart is fierce, but this is not a fight of equals. These demons from the sea come with weapons we do not understand, shields of iron, and numbers that will grow with every ship. They have beasts that carry them faster than we can run, and their fire can strike from far away. We may destroy the mine, but at what cost? Will our clans be left in ashes?

"Yes, the forest fights back, but it does not fight blindly. It takes its time, grows silently, and overwhelms through patience. What you propose is bold, but is it wise? We must ask ourselves, can we truly drive them away forever, or will this only make them strike harder, take more, and crush us beneath their heel? What does your Uwishin counsel?"

Wajari did not expect such resistance. A sudden bolt of anger surged through his body but he managed to tamp it down before responding.

"Our Uwishin, Tsewa, my own father, counsels that we should run away like scared women and children at the sight of a snake. He cares much for the spirits, but less for the bodies which carry those spirits." With renewed energy, he said forcefully, "Let the mine be a test then. If we cannot rise to destroy this wound upon our land, how will we defend against greater wounds? If we wait, the demons will grow bolder. Their numbers will increase, their chains will multiply, and their greed will devour everything.

Every tree, every river, every child.

"Kuntui teaches us not only patience but also action when the time is right. The jungle does not wait forever to reclaim what is hers. It sends roots to crack stone, vines to choke the invader, storms to wash away what does not belong. This mine, this single place, will show us who we are. If we fail here, they will believe we are weak. They will take our lands, our people, and our future. But if we succeed, it will be a warning they cannot ignore.

"I do not ask for blind sacrifice. I ask for unity, for strength, for courage. The forest is vast, and its people are many. Together, we are stronger than any iron, sharper than any blade. Will you stand with me, or will you wait for their chains to bind us all?"

Those around the ring were mostly silent, with a few muttering here and there. At length, another warrior entered the ring and faced Wajari. He was a large man, even among the warriors. Well respected and revered, he was Shakaim, of the Awaru, and like the Shuar spirit of strength and work, he seemed to embody the physical and spiritual might of the Shuar.

"I know you, Wajari," said Shakaim. "Our clans have had their disagreements in the past, we have fought each other, bloodied each other and taken the heads of the fallen. But I know you Wajari. You speak truth here, how could it be otherwise? The Awaru clan will follow you and help close this wound the demons have inflicted."

Slowly, but with ever-increasing frequency, shouts of acceptance filled the glen. Wajari had won this first fight.

The mine would be destroyed.

Chapter Twenty Nine

There is a time for everything, and a season for every activity under the heavens: a time to be born and a time to die, a time to plant and a time to uproot... a time to search and a time to give up, a time to keep and a time to throw away, a time to tear and a time to mend, a time to be silent and a time to speak.

Ecclesiastes 3:1-2, 6-7

Pedro trembled in fear. He knew today was the day he was going to die. The other slaves knew it too. They kept their distance as they hastily ate their breakfast before the shift began. He was a stranger to them, an unknown quantity, a potential problem if any dared get too close. Pedro was all alone, there was no one here to protect him, only the ones intent on tormenting him. And killing him.

He shuffled, staring at his own feet, as he slowly made his way out to the camp. Every muscle in his body ached, even his bones seemed to scream in agony. When he dared to look up, he saw them. The bosses were waiting for him, their lashes at the ready. Pedro felt his knees buckle, but to his surprise, the overseers took him by the arms and dragged him out of the camp. Were they just going to execute him away from curious eyes?

They took him to the building that served as the foreman's quarters.

Opening the door they thrust him inside into a darkened room. When Pedro's eyes adjusted, he saw that he was not alone. Fear gripped him then as he saw that it was Almagro who waited there, seated in the dark.

"Señor de Arobe! How pleased am I to have you visit," drawled Almagro mockingly. "It trust you had a restful night's sleep? I, myself, slept poorly, consumed by a thought. Yes, a thought. I gather that you may think this is a rare occurrence for me and you are right.

"You are the son of a nobleman, born into leisure, and afforded the education that corresponds to your status. I had none of these things. My education consisted of hard work and beatings when that hard work was lacking. Hardship was my only teacher, my companion and my friend. And yet, I had a thought, an inspiration, you might say. Do you not find that curious?"

Pedro said nothing. He stood, shifting his weight from foot to foot, not daring to look at the big man's face.

"Would you like to hear what it is?"

In a shaky voice, barely above a whisper, Pedro replied, "Yes."

"What was that?"

"Yes please, Señor," he said a little louder.

"Better. Well then, it is my thought to offer you two things. Here is the first: you, as I said, are the son of a nobleman. Perhaps you should be treated as one. You would still have to work, of course, but I could see to it that your tasks are light and you would be safe from beatings and the lash. Better food, longer rest periods and the secure knowledge that you will live out the term of your sentence. All I would ask is that you remember poor Almagro after your release, and afford him the same kindness I am prepared to afford you. A few more coins in my coffers, a line of credit at the tavern...that sort of thing. What do you say?"

Pedro would have laughed if he had the strength. Since the shipwreck, the de Arobes had no wealth on hand to comply with Almagro's demands. That wealth only existed within their own lands and at the moment those lands were far away. The de Arobes enjoyed the status of nobility in Santa Maria only on reputation. They still had to rely on others to provide housing and food. In time, debts would be repaid, but at the moment they were literally penniless.

Pedro was not about to share this information with Almagro, instead he asked, "And what is the second thing?"

"Why, you experienced that yesterday. Now imagine that every day until you drop, which will be sooner than later. Perhaps even today. But you *could* stay here today, in a bed recovering your strength, later a warm meal and start your day tomorrow without a care in the world. Tell me, what are *your* thoughts? I will not make this offer again."

Almagro clearly thought he had won this round, and indeed he had. A year from now when he found out the lie behind it, Pedro would be safe with his family in Santa Maria.

"You have had a very good thought, Señor," said Pedro, laughing inwardly. "I accept your offer, the first one, of course."

"Ha ha," laughed Almagro. "You and I will become good friends, I deem, and we will laugh about this next year when we are seated at your father's table!"

I will be the one laughing when you are brought down, you villain. I can wait a year.

As graciously as he could muster, Pedro said, "Thank you for your kindness, Señor. I look forward to that day."

* * *

Bahati, Obadele and the other slaves watched as Pedro was led away. The was no room for speculation or discussion however, as the bosses got them working. A short time later, something unprecedented happened. The door to the foreman's quarters opened and Almagro called the bosses to him. It was a rare occasion to leave the workers unsupervised and they quickly took advantage of it.

"What do you think is happening?" asked Bahati, putting down his shovel.

"I do not think I want to know the answer to that," replied Obadele. "Either the boy has met his end or something more nefarious is happening."

"You told me he was here to be punished. Surely they will not kill him without cause after one day. The bosses, even though they have complete control over the camp, still have their own bosses in the town that they must answer to."

"Perhaps. But they can just make up any story they want about the boy's fate. That is probably what they are conspiring right now. Who would we be to make claims to the contrary?"

"I do not understand. It would be easier to work and beat him to death in the course of his sentence. They almost did that yesterday, there was no one to stop them, and he was nearly dead when he was brought to the barracks."

"The bosses are evil, twisted men. Whatever the young man did, I am sure he deserves whatever they are inflicting on him."

"Why do you say that?" asked Bahati. "Do you know something of his crime? Did he say something to you about Amina?"

"The boy, Pedro is his name, was out of his mind with pain and terror, but he made an admission to me when he was calmer. Without stating it for fact, he told me of his crime, and I do not know the details but I will not hide what I know from you any longer. Bahati, he killed Amina."

Bahati reeled as if he had received a blow.

"He told you this?"

"In an indirect way, yes, but in his state I was forced to piece it together, yet I have no doubt it was the truth."

Bahati became the embodiment of fury. He swung his shovel, striking the pile of rubble over and over until it splintered. He turned on Obadele, his eyes flashing red.

"You! You should have told me this last night when he was within my grasp. The bosses will not cheat me of my revenge!" He made to charge the building where the bosses were, but Obadele jumped in his path and blocked him. They wrestled fiercely as Bahati tried to get by.

"No! You must not!" cried Obadele. "They will kill you before you can get close to him! You must put aside your anger or your life and that of Amina will be wasted."

Bahati release his friend and stepped back. He bent over and took in several deep breaths.

"I know that Amina was lost to me when they took her away," he gasped between heaves, "but I took solace knowing she was at least safe. She was not, was she? To think that that whelp, that sorry excuse for a man, has taken her is more than I can bear!"

He fell down to his knees, kneading his hands into the dirt before him in grief.

"He had better be dead, for if I ever see him again I will kill him without a thought, even if the bosses kill me afterward."

Obadele looked at his friend, unsure how to comfort him. It had been his own words after all, that put the man in his current state, but he could not continue to keep the truth from him. All he could do now was protect Bahati from himself.

The overseers returned from their barracks, some of them with smirks on their faces as if they were privy to some secret. Obadele rushed to Bahati's side and thrust another shovel into his hands.

"Get up," he entreated Bahati. "The bosses are returning. They looked quite pleased with themselves. Do not give them a reason to notice you."

"Is the boy with them?"

"No, he is not, and it is better if you remove those thoughts from your head. You must look and act as you always have. Enough! Here they come."

Bahati leaned on the shovel to raise himself up, then attacked the rubble pile with a vigor fueled by his rage. Obadele turned to help him.

"Slow down," he whispered to Bahati, "They will wonder why you work so hard when there is no reason or whip to spur you on."

But there is, Obadele, there is. The whip of my own anger drives me. My revenge will not be denied, even if it only expended on these rocks.

* * *

Rosa had planned to meet Ignacio when he returned from the mine, but she had learned that the *Santa Victoria* was preparing to leave. *They were here barely two days!* She decided to write a quick letter to Isabella as she would not have another chance for several months. *So much to tell, but so little time!*

Dear Esperanza, she wrote. *I scarcely know where to begin! My journey has been full of surprises, the most unexpected of which was meeting your brother Ignacio aboard the very ship that brought me from Perico. What a small world this is! He remembered me and his time with us as a boy. He spoke of you with such warmth and admiration, and I felt instantly at ease in his company.*

Tragically, our ship ran aground before we had gotten very far. It seems I will not be residing in Callao as I had planned, but in a small frontier town called Santa Maria del Oro. Many lives were lost but Ignacio was instrumental in saving a great number of us. Despite the chaos, Ignacio's presence after the wreck was a steadying force for many of us. He proved himself a man of both strength and kindness, helping where he could and offering comfort to those who were frightened.

Since our arrival in Santa Maria, I have been trying to piece together a new life, though it has not been without its challenges. The town is peculiar, as if caught between its aspirations and its realities. The people here are kind in their way but guarded, as though the jungle itself has taught them to be wary. Yet, it has a promising future as a source of gold and other precious metals that have put it on the trade routes.

I had hoped to tell you all of this in greater detail, but I have only just learned that the Santa Victoria, the ship that will carry this letter, is leaving today. How I wish I could sit with you and share these tales properly! I am eager to hear from you and to know how you are faring. Please write to me when you can.

With warmest regards, Rosa.

Rosa sealed the letter and hurried down to the waterfront. She managed to press the letter into the hands of an officer, although he assured her she had plenty of time. The ship would not depart until the morning. She immediately thought that Ignacio might want to write his own missive and so she hurried to the church.

She entered the church, and not seeing any sign of Ignacio, went to his quarters. Without knocking, she entered the small room. There was a dim figure by the outer door.

"Ignacio, here you are at last! I..." She faltered as she realized the figure was not Ignacio. "Why, don Juan! I was expecting to find Father Ignacio."

"As was I, Señora Alvarez. I was to offer my apologies to the good Father...we had some harsh words as we returned from our excursion, but it seems I have missed him."

Rosa looked about the room and frowned.

"Look," she said pointing, "that is his journal on the floor! And under the table, his pouch. Its contents have spilled. Even Ignacio is not that careless with his things."

"Most odd," said Yllescas, picking up the journal. "It seems he was here, but hastily left." He thumbed through the book. "Perhaps there is a clue within these pages. Ah here! He made an entry last night. Before we squabbled. *'The journey to the mine was grueling,'* he says, *' not for the road itself but for the weight of what we carried. Pedro, broken in spirit, was like a man condemned, though I still wonder if he deserves such pity. His defiance concerns me, as does the one called Almagro, whose reputation precedes him. The man seems to thrive on the suffering of others. The jungle looms heavy around us, an indifferent witness to all this cruelty. I feel unease about Pedro's fate, the mine, and this growing sense that I am complicit in something far darker than I yet understand.'* This was well before his final appraisal of the place."

"We should not so eagerly rifle through a man's personal thoughts," Rosa said reproachfully. "In any event, it does not tell us anything about his hasty departure, if indeed that is what it was."

"My apologies, Señora," he said, placing the book on the table. "It was not my intent to pry. Forgive me."

"You seem to be rife with apologies today, Señor," she said guardedly, gathering the pouch and its effects. "I will return to town and see if I can find him. Perhaps he provides comfort to don Francisco."

"I will accompany you. The sooner I lift this burden from my shoulders, the better."

* * *

Ignacio was in darkness. For some reason he could not open his eyes and his thoughts were muddled. He became aware of a droning voice, but he could not understand the words. They drifted in and out, like a snake through the underbrush. Just when he thought he could make some sense of it, it would escape him.

"The process," the voice droned, "ghastly as it is, begins by slicing beneath the scalp, peeling away the skin to preserve the face. The rest of the flesh is discarded like refuse. The skin is boiled in their infernal brews of leaves and roots, shrunken but not destroyed. Then they fill the empty head with heated stones and sand, sewing shut the eyes and mouth to 'trap the spirit.' They claim it binds their enemy's soul, but to me, it is a desecration. A mockery of God's creation. What savagery it takes to defile the human body in such a way! We are made in His image, and to mutilate it like this is to spit on His divine work. It is not enough that they kill, no no no. They seek to imprison the very spirit. Such blasphemy is beyond redemption."

Ignacio's mind swam up toward the voice, grasping some of what he heard. Visions of the heads they had encountered flooded his thoughts, the revulsion he had felt when he first saw them, the fear they had infused in the survivors lost in the perilous wilderness. The voice went on:

"And then there is their vile communion with spirits through their drugs! Ayahuasca, they call it. A devil's potion, if there ever was one, brewed from twisted vines and bitter leaves. They drink it to summon visions, to claim they can walk among the spirits. But what spirits? Certainly not the angels or saints of heaven! They open their souls to demons, to false gods that whisper lies into their ears. Years I have spent showing them the way, yet they persist! They tried, many times, to get me to drink it, but I was resolute! It is a flagrant rejection of the sacraments, an affront to the only true communion, the body and blood of Christ. They seek enlightenment not through the Word but through the poison of their jungle. It is no wonder they are lost in darkness, clinging to their heathen ways! They willingly court damnation, and for what? To speak with shadows and phantoms? What could they ever learn from such abominations that they cannot find in the Gospel?

"Then there's that demon-clad charlatan they call Tsewa, a man cloaked in feathers and bones, claiming he communes with the gods of the forest! Ha! He is no more than a peddler of lies and sorcery, leading his people astray with his devilry. He twists the minds of his followers with his chants and potions, convincing them that his visions come from the heavens. But mark my words, they come from the pit of hell! Tsewa's so-called wisdom is nothing but heresy wrapped in superstition. He rejects the light of Christ for shadows and false idols, calling upon powers that no Christian should ever dare to name. It is men like him who keep these people chained to their ignorance, refusing the salvation of the Lord and dragging others down into their heathen darkness!"

Abruptly, Ignacio awoke from his stupor. The mention of Tsewa's name bolted him up into a sitting position. He had been laying on a grass mat and saw that that he was in a wall-less hut, no more than a roof really, supported by thick wooden beams. He cast about, seeking the source of the voice that had been haunting him. Nearby, in a cage made of wood, was a man. Ignacio focused on him.

"Burgos? Is that you?" he asked groggily.

"Ah, good! You are awake! That sting they use has quite a punch to it, does it not? You have been insensate for some time. I am getting tired of talking to myself."

Ignacio's hand went to his neck, remembering vaguely the prick he had felt before succumbing to darkness. He felt a small scab.

"How did I get here? Where am I?" Then, with more focus, "Why are you in a cage?"

"So many questions, very few answers. We are prisoners, you see, although they seem to like you more than they do me. They have tended you in your slumber, while I am lucky to be fed every so often."

"Are we alone here? Where are the 'they' you speak of?"

"Again with the questions. For the moment, yes, we are alone. Most of the warriors have left, no doubt on one of their interminable raids. But Tsewa and the women are here. You will see him soon. It was his will that you be brought here. I would flee if I could, but they need me, for the moment. Tsewa does not speak our language. I am to be his mouthpiece."

"Then tell me what he wants of me."

"Oh, I have no idea. Perhaps he wants to hear the Word of God from someone other than myself, but until he makes his needs known, I have no way of knowing."

"I am free," Ignacio said, looking around wildly. "I can escape, make my way back to town."

"And leave me here to rot? Thank you very much."

"Certainly not!" Ignacio exclaimed, making his way to the cage. "I will get you out of there one way or another."

"Do not bother. The cage is well made and without a sharp knife you will never get it open. Even if you did, we would not get very far. These lands are theirs and they would be upon us before we took a dozen steps. You may not see them but we are always watched. Go back to your mat. Already someone comes."

Ignacio looked back toward the hut. Several women had entered bearing bowls of water and food that they placed by the grass mat. Ignacio took his seat and looked at the offering. He was suddenly ravenous and without hesitation began to eat what was placed before him.

"Hmmph," said Burgos. "At least *you* get breakfast."

Ignacio pointed to the food and then to Burgos, but the women shook their heads vigorously. It was clear that Burgos was the prisoner while Ignacio was somewhat of an honored guest. He tried again to get the women to give Burgos something, but, even without a common language to communicate, the answer was made clear. Burgos would be fed just enough to keep him alive and no more.

"Do not worry about it, Father. I will consider this an early Lenten fast."

Chapter Thirty

In the forest, the mighty jaguar may sleep unbothered, but even the smallest ant, with a whisper to its kin, can awaken the leaves and set the trees trembling.

-Shuar parable

The day in the camp began like any other. The morning bell was struck, a meal was hastily eaten and the workers went to their assigned tasks. There was no time for yawning or small talk. This was not Santa Maria. It was a slave camp, no more, no less. The fact that something was actually produced here was secondary to the cruelty that presided over the resident's lives. Here, the only thing that mattered, the only thing that would be tolerated was work. The sun had not yet risen, but soon its scorching rays would be burning their backs. An unrelenting fire that burned more than backs.

The fire raged in Bahati's heart. He threw himself into his tasks with a fervor that bordered on the manic. Obadele watched him discreetly fearing his friend might hurt himself in his frenzy. Perhaps Bahati did it in an attempt to burn out the fury that engulfed him, but while the bosses might observe his actions with approval, it was clear he would not be able to maintain it. Then the overseers would notice that his pace had slackened, and then there would be trouble.

Obadele risked a harsh whisper when the boss' attention was elsewhere.

"What are you doing? You are going to get hurt if you do not slow down."

"I do not care," said Bahati without concern about being heard. "I cannot contain the pain I feel, I can only bury it under even more pain. Until that Pedro is dead, by my hand or theirs, I will not rest."

"Quiet! They will hear!"

Bahati went silent, not because he had fear he would be overheard by those who would, in any event, not understand his language, but because he had nothing else to say. The time for words was past. It was time for action, even if it were only at his job. The grueling sun was hot, mosquitoes swarmed on sweating skin, but Bahati felt none of it. His world had contracted to just one thing...Pedro's dead face.

In any slave camp, there were slaves who were not physically capable of heavy labor, usually older slaves or the disabled, and these were usually tasked with carrying water to the workers. Bosses had flasks of water with them at all times, but these also had to be replenished and it fell upon these few to fulfill those needs. Today, the old man that routinely filled this role was nowhere to be seen. Obadele felt his strength flagging even if Bahati worked on like a machine, and he scanned the area for the water-bearer. Finally he spotted someone distributing water at the other end of the camp. It was not the old man. It was someone much, much younger. Obadele's jaw dropped.

Obadele went back to his work, his mind awhirl. *What do I do? What do I do?* He realized there was nothing he *could* do. Pedro, with his bucket of drinking water would come to them eventually.

"Bahati!" he croaked. "The water! The water bearer is coming!" Bahati ignored him and continued at his task as if he had not heard. If anything, he redoubled his pace.

"Bahati! Look! The water bearer is nearly here!"

"I do not need water. Leave me be."

Obadele reached out and grabbed Bahati by the shoulder. "You must look!"

Bahati brushed off Obadele's hand brusquely, but in doing so, saw past his friend and grasped his meaning. Bahati's jaw did not drop open as had Obadele's. Instead, his eyes drew into grim slits that danced with flames.

"The bastards did not kill him! Instead they have rewarded him! I shall reward him as well!"

Once again, Obadele found himself between Bahati and his intended prey. He strained against Bahati with all his might, but it was like trying to hold back a bull.

"Please stop!" he pleaded. "They will kill you for even trying!"

"I will kill *you*, if you do not get out of my way!" In his rage, he threw down Obadele and recovered his shovel. Hearing the commotion, the overseer turned and strode toward them.

"You two! Get back to work! Save your bickering for the barracks!" He was rewarded with an immense clout to his face that sent him sprawling to the ground. Stepping over him, Bahati closed the distance to Pedro. Pedro looked at him and offered a small smile that quickly turned to a look of fear. Then the shovel struck him in the head. He dropped like a stone.

Bahati stood over him, his shovel raining blow upon blow. Once, the shovel's blade turned and caught Pedro in the neck, nearly severing his head from his body. Bahati did not stop. Nothing would stop him from turning Pedro into nothing more than a bloody pulp.

It was not until several bosses had tackled him and wrestled him to the ground that Bahati's attack was stopped. It took several blows to subdue him and when they finally had him pinned to the ground, the overseer that had suffered Bahati's first blow towered over him, his face bruised and bloodied. He raised his musket, its butt aimed at Bahati's face, but the blow never landed. Instead, something peculiar happened. As if by magic, a spear sprouted from the man's chest, its bloody petals a gruesome flower.

The camp erupted into chaos.

* * *

"I understand your concern, Señora Alvarez, but I am not sure what you expect me to do."

Rosa stared at don Alonso in disbelief. After searching high and low for Ignacio, she had come up empty. As a last resort, she had gone to Santa Maria's Chief for help.

"What I expect you to do, Señor," she said coldly, "is to look for him. This is no longer the peaceful little hamlet that it was. There has been drunkenness, thievery and even murder! Just because the *Santa Victoria* has sailed away does not mean things are back to normal."

"That is true. Things have not been normal since you and yours arrived at our shore." Rosa stiffened at this as don Alonso continued. "All these things you mentioned, the thievery and so on, were perpetrated by members of your company. Now, I cannot ascribe blame for recent mishaps upon you as a whole, indeed I am grateful to have persons such as yourself and the good Father among our community, but you cannot deny the truth of what I say. The balance has been upset and now that we have had a period of adjustment, we will find our footing together."

"That was a rather long-winded way of saying you will do nothing," she said hotly.

"Señora, this is a small town. If he is indeed here, he will turn up."

"Where would he be if not here? Do you think he went mad and ventured into the forest? He accompanied your own son to the mining camp and, as far as I am concerned, never returned. You would have me wait until somebody trips over his body."

"I would not wish that to be so," he replied with a sigh. "Very well. Captain Salazar left a number of soldiers here. I will set them on the hunt. Speaking of the Captain, have you considered that Father Ignacio may have left with them?"

"Unless you have direct knowledge of his departure, you should not say such a thing. I have searched his chambers. If he had left, as you suggest, he would have taken his few possessions. His journal, which he is never without, I found on the floor of his room."

"I am sorry, Señora, but that is something that had to be considered. As I said, I will set the soldiers on the problem."

"Thank you, don Alonso," she said with a huff, "for doing the very least you can do. I will see myself out."

Rosa left the Administration building, resentful of don Alonso's lack of interest in Ignacio's fate, slamming the door for good measure. *Oh, I wish Rodrigo was here,* she thought. *He would not hesitate to help, but he too, has been caught up in this web of deceit and malfeasance. What am I to do?*

She began to wander the town, with no clear destination in mind, letting her eyes search for something, anything, that would be of help. The first thing she encountered was the square, now littered with tents that housed the workforce Salazar had left behind to build the infrastructure he required. It was a noisy, disorderly affair with strange languages and even stranger smells wafting through the air. *Yes, don Alonso, I can see the town has struck a balance.* Suddenly, she felt fatigued, mentally and physically. She would go home now and gather her thoughts. Perhaps she could think of something useful.

Señora Fernandez was the first person to see her when she arrived at the house. She could tell right away that something was wrong with Rosa and pressed her for details. Rosa broke down and fell into a nearby chair. Between sobs she began to tell her tale, but Señora Fernandez stopped her.

"Wait, dear Rosa. Pull yourself together. I will gather the others as I feel we all need to hear this."

Soon, the other women of the household, Inéz, Maria and Carmen came into the room. Luckily they had all been home doing assorted chores and not at market. As soon as they saw Rosa, they huddled closer to offer her comfort. Her sobs had subsided and she told them of everything that had happened from the moment Ignacio left at the road to the mine.

"What a brute, that don Alonso," said Inéz. "He more than anyone should have done all that he could to help you. And the way he treated you! He should be ashamed."

"He is a politician," said Señora Fernandez. "He will indebt himself to no one until he can determine how it is to his benefit. If there is no benefit, then the matter dies."

"Then so does Ignacio," sniffled Rosa. "Nobody cares."

"No, no," said Señora Fernandez, hugging her closely. "That is not true. *We* will undertake this matter, the five of us. We will leave no stone unturned, no place unsearched, no politician unconfronted until we find Father Ignacio. And find him we will."

"Really?"

They all replied in unison.

"Really!"

"It is a woman's duty," said Señora Fernandez, "to fill the space where men fail."

"Oh, why did I not come to you first? For the first time I have hope. You are truly good friends."

* * *

Ignacio was not prepared to meet Tsewa. The reality of the man was far different from the one he had seen in visions. Even though Burgos had previously told him what to expect, it was still a surprise. Ignacio had never seen a man as ancient, a man who seemed more a resurrected corpse than a living breathing man. Yet he had come to the hut on his own feet, only somewhat assisted by his wives. The next thing that Ignacio noticed were his eyes. They, in contrast to everything else, shone with vibrancy and intelligence.

Tsewa was seated on a stool across from Ignacio. The old man uttered a long string of words in a tongue completely foreign to Ignacio and he listened with bewilderment. He soon realized that the words were directed at Burgos, although Tsewa never once looked in his direction.

"It is as I have told you before," said Burgos. "I am here only to relay Tsewa's words to you. I am forbidden to offer my own opinions or to offer explanation upon pain of death. You will not look at me at any time. Anything you say is to be directed at Tsewa directly. I am to be ignored. So says Tsewa."

Ignacio nodded to Tsewa, indicating that he understood the rules of engagement. He quickly gathered his thoughts and addressed the timeworn man before him.

"I am Ignacio de Montemayor, a servant of God and a seeker of understanding. I suspect you already know much about me, perhaps more than I know about myself. I have traveled far, endured trials, and now find myself before you, not by choice but by destiny, it seems."

He paused, searching for the right words, then continued, "It is clear that I am here for a reason. You, revered Tsewa, hold the answer to why. I humbly ask, what do you seek of me? What purpose do you see in my presence here?"

"It is true," said Tsewa through Burgos, "I know much about you and yet there is much I do not know. The name you use for yourself, I did not know. I think of you as *Nantá Iwia,* the Wandering Spirit. It is strong, your spirit. So strong that I sensed your presence from far away. So strong that I sought you out as soon as I was able. You have much in common with the spirits of my world, and they have counseled me to seek you out. I suspect the true purpose of your presence here, yet I leave that to the spirits to reveal. We will learn the truth together."

"I am a man of God. My world is filled with His Word and those of His calling. My faith does not hold with spirits lest they come from Him. Yet that faith has been shaken of late. The dreams and visions I have had...tell me, was that truly you? Your visage is very different."

"You saw me as I see myself. This body is old but my spirit remains strong. But as you can see, that alone will not be enough to keep me in the world of the living. Soon, I shall join with the spirits."

"Then I must ask again, revered Tsewa...what need have you of me? As you say, we are of different worlds. Our beliefs are at odds."

"You limit your spirit to only embrace the words of your god. This I have learned from the man in the cage. There is a greater reality to espouse without abandoning what you already know. I offer only for you to explore it, then you can come to your own reality. I offer to be your guide."

Ignacio sat back, not knowing what to think or even reply. *Could this be the work of God?* he wondered. *Could He have brought me here, to this strange place, to sit before this man whose beliefs seem so alien, so at odds with the Word? And yet...Tsewa speaks of spirits as if they are as real as the earth beneath us, and perhaps they are. How else can I explain the visions that have haunted me? The dreams that felt as real than my waking moments? To explore without abandoning what I know. Is that even possible? Can faith and discovery coexist? Or is this a temptation designed to test my resolve?*

He glanced at Tsewa who waited patiently, like a figure carved of stone. The air had grown silent, holding its breath, it seemed, and Ignacio was no closer to an answer.

Finally, he said, "And if I were to decline your offer?"

"Then," replied Tsewa, "you would be returned to the world you know, but I would counsel against that. Your world is changing and you will not recognize it or be able to control it. You will forever feel incomplete, your spirit unshaped."

Ignacio could not deny to himself that he was at a crisis point in his life. He was already feeling 'unshaped' since he first arrived in this strange and exotic land, yet he felt confident that at his core he would remain unchanged. If nothing else, this would mark the end of his visions and dreams. He would be free of it.

"Very well," he replied with a deep sigh, "I accept your offer. What do I have to do?"

* * *

It was several moments before Bahati realized what was happening. The arms that were holding him down had fallen away leaving him laying in the dirt. Once the shock of seeing the overseers skewered had passed, he sat up quickly and surveyed the scene. From every side of the forest, Shuar warriors were pouring into the camp. The air was filled with yells and screams. He jumped to his feet, regained his lost shovel and joined the fray.

Some of the bosses that had held him down were still nearby, stunned by the sudden eruption of violence. Bahati did not hesitate and he employed his weapon as efficiently as he had on Pedro, catching two of his oppressors virtually unaware of the danger they faced. Bahati struck the first with an upswing to the man's chin that sent him flying backward. The second received the edge of the shovel on his head, splitting it. When the man fell, Bahati put a foot on his shoulder to wrench the shovel free. No finding any more enemies near him, he ran to where he had left Obadele.

The soldiers fared a little better initially, positioning themselves behind assorted barrels and carts, firing on anyone black or feathered but quickly found themselves outflanked. They hurriedly retreated to the foreman's quarters and took up positions in the windows.

The chaos was in full swing and Bahati had to duck and dodge several times to avoid the arrows and spears that were flying. He reached Obadele intact but the man was standing there dumbfounded.

"Obadele!" he cried, shaking Obadele by the shoulders. "It is here! The signal we have been waiting for! It is time to fight!" Bahati pressed his shovel into Obadele's hands. Once he had weapon in hand, Obadele's eyes lit up and a grin came across his face. Bahati took hold of a spear that had fallen nearby, and together, he and Obadele raced toward a knot of bosses that were racing toward the relative safety of the mine entrance.

A party of warriors charged the foreman's quarters, several of them brandishing flaming torches. Many fell from the volleys of gunfire erupting from the building, but a few managed to thrust their torches through the windows. Others set fire to the woodpiles piled against the building and soon it was engulfed in flames. The soldiers, panicked and overwhelmed by smoke, began jumping from the windows and even the front door, where they were picked off without too much effort.

Last to exit the building was Almagro, singed and disheveled, brandishing a machete in each hand. His eyes blazed in fury and he hewed many that were in his path, but many more awaited. Soon, even he was overwhelmed by the sheer numbers he confronted, and he fell, riddled with arrows and spears.

Throughout the melee, Wajari searched for his target, the little man who he had marked as 'Gold Chief'. To him, the little man was the embodiment of the invader's greed. He would bear the brunt of Wajari's wrath. He would be the example.

"Do not kill them all!" he roared. "The little fat one! I want him alive!"

Pinchu came running up to his side with several other warriors. "Many of them have taken refuge inside the mine," he said to Wajari. "We cannot get to them easily."

"Take me there!" Wajari growled. "I will show them how mistaken they are!"

Though his lungs were bursting at the effort, Bahati managed to catch up to the overseers. With spear in hand, he thrust it into the back of the one nearest him. The man howled in pain and fell. With a yank, Bahati pulled out the spear and threw it at another. It was more anger than skill that made the weapon find its mark, as Bahati had never done such a thing in his life, yet the man fell dead and the ones running behind him were tripped up by his body. By now, Obadele had caught up to him and between them they overcame the remaining men, using shovel and spear unsparingly.

The mayhem had subsided to nearly nothing. There were minor scuffles here and there but the resistance to the incursions failed. Slaves, now free, danced and pounded each other on the back in celebration, while others looked at the warriors with trepidation, not fully trusting the outcome and fearing retaliation.

At the mine entrance, Wajari peered inside but could not see anything.

"Is there another way in?" he asked "Or worse, is there another way out?"

"I do not know," said Pinchu, "but we have watched this camp a long time and never seen hint of such. I think this is the only way."

"Then gather what leaves and wet wood you can find. Build a great fire here at the mouth and we will smoke them out. We will make them choose between breathing and living what little life we will grant them."

Chapter Thirty One

The earth shakes beneath our feet, Spirits rise to meet the call. We are the jaguar's roar, The serpent's strike, The eagle's eye in the darkened sky.
Our roots are deep, unbroken, unseen, Our hands hold fire, our hearts hold truth.
To those who wound our mother's skin, To those who bind our people's strength, Your time is done, your sun has set.
We are the forest, we are the storm, We are life reborn in the warrior's form!

-Shuar War Chant

Ignacio regretted his decision as soon as the potion hit his tongue. The smell of it was bad enough but the taste was much, much worse. The brew was bitter and acrid, burning as it slid down his throat, and he struggled not to vomit. He forced himself to swallow, then forced himself again to drain the bowl. It left behind a taste that seemed to linger not only on his tongue but in his spirit. It was as if the concoction itself carried a warning, a harbinger of what was to come. Around him, the dim light of the setting sun lit Tsewa's hut with fingers of light that flickered like restless souls. The air was thick and heady, the mingling scents of earth, smoke, and decay enveloped him as if to weigh him down.

He tried to steady his breathing, as Tsewa had instructed him, but it was as though the air itself was resisting his lungs. He was aware of Tsewa sitting across from him, his frail body still, his ancient eyes piercing. Around him, his wives moved like silent phantoms, tending to the ritual. They chanted softly in a language he could not understand but which resonated somehow deep within him, stirring something he could not begin to name.

As the minutes passed, the world began to shift. At first, the change was subtle; colors in the hut seemed more vibrant, the sounds of the wives' chanting richer, as if the ordinary had been stripped away to reveal something truer beneath. Then the visions began.

They came slowly, like a dawn breaking over a strange horizon. Swirling colors emerged, forming and dissolving, refusing to settle. Shapes took form, fleeting at first, a cross, stark and radiant, before it melted into the undulating body of a serpent. The serpent's scales shimmered with iridescent light, its eyes, piercing and golden, suddenly fixed on Ignacio. He recoiled, terror gripping him as he thought of Eden, of the serpent in the Garden, of temptation and sin.

He had no choice but to stare back, paralyzed, at the frightful reptilian face, its tongue darting in and out in rhythm to his own heartbeat. Yet the serpent did not strike. Instead, it spoke. Not with words but with a presence that filled the space around him. *"Not all serpents are your enemy,"* it seemed to say.

The scene shifted violently, and he was no longer seated in Tsewa's hut but soaring high above a vast jungle. His arms were outstretched, as though he were being crucified, his body suspended in the heavens. Below him, rivers carved their way through the endless green, shimmering like veins of silver in the moonlight. As he watched, faces began to emerge from the water, human faces, animal faces, and faces that were both and neither. They cried out, their voices a haunting chorus of suffering, defiance, and hope.

They called him by name, but not the name he knew. They called him *Nantá Iwia*, the Wandering Spirit. Their voices swelled, enveloping him, and he felt as though he were being pulled into the very river they rose from.

Suddenly, he was no longer flying but standing before an immense tree. It towered impossibly high, its roots spreading deep into the earth as if anchoring the world itself. Its branches stretched skyward, touching the stars, each leaf shimmering with a light of its own. The bark of the tree was inscribed with symbols, intricate and ancient, that he could not read yet felt he should understand.

At the base of the tree sat a jaguar, its golden eyes unblinking and intense. The creature radiated power and wisdom, its presence both majestic and terrifying.

"You fear what you do not know," the jaguar said, its voice a low, resonant hum that seemed to vibrate within his chest. "You cling to the cross and reject the circle. You must see the whole."

Ignacio wanted to respond, to ask what it meant, but before he could speak, the jaguar leapt toward him. He recoiled against the attack. But instead of sinking its claws into him, it passed through his body, and he began to fall, falling endlessly, tumbling through darkness and light. His body fragmented, shattering into shards of glass, each piece reflecting a moment of his life.

In one shard, he saw his ordination, the day he had devoted himself to God. In another, he saw the confessional, his trembling hands as he offered absolution to his first penitent. Then came other shards: his encounters with Rosa, her face illuminated by moonlight; the desperate eyes of Pedro as he pleaded for forgiveness he would never receive; the faces of the enslaved, hollow and broken, etched into his soul.

The shards began to reassemble, but the image they formed was incomplete. Whole pieces were missing, leaving gaps that pulsed with an emptiness he could not bear to face.

He awoke slowly, his body drenched in sweat, his heart pounding as though he had been running for miles. His vision was blurred, but he could tell something was wrong. The sun had been setting but now it was high overhead. How long had the potion imprisoned his mind? The hut was swimming in and out of focus. Tsewa sat across from him, as if he had never moved from his perch. His expression was inscrutable, his eyes gleaming with the same ancient wisdom Ignacio had seen in the jaguar.

"What did you see?" Tsewa asked through Burgos, his voice calm yet probing.

Ignacio hesitated, his mind a storm of images and emotions, unable to form a coherent response.

"I... I saw the truth," he said finally, voice hoarse. "But it is not yet whole."

Tsewa nodded, as though he had expected the answer. "Truth is never whole, Nantá Iwia. It is a path, not a destination."

Ignacio wanted to argue, to cling to the certainty of his faith, to the absolutes he had been taught to believe, yet the words would not come. The jaguar's voice echoed in his mind: *"You must see the whole."*

He looked at Tsewa, this ancient man who seemed to straddle the line between the living and the dead, and for the first time, he wondered if the light he carried in his heart was but one of many, and he had been blind to the others all along. The jungle seemed to hum with life, a cacophony of sounds that now felt like a symphony. The faces he had seen in the river lingered in his mind, their cries resonating deep within. He did not yet understand what they meant, but knew they were not to be ignored.

Tsewa's words broke the silence. "Your journey has only begun, Nantá Iwia. The spirits have spoken to you, and they will speak again. Listen, and you will find what you seek. Sleep now. When you wake, you will try again."

* * *

"Don Juan, you must take me. I have to see for myself!" Yllescas looked at Rosa with a skeptical eye. She had cornered him at La Posada while he was entertaining a woman companion. Said companion left in a huff when Rosa arrived, pointedly ignored her and started talking to Yllescas.

"Believe me," he replied with resignation, "you do not want to go there, Señora. It is not a place for refined women such as yourself. It is a place of toil, pain and misery, and I seriously doubt Ignacio would have returned there under his own volition, let alone unescorted and unprotected."

"He must have, don Juan. He is not anywhere in the town, and believe me, I have looked. Even in places such as this," she said, letting her eyes roam about the tavern with distaste. "Ignacio is a man of compassion. He would have felt a need to minister to their needs."

"And so he left on his own," Yllescas said with a chuckle, "leaving no word with anyone who may miss him, to minister slaves? That is absurd, to say the least. In any event, he would not be allowed to do such a thing. The camp's officials keep a very tight ship."

"You are just like your father! Unable to put the needs of others ahead of your own!"

Yllescas sighed heavily and gave Rosa a stern look. "That is patently untrue, Señora, and you know it. My father's position in this town is predicated on putting the people first, otherwise Santa Maria would fall into chaos and ruin."

"Ignacio may well be missing because of chaos," she cried. "And as for ruin, have you looked at the town square lately? Crawling with soldiers and slaves who have no other duty than to protect and work for the gold produced at the mine. They care not for the town!"

"Rosa," replied Yllescas calmly, "what you see as chaos, I see as progress. That gold you denounce will turn this town into a city. Peasants into nobles."

"Then Ignacio is a small price to pay for your ambitions, is that it? How many more casualties will you justify to achieve this progress? Fine!" She pounded the table with her fist, making the cups jump. "If you will not take me, then I shall go myself!"

Yllescas looked around at the faces that had suddenly turned toward them. With a small wave and a smile, he turned back to Rosa.

"Señora," he said grimly, "you will not. Nor will I take you there. I have told you repeatedly that the camp is not for one such as you. I have no doubt that you will come to great harm if you do." Rosa was about to argue again, but Yllescas stopped her with an upraised palm. "And if you were to go and he was still not to be found, what then? Will you then turn over every tree and bush in the forest to find him? I too, have great affection for Father Ignacio and pray for his return. I do not know where he is, but I can tell you where he is not, and that is the mine. I was with him, remember, and I do not think there is anything in the world to compel him to go back."

"Not even Pedro?"

"Especially not. He knows the boy is serving a sentence, that he is not to be coddled in any way. No, wherever Ignacio is, it is not there."

"Yet you refuse to make sure." She stared at Yllescas with blazing eyes. She slammed the table once more for good measure and walked away. It was Rosa's turn to leave the tavern in a huff.

Her angry footsteps led her from the tavern, and once again without purpose or destination. She gave no heed to those around her, her eyes focused on the ground ahead of her. Once, she bumped into a man who apologized profusely, but with a curt wave, she walked on.

Her heart and mind still fuming, she found herself facing the church. She realized that the reasons her feet had propelled her there were many; faith, despair...Ignacio. She slipped through the door and stepped inside. The sound of her footsteps echoed through the stillness, a stillness that screamed of emptiness. Was there more missing in this space than its pastor? Once this was a source of comfort, of strength, and yes, even happiness, but now it felt vast and hollow.

Her attention was held by the crude wooden altar and she made her way toward it. Crossing herself, she dropped to her knees and clasped her hands tightly.

"Dear Lord," she began, her voice trembling, "I come to You as a woman desperate for answers, for guidance. If there is a path, I cannot see it. Help me to find Ignacio. Bring him to safety. He is a man of great faith, a servant of Your will, and yet he is lost to me, to all of us.

"Ignacio..." she whispered, the name catching in her throat. "I love him, Lord. I love him with a depth that terrifies me, that shakes the foundations of who I am. I have tried to keep my feelings hidden, to keep them proper, but they overwhelm me. And now, I fear I may never see him again."

Her hands gripped each other harder, her knuckles whitening as she poured her anguish into her prayer. "If he is gone, then let me know. Let me find peace in the certainty of his fate. But if he lives, I beg You, show me how to reach him. Show me how to help him, how to bring him back to where he belongs."

Her shoulders slumped as she surrendered to the grief in her heart. "Ignacio, if you can hear me, if you can feel me, know that I am searching for you. Know that I will not give up." Her voice broke, and she leaned back on her heels, her head tilted upward toward the crucifix hanging above the altar. The hand carved figure of Christ gazed down at her.

"Lord, You suffered for us, for our sins, for our salvation. You endured the ultimate pain so that we might have hope. I know my pain is nothing compared to Yours, but it is all I have. Please, use it. Use me. Let me be a vessel for Your will, so that Ignacio might be saved."

Rosa felt the weight of her helplessness settle over her once more. Her thoughts turned dark, filled with fears she could not voice. *What if Ignacio is dead, his body lost in the jungle or buried in some unmarked grave? What if he chose to leave, to escape the burdens of his faith and the weight of my love?*

"No," she said aloud, shaking her head fiercely. "He would not leave. He would not abandon his flock, his duty. He is out there, somewhere, and he needs me. I know he does." She rose and stepped close to the altar, bowing her head as tears rolled down her cheeks. She struck a flint and lit a candle that was there.

"This," she whispered, "is my prayer, Lord. This flame is my hope. Keep it alive, even when I falter. Let it guide Ignacio back to us, or guide me to him."

She crossed herself again and left. To her dismay, the burden was still upon her.

* * *

It did not take long. Once the warriors got the fire started it was just a matter of keeping it smoky enough and then to fan it into the opening of the mine. After just a few moments they were rewarded with the sound of coughing coming from the darkness.

"Get more wood!" Wajari shouted. "Fan the smoke harder! Make them run into our arms!"

While not precisely running, those that had sought refuge in the mine soon began to stagger out, cough and wheezing, trying to expel the smoke from their lungs. They came out singly or in pairs with great reluctance knowing what awaited them outside, trading one death for another. They were taken forcibly and bound as they emerged, set seated by the mouth of the cave to watch as the rest of their compatriots were given the same treatment.

"Haha!" Wajari crowed jubilantly, "Fleeing the jaguar, only to meet the anaconda! Where are the rest? Where is the little fat one?" A total of six men had fled the cave but Luján was not among them. "Stop fanning the smoke," said Wajari. He then pointed to two warriors. "Get in there and pull him out. I will not have him dying and depriving me of my prize!"

Presently, a squealing came from the mine, sounding more like a wounded peccary than a man. The warriors came into the sunlight, dragging Luján by his arms. The assessor dug his heels in the dirt, resisting with all his might.

"No, No!" he pleaded. "I have done nothing to you! Spare me! I will do anything you say!" He kept on, his words becoming incoherent in his terror, finally falling to sobs and more squealing.

Wajari struck a comical pose, his cupped hand pressed to his ear, as if he were trying to hear Luján better.

"What does he say, Pinchu? I cannot understand *anything* he is saying." The other warriors began to laugh.

"I believe he is saying he is the gold-chief," said Pinchu, joining in the humor. "He says he will give you all the gold you want if you let him go."

"Ah, my greatest wish," said Wajari as Luján blubbered on. Wajari struck another pose and cupped his other ear, making the warriors laugh harder. "Tell me, what else does he say?"

"That he is thirsty from all the smoke and that you should give him a drink!"

"A drink! Why did I not think of that?" He gestured to the warriors holding Luján. "Bring him over here!" he cried, very serious now. They followed Wajari a short distance to the smelter where a cauldron on the flames still bubbled. "Hold him down. Open his mouth." Luján's eyes went wide with terror but his screams were dampened by the warriors prying his jaw open. Wajari filled a long handled cup with the molten ore.

"You love gold so much, I will make sure that you are filled with it!"

Luján tried again to scream but it was drowned out by the pouring of the hot metal down his throat. Cup after cup Wajari poured into him, even though Luján was probably dead after the first. He did not stop until the man's belly swelled and the molten ore erupted from it.

"There!" said Wajari. "That should satisfy even a glutton like you! Now you will forever be the gold-chief!" Wajari dropped the cup and walked back to the other prisoners.

"What shall we do with them?" asked Pinchu. Wajari looked them over, assessing the amount of fear in each man's face. Some were clearly fearful, but there were a couple who gave back a defiant glare.

"Cut them loose," said Wajari after several minutes. "Let them return to their people to tell them of our great triumph here. Let them tell their people to be afraid, very afraid, for we will come for them next!"

Chapter Thirty Two

Is not this the kind of fasting I have chosen: to loose the chains of injustice and untie the cords of the yoke, to set the oppressed free and break every yoke?

Isaiah 58:6

Now that he knew what to expect, Ignacio's fear of the ayahuasca experience was greatly diminished. He had only a slight hesitation as he drank, and that was due in part, to the taste, which still triggered his gag reflex. Even so, he felt curious and a quiet resolve to understand the visions.

The ayahuasca took hold. Ignacio closed his eyes and let himself fall into the abyss of his mind. The descent was gentler this time, less chaotic. Colors blossomed behind his eyelids, hues of green, blue, and gold merging and swirling in harmonious patterns. He was no longer a lone traveler stumbling through unfamiliar terrain; he felt welcomed, absorbed, and intertwined with the flow of energy around him.

He found himself standing in an endless jungle, its canopy so dense that it seemed to merge with the sky. Yet, there was light, soft, golden beams that danced on the leaves and illuminated the intricate web of life below. Every leaf, every insect, every root and vine pulsed with a quiet, vibrant energy. Ignacio felt it coursing through him, as if he were no different from the trees or the creatures scurrying beneath them.

He knelt and placed his hands on the soil, rich and damp. Suddenly his perspective shifted. He could feel the roots of the jungle beneath him, spreading out like veins, connecting tree to tree, plant to plant, the entire forest a single, living organism. He sensed its pulse, its rhythm...a slow, steady beat that mirrored the heartbeat of the earth itself. And in that moment, Ignacio realized that humanity was but one small part of this vast, interconnected web.

The jungle spoke, though not in words. It communicated through sensations, images, and a deep knowing. Ignacio saw the cycle of life unfold before him: the birth of a sapling, the quiet decay of a fallen tree, the way every death nourished new growth. Nothing was wasted; nothing was lost. It was a perfect balance, an eternal dance of giving and receiving.

"You see now," a voice whispered. Ignacio turned, but there was no one. The voice continued, *"You are not apart from this. You are of this. You take, you give, and so the cycle turns."*

Ignacio's vision shifted again, and he found himself by a river, its waters clear and teeming with life. Fish darted beneath the surface, their scales flashing like silver. Birds called from the trees, their songs a melody that harmonized with the flow of the water. The now familiar jaguar emerged from the undergrowth, sleek and powerful, and it regarded Ignacio with piercing eyes. *Was this Tsewa in this dreamworld?* There was no fear...only awe. The jaguar was a predator, dangerous, but also a protector, a vital part of the jungle's balance. As he watched, the river began to change. Its waters darkened, filled with silt and debris. Trees along its banks fell, their roots exposed and helpless. Ignacio felt a pang of sorrow, a deep ache in his chest, as he saw the life around the river diminish. The fish disappeared, the birds fell silent, and the jaguar slinked away, its golden eyes filled with accusation.

"You must remember," the voice whispered again. *"You take more than you give. The balance is fragile. Without care, it will break."*

Again, he turned toward the voice finding he was no longer in the jungle but in a barren wasteland. The ground was cracked and dry, the air heavy with ash. He saw figures in the distance coming near, men and women, their faces weary and hollow. They stumbled through the desolation, searching for something they could no longer find. Ignacio understood their plight. They had lost their connection to the earth, to the balance that sustained them.

Tears filled his eyes as he reached out to them, but his hands passed through their forms like smoke. He was powerless to help. *"What can I do?"*

he asked, his voice trembling with despair. He looked down and saw that his body was glowing. Glowing with the same golden light that he had seen in the jungle. He realized that he carried the jungle's energy within him, that it was part of him, as it was part of everything.

"Now you carry the truth," the voice said. *"Embrace it. Live it. Be the balance."*

With those words echoing in his mind, Ignacio suddenly felt he was straddling two worlds, the world of truth and one of shadows. He felt the shadow world reach up to grasp him. He felt hands on his face, felt more potion being poured into his mouth. He drank eagerly. The void leading to the world of truth opened once more and swallowed him whole.

* * *

"And now you see how easily they fall!" shouted Wajari to all the warriors and freed slaves of the mining camp. "Without numbers they will not last. But if we allow them to go further, when will it stop? Shall we wait until they double their numbers in the town? You, Shakaim! How long do you think they will sit on only one side of the river? More ships will come and soon they will build a town and begin new searches for gold on your lands to the north.

"Lucky we were to strike when we did. That ship that came had many more soldiers and men. Were they still here, much harder would we have to fight to push them away. We have proved to ourselves what we have known for many years, that they are weak, blinded by their greed, blind to nature...blind to *us*! Never should we have allowed them to first set foot on our lands!"

"Strong words have you, Wajari," Shakaim shouted back. "You are right in everything you say, but it is not enough! We should not have allowed them to gain a foothold or to build a town, yet here we stand with outsiders, these slaves who have no home but here. Are we to allow them the same opportunity? How long will it be before they betray us and build a town of their own? I say we relieve ourselves of the burden *before* it becomes a burden."

"And yet we will risk it, as they have risked much to help us. They are as much the enemy of the invaders as we, perhaps more. These men," he said, waving his hand over the Africans, "are no more than animals in the eyes of the invaders. Less! We kill animals for food, we do not torture them, we do not make them work until they die. No, these men fought with us and they are friends. Their world is not the invader's world.

"This camp is on our clan's lands and so I will decide for them. They will continue to live here in our shadow. We will teach them the ways of our people. They will live as part of the clan, living as we do, hunting as we do. And they will fight with us when we destroy the town and push its people back into the sea!

"By now, the demons we have set free will have made it back to the town and told them of has happened here. Some will prepare a defense, but most are like the little gold-chief. They will cry and cower and their defenses will mean nothing! Are you ready?"

Wajari raised his arms high and cried, "We are ready!"

"The jungle speaks, and we answer!" he shouted. The warriors chimed in in unison, stamping their feet and striking their spears against the ground, creating a terrible drumbeat. The Africans among them stared wide-eyed, unsure whether to add their shouts or be frightened.

The earth shakes with our footsteps!
We are the jaguar's roar,
The serpent's strike,
The storm that bends the trees!
Our spears are the claws of the earth!
Our hearts are the fire of the ancestors!
We fight for the land,
We fight for the spirit,
We fight for the freedom of our people!
Who can stand against the jungle's fury?
Who can silence the voice of the Shuar?
No chains will hold us
No walls will stop us!
We are the storm that devours!

As the tumult died down, Wajari once more spread his arms.

"Go you, Northers! Gather your warriors! In two days we reclaim what is ours. Two days for the town to fester in despair. Two days and then the dawn will bring our freedom!"

* * *

Rosa had had enough and she was determined to find out what she could on her own. She had found constant resistance from everyone, and now, most recently, even her housemates. When she had told them of her plan to make the journey to the mining camp herself, none of them were willing to go with her.

"There is much I would do for you," Señora Fernandez had said, "but what you are contemplating is suicide. Even the men take extreme precautions when they make the trip. How do you think you can make it through safely? Surely you can find some men willing to escort you."

"I cannot." she had replied. "I am turned back at every request. I am forever being told that I will have news of the camp when the next shipment arrives. That is not for another four days!"

Alone and despondent, she returned to her room. None of her prayers had been answered, no guidance or sign had been given. It was as if the entire world had turned its back to her and shown indifference to Ignacio's fate. As she sat there, her resolve solidified. *Ignacio would do it for me, were I missing. He would do it for anyone he felt was in danger. I can do no less.* Packing just a small bag, she left the house stealthily, making sure none of the household saw her leave.

The sky made some rumblings as she made her way to the mine road, but she was not to be dissuaded. She stepped out onto the road and had perhaps taken a dozen steps, when a shadow came out from behind a tree.

"And were do you think you are going?"

Startled, Rosa stopped in her tracks as the figure walked toward her. In her current mania, it was a moment before she realized who it was.

"Don Juan!" she cried, regaining her composure. "You refuse to help me, and instead direct your efforts to spying on me?"

"It was my thought that you might attempt something like this. I have watched, not you, but the road, hoping against hope I would not have to confront you in such a way."

"Well, you have made your point...repeatedly," she replied, scowling. "Now stand aside and let me do what you would not."

"Señora," he said, blocking her way, "I am loathe to have this argument with you again. If need be, I will drag you bodily to your abode until this madness of yours passes."

"Try it, you arrogant mule! I will gouge out your eye...I will..." Her tirade was cut short as the sound of running feet came to their ears. They both looked up the road fearfully, expecting the worst to appear from the forested end of the road. They relaxed when they saw it was not savages, but men of their own kind. Six of them, bloodied and bedraggled, one limping and supported by another. Upon seeing the pair they began shouting, six voices overlapping each other.

"They are coming!"

"They are coming to kill us!"

"Soldiers! Send the soldiers!"

"Help us!"

"Run! They will hunt us!"

"Hundreds of them!"

"Quiet! All of you!" shouted Yllescas, waving his arms before them. "Control yourselves! Tell me what you are running from!"

Immediately all six started talking and shouting at the same time.

"Stop!" Yllescas commanded. Then, pointing at one man randomly, said, "You! Tell me what is happening."

The man took several deep breaths before replying, calming himself as best he could. "The savages, Señor. They came pouring out of the forest, catching us unawares. They killed nearly everyone barring the slaves."

"What? Why not the slaves?"

"Those miserable black dogs rose against us, siding with the savages. We were overwhelmed!"

"How did you escape then?

"Ignacio!" shouted Rosa, interrupting. "Was Father Ignacio there?"

"What...?" the man started, confused. He turned to Yllescas. "No, the priest was not there. He left with *you*, long before the attack came."

Yllescas turned to Rosa with a glare. "Did I not tell you as much? Do you still want to go, knowing now what awaits?" He addressed the man once more. "Your escape. What happened?"

"We did not escape. We were captured, bound, awaiting death. They made us watch as they killed the assessor brutally." The last word caught in the man's throat and he sobbed. "It was terrible! So very terrible. We thought we were to be killed the same way, but they cut us free and bade us to run."

"To spread the terror all the faster," said Yllescas. "Come then. We must return to Santa Maria and warn the others."

Chapter Thirty Three

Proclaim this among the nations: Prepare for war! Rouse the warriors! Let all the fighting men draw near and attack. Beat your plowshares into swords and your pruning hooks into spears. Let the weakling say, 'I am strong!

Joel 3:9-10

The tents were cleared from the square and a stage, hastily constructed from crates and boards, was erected. A call had gone out to all the people in the town and they were now assembled, looking anxiously at each other, awaiting the announcement. Rumors had already been flying and several people were near hysterics, which did not help the mood. Finally, don Alonso Yllescas mounted the stage and waved everyone to silence. His face was stern, alerting the crowd of the gravity of the situation.

"My friends," he began, his voice steady. "I will not waste your time with pleasantries or assurances of peace. You deserve the truth, and the truth is this: danger is upon us." A ripple of murmurs began to spread through the crowd. Yllescas raised his hand, demanding silence.

"It has come to my attention," he continued, "that an attack is imminent. A force unlike any we have faced before is gathering strength, and they may be at our door at any moment. We will do what we can in whatever time we may have. Our attackers are not some distant threat. Though we have lived somewhat peacefully, with few interactions, the savages are here, in the forests that surround us, watching, waiting. They are warriors, fierce and determined, and their goal is nothing less than our destruction. Apparently, the arrival of the galleon, *Santa Victoria*, has unsettled them. Our friend, Fray Daniel Burgos, has lived among the heathens for years, spreading the word of Our Lord and instilling in them our morals and virtues. It appears, that in this, he has failed.

"But hear me now, and hear me well: we are not helpless. Although Captain Salazar and his men have left, we are not without strength or resolve. Santa Maria has stood for years against hardship, against famine, against threats from within and without. And we will stand again, united, as one people.

"This is what we must do," Alonso said, his tone sharpening like a blade. "First, the safety of our women and children is paramount. They will be sheltered in the church and other strong buildings at the heart of the town, under constant guard. Those who cannot fight will protect them with their lives. Mothers, fathers, I understand the fear you feel, but know this: every effort will be made to ensure their safety."

He gestured toward the soldiers gathered at the edge of the square. "Second, our defenses must be fortified. Though we are few in number, we are resourceful. Every musket, every blade, every tool that can be fashioned into a weapon will be put to use. Hammers, axes, scythes...well, if it can be wielded, it *will* be wielded. And for those of you who have never held a weapon before, our soldiers will train you. There is no time for hesitation or doubt. You must learn, and you must learn quickly.

"Third," he said, "we must work together. This town is not just a collection of houses and businesses. It is a community. Every one of you has a role to play, whether it is guarding the women and children, carrying supplies, tending to the wounded, or simply offering a comforting hand to those in despair. We are stronger together than we are apart."

He stepped closer to the edge of the stage, his voice lowering but gaining intensity. "This will not be easy. It will not be without loss. Yet, we will fight, not just for our lives, but for our future, for the future of Santa Maria. This is *our* home, and we will *not* surrender it.

"Finally," Alonso said, his voice rising again, "we must remember what we are fighting for. Look around you. Look at your families, your friends, your neighbors. These are the people you are protecting. This is the life you are fighting for. Do not let fear consume you. Let it fuel your determination. Let it strengthen your resolve."

He paused, letting his gaze sweep over the crowd. "I cannot tell you how long we have to prepare, to fortify, to train, to pray, but when the time comes, and, for all we know, it might be tonight, we will face our enemy not with fear, but with courage. Not with despair, but with hope. Not as individuals, but as one people."

Don Alonso took a deep breath, his voice softening. "I cannot promise that this will be easy. I cannot promise that we will all see the dawn after this battle. But I can promise you this: we will fight. We will endure. And with God's grace, we will prevail."

As Yllescas concluded his speech, one of the soldiers took the stage and began speaking to the crowd.

"Not many of you know me," he said, "but I am Lieutenant Miguel Estrada. It is Señor Yllescas wish that I lead the military portion of the impending battle. Let us not delay. All women and children will gather what they need and get to the church. Please! Only what you need!" The townsfolk sensed the urgency in his voice and began to disperse. "Men! Gather your weapons and meet me outside the tavern. We need volunteers to build barricades around the church, volunteers to stand watch on the tallest buildings and others to gather provisions. Everyone! Get moving! There is no time to waste!"

The town quickly became a beehive of activity with everyone scrambling to get what and where they needed. On the stage, Yllescas spoke with Estrada. "What of the slaves under your command? The slaves at the mining camp cast us aside and joined the savages. Will you arm them and hope they do not betray us?"

"I will make it clear to them that the savages are their enemy as well as ours. I will offer them their freedom if I have to. They will have nothing to gain by failing us."

* * *

Once the crowd began emptying the square, Rosa approached the Lieutenant. "I want to fight," she told him. "I will not huddle fearfully with the other women while the battle of our lives ensues. Give me a weapon, any weapon, and I will fight in our defense."

Estrada looked at her appraisingly, a hint of mirth in his eyes. "Señora," he began with a smile, "I do not have time to jest. You will be of much more worth in the church. Your spirit alone will bolster their morale."

"I do not jest. You will not think it funny when I knock your teeth down your throat. Give me a weapon or give me your teeth!"

Don Juan Yllescas had strayed within earshot and immediately decided to intercede.

"Espera, espera, espera," he said, putting himself between the pair. "Lieutenant, this is *not* the battle you want to fight. I suggest you give her what she wants and be done with it."

"You cannot be serious, Señor! I will not have her death on my hands!"

"She may die whether you say aye or nay...we *all* may. Do not waste the little time we have. Give her a weapon and send her on her way!"

Estrada frowned and stared at the grim and defiant faces before him. "Very well," he said at last, "I will see what I can find." He turned on his heel and strode away.

"I did not need you to rescue me," Rosa said to Yllescas.

"Apparently not, but at the very least I needed to rescue the man's teeth." He put his hands on her shoulders gently. "Listen, this is the last time I intervene in your persisted efforts to harm yourself. You are a strong woman, of that I have no doubt, but please, take a moment to think before you propel yourself into another ill-conceived action."

"I merely attempt to do the things that should have been done from the outset," she replied. "But far be from me to tell a *man* what to do!"

"Yet here you stand, instead of lying dead, or worse, at the mining camp. No, Señora, from now on, do as you please. My only aim was to protect you, but I cannot protect you from yourself. And no longer will I try. Your destiny, your *fate*, is yours alone."

The sky continued its rumblings. A light rain began to fall, the raindrops masking the tears that rolled down Rosa's face. Whether from anger, fear or despair, she could not tell. *Ignacio, this is all your fault,* she thought. *Without you, my thoughts betray me. If you are dead, then part of me feels I should be dead as well. The only thing that keeps me going is the thought that somewhere, somehow you are still alive.*

As the night wore on, chaos began to take on the appearance of discipline. The church was emptied of anything that could be removed save the altar and wall hangings. With provisions taking up much of the space, a decision was reached to use the adjacent building, that had temporarily housed the prisoners from the *Santa Estrella,* as a second refuse for the women and children. Men were assigned to rooftops to act as lookouts and weapons were gathered. There were few firearms beyond what the soldiers carried, and so the distribution of gunpowder and ammunition was rationed to the handful that needed them.

Lieutenant Estrada made the rounds, gathering small groups of men and pressing them through drills, teaching them to make the most of the weapons they had be it shovels, hoes and even hammers. Fortunately, there was an abundance of blades: knives, machetes and scythes, to complement the arsenal. Among these were Rosa and a few other women who had decided that fighting alongside the men was preferable to hiding in fear. After Estrada's encounter with Rosa, he did not even try to dissuade them from their choice. But that did not mean he did not drill them all the harder. He treated them, with sharp orders and even some profanity, as he did with the men he now commanded.

At last the town achieved a sort of order. There were refinements to be made, to be sure, but these would wait later, if there was time. The rain abated and the sky began to clear. Estrada was relieved, having feared the rain would compromise the gunpowder held by those who were not soldiers.

With the cessation of the rain, an eerie quiet descended on the town. Even the jungle beyond seemed to be holding its breath, causing everyone to become extremely vigilant. The only ones who managed to get any sleep that night were huddled with their children and surrounded by armed men.

Chapter Thirty Four

But everyone who hears these words of mine and does not put them into practice is like a foolish man who built his house on sand. The rain came down, the streams rose, and the winds blew and beat against that house, and it fell with a great crash.

Matthew 7:26-27

The night passed without incident. The morning broke with clear skies and a bright sun, already the promised heat of the day was beginning to be felt. Don Alonso had refused to sequester in the town proper, resolutely insisting to stay at his home, which also meant his house staff. He had sent for his son, don Juan, and Lieutenant Estrada and they arrived as don Alonso finished his breakfast. After hearing their reports, don Alonso sat back, ruminating, his gaze focused on them both.

"I will have you know," he said, "I slept fitfully this night. Many conflicting thoughts ran through my mind, but eventually one became strong enough to push the others from my head. I believe we are going about this all wrong."

"I do not understand," said Estrada, "The town is now fortified to the extent we can manage. Some things can be improved, such as building barricades and securing our perimeter, but I have assigned the tasks and they are underway as we speak."

"I think I know you well enough, father," said don Juan, "to guess where you are headed, but I implore you not to follow that course."

"You do, indeed, know me, my son, yet be assured I have given this much thought and do not take this position lightly." Estrada gave him a puzzled look, then looked from father to son. "I sense your confusion, Lieutenant," continued don Alonso. "You have done a remarkable job shoring up our defenses, given the limited resources and time at your disposal. Yet perhaps defense is not enough. Perhaps a bit of offense is called for. I propose we make an effort to retake the mine."

"Surely, you speak in jest, Señor," exclaimed Estrada.

"I knew it," said don Juan quietly, "I knew it as surely as I know fruit falls from a tree and not the other way around."

"Listen, you two. Hear me out." said don Alonso. "For all we know, the mine still stands. All we have is the word of a few men who perhaps panicked at the mere sight of a savage. Those men are accustomed to bossing the blacks around but they are cowards at heart. Think on it! They returned with their heads securely fastened to their necks! When has *that* ever happened?"

"I have faith in their testimony," countered don Juan. "Far be it from us to know why savages do the things they do. I believe the men to be truthful."

"Ah...no doubt they *believe* it is true, but *is* it true? That mine represents a future for Santa Maria, a future that will be forever denied us if it is lost to us. The town is nothing without it and we will end up living in huts without the interest of the Empire."

"If we should survive until such a time, said Estrada, shaking his head. "We cannot, in good conscience, take men away from our defenses to launch such a foray. It will leave the town undefended!"

"You forget, Lieutenant, that in the absence of Captain Salazar, you answer to me. I am the Chief here and if I say 'launch an offensive', you will do just that!"

"Stop, you two!" exclaimed don Juan, as the two men stared each other down. "Let us not get into a cockfight of words. Father, you are putting the Lieutenant in an untenable position. We cannot just mount an impetuous offensive without a plan in place."

"One thing we can do is send those six men back as scouts."

"A moment ago, you called them cowards!" said Estrada. "At any rate, they are working for the town's safety. Don Juan is right. A plan for such an endeavor requires planning and we have scarce little time for plans."

"We do not know that!" bellowed don Alonso. "What if we find ourselves here tomorrow, in this very room without having been attacked and have done nothing in the meantime? Will you then concede you may be wrong?"

"In the realm of possibilities you have offered us," said Estrada, "that is one I can embrace." He continued in a conciliatory tone, "Señor, let us confer together and discuss these options in a civilized manner. If a plan is needed, then we shall draft it, and if the morrow comes with circumstances unchanged, I will consider your proposal."

"For an armed offensive to retake the mine?"

"Perhaps first a scouting expedition, but please, let us cool our heads and approach this with some logic."

* * *

Rosa was watching as the barricades were being constructed when Carmen approached. She was surprised to see her, thinking the others from her household had sought refuge with the other women. They embraced, Rosa quickly noticing that Carmen was armed, with a knife fastened securely to a wooden pole.

"You armed yourself," Rosa said, eyeing the makeshift weapon.

Carmen nodded. "I had to. They pointed me to a table full of blades and told me to pick one. But I don't intend to let a savage get close enough to use it. So I found a pole." She adjusted her grip. "The farther away I can keep them, the better."

"That is wise," Rosa admitted, then gestured toward the weapon. "Perhaps you can help me find a pole as well. Two, actually. I have two knives."

Carmen frowned. "Two spears? Would that not that be a bit unwieldy?"

Rosa forced a small smile. "One to throw. One to stab."

Carmen exhaled sharply and glanced toward the growing fortifications. Men were hammering, sawing, sharpening wooden stakes. The town was becoming a battlefield. She hugged her arms as if warding off a chill. "I never imagined this."

"None of us did."

"Rosa," Carmen hesitated, lowering her voice. "Do you really think we can do this? Fight them? Kill them? I mean, look at us...a week ago we were baking corn cakes and bread!"

Rosa's fingers tightened around the hilt of her knife. "I think we have no choice."

Carmen swallowed hard. "But... I do not know if I can. Not when the moment comes." Rosa looked at her friend, seeing the fear she herself was trying to suppress.

"Neither do I." Rosa replied quietly. "But I had no doubt of what we will do when the hordes are upon us. We will not have time to ponder whether we can or cannot. Not when our very survival is on the line."

A long pause passed between them. Then Carmen squared her shoulders, shifting the spear in her grip. "I suppose we will find out soon enough."

Rosa nodded. "Yes. We will."

The air in Santa Maria was thick with tension. Even with the noise of the hurried construction of barricades, there was an eerie quiet in the streets. No drums of war beat in the distance, no battle cries echoed through the trees, no indication that there was any danger at all. The barricades were taking shape, encircling the center of town, forming at best a crude defense. Fires flickered in hastily assembled fire pits, illuminating the tense, restless faces of those who had taken refuge here. Elderly men, too old and weak to work, stirred pots of food over open flames.

Rosa and Carmen found themselves standing near one such fire, their weapons still in hand. Rosa felt more restless than ever. She hated being penned in, useless, when danger loomed just beyond the edge of town.

Carmen shivered beside her. "I do not like this," she whispered.

Rosa glanced at her. "None of us do."

"I mean being here, out in the open. It makes me feel like an animal waiting to be slaughtered."

Rosa exhaled. "We are not waiting for slaughter." She gestured toward the men sharpening tools into makeshift weapons, the men hammering and bringing in ever more wood. A nearby house had been essentially dismantled to provide the necessary materials. "We are preparing to fight."

Carmen looked away. "And yet, there is nothing we can do to help." As if to punctuate her words, a frustrated voice rose from a nearby fire.

"What is this?" a soldier snapped, holding up a ladle filled with thin broth. "This will not sustain anyone for battle! We need something stronger!"

"We must make do with what we have," replied the old man stirring the pot. "There is no one to hunt or harvest. We are left with scraps."

Rosa stepped forward. "Then let us make something of those scraps." The men around the fire looked up at her, skeptical. Rosa folded her arms with indignation. "Do you have maize? Beans? Anything hearty?" She was offered a reluctant nod.

"A little," the old man said, grudgingly. "There is perhaps a little meat, but not enough for everyone."

"Just for you then? Get out what you have and let us use it. If the we must fight, we need strength, not water pretending to be soup." The old cooks exchanged glances, then, one by one, they set to work, pulling out what little they had. Carmen, without hesitation, hesitated, joined in, rolling up her sleeves.

The fire crackled as they worked. Rosa diced what few vegetables they had while Carmen stirred a second pot, thickening the broth with whatever grains could be spared. The scent of roasting corn and spices filled the air, cutting through the stale smell of fear that clung to the square.

"Carmen," Rosa murmured after a while.

"Hmm?"

"If we die tomorrow, I do not want my last night to be spent in silence."

Carmen paused, then gave a small, shaky laugh. "What do you want, then?"

"To talk." Rosa glanced at her. "To remember why we fight."

Carmen exhaled and leaned on her stirring spoon. "Then talk. Tell me something good."

Rosa thought for a moment. "I remember when I was little, my mother would bake sweet bread on Sunday mornings. She would wake before dawn, and I would wake to the smell of cinnamon and sugar in the air." She smiled faintly. "It felt like the world was safe, as long as that scent filled the house."

Carmen's face softened. "That sounds nice."

Rosa tilted her head. "What about you?"

Carmen stirred the pot absently. "My father used to take me riding," she said quietly. "We would go to the hills beyond town, where you could see the whole valley spread below. He would point to our little town of Albarracín and say, 'There is your home, Carmen. You must always know where home is.' Carmen paused for a long moment, then she continued, "I miss Albarracín. I thought the world too small and I set my eyes on Callao, where I thought there would be untold opportunities beyond what Albarracín had to offer. A greater will than mine set me here in Santa Maria. Now this is my home." A silence stretched between them, heavy with unspoken words. Carmen sighed. "And tomorrow, our home may be gone."

Rosa met her gaze. "Then we will make sure it is not."

The food was ready before long, and bowls were passed around. It was not much, but it was better than the thin broth that had first been offered. The Rosa and Carmen ate slowly, savoring the stew, not knowing when their next meal would come.

As they finished, Rosa turned to Carmen and smirked. "Come, show me where I can find some poles to make a weapon such as yours." Carmen led her to a pile of lumber near the dismantled house. They soon found what they needed as well as a spool of strong twine. In very short order, the spears were ready. Rosa felt the heft of each weapon in turn, jabbing the air with a grunt. "That is not enough," she said to Carmen. We need to find a place to practice."

Carmen groaned. "Must we?"

"Yes! If we are to fight, I would rather you not skewer yourself, or me, before you skewer an enemy." Carmen rolled her eyes but followed Rosa to a clearer area near the barricades. They found a post that had been discarded by the workers, and Rosa jammed it into the ground.

"This will be our enemy," Rosa said, mirroring the words she had spoken earlier. The two women took turns jabbing at the post, their makeshift spears clumsy in their hands. Carmen flinched with every strike, but Rosa forced her to continue.

"Again," Rosa commanded. "And stop wincing. You cannot afford hesitation." Carmen set her jaw and thrust the spear forward, this time with more force.

Rosa nodded approvingly. "Better." They continued until Carmen's strikes became more confident, until the fear in her grip lessened. Finally, exhausted, they lowered their weapons.

Carmen panted. "If nothing else, I will at least wound someone before they kill me."

Rosa placed a hand on her shoulder. "No one is dying tomorrow."

Carmen gave her a sad smile. "You cannot promise that."

Rosa hesitated, then shook her head. "No, I cannot."

After catching their breath, they gathered their weapons and returned to their spot by the fire. They sat side by side, neither speaking, both listening to the ongoing work. Perhaps tomorrow, everything would change, but for now there was an uneasy peace. All they could do was wait.

* * *

Tsewa watched Ignacio sleep. This was a true sleep, not one brought on by the potion. Ignacio's breaths were regular and even and his face bore a semblance of peace. He had been under the ayahuasca's influence for two days now arising from his trance only briefly for sustenance and water. During those times, he was withdrawn, speaking to no one or even making eye contact with Tsewa. Since then, he had been resting comfortably.

But now, it was time for Ignacio to embark on another journey. The final one, for now. Tsewa was loathe to rouse the man again but he felt his own time growing short and any pretense of patience had abandoned him.

He signaled to one of his wives and this time she brought two bowls, one for Ignacio and one for Tsewa. Propping Ignacio's head on her lap, she put the bowl against his lips. Still asleep, he mechanically drank the bitter liquid. He began to moan as his already saturated body accepted another dose. From his perch, Tsewa could see that Ignacio's eyes had begun to twitch beneath his eyelids. He knew then that it was time and drained his own bowl. His wives caught him as he slumped over and gently moved his frail form to his pallet. There, they gently bathed Tsewa's body first with water, then with a fragrant oil. They placed his arms, crossed, over his chest and, each in turn, kissed him on the forehead

They began to chant then, a slow heavy toned song full of grief and mourning.

The river calls, the river takes,
A path unseen, a journey made.
The wind that spoke now whispers low,
Its voice is fading, soft as rain.

As they sang, they placed his few possessions about his body.
Oh, great one, drift beyond,
Oh, strong one, hear the song.
The sky awaits, the earth lets go,

The stars will light your way.

They laid garlands of flowers next, one a crown that was reverently placed on his head.

Rest now, father, warrior, guide,
Your hands have shaped, your words remain.
The jungle hums, the night is full,
We send you forth, yet hold you near.

They knelt then by his pallet and began a vigil that would not end until Tsewa drew his last. His instructions to them had been clear: he was not returning from this last vision-quest. His pallet was to become his funeral bier.

Your steps were deep upon this land,
The trees still bow, they knew your name.
The spirits watched, they called to you,
And now you walk among their ranks.
Oh, great one, drift beyond,
Oh, strong one, hear the song.
The sky awaits, the earth lets go,
The stars will light your way...

Tsewa had given them instructions regarding the white man as well. They would continue their vigil patiently until one departed and the other returned.

Chapter Thirty Five

Never interrupt your enemy when he is making a mistake.

Napoleon Bonaparte – circa 1805

The next day was an almost exact duplicate as the previous. The sky was clear, the sun was exceptionally hot and what remaining fortifications could be made were underway. The labors came to a pause however, when don Alonso Yllescas once again mounted a makeshift stage. A hush came over the townsfolk and soldiers as he called for their attention.

"My friends, brave men and women of Santa Maria," he began, in a loud, commanding voice. "We stand here once more, under the same sun, on the same earth, and yet today is unlike any other day. In the time since learning of the attack and plunder of the mining camp, I have given this much thought and it has become clear that we have but one path forward. Today, we will make a choice, not just for ourselves, but for our children, our homes, and our future. We have built this town with our sweat, defended it with our blood, and cherished it with our hearts. But now, shadows threaten our home, and whispers of fear seep into our homes. I will not allow it. *We will not allow it!*

"The savages have taken our mine, our lifeblood. They threaten our livelihood and our safety. They believe we will cower, that we will sit idly by and watch our hard-won prosperity be stripped away, but I say no! We are not a people who yield, not to any man, not to any tribe, and certainly not to fear.

"There are some who have argued," he said pointedly looking at Lieutenant Estrada and his own son, "that we should wait, that patience will protect us. But patience in the face of such aggression is nothing but surrender. Make no mistake! The heathens have declared war upon us, not with words, but with actions. By taking our mine, they have struck at the heart of our town, our economy, our way of life. They believe they have weakened us, that we will crumble. But we are stronger than they know

"And so, I call upon you—not to wait for their war to reach our gates, but to take the fight to them. Let us be the storm that they did not foresee. Let us be the thunder that shakes their confidence and the lightning that ignites their fear.

"We will strike first! Not out of recklessness, but out of necessity. We will reclaim what is ours, not just for the wealth within the earth, but for the dignity of our people, for the message it sends. We are not victims. We are not prey. We are the defenders of Santa Maria!"

Adopting a softer tone, he continued. "Our town is small, our numbers few, but our hearts are fierce, and our will unbreakable. Let them see that when they look upon us. Let them see that we do not fear their arrows or their spears. Let them see that we are united, resolute, and ready to defend what is rightfully ours. The mine is not merely a place where gold and silver are drawn from the earth. It is a symbol of our perseverance, our strength, our unity. It is the sweat and toil of every man who has descended into its depths, every woman who has supported this town, and every child who dreams of a brighter future. If we allow them to hold it, if we permit their claim to stand unchallenged, we are admitting defeat before the battle has even begun." His voice again regained its volume, thrusting his finger into the air. "We cannot, nay, *we will not,* let that happen. By retaking the mine, we do more than reclaim our property. We send a message that Santa Maria is not to be trifled with. That we are not a people who bow to threats or succumb to fear. We are a people who stand, who fight, who prevail.

"And let this be known, not just to those godless savages, but to all who would think to test our resolve...Santa Maria is a bastion! We are a people forged in the fires of hardship, tempered by the trials of the New World, and we will not break. We will rise, and we will conquer the challenges set before us. The forest people think they can divide us, make us question our strength. Let us show them they are wrong. Let us show them that every man, every woman, and even our children know that freedom is worth fighting for, that peace is worth defending, and that Santa Maria is worth every drop of sweat, every heartbeat, every breath.

"So I tell you now, we will bear arms, not just for gold, not just for land, but for honor, for pride, for the very soul of our town! We will fight so that our children can sleep soundly, knowing that their parents did not yield to fear!

"This is our time to prove that we are more than settlers on this foreign shore. We are its masters. We are its protectors. And we will not be driven away. We will not be made to fear the shadows that dance beyond our walls. We will drive them back. We will retake our mine. We will defend Santa Maria.

"Stand with me now. Let us march not with fear, but with courage. Let us meet them not with trepidation, but with unyielding strength. Let us reclaim what is ours, and show the world what the people of Santa Maria are made of.

"To victory, my friends—to victory!"

Don Alonso was greeted, not with the thunderous applause he expected, but with a chorus of murmurs and raised voices. One of the voices became suddenly louder.

"The gold is more important to you that the people? Your plan will leave the town undefended!"

"Are you leading the march yourself or will you be huddled here with the rest of us?" shouted another. The outcries sparked a chorus of boos as well as loud arguments breaking out among the assembled, some for, many more against. The crowd was quickly losing control. Don Alonso gesticulated wildly and called for order.

"Quiet!" he bellowed. "Quiet! I did not come to you for debate or for your permission! As the Chief of Santa Maria, I will dictate when and how we will do things. Firstly, the expedition will be led by Lieutenant Estrada. He and his soldiers will be the tip of the spear. Secondly, I conscript all the slaves among us into this expedition. Hear me, bondsmen! Any among you who fight valiantly and survive to return, will be granted freedom. You will all be free men in Santa Maria, free to own property, free to live and work as you please!" This last declaration stunned the crowd into a hush, although murmurs continued. "All that I ask now is for volunteers among you to fill the rest of the force. Any of you who wish to be part of our righteous cause will come forward and stand with Lieutenant Estrada and his men."

"And what will you offer us?" someone shouted. "We already have our freedom!"

"That is right!" offered another, "are we less than slaves to you?"

Don Alonso declined to respond to these protests, and said instead, "These brave men will embark on their mission at dusk. They will then retake the mining camp at dawn, surprising the savages unawares. Come, you brave men of Santa Maria, be free of the fear of savages forever! That well be your reward!" He descended from the stage and joined Estrada. Surprisingly, roughly a quarter of the men in attendance joined him as well, leaving the rest to stare in disbelief.

In short order, the volunteers set about gathering all the slaves they could find. They pushed them together and started handed them weapons, not muskets or blades, but farming implements and clubs. Conscripted, armed and pledged, but not trusted.

As the dust settled, Rosa and Carmen stood to the side, watching the scene unfold. The slaves, their faces a mix of confusion, fear, and anger, accepted the crude weapons given to them. The soldiers and the volunteers did not even look them in the eyes as they pressed the crude weapons into their hands. It was clear enough that these men were not comrades in arms, but tools for a desperate and perhaps foolhardy cause.

Carmen folded her arms and exhaled sharply. "Freedom, he says."

Rosa's eyes narrowed as she watched a volunteer shove a rusted spade into a slave's hands. "A freedom bought in blood and for someone else's interests," she said grimly.

Carmen turned to her. "Loathsome, is it not? How many of them will live to claim it?" Rosa did not answer immediately. Instead, she observed the way the slaves looked at each other, some murmuring in their own tongue, others casting dark glances at the men who now commanded them.

"That is the point, no?" she said finally. "Don Alonso grants them their freedom, but only if they survive this madness. He does not care that most will not. Even the volunteers and soldiers. He hopes to be able to keep his gold and the hell with anything, or anyone, else."

Carmen shivered despite the heat of the day. "This is not well reasoned.

It is suicide. And they will have us share in their doom." Carmen glanced at the ragged formation of men standing near Estrada. Some looked eager, gripping their weapons tightly, their jaws set. Others, though, were hesitating, shifting their weight, casting uncertain glances at the slaves and back at the town. "The men who volunteered," she continued, "do they really think this to be the best course?"

"They do," said Rosa. "The fools. They think this will be some grand victory, that they'll return as heroes." She scoffed., as she watched Estrada barking orders. The preparations were moving quickly now, and dusk would come soon enough. She looked at Carmen with an amused smile. "Would you go, if they asked you?"

Carmen blinked in surprise. "Me? Of course not! I would sooner throw myself into the river. And I *was* asked. We *all* were. I was in the crowd as well as you."

Rosa's smile faded quickly. "I know and now here we stand, waiting for them to deliver us from evil. When the evil does come, and they are not here to help with the defense, we will not be given any choice but to fight." Carmen was silent for a long moment. Then she whispered, "Do you think the savages *will* come? It has been two days since the initial panic and we have seen no sign that we are truly in danger."

Rosa turned back toward the gathered men, the slaves gripping their pitiful weapons, the volunteers making hurried plans. She did not know many of them personally. She did not know if she would know any of them ever again.

"Yes," she said quietly. "I think they will."

The day wore on at an unhurried pace. Nothing truly had changed from the day before save that there fewer men working in the square. Those that remaining continued with the chores required of them. The building of barricades kept going apace, while a wall of questionable strength started to sprout along the town's perimeter. It would not keep invaders out but certainly would hinder their momentum before reaching the subsequent barriers and the town proper.

At length, the sun westered and shadows lengthened. Don Alonso's makeshift army had assembled at the mouth of the mine road. The trees bowed menacingly over the road and beyond them darkness awaited ominously. A few looked that way with trepidation but most were stone-faced and grim. Before embarking, don Alonso provided what he hoped were inspiring words to those willing, and unwilling, to follow his orders.

"To those of you who march willingly," he began, "you will be remembered as heroes. Your names will be spoken with reverence. To those of you who march because you must, know this: fate has given you an opportunity. Prove yourselves. Fight bravely. You will not only live, but live as free men. No more chains. No more masters. Only the dignity of those who have fought and won their place in this world. There will be no retreat. No mercy. Strike them down before they strike you. Show them no weakness, for they will show you none. If you hesitate, you die. If you falter, you doom the man beside you. So be strong! Be ruthless! And when the sun rises, let it shine upon a victory that will echo through these lands for generations to come!"

With that, Estrada took the first steps onto the road with his soldiers while the rest followed behind. Don Juan, who had been standing with his father felt compelled to comment.

"Fine words that they will no doubt carry in their hearts as they march. They will think of you, cozy in your house while they risk their lives for you."

"Mind your words lest I send you scrambling after them!" said don Alonso in retort. "They go at my command, but it is for themselves they do this thing. Is it my fault the savages chose the mine for their show of hostility? To align my strategy with the gold that now resides in their hands is an unfair characterization. If they had instead invaded our farms, everyone would say I was more interested in maíz than their lives."

"You *do* enjoy one or two bollos de maíz every day for breakfast," chided don Juan. "You know this will do nothing but stir the hornet's nest. Just remember, when all this is said and done, that I opposed what I see as a rash and impetuous action. You will remember the heroes should they prevail but will you remember those that die at your whim?"

Don Alonso's face darkened at his son's words. He turned his feet to his home, offering "Hmmph," as his only reply.

* * *

There are always watchers in the forest. As soon as Estrada and his contingent embarked on their mission, runners were sent to Wajari, running along paths unseen and unknown to those on the road.

Wajari received the news with his customary grin. "This is better than I had hoped for," he said to Shakaim and Pinchu. "They unknowingly send us an offering and we will take it! It will be nothing to cut them off and cripple them before they know what has happened. Take warriors back with you." he said to the runners. "Secure the road behind them and close their retreat. Let this place be the only choice they have, but they will never reach it!"

As the runners went to do as they were bid, Wajari turned to his compatriots and said, "This group on the road is largely made up of slaves. Let as many of the black men with us join the party we will send to meet them. Let the slaves see their brothers arrayed against them and we will see how many of them will still follow the commands of the demons. All else remains as we planned. The town falls at dawn!"

* * *

"Is this another of your well-thought ideas or something else entirely?" asked don Rafael Montoya. The Magistrate was seated in don Alonso's office along with the other town officials.

"I must admit that it is more of a feeling, but do not discount it out of hand," said don Alonso. "It is a contingency that I think we should consider."

"A contingency that will forever mark us as pariahs in the community. You propose to move the town's leaders to the *Santa Estrella* to wait out the storm? Tell me, how will any of the townspeople view that without labeling us as cowards? And what of our families? My own wife is one of the many stored away in the church."

"Well, I suppose that immediate family could be considered as well, but remember, the vessel is rather small. There will have to be few exceptions."

"And then what, Señor?" asked don Rafael. "We will still be lashed to the dock. None among us are sailors. How would that be any safer than anywhere else in the town?"

"A contingency, as I have said. If needs be, we could loose ourselves from the mooring and trust to the currents to push us from the shore."

Don Rafael crossed his arms and took a deep breath. "The only thing that has been loosed from its moorings is your mind. I, and I hope I speak for the others present, plan to remain where I am and take up arms if that is what is needed of me. Take yourself and your household and hide on the ship if you like. I will have no part of it."

Don Alonso looked about the room at the other officials. Many had their eyes downcast, their manner sullen and quiet. None were clamoring to join don Alonso.

"So be it," he said. "I will safeguard my family and household. We will be alone, I warrant, but they will be safe with me come the storm."

Don Rafael rose and made to leave. The other men in the room seemed to be of like mind. As he left, he addressed don Alonso one more time.

"You are mad," he said, "and even worse...you are a coward."

Chapter Thirty Six

See, I have this day set thee over the nations and over the kingdoms, to root out, and to pull down, and to destroy, and to throw down, to build, and to plant.

Jeremiah 1:10

All was darkness. It was not a mere absence of light. It somehow pulsed like a living thing, vast and infinite. It did not press upon Ignacio like the heavy black of a moonless night, nor did it swirl like the shifting void behind closed eyes. Instead, it simply *was*, stretching in all directions beyond comprehension, a boundless abyss where time itself seemed to unravel.

There was no up, no down, no sense of distance or proximity. He reached out, to wave his hands before his eyes before realizing...he had no hands. He had no sense of body other than his awareness. Had he gone blind? Had he died? The fear suddenly bloomed within him and he fought desperately to push it down. He calmed himself, unable even to take a deep breath. He seemed to not need air, just as he had no other sense other than just *being*. Again, the panic threatened to overwhelm him, when a spark suddenly ignited before him. It was small and dim, and now that he had something to focus on, he gained a sense of how vast the abyss was. The spark was incredibly far away, but even as he thought this the spark began to come toward him, growing brighter and larger.

Ever closer the spark came. It began to elongate until it began to appear as a rip in the very fabric of the void. Ignacio had no choice but to watch as the spark came ever closer, ever brighter. With a start, he noticed there was a shape of sorts within the spark, darker than the surrounding halo, yet bright in its own manner. The shape began to undulate, stretching this way and that until it settled on a definite form. It took on the general appearance of a man-like figure, and now that it was closer, Ignacio could see that the figure was striding toward him.

Tsewa! The thought came to Ignacio unbidden. Although the figure seemed unformed, like a crude figure made of clay, he had no doubt that he was correct. Ignacio wanted to shout out, in greeting or alarm, he was not sure which, but nothing came forth.

Again, Ignacio was overwhelmed, not by panic but by a feeling of calm and serenity that emanated from the manifestation. *Do not fear,* a voice said in his mind, *you will be made whole.* The image coalesced further, taking on definition and Ignacio could see that it was indeed Tsewa as he had seen him in his visions; a strong, youthful warrior full of life. Yet, in Tsewa's eyes, Ignacio could see a sort of sadness and he realized this was an end of sorts. He would never again see Tsewa in the flesh. While this realization was still in his mind, Tsewa's figure contracted, becoming a dark mote somehow even darker than the surrounding void. Ignacio's perspective shifted abruptly. No longer was the apparition coming toward him, he now sensed he was falling into a shining well with the mote at its bottom.

Bright ribbons of light streamed by him at a feverish speed as he fell. And fell. And fell. If not for the streamers flowing past, Ignacio could not tell that time was passing. The mote suddenly grew and Ignacio plunged into it.

There was no landing. He did not crash into the darkness as he had expected. Instead, he passed into it, through it, becoming a part of it even as it became part of him. There was no sensation of impact, only an overwhelming flood of experience, as if an entire life was being poured into his mind, saturating his very essence.

At first, all was chaos. Flashes of color, sounds that had no meaning, emotions that were not his own but coursed through him as if they had always belonged to him. Then, like a river settling into its bed, the torrent began to take shape. He was no longer Ignacio. He was a boy, standing at the edge of a river, its surface shimmering under the sun. His mother was beside him, her hand on his shoulder, pointing at the water where fish darted beneath the surface. He felt the warmth of her hand, the comfort of her presence, the smell of earth and vegetation thick in the air. This was Tsewa's memory, Tsewa's childhood, but Ignacio *was* him now, seeing through his eyes, feeling his emotions.

The scene shifted, and Ignacio was running through the jungle, feet bare against the damp earth. His heart pounding, not from fear, but exhilaration. He was chasing something, a howler monkey swinging through the branches above, its cries echoing through the trees. His lungs were burning, but he did not stop. The chase was life, movement was life, the jungle was life. He could feel the rhythm of it, the pulse of the world around him, as if he were one with the roots and the leaves and the creatures that moved unseen.

Another shift. He was older now, standing in the circle of warriors, their bodies painted, their faces solemn. A test of courage. He gripped his spear, feeling its weight in his hands, knowing that tonight he would prove himself. The elders sang their chants, their voices deep and rhythmic, weaving through the night air like the smoke of the fire that flickered before them. His pulse was steady, his resolve firm. The jungle watched, the spirits watched. He stepped forward.

The flood of memories came faster now, each one a thread in the great weave of Tsewa's life. The hunt, the battle, the love, the sorrow. He felt the sting of loss when his father did not return from war. He felt the pride of standing beside his brothers, painted and ready to defend their home. He felt the warmth of a lover's embrace, the soft whisper of her voice in the stillness of the night. These were no longer just images. They were experiences, lived and real, as much a part of Ignacio as his own memories.

Then came the knowledge. The wisdom of generations passed down through spoken word, through ritual, through the silent teachings of the jungle itself. He understood now the language of the wind through the trees, the way the earth whispered secrets through the movement of animals, the song of the river as it carved its path through the land. He understood the cycle: the birth, the growth, the death, and the rebirth. He saw how man was neither above nor apart from this cycle, but within it, a single note in the great song of existence.

Tsewa's voice enveloped him. *No longer are you only yourself. You carry me now, as I have carried those before me. Our spirits are not lost, only given.* Ignacio felt his own sense of self flickering, as if he were dissolving into this vast ocean of memory. He struggled, clinging to his identity. He was Ignacio, the foreigner, the outsider. He was not a warrior, not Shuar, but even as he resisted, the flood did not cease. The river of memory did not yield. And then, finally, he let go.

And in letting go, he understood.

He was Ignacio, but he was also Tsewa. He was the jungle, the river, the sky. He was the hunter and the hunted, the living and the dead. And now the knowledge of generations began to course through him. Nantu, Tayusha and Yankuam...all Uwishin before Tsewa...Etsa, Kuwi, Ampush...they were all there in a line that stretched back to the beginning of time, and now Ignacio was part of that never-ending chain. It would take Ignacio a long time to reconcile everything he had absorbed. He rested and willed the void to take him again. Floating everywhere and nowhere, the darkness embraced him and held him. This was a womb nurturing and protecting him as he prepared for his rebirth. He took comfort in its safety. He would take as long as he needed.

But then... another spark appeared.

* * *

Wajari was not a prognosticator. He was not a prophet. In many ways, he was not very bright. But he *did* know the things that were important to him: hunting and warfare. Thus he accurately predicted the events surrounding the battle of the mining road.

It was full dark as the expedition marched up the road. Stops had been made along the way for water and provisions, and the breaks, though necessary, took longer than Estrada would have liked. If they were to make the camp by dawn, they would have to get moving. Estrada had grudgingly allowed the breaks, but now he set them on their feet and on their way saying, "We are not stopping again. We are a war party and the war awaits us."

Wary eyes darted left and right at the surrounding foliage as much as they looked ahead. The jungle was hushed and the troupe made an extraordinary amount of noise as they traveled. It was unavoidable, of course, armor and armaments are not necessarily made for stealth. After a while, a measure of comfort descended among the men as no threats to their advance materialized and they began talking quietly. The soldiers behind Estrada became more emboldened, speaking louder than necessary.

"I cannot see a wretched thing," one soldier muttered, squinting into the gloom.

"Stop griping," his companion grunted.

"I like griping," came the immediate response. A few of the men chuckled softly, the tension bleeding away as the exchange continued.

Estrada, marching at the head of the column, shot a glare over his shoulder. "Stow it, that is enough!" he snapped, his voice low but firm. "The next man that speaks will be pulling rear guard alone in the dark."

The laughter died instantly. The jungle remained silent, its unseen eyes watching.

After a while, one of the volunteers made his way forward to Estrada.

"Lieutenant," he said, "I know this road. A little further it curves to the left, then the road becomes quite steep but leads straight to the camp. We can be there in minutes."

"Excellent!" said Estrada. "Prepare yourselves, men! The time has come for us to fulfill our duty. Forward!"

The host negotiated the turn and found themselves on a straight path just as the volunteer had said. It was steep but not impassable. They looked up, eager to see the camp but they were greeted with a far different sight.

A lone man, a black man stood at the crest bearing a torch. He began shouting in a tongue unfamiliar to the soldiers and volunteers. He was addressing the slaves among them.

"Brothers! Sons of Africa! Sons of suffering! I am Bahati! The time of chains is over!" Bahati raised his torch high, the flickering flame casting wild shadows across his face. His voice rang out, strong and commanding, cutting through the humid night air like a blade. A murmur rippled through the ranks of the slaves below. They glanced at each other, uncertainty warring with something deeper.   Bahati's voice swelled with fire. "I know your hearts beat fast! I know your hands shake at the weapons they have given you! I know because I was once like you. Beaten, bound, used as a beast of labor for their gold, for their hunger, for their power! But I am a beast no longer!"

He struck his chest with his free hand, the sound like a drumbeat in the night. "Look at them!" he shouted, thrusting the torch toward the soldiers and volunteers. "They do not arm you because they trust you! They do not march you here because they see you as men! They drive you forward like cattle to die in their fight!" A few of the enslaved men shifted uneasily, gripping their makeshift weapons. The soldiers among them stiffened, not knowing what was transpiring.

"Who will you bleed for tonight? The men who whipped your backs? The men who stole your names? The men who will throw your bodies in a ditch when you fall? Or will you stand with your true brothers? With the men who have broken their chains, who have seized their freedom, who will never again bow to any master?"

He swept his torch in a wide arc, illuminating the crest of the hill. Shadows moved. Figures emerged from the darkness. More freed slaves, armed, waiting.

"Come to us! Come to your own! Raise your weapons, but not for them! Turn them upon your oppressors and walk with us into freedom!"

The soldiers were taken aback. "Who is that?" one exclaimed. "What is he saying?" cried another.

"It matters not!" shouted Estrada. "Train your muskets! Cut him down!"

Shots rang out and Bahati stumbled. But before another volley could be sent his way, the forest on either side of the expedition erupted. Scores of Shuar warriors and freed slaves descended upon them. The bonded slaves among the volunteers did not hesitate in the least. They fell upon their erstwhile companions with a frenzy, shouting over and over, "Freedom! Freedom!"

Bahati nursed his arm where a musket ball had grazed him. It was nothing and he felt no pain. He looked upon the melee below and smiled. He longed to join the fray, but it was over almost before it had started. Another victory for freedom.

* * *

All through the night the sentries on the rooftops kept their attention on the wall of forest surrounding the mine road. They relied on logic that offered two alternatives. One, that the expedition would return victorious, or second, if the expedition had failed, then the main force of savages would be emboldened and come from that direction, using the road as the path of least resistance to the town.

For two days Rosa had done what she could to help the townsfolk, particularly the women, cope with the impending threat. Although she and Carmen ran through their drills whenever they could, she found that a large amount of time was spent seeing to the needs of those sequestered in the church and the adjacent building. She was making sure they had the provisions they needed and, more often than not, managing the cooking of meals.

She awoke well before dawn and set about starting the fire in the stone-lined pit and gathering items for the morning meal. *I might as well have been a scullery maid*, she thought to herself. In reality, she did not mind the work. It gave her a sense of purpose and more importantly, kept her busy. The fire was just starting to catch when Carmen joined her.

"Good morning, Rosa," Carmen said, her arm over her mouth as she unsuccessfully tried to stifle a yawn. "Are we ready for yet another day of abject boredom and drudgery as we wait for something that may never materialize?"

"Enjoy the boredom while you can, sister," replied Rosa. "Those foolish men are kicking the anthill even as we speak. Who knows what the day will bring."

"If it brings a hot cup of chicha that will be enough to start."

"I know you are barely awake," said Rosa crossly, "but it would do you well to not be so flippant." Carmen plopped down on a nearby stool, rubbing the sleep from her eyes as Rosa fed more wood into the fire. The flames caught, flickering against the pre-dawn darkness, casting their shadows large against the walls. Rosa handed her a small cup of chicha, which Carmen accepted with a satisfied hum.

"Thank you, my ever-dutiful mother," she teased before taking a sip.

Rosa rolled her eyes. "Please take this more seriously. Whatever transpires at the camp, we should know before nightfall."

Carmen blew on her drink. "They will probably drag their feet, trying to haul back as much gold as they can carry. That is the real reason Yllescas sent them"

Rosa shot her a sharp look. "Don't be naive."

Carmen sighed and glanced around. The town was beginning to stir. A few women shuffled out from the buildings, eyes heavy with sleep, cradling their shawls around themselves as they prepared for another day of waiting. The air was thick with tension.

"I *do* take this seriously," Carmen said, her voice lower. "But what else am I to do? We drill, we watch, we work, and yet we are still here, waiting. If I let myself dwell too much on what could happen, I will go mad."

Rosa softened slightly. She understood. The waiting was almost worse than the fight itself. At least in battle, there was action, decisions to make, something to do. But here, confined to the square, all they could do was brace for whatever came.

"I just hate feeling useless," Carmen admitted, resting her chin in her palm.

Rosa exhaled and stood, brushing the dust from her skirts. "Then don't be. Come, help me finish the meal. The children will be hungry soon, and I do not want to hear them crying this morning. It makes the women all the more fearful."

Carmen nodded and rose, stretching her arms over her head. "Yes, yes, nothing like labor to keep the mind occupied." She gave Rosa a small smirk. "At least until we get to run some more drills and pretend we're proper warriors."

Rosa handed her a ladle. "There is no pretending, sister. When the time comes, we will be."

Above them a sentry looked down on the fire. The smoke came up to him carrying the first odors of the morning meal. His stomach began to growl. *I hope my relief comes soon,* he thought. *First a hot meal then bed.* He stepped forward slightly to catch more of the aroma. He realized with a start that there was *too much* smoke for such a small fire and that the smell was much more than wood burning. He whipped around and saw behind him the reason.

"Fire! Fire!" he shouted. "The savages are burning the farms!"

Chapter Thirty Seven

They hunted our steps so that we could not walk in our streets; our end was near, our days were fulfilled, for our end had come. Our pursuers were swifter than the eagles of the sky; they chased us upon the mountains, they laid wait for us in the wilderness.

Lamentations 4:18-19

By the time the alarm was raised, the fire in the fields was already spreading quickly. The farm houses and outlying buildings were already engulfed, and as the sky lightened with the dawn, it was dimmed by the thick black smoke. The field where maize was planted seemed to be the epicenter but the fire had already spread beyond its borders. All the crops were in danger now and the flames were dancing their way toward the town.

There was nothing to be done. The farmers and their families had been moved to the relative safety of Santa Maria and they now stood horrified as their livelihood was consumed. A granary and storage building still stood between the farms and the town but the flames were already licking their sides. Their destruction was inevitable.

Panic ensued as the wind began to push the smoke in their direction, bringing the reality of the tragedy to their very doorstep. It seemed no one recalled the danger of the impending attack, more concerned about the lose of their food stores. Without crops, the town would face decimating hardship. Chaos took hold as people rushed to and fro without purpose. Some were stricken to the spot they stood, wailing and sobbing in fear. Rosa, however, kept her head and took charge of those around her.

"Women!" she shouted as she began herding them. "Gather up your children and get back into your shelter! The danger is here! Move!" Some she waved forward, others she had to take by the arm. As soon as the flow started going in the right direction, she cast about at the nearby men. "Get buckets! Get water!"

"What good will that do, woman?" a man shouted back. "We cannot put out the fields with buckets!"

"Forget the fields, you dolts! The crops are gone but the flames are getting closer! Soon the buildings will burn unless we begin dousing them now!" There were no further arguments and the men scrambled for the buckets as if it had been their own idea. Carmen was standing nearby with a dumbfounded look on her face, dazed and immobile. Rosa grabbed her by the arm and shook her.

"Carmen!" she shouted into Carmen's face. "Where is your spear? The time has come!" Carmen looked at her blankly.

"Is it time to practice our drills again?" she asked numbly. Rosa gripped her tighter, and with her free hand, slapped her hard across the face. Carmen winced and fell to one knee. "What was *that* for?" she cried.

"Get on your feet and get your spear! There is no time! The savages will no doubt follow the flames!" Their spears had been leaning on a tree near the fire pit. They picked them up and looked at each other briefly. Carmen had tears in her eyes, her cheek blazing red. Rosa looked at her kindly. "I am sorry to have struck you Carmen," she said tenderly. "The time has come to do what we have dreaded, but we will do bravely, together. Right?"

"I changed my mind," said Carmen, a slight smile coming to her lips. "I want to go back to being bored."

Before either could make another move, war cries erupted all around them. Shouts of 'Ajaá!' and 'Neká!' mixed in the air with 'They are here!' and 'The savages!'. Rosa and Carmen took off at a run.

Shuar warriors erupted from all sides of the town, howling like the spirits of the dead. The ramshackle wall the defenders had erected fell ineffectually at the feet of the warriors, not slowing them in the slightest. The few sections that remained upright were set afire, further encircling the town with flames. Most of the men on the roofs had muskets, and while many found their mark, there were many more warriors to replace them, too many to stem the flow. Still, they did what they could as the Shuar came up against the barricades, but ultimately it was not enough as these too, once breached were ignited by the brands carried by the invaders.

To the Shuar, the priority was the muskets. Several of them were set to climb the buildings and disable them. They scampered up the backs where there was less resistance and scampered up like monkeys. Many of the snipers were caught off guard as they were suddenly attacked from behind. Most were killed unawares by a stealthy spear in the back. Some were able to give fight briefly, but these too were overwhelmed. In short order, the few guns at the town's disposal fell silent.

The warriors quickly set about putting the buildings they had conquered to the torch. The few townspeople that were still inside them came streaming out from the doors and windows only to be met with spears and knives. The defenders came at the warriors fiercely, temporarily turning the tide of the slaughter. Many warriors retreated to their ranks but not before severe damage was caused.

The wall had failed, the barricades were breached, the gunmen had been silenced, and now a new threat was at the door. A second wave came behind the Shuar...the freed African slaves. While the warriors were merely fierce, the Africans came at the defender not just fierce, but with a hatred and anger that had been bottled up for years. They fell on their former masters with a ferocity that belied their former complacence and drove the defenders back

Chaos descended into the streets of Santa Maria. Without the soldiers or Lieutenant Estrada to coordinate their efforts, the people of the town fought without strategy, without leadership. They fought bravely although they were forced into isolated skirmishes throughout the town, but the Shuar, for all their savagery, had a plan. Foot by painful foot, they were driven slowly toward the square, away from any place that might offer shelter or concealment.

Rosa wiped sweat and blood from her eyes. When the fighting had broken out she had dived in without reservation. She had wounded more than a few of the warriors but had not killed any. It was strange that any time she entered a fray, the warriors had pointedly avoided confronting her. More than once they had backed away at her approach and another time a group of them ran by her to join another skirmish without trying to harm her. She was not so reserved and swung her spear whenever she could.

It was she who first noticed the flames had reached the church. She ran to the doors and flung them open. "The church is on fire!" she screamed, "We must get them out!" A semblance of organization came upon the defenders nearby, holding off the horde as the women and children poured out. The same was done for the adjacent building although that had had not yet been touched by the flames. The protectors shoved the escapees behind them even as the warriors threatened to surround them.

"To the ship!" shouted a voice. "Women, children! This way to the ship!" It was don Juan Yllescas, appearing seemingly out of nowhere. He waved to those who had sought asylum, "Hurry! There is no time!" The refugees, crying and near hysteria, ran toward his beckoning figure, the defenders pushing back against the swarm.

The last of the escapees exited the church and Rosa turned back to the conflict. She bore down on a warrior before her, her spear held high. He glared at her and knocked her spear aside with his own. Rather than following up his attack, he shoved her violently out of the way and moved on to find more acceptable prey. In his wake, several more warriors followed, stepping over Rosa without harm. Rosa was dazed from her fall, her head had made brief contact with the ground and stars danced in her eyes. When her vision cleared, she saw a hand reaching down to help her up.

"Are you alright?" asked Carmen as she pulled Rosa to her feet. Rosa brushed herself off, her eyes flitting over Carmen. She was disheveled and dirty, but whole.

"Of course I am," Rosa snapped. "I have been running around to no great effect. They will not engage me in battle."

"We are not a threat to them, apparently. They ignore me as well."

"Well, they do so at their own peril. I will stab them in the back if I have to!"

"Should we run for the boat? For all the good we are doing here?"

"Never!" Rosa shouted defiantly. "This is *my* home. I will not be driven from it!" She turned and ran back to the knots of fighting men. Carmen sighed deeply, took a firmer grip on her spear and followed.

Don Juan Yllescas waved the mob of women and children toward the waterfront. He had been opposed to using the *Santa Estrella* as a refuge initially because it had been proposed by his father as a retreat for the town's elite, but now there was no choice. The only question was, would there be enough room for everyone. His father had taken possession of de Cuellar's cabin immediately after the meeting with the officials and he was still there taking up precious space. *Damn him! He cannot object to harboring these people to save his own skin!* Luckily, the gangplank was still in place. Don Juan had feared that his father may have removed it at the first sign of trouble. The throng made its way swiftly onto the deck as Yllescas waved them on, helping those who stumbled or fell.

Finally, the last of them boarded the ship and Yllescas set about clearing the mooring lines. He was cutting it close...the fighting was coming nearer. Running up the gangplank, he wondered how he was going to deploy the sails alone. He was the only one aboard with any knowledge of watercraft. *Well, they are going to have to learn fast!* He was about to start shouting orders at the refugees when something caught his eye. He turned to look out over the water.

There were hundreds of Shuar canoes making their way from the northern shore.

It was over all too quickly. The sun had barely reached its zenith and the sounds of battle had faded away. The warriors now spent their time putting the remaining structures of the town to the torch. The church was nothing more than a burnt husk as well as everything that once ringed the square. The flames rose higher and higher as if challenging the sun itself. Gone were the Administrative building, the tavern and the others. Now the attention was focused on the homes that circled the town.

Both forces had suffered losses but by far the Shuar had had the advantage through sheer numbers. There were yet a few survivors among the defenders. These were now being dispatched systematically. Two of them stood now, back to back, spears facing the ring of warriors that surrounded them.

"This is it, Carmen!" shouted Rosa. "Give them Hell!"

Chapter Thirty Eight

There was once a great serpent who lived in the depths of the river. It was older than the trees, older than the mountains, and it knew the ways of the world. The serpent did not hunt, nor did it hoard. It moved with the water, never fighting the current, never taking more than what was given. One day, men came to the river's edge. They saw the serpent's home and marveled at the richness of the land. They cut the trees to build their houses. They trapped the fish, taking more than their hunger demanded. They dug into the earth, pulling its treasures from the soil. The serpent watched, but it did not move. It listened, but it did not speak. As time passed, the river grew restless. Its waters, once clear, turned thick with mud. Its fish, once plentiful, grew scarce. The serpent's body ached, for the river was its home, and the home was unwell. One night, the river called to the serpent: "You are the keeper of the balance. Will you remain still while your home withers?" The serpent did not answer. It only moved. When the men woke, the river had changed. The banks where they built their homes were gone, swallowed by water. The land where they had planted their crops had turned to stone. The forest, once open, was thick again, its vines and roots sealing the paths they had walked. The men searched for what was lost, but they could not find it. The river had taken back what belonged to it. The serpent was never seen again. Some say it swam far away. Others say it became the river itself, watching, waiting, knowing that all things must flow as they should.

-Shuar Parable

It was different this time. It was far dimmer than the spark that carried Tsewa's essence. More than that, it had a definite shape, a circle without halo. Once again, Ignacio felt himself propelled to it and the circle increased in size as he watched.

Now he became aware of other sparks in the darkness. They were small specks of light that surrounded him like stars. Ignacio realized with a sudden understanding that they *were* stars and that there arrangement was quite familiar. There was Orión and Escorpión! And further yet La Cruz del Sur. A tight knot of stars caught his eyes, captivating his attention. Never had he seen Las Pléyades so clearly and distinctly.

Looking back at the circle, he saw it was now blue and white with some areas of brown, and he understood what he was seeing. It was a world. His world. And he was falling toward it. It filled his view, its brightness drowning out the stars. He could see now the familiar outlines of continents. There, to his extreme left was his long-lost Spain, below him New Spain swelled ever larger. A deep green was now added to the palette covering nearly the whole of the continent. *Trees*, he thought, trees upon trees covering the land in a great jungle that spread from coast to coast.

He descended through clouds and now the inky blackness that had encompassed him was filled with a cerulean blue. To his left, the ocean sparkled. He saw the river that marked the border of his new home. He looked for Santa Maria but all he saw was a blackened stain.

Abruptly, he was standing on the ground. Ignacio shook his head and felt his arms. This was not his dream-self which he had become so familiar with. This was his own true body. How had he had gotten from Tsewa's hut to the edge of Santa Maria? The question bothered him greatly, even after all that he had experienced on his spiritual journey. Another mystery to be pondered and sifted through the filter of his altered reasoning.

Instead of the familiar buildings of the town, he stood before a great column of black smoke drifting lazily into the sky. He walked toward where the town had stood numbly, his mind threatening to collapse under its own weight. One thought broke through the fog: *Something terrible has happened here.* He found a street and as he walked found himself surrounded by utter devastation.

The flames had long burned out, but piles of smoldering ruins still smoked, adding their own vapors to the dark cloud overhead. There was nothing standing that was taller than couple of feet. From his vantage point, Ignacio could see straight to the river. Nothing encumbered his view.

Now he saw the bodies. Warriors, townspeople, Africans. They lay here and there, causing him to swerve from his course to avoid coming near. Some lay in pools of blood, weapons piercing their bodies, others burnt by the fiery tempest that had swept the village. He felt his gorge rise and did not try to stop it.

Ignacio stood now in front of the remains of his church. He only recognized it because the altar still stood, smoking and crumbling in the remnants of the structure. Here, he was finally overcome by emotion. He fell to his knees and sobbed. Not for the church, but for the senselessness of it all. Pounding his fist into the ashes, he cried out, "No!" then with more force, "Rosa!"

He thought of Rosa and all the others he knew from the shipwreck to Santa Maria. "Gone!" he screamed, "Everyone and everything is gone! I was not here! In their moment of greatest need, I thought only of myself!" He collapsed then, curling up on the ground as the sobs came in overwhelming waves. Exhausted beyond measure, he laid there there unmoving and insensate until he felt a hand on his shoulder.

"Come, Nantá Iwia," a voice said tenderly, "There is nothing more for you here. Let me take you back to Nunkui Nampet."

Ignacio allowed himself to be pulled to his feet. He looked fuzzily at the man before him.

"Wajari, what happened here?" Ignacio asked, never wondering how he knew a man he had never met. How he had spoken to the man in his own language. It was all there in Tsewa's memories.

"Balance has been restored," replied Wajari. "For years we struggled with an imbalance when the first settlers of the town arrived but as we became accustomed to their continued presence, we allowed this imbalance to persist. But when they reached out to the greater world, when the other white men came to the town, no longer could we tolerate the imbalance and its potential to be far greater."

"So, they are all dead," said Ignacio, stating it as fact, wiping the tears from his face.

"No. Many still live. I admit most of the men are dead, but many of the others still live. What is important is that the town and the mine are dead. Without them, the white men will stop coming here."

For a time, perhaps, thought Ignacio. "What will happen to them?" he asked, "The survivors?"

"They will learn to live in balance with the forest, and with us."

Ignacio nodded slowly. "I would like to meet with them, talk to them, perhaps guide them."

"That will not be possible, Nantá Iwia. They are being dispersed among the clans. Keeping them together would be too great a risk." Wajari then gave a short laugh and clasped Ignacio's shoulder. "There *are* two waiting for you at Nunkui Nampet. One of them is particularly troublesome."

Ignacio took a long look at the remains of Santa Maria, then he turned back to Wajari with a smile. "Yes, I suppose she is."

Chapter Thirty Nine

My skin grows black and peels; my body burns with fever. My lyre is turned to mourning, and my pipe to the sound of wailing.

Job 30:30

Captain don Rodolfo de Salazar of the *Santa Victoria* stood on the deck and swept the coastline with his glass. The layover at Valdivia had taken much longer than he had anticipated. The delivery of Captain de Cuellar and subsequent trial had taken most of the time as Salazar had been determined to be a material witness to the proceedings. Although he did not care much for de Cuellar on a personal level, he was loathe to give testimony against a fellow Captain. In the end, being an honest man, he was instrumental in providing crucial evidence that sealed de Cuellar's fate. Ultimately, concisely and unanimously, de Cuellar was found guilty of acts of piracy, conspiracy, mutiny, and high treason. As as piracy and theft from the Crown were capital offenses, de Cuellar and his cohorts were sentence to death by hanging.

Salazar was not willing to stay for the public spectacle and left port as soon as his testimony was no longer required, his duty to the court fulfilled. The weight of the proceedings had sat uncomfortably on his shoulders, and he had no desire to witness the grim conclusion. As soon as the final signatures were inked onto the official documents, he ordered the *Santa Victoria* to set sail, eager to put Valdivia behind him and return to the open sea. In all, Salazar was now more than a month behind schedule.

He scanned the waters near the mouth of the river again. Where were the fishing boats that had previously greeted the galleon's arrival previously? The great ship entered the river and the silence persisted. As before, the jungle presented an impenetrable wall on both sides of the river. After a while came a break in the foliage on the southern shore. It took Salazar a moment to realize what he was seeing. The jungle is very quick to reclaim its own and the break revealed an area which was quickly filling in with brush and saplings. He turned to Velasco, his First Officer.

"Look! Are these not the farmlands we marveled at upon our last arrival? They have all gone to ruin!"

"Perhaps, Captain," Velasco said cautiously, "we are misremembering this part of the landscape. A town like Santa Maria would not be prone to destroying their own supply of food."

"No, no," said Salazar, "this indeed was it. There is nothing wrong with my memory. Look ahead," he said pointing, "there is the bend that, once rounded, will bring us into the town proper. It was near this very spot that we apprehended de Cuellar, curse him!"

"Aye, Captain, I concur, I see it now." replied Velasco. "We will know the truth of it soon enough."

As the *Santa Victoria* rounded the bend, a hush fell over the crew. Where once had stood the bustling town of Santa Maria, there was now only ruin. Smoke no longer rose from chimneys, nor did the sounds of hammers and voices carry over the water. Instead, the remnants of a great conflagration lay before them.

The town had been razed to the ground. Blackened beams jutted from the rubble like skeletal remains, and the once-orderly streets were now little more than pathways choked with ash and debris. The church, which had stood proudly at the town's center, was a hollowed-out shell, its altar barely recognizable amidst the charred wreckage. Over everything, the jungle had encroached the town, the streets were now flourishing with growth, vines draped over anything over a few feet tall.

The dock was gone, reduced to little more than scorched pilings jutting from the water. The hull of the *Santa Estrella* was visible, its main structure burned to the waterline. A single mast rose in defiance. There was no sign of life, even the scavenging vultures had left.

Captain Salazar let his spyglass drop to his side, his face grim

"Madre de Dios..." he muttered.

Velasco crossed himself, his voice barely above a whisper. "It is as if the jungle itself rose up and swallowed them whole." He regained some of his composure and added, "I will assign an expedition crew immediately."

"To what end?" asked Salazar. "Whatever happened here...we missed it."

"There may be survivors. Surely the mine..."

Salazar stopped him. "I do not believe there is anyone left. We will drop anchor and stay the day in case any come forward or some signal is given, but I believe they are as dead as the town. As for the mine, that is lost to us. There is no one aboard this vessel that knows of its location and even if we were to find the road that leads to it, the jungle has surely reclaimed it. Just look at the town if you need further proof. I will leave it to those with greater authority to decide what to do about the mine."

Salazar grew quiet. He thought of the men he had left here. He thought of the assessor, Domingo Luján, whom he had sent to the mine under the man's vociferous protests. *God rest your souls,* he thought. *May your deaths have been met with little suffering.*

At the rail, Rodrigo wept.

Chapter Forty

In the time before memory, there were two hunters who set out into the jungle in search of game. One was skilled and strong, his spear always true, his feet swift and sure. The other was patient and quiet, listening more than he spoke, watching more than he moved. As they walked, the jungle grew strange around them. The trees twisted in ways they did not recognize, and the rivers ran in silent currents. Still, they pressed on, for they had come too far to turn back. Then, in a clearing where the earth was red as blood, they saw a great jaguar with eyes like burning coals. The strong hunter gripped his spear, ready to strike, but the quiet one placed a hand on his arm. "Wait," he said. "This is not a beast of the hunt." The jaguar stared at them for a long time. Then, without a sound, it turned and walked into the trees, leaving behind only a single black feather resting on the ground where it had stood. The strong hunter scoffed and shook his head. "What good is a feather?" he asked. "We came for meat, and we leave with nothing." He turned and went back the way they had come, cursing the empty sky above him. But the quiet hunter picked up the feather and held it in his hands. He did not understand its meaning, but he carried it with him. Many years later, when his hair was white and his strength had faded, he still had the feather. And though he had never spoken of it, those who sat by his fire often found themselves dreaming of a great jaguar leading them through the dark places of the world, where paths are lost and found again. It is said that the feather remains, passed from hand to hand, always waiting for the one who

will understand what it truly means.
- Shuar Parable

Ignacio was old. Older than he had a right to be. In his being, he still thought himself a young man and he longed to roam through the jungle with the vigor of his youth, to feel the earth firm beneath his feet and the sun warm upon his face, unburdened by the weight of years and memory. But it was not to be. Too long had he been Uwishin. As the spiritual leader of the clan, he felt a closer relationship to the forest world than any of his fellows could ever experience. But that time was becoming short. It would soon be time to move on. This did not trouble him greatly but he knew things were about to happen. Things that would need a strong Uwishin to guide the people, a strength that was waning day by day.

Rosa had gone to the spirits long ago and Carmen would soon follow. These two were the only wives he had taken although only Rosa had borne his children. They were fully grown now, wives and warriors in their own right.

He had considered his children, but not one of them exhibited the aptitude to follow in his footsteps. He would have to seek elsewhere. And he *had* been seeking. The use of the trance potion had taking its toll on him and he used it only rarely. More often than not, he relied on his oracle that was imbued with the power to give him insight.

He turned to the oracle now. The sight of it never ceased to cause him unease but he accepted it as a representation of the Great Balance. The oracle was a cage. A cage that housed the bones of the long-dead Fray Burgos. Ignacio never learned the manner of Burgos' death and that mystery was a major cause of his unease, but the years had softened the impact.

He stared at it now, focusing on the empty eye sockets, calming his mind and accepting whatever would present itself. He had tried many times, but today it came almost instantly. In his mind, he saw the spark he had been searching for and he smiled.

Far away, in another part of the vast jungle, a young boy wandered the forest wielding his spear and following the trails as his father had taught him. He stopped abruptly. Something had caught his eye. There, through the trees he saw something he was not expecting: a white man dressed in black robes.

The white man smiled at him.

ABOUT THE AUTHOR

Anthony Garcia tells stories. He has always told stories—on paper, in ink, in the spaces between words where ideas flicker like firelight.

Once upon a time, he ventured into the world of comic books, founding a publishing company and crafting *Professor Roentgen's Mysterious Rays*, a tale of discovery and wonder, and *Project Dark Matter*, a story of heroes and the shadows they cast. He edited and contributed to *The Hierograph*, a gathering place for emerging comic creators, and his words found their way into *The Compendium*, where Steampunk dreams take form.

For more than thirty years, he spent his days as a radiologic imaging specialist, peering into hidden places, unraveling mysteries of bone and shadow. But that, he insists, was only ever the side job. The real work—the heart of it—was always in the stories.

Now, he turns his hand to prose, weaving tales that unfold in new and unexpected ways. He lives in Tucson, Arizona, with his wife, two dogs, and an ever-growing collection of books—because what is a home, really, without too many books?

MORE BOOKS BY ANTHONY GARCIA

Professor Roentgen's Mysterious Rays
ISBN-13: 979-8864462539

Project: Dark Matter
ISBN-13: 979-8873775156

FOLLOW ON SOCIAL MEDIA

email - twenty2six@gmail

https://www.amazon.com/author/agarcia.burningplanetmedia857

https://www.facebook.com/AnthonyGarciaBooks

@anthonygarciabooks.bsky.social

Instagram - @T2sBooks